D1425892

About the Author

AJ Waines is the number one bestselling author of *Girl on a Train,* which topped the UK and Australian Kindle Charts in 2015. She was a psychotherapist for fifteen years, during which time she worked with ex-offenders from high-security institutions, gaining a rare insight into abnormal psychology. She is now a full-time novelist with publishing deals in France, Germany (Penguin Random House) and USA (audiobook).

Her first novel, *The Evil Beneath*, went to Number One in 'Murder' and 'Psychological Thrillers' categories in the UK Kindle Charts and *Dark Place to Hide* reached Number One in 'Vigilante Justice'. In 2015, the author was ranked in the Top 20 UK Authors on Amazon KDP (Kindle Direct Publishing).

Alison has also written two self-help books: *The Self-Esteem Journal* and *Making Relationships Work* (Sheldon Press). She lives in Southampton, UK, with her husband.

Find out more at **www.ajwaines.co.uk** or follow her Blog at **www.awaines.blogspot.co.uk.** She's also on Twitter (@ajwaines), Facebook (AJWaines) and you can sign up for her Newsletter at: **http://eepurl.com/bamGuL**

Also by AJ Waines

The Evil Beneath
Girl on a Train
Dark Place to Hide

Writing as Alison Waines

The Self-Esteem Journal
Making Relationships Work

No Longer Safe

A J WAINES

No Longer Safe
A Novel

ISBN 13: 978-1517350710
ISBN 10: 1517350719

Find out more about the author and her other books at
www.ajwaines.co.uk

For Ruth and Mike Holmes
You are both amazing

Chapter 1

15 November

You were the last person I expected to hear from. After all this time. After all the cards and letters that had come back marked 'return to sender'.

I drifted from the hall into the sitting room, carrying the envelope on both outstretched palms, like a piece of newly discovered treasure. One slice from Dad's paper knife and it was open. At first I thought it was an invitation to a wedding, but there was no card; instead it was a letter wrapped around a glossy brochure of a castle nestling amongst snow-capped mountains.

It was your handwriting for certain. I looked straight down to the bottom of the second sheet to confirm it. Karen Morley. That's when I had to sit down.

My head was suddenly too big for my body and I couldn't trust myself to read without feeling giddy. Was it really you? I checked the address – Brixton – in London-terms that meant you were practically on my doorstep. No distance at all.

I made my brain slow down so I could trail my eyes across the curves of your fountain pen. That was a novelty in itself – the personal touch – when nearly everything that landed on our doormat these days was typed. But that was very much your way of doing things,

Karen – making people feel special, making that extra effort to show you cared.

Would be wonderful to see you again…remembered your birthday…love to invite you…important time for me…

I read the first part again. It *was* an invitation, but not to a wedding. You were inviting me to a cottage in the Highlands – on holiday.

I slid from the arm of the sofa into the seat. Nearly six years without a word and now this. I tried to reach you after we finished Uni, of course I did. You were the one who stood out, the friend I thought I'd found for life. Once Uni was over, other associations tailed off and calls were replaced with Facebook updates with the odd round-robin email. But ours was different.

To be honest, I hadn't expected you to fall away like you did, Karen. We'd established a real bond – or so I thought. Afterwards, you moved to Bristol while I moved back to London, but I was certain we'd visit each other; I'd travel one weekend, you'd travel the next. I had my heart set not only on keeping in touch, but staying best friends.

I did go to stay with you at the start – just once, remember? You replied to my emails for a while, sent a cheery card that first Christmas, but then, like the rest, you drifted away from me and I never heard from you again. Until now.

I held the letter under my nose, stupid I know, just to see if there was a trace of you left on the paper. Then I held it to my chest and allowed your presence to sink into me again. You were my inspiration, the person I wanted to be. I'd never felt that kind of admiration about anyone before. You brought everything alive and coaxed me out of my shell.

With no siblings and a small disjointed family, my only proper relationships were with my parents and I'd always found them impossible to talk to. It had never occurred to me to bare my deepest feelings to them. You were different. I knew straight away the first time I spoke to you. All my doubts and failings came tumbling out, because you made me feel so safe, without any sting of judgement.

No one had ever offered that to me before. No one else ever seemed to notice when something was wrong. I'd spent most of my life going it alone, because I was awkward and shy and people didn't know what to do with me.

I brought my hand to my mouth. It must be a mistake. You must have mixed me up with someone else and posted the invitation to the wrong person. That would explain it. This was too much to expect after almost six years of silence; it was too big a deal. An invitation to spend fourteen days together out of the blue, without any preamble? But then that was you, Karen – always surprising people, keeping us all on our toes.

I heard the bread ping out of the toaster and hurried into the kitchen. Batting away coils of smoke, I retrieved the end result – crispy black, again. The setting button had fallen off the ancient Morphy Richards weeks ago. I dropped the charred slice in the pedal pin.

I was late. I ducked into the fridge and snatched the bundle wrapped in cling film. Mum still insisted on

3

making tomato sandwiches for me every day for work. Nothing else on the bread, just tomato – they were always limp and soggy.

On the way back to the hall to grab my duffel coat, I passed the school photo of me, with buck teeth and pigtails, that my parents insisted on hanging on the door of the cupboard under the stairs.

I'd desperately wanted a sister when I was growing up, someone to share my family's idiosyncrasies, of which there were many. I discovered how different we were from other families at around the age of six. Crisps, biscuits, sweets, soft drinks, for example, were forbidden. *What's wrong with fruit and water?* my father used to say.

Mum never left the top button undone on her blouse, never wore shorts, never went bare-legged or open-toed even around the house; there were no low-necklines or miniskirts allowed. A female revealing flesh was seen as vulgar and 'asking for trouble'.

The subsequent labels I started to collect in school reflected the indoctrination I was subjected to at home: 'prude', 'religious freak', 'holier than thou', 'goody-goody', 'old maid'. Being around other people – Brownies, then Girl Guides, the church choir – became lonely and hostile territories and I'd have given anything to have had an older sister holding my hand.

I picked up my scarf and gloves, but didn't go any further. Hearing from you like this had shaken it all up again and instead of reaching for the door, I stood still. Then I went back; thinking, remembering.

I never understood why you took a shine to me. You

and I were from different ends of the spectrum – you were way out of my league in every respect. Bright, charismatic and larger than life – you got a first in Anatomy and Human Biology (no surprises there) and I scraped through in English and History (ditto, regarding the surprises).

You were the sort of girl whose eyelashes curled up into long sexy sweeps without mascara, whose teeth were marble white without dental intervention. You were slim, but had shapely curves whereas I was 'skinny' in a way that made my bones stick out. If you were a Porsche, I was a clapped out Morris Minor – with an emphasis on the 'minor'.

I was always in awe of you. You seemed to know something everyone else didn't. I often wondered how you'd become like that – the one who naturally stole all the attention in the room.

I went back into the sitting room for the letter. Reading it again to the end, I was satisfied that it *was* intended for me; you'd actually got my birthday right – and you were hoping to use the holiday as a way to mark the occasion. With me. I could barely believe it. I checked inside the envelope expecting to discover the invite was some kind of trick, but it was empty.

The last time I'd heard from you was through a postcard. When was that? 2008? I couldn't remember, but it was pressed inside my diary, so I could find out. It said something like, *Hi – just back from a trip to Venice with Roland. Leaving Bristol soon, will let you know…*

I never heard any more. Now, your letter was addressing me like there'd been no gap at all, as if we were best friends again and you were offering to pay (yes, *pay* – I hadn't spotted that at first) for a two-week break together in the mountains. *You could take photos*, you wrote, scoring another point for remembering my favourite hobby. *Can't wait to catch up. You must fill me in on everything!* you'd added.

I hadn't taken in the penultimate paragraph until then. There was some very important news – how could I have missed it? You were a *mother* now. There was a baby girl! Nine months old. Crikey. There was no mention of the father.

It sounded like you'd been through a rough time. Melanie had been a very sick child; problems with her breathing. She was in a specialist children's hospital in Glasgow and was finally going to be coming out after months of intensive care.

Hence the trip to Scotland. It made sense – you wanted to celebrate, while also being close at hand for a time in case there were complications. And you wanted *me* to be there. I shook my head, still woolly with disbelief. You suggested we travel up together – all I had to do was give you a call on the number you'd given.

I felt for my mobile in my pocket, then withdrew my hand. I'd ring later. I didn't want you to think my life was so thin that your letter was the only thing on my mind. Then I remembered my new rules.

In the years since we met, I'd been putting into practice all I'd learnt from you. I'd stopped trying to fit in, stopped going along with things, hiding my real self. I'd been braver, standing up for myself more, saying what I thought and being more – what's the word they kept using in the books? – *authentic*, that's it. I'd been trying to be more real. I'd had a terrible set-back lately, I would tell you all about that, but I was still doing well. *Karen – you'll be proud of me.*

My new rules meant I was going to call you straight away and let you know how thrilled and touched I was with your invitation.

By then, I knew I was definitely going to be late for work. Mr Domano would cut my lunch break, but I didn't care. I pulled out my phone and dialled the mobile number you'd given. My shoulders fell when I reached your voicemail. I hadn't rehearsed anything and was about to end the call when I remembered that the new me was meant to respond in the moment and be true to herself.

I babbled something about how much I'd missed you and what a treat it would be to catch up. It came out like a long, loud explosion, until I finally got to the point. 'anyway…yes…I'd love to spend—' I was interrupted by a shrill screech; the voicemail had run out of patience. Never mind, I'd try later.

As soon as I got to work, I marched straight past the lift and carried on along the corridor in search of an empty seminar room. Once inside the small room at the end, I put my bag on the desk and delved inside for the letter. I drew it out and pressed it to my cheek. You and I *were* good friends, Karen, weren't we? Good friends could do this – have long breaks then pick up exactly where they'd left off.

With the vision of you fresh in my mind, I tried the number again. It rang three times and then your voice broke through. As soon as you spoke I felt the air warm up around me.

'It's Alice,' I said. 'Alice Flemming.'

'I *know* who it is! I just got your message. It's brilliant to hear from you.' Your voice was just as I remembered it; sparkling and full of life. Your words seemed to flood into my bloodstream like a hit of alcohol.

'I'm sorry it's been so long,' you said. 'My fault entirely. Can you forgive me? I'll tell you all about it. Still – you're definitely coming to the cottage in two weeks' time? You like the idea?'

'Absolutely. Sounds amazing.'

'Not too short notice?'

'No – I'm owed leave.' There was so much to say, to ask about. 'You have a little girl – Melanie. How is she doing?'

'Good. Really good. I can't wait for you to meet her. We'll have a wonderful time, Alice. I'm so pleased you can come.'

We made arrangements to meet at King's Cross and then you said you were getting into your car and had to go.

The following week I had an email with an amendment to the plan. Karen was now driving up to Scotland on her own, a day earlier, to check in at the hospital and she suggested it would be better if I went up under my own steam.

I'd already envisaged us sitting together on the fast train from King's Cross, spreading ourselves out across four seats, our table piled high with crisps, cups of hot chocolate and magazines we didn't read, because we had so much to talk about. She would have told me how much she'd missed me since those days we lived in the condemned house in our third year at Leeds. I would have reminded her about the slugs that got into our bedrooms and slithered across the carpet because of the faulty damp course. Joked about the hole in the bathroom floor that gave a panoramic view of Randy-Andy's bedroom below. I would have made her laugh and she would have put her arm around me.

But that wasn't to be. I was going up on my own.

I sent a tentative text saying I didn't mind tagging along to the hospital one bit, hoping she might change her mind, but the reply was short and to the point. *It's better this way,* she wrote. *See you Saturday.* There was an innocent 'PS' at the end after her name. *Hope it's okay if you do some of the cooking, as I'll have my hands full with Melanie.* It was followed by three 'X's – big kisses, her trademark.

I sent a reply saying I'd be delighted to help out and meant it.

You and me, Karen – like it was meant to be.

Only later, with the glaring beam of hindsight, did I see how easy it was for me to be swept along. Everything on the surface seemed perfect. All I could think of was that our bond hadn't died after all; it had just gone into hibernation for a while. Inside I was smiling and couldn't stop. *Just think – you chose me!*

Chapter 2

Alice is on board. I've done it! That's another major result under my belt.

I knew I was pushing my luck after all this time. As soon as she realised the letter was from me, I thought she might rip it to shreds, but no – she's come good.

Surprising really – it was a pretty tall order to expect her to head all the way to Scotland for two weeks, even though I did offer to pay for the whole thing. I was expecting her to dismiss me for being such a crap friend, but she said yes, straight away. She didn't even suggest we meet in London first – for a drink, say, to catch up and re-establish things between us. She didn't need any persuading whatsoever! She jumped at the chance to go away together.

I should have trusted that her attachment to me went deeper than I'd dared hope. She always thought highly of me – even put me on a pedestal.

Only a few more loose ends to tie up and everything will be in place. I can't believe I'm this close.

It'll be just like it used to be. Good old Alice! I know I can depend on her. Let the party begin!

·

Chapter 3

The very act of getting to the cottage turned out to be a massive undertaking. I should have recognised that as an omen that our little escapade was going to be far from plain sailing. I didn't know travelling from London to Fort William would take *eleven* hours – and by the time I'd tried to make a booking on the overnight sleeper, all the cabins had gone. Even though I caught the train at 5.00am, the day was almost over by the time I arrived.

Snow was on the way; I could smell it, feel the weight of it in the air as I finally stood on the station forecourt waiting for a taxi for the last leg of the journey. A few hardy types had alighted with me with stuffed rucksacks, their trousers tucked into thick woollen socks, but no one else. This place really was in the middle of nowhere.

What I noticed most was the severe drop in temperature. London felt like it belonged to a different season, as if during the train journey I must have crossed through an invisible curtain into another world.

After around fifteen minutes in the taxi, the cab driver pulled off a main road into the grounds of Duncaird Castle, then into a side road, then a track along the edge of a copse of dense trees. I watched the meter whizz round with the speed of a one-armed bandit, whittling away half the money I'd brought with me.

Eventually, the cabbie pulled up at the end of a track beside a broken wooden gate. He touched his cap as I handed over a couple of notes. He was keeping the change. Right. Fine.

He put the car into first gear and skidded away sending clumps of mud over my new boots; the ones mum didn't approve of. Heels too high apparently. *You'll end up with bunions,* she'd warned when I'd brought them home from a trendy shop near Sloane Square. In the old days, I'd have taken them straight back for a refund, but not now. I loved them; they made me feel elegant (which is difficult at five feet two) and they made me walk differently. Like a woman, not a child. Mum was grumpy for a while, but she didn't say anything else.

I'd brought hiking boots to the mountains too, of course, but I wanted Karen's first impression of me to be at my elegant best.

As I turned towards the cottage, I fought against the tugging wind. It was like being blasted by a fire extinguisher. I grappled with the toggles on my coat to force it to wrap across my body. My lovely shiny boots were being sucked down into squelchy sludge with every step. Then there was long grass, solid ground and several steps. Before I raised the knocker, I heard a key clunk into the lock on the other side.

Karen opened the door. 'Alice – it's really you!'

She swamped me in a hug that nearly swept me off the ground. The interminable journey, the savage weather was forgotten; I was home at last.

'I'm *so* glad you could come – you can't imagine,' she said. 'You look amazing!' She looked down at the short denim skirt under my coat, my trendy boots. 'Look at you – all feminine and gorgeous. Your hair is longer now – I love the shaggy fringe – my goodness, how grown up you look!' My heart flipped.

She looked radiant. Her long golden hair was glossy – a field of corn in a midday sun – her skin tight with no blemishes in sight.

Before I could catch my breath, she'd reached down and humped my suitcase and backpack into the hall.

I couldn't hide how moved I was; half a decade of sadness, hurt and grief at having lost her – and then the joy of finding her again – it was suddenly too much for me.

She gently stroked a tear away from my cheek. 'It's been such a long time,' she said, fixing her gaze on me like I was the most important person in the world. As if she'd been waiting a lifetime for this moment. 'Come and get warm. You must be frozen.' She took my coat and gloves. She peeled off my boots as I clung on to the newel post and left them on the mat to dry. Then she led me by the hand through a door that resembled a wooden gate into the sitting room.

'Look – isn't this place adorable?' she exclaimed.

The cottage certainly had 'rustic charm', with its quaint low beams decorated with horse brasses, a sturdy Welsh dresser in the corner displaying willow-pattern plates and a crackling log fire. I knew it wasn't possible, but nevertheless it felt several degrees chillier inside than it did outside.

'I managed to get the log fire up and running,' she said.

Chunks of fresh firewood were hissing and spitting in the grate. I shivered and reached out towards the flames.

'Listen – I made a terrible mistake,' she confessed. 'Total idiot, I thought there'd be central heating. But we can snuggle up in front of the fire. It'll make things even more cosy.'

'I'll warm up in a minute,' I said, slapping my cheeks. I knelt down on the hearthrug, the heat from the quivering flames making my skin tingle.

She clapped her hands together. 'Right. Next big thing. Mel is in her highchair – you stay by the fire while I go and fetch her.'

Karen came back jiggling her daughter on one arm, pulling a little trolley with the other. Fastened to it was an oxygen tank, the size of a large bottle of Coke.

She didn't give me time to react. 'And here she is!' she said, stroking her daughter's earlobe. Melanie had a tiny plastic mask over her nose and mouth. 'This is my wonderful friend from University – Alice,' she said, adjusting the tubes away from her clawing fingers.

I took hold of her plump little hand. 'She's gorgeous.' She had Karen's alert silvery-blue eyes, but with darker, cropped hair the colour of mahogany, under a pink crocheted hat.

Karen tapped the oxygen tank. 'She has to have this for the time being – about ten times a day – to make sure she's breathing properly, don't you, sweetheart...?' Karen planted a kiss on the child's cheek and kept her eyes shut, her forehead crumpling for a split second.

Melanie tried to pull the mask away from her face. 'I know, darling – it's very annoying, isn't it?' Karen looked up at me. 'She's still getting used to it. It'll be fine.'

Karen's voice was too light and airy; I could tell she

14

was bluffing, making everything seem hunky-dory, but I wasn't convinced at all.

'I was so thrilled to hear from you,' I said, not wanting to burst the bubble.

'About time, eh?' She tossed back her hair. 'Anyway, I'm being a terrible hostess. I must get you a drink. What do you fancy?' She didn't wait for my reply and headed off into the kitchen. 'Coffee with a splash of milk?'

She came to the doorway. 'Still one sugar?'

'Spot on.'

'I've bought some prunes and sultanas, specially,' she called out, as the door swung shut between us.

She'd remembered.

I cringed. I knew she'd had a penchant for After Eight mints and now wished I'd thought to bring some. Then I caught myself; Karen wasn't the sort to have a favourite *anything* for very long.

I stood up to take a proper look around me and realised just how basic the place was. No double-glazing, no television or DVD player. The wallpaper was peeling away at the skirting boards and a sunken sofa stood limply in front of the fireplace. I didn't dare touch the curtains, they looked like they might disintegrate, and the heavy musty smell reminded me of the crypt at Dad's church.

The latch on the bare wooden door, more at home on a garden shed, clunked as I went through to join Karen. A smell of root vegetables and apples, slightly buttery, hit me. I had a look around: no washing machine, toaster or electric kettle.

Karen poured the hot drinks while I tried to look

impressed by the chipped earthenware terrines, dented copper pots and antiquated stove.

'We got here a couple of hours ago,' she said, nudging me back towards the hearth with a mug. I pulled up a worn leather pouffe and huddled into it, my hands reaching for the flames between sips of coffee.

'I've brought loads of jumpers you can borrow and there are spare blankets if you need them,' she said. 'I put a heater on in your room to take the edge off and there's a hot-water bottle on your bed. *Anything* you need, just say. Okay?'

She sat Melanie on the sofa alongside a floppy blue rabbit that was wearing a mini version of her face mask – and disappeared for a moment. When she returned, she knelt beside me holding a pair of fingerless gloves. 'I don't know whether you brought any, but these are for you,' she said, pressing them over my hands. They were made of Icelandic wool with a zigzag pattern on them. Exactly the kind I would have bought for myself if I'd been more on the ball. I grabbed her arm as she sat back on her heels.

'You're amazing. Thank you.'

As if on cue, Melanie clapped her hands together and squealed. She threw the rabbit on to the floor and Karen picked it up and made it dance. Melanie gurgled something along the lines of, 'Blaba nowa mowa…' and took a plastic block out of the bucket on the sofa and flung that on the floor, too.

Karen and I looked at each other and laughed. 'She's changed so much,' she said, pressing her hand to her chest as if holding back a surge of loss and joy, all in one.

'I've missed watching her grow.' She pulled the hat down over Melanie's ears.

She looked at me, then nipped her lips together and tipped her head to one side. 'Oh, Alice – it's been so long. I was useless at keeping in touch. I thought you'd have given up on me.'

'No way,' I whispered, barely able to speak.

'We need to say a proper hello,' she said, opening her arms. I let myself fall against her and she caught me, wrapping me up and holding on tight. It was awkward on the rug; we were in danger of toppling over, but I noticed her skin smelt the same and the lemon-honey scent of her hair was just as I'd remembered it.

'I missed you,' I whispered.

I wanted to tell her how desperately disappointed and upset I'd been when she'd failed to reply to my cards and emails, how hurt I'd felt when we'd drifted apart, but I didn't want to moan.

She must have had her reasons.

I was certain it would all become clear during our stay. Besides, as the holiday unfolded, I wanted Karen to see how much I'd moved on and grown up. That's where I wanted my focus to be, not on the way I'd felt so snubbed.

I cleared my throat. 'What exactly is this place?'

'It's a crofter's cottage.' She got to her feet and pointed out of the window. 'Glasgow is about ninety miles that way.' She leant down and tossed another log onto the fire. 'Sorry it's not The Ritz.' She pulled an impish face. 'It was the only cottage the owner had left at short notice. She was about to give it a complete makeover.'

'Ah…I'm sure it'll be fine…it's such a lovely idea.'

She picked Melanie up and adjusted the mask. 'What shall we play with now Alice is here?' Karen manoeuvred a box of toys towards me with her foot. 'We've got everything in here,' she said.

Melanie chose a wooden train, so the three of us took up positions on the floor and wheeled it back and forth. I had no experience with babies, only older kids, but Karen seemed completely in control and at ease. It didn't surprise me. I don't think I'd ever seen her flustered.

I looked from one to the other. 'Can I take some pictures?' I asked, thinking of the camera in my backpack.

Karen scrunched up her nose. 'Not while she looks like this. Wait a few days and she won't need the oxygen so much – then you can get some lovely shots.'

'Of course.'

Melanie sat flapping her hands down onto the carpet. 'Do you want to hold her?' Karen carefully passed her over, hooking the tubes around my shoulder. The child bawled uncontrollably at the disruption, so I handed her straight back.

'She's tired,' said Karen, kissing her cheek.

'How long was she…? How long has she been ill?'

'It's been awful,' she admitted. 'Mel nearly died soon after she was born. She was at Great Ormond Street Hospital first, then they took her to the specialist unit in Glasgow after she developed problems with her breathing. She's been in intensive care for months.'

'I'm so sorry. You must have been desperately worried.'

'It hasn't been easy. I'm over the moon about bringing her home – well, here first for a bit, to make sure she's okay – then finally home, to London.'

I went over to the tiny square window that looked out across the front garden. It was almost dark by now, but when I cupped my hands against the glass I could make out two bare apple trees near the centre and a cluster of bushes within a tumbling stone wall. It looked like the place had once been respectable, but it was now entirely overgrown.

'The view from the track at the back is amazing,' she said, blowing a raspberry into Melanie's cheek and making her laugh. 'There's a loch nearby...oh...and a byre.'

'A byre? What's that?'

'A sort of cowshed, by the look of it.' She checked her watch. 'Right – time for a bath, then bed for this little one.'

'Can I help?'

'Maybe next time. She's not used to new people and don't forget, I'm out of practice – I haven't done this for a while.' She laughed.

'Of course – you've only just got her back.'

She put her arm round me. 'I want you to be part of this, though. Why don't you unpack? I'll show you upstairs.'

The stairs were located inside the narrow chilly hallway and led to two bedrooms either side of a tiny bathroom, which had a freestanding bath on clawed feet, a loo and basin. There was no shower and an electrical water heater hung precariously on loose wires above the taps.

As I turned away from the bathroom, I noticed another set of stairs at the far end of the landing.

'More rooms?' I said.

'Just one – a dormer attic conversion.'

She led me to my room. Like everywhere else in the cottage, it was quaint but basic. There was an old washstand on a dressing table, a wardrobe that didn't appear to close and a scattering of rag rugs covering the threadbare carpet. The bedstead was the only piece out of context, with its bold and ostentatious black cast-iron frame topped with what looked like small cannon balls.

'No one will bother us,' said Karen, pulling my curtains closed for me. A small heater on the floor was rattling, but wasn't making much difference to the air temperature.

I peeked inside Karen's room. It was strewn with baby things: a changing mat, piles of nappies, sleepsuits, lotions, bottles – and there was a cot in the corner.

As Karen bathed Melanie, I hung up my gear, listening to the splashes and squeals. There was a clunk followed by the swoosh of water gurgling down the pipes, and shortly afterwards, I heard her footsteps pass my room and a door close. She came out humming to herself, swept into my room without knocking and flopped down on the bed.

'She's all sorted,' she said. 'I want you two to get to know each other.' She sat up, smiling at me. 'You'll be changing her nappy before you know it.'

I bit my lip. This was Karen as I remembered her. She'd had her baby torn away from her for months – not knowing if she was going to live or die – and yet she was still keen to make me part of their intimate reunion.

Nevertheless, there was something about her that was trying a bit too hard. So far, our conversation sounded straight out of a woman's magazine, where a celebrity invites cameras into her home and gives a trite interview to promote her new film. I wanted her to let down this 'everything's wonderful' façade and tell me how things really were for her. I knew enough about hiding feelings to know something wasn't right.

I shivered and she reached out her hand, inviting me to pull her to her feet. 'Let's get you warmed up,' she said as she led me to the stairs.

'I want to hear *everything* about you,' I said, as we hunched up close to the fire. 'The baby…and…' I stopped short, realising I didn't have a clue about what else she'd been up to over the last six years.

'We'll have all the time in the world for that,' she said, rubbing my arm.

London life already felt like it belonged in my past – it was built of a tighter, rougher fabric, where everyone was happy to elbow you out of the way. Perhaps the back-to-basics living here would help me reconnect with simple things. I could stretch my legs and explore a new landscape, take photographs; I might even write some poetry. It would be like a retreat; a chance to get back in touch with myself again. Most of all, however, I wanted Karen to trust me, open up to me and stop treating me like a guest.

'Let me show you the rest of the place,' she said on cue, just as the warmth was starting to penetrate my outer layer.

It was like visiting a museum. Under the kitchen window was a small cream-coloured fridge and, further along, there was a low tap over a drain in the floor. In between, there appeared to be the one concession to modernity; a stainless-steel sink unit and draining board.

'There's a big chest freezer in the scullery,' Karen said, pointing to a door in the corner. 'I bought a few pieces of fresh meat from the village.' She brushed a cobweb away from the draining rack. 'We've got milk and butter – all the essentials to keep us going. The corner shop is three miles away.'

She swung open the fridge door and a cauliflower fell out with a thud onto the flagstone floor.

'Crikey – there's enough here for the whole winter,' I said, taken aback. Each shelf was stuffed with packets, fruit, vegetables and jars. She shrugged, giving a clipped laugh.

We retreated to the comfort of the dancing fire again. The last of the daylight had been snuffed out and Karen switched on a lamp by the bookshelf. I couldn't help thinking, with its distinct lack of modern appliances or home comforts, it bore rather too much of a resemblance to where I lived in Wandsworth. Palace Gardens – it sounded posh, but it wasn't. It was a row of rundown terraced properties running alongside the grimy railway line.

I was twenty-seven and still lived with my parents. Dad worked as an undertaker and mum spent most mornings serving in a book shop. She was involved in local volunteer groups too, alternately fundraising for neglected animals, wild birds and humanitarian crises overseas.

Neither of them had grasped the concept of twenty-first century living; Mum still made her own clothes and

Dad smoked a pipe. The most high-tech appliance we had in the house was a television, but they still seemed to prefer listening to the radio. Our home wouldn't have looked out of place re-created at the Victoria & Albert Museum – to show what living in the tough 1940s was like.

Here, the tapestry fireguard, the broken grandfather clock, the rickety wooden clothes horse – were all embarrassingly familiar. Bare essentials instead of luxuries; it wasn't going to be the least bit comfortable, but at least Karen was here.

I glanced over and her eyes had fallen shut; her belly rising and falling under her clasped hands. I watched her for a few moments, relishing her presence, not wanting to disturb her.

I always felt I'd let my parents down; at best I scraped average at everything – school work, baking, sewing – and for most things I didn't even get as far as 'average'. I tried hard; I just always seemed to be behind.

By the time I was about eight both Mum and Dad had lost interest in me, giving me menial tasks to do around the house to make up for the fact that I never excelled. One year they asked me to decorate our Christmas tree and I stood my masterpiece too close to the door, so when Dad came in the whole thing fell over, smashing baubles and sending pine needles everywhere. I can still hear the contempt in my mother's voice when she told a neighbour about it: 'She can't even get *that* right.'

With Karen, I never felt like I was a disappointment. That thought brought another memory of what Mum had said on meeting Karen that one time at our graduation ceremony. 'She's something special that young lady,' she'd said wistfully. 'She's going to go far.' Then she'd given me that earnest look of hers and said, 'Stick with her, my girl, she's worth having on your side.'

Karen got up with a start. 'Better just check something,' she said. I followed her into the kitchen, where she opened the door to the space under the sink. 'The landlady said there was a bit of a leak in the U-bend and we'd need to keep an eye on it.' A squashed-up cloth was already saturated at the back. 'Damn – it needs a bucket,' she said, tutting. 'There's one in the scullery.'

'I'll get it,' I said. I wanted to show her how helpful I was going to be; to prove to her that inviting me was the right decision. I found one next to a sack of logs and brought it through.

She reached out to take it, but I held on. 'It's okay, I can do it.'

'The bucket's quite tall,' she said, as I got down onto the ice-cold slabs. 'You'll need to tip it to get it right underneath.'

It was a tight fit and I strained and stretched to get it upright in the right spot, half my body squashed inside the cramped space. Finally, I heard a plunk as the first drip slapped against the tin base. 'Done it,' I said, starting to back out.

At that moment, Karen said something, but I didn't catch her words. In my concern not to miss anything, I snapped my head up – and bam! There was a stab of excruciating pain as the tap of the metal stopcock rammed into my temple. I cried out, then felt my body dissolve under me before tiny pinpricks of light gave way to blackness.

Chapter 4

Karen was slapping my face, calling my name.

'Alice, Alice…are you okay?'

I blinked, trying to sit up. I was on the sofa under a blanket.

'Bloody hell,' I said taking my hand up to the side of my forehead. A bad taste like burnt metal was clinging to the roof of my mouth. I must have bitten my tongue. 'What happened?'

She was hovering over me, a dripping glass of water in her hand. 'You banged your head getting out from under the sink,' she said. 'You'll be fine in a minute.'

I rolled my fingers gently over the tender spot. 'It really hurts…'

'It's not cut or anything,' she said, peering over me. 'Just a bump. I'll get some ice.' She came back with cubes wrapped inside a tea towel and held the bundle carefully against my head.

'How long was I out for?'

'Only a few seconds,' she said, without concern. 'I got you straight in here.'

I sat up trying to convince myself I was okay. Karen shook a packet of painkillers in front of me. 'Have a couple of these and get an early night. If you feel awful in the morning I'd better get you to A&E.'

That was the last thing I wanted. Poor Karen had spent most of the last few months tramping up and down hospital corridors and I was determined not to drag her back there for my sake. I hated the idea of spoiling things.

I swallowed the tablets and rested my head against a cushion. I glanced at the clock on the mantelpiece – it must have been fast. Karen said I'd only been unconscious for a few seconds.

'It's just a little bump,' she insisted. She made a cup of tea and ladled sugar into mine.

'Thank you,' I said trying to hide my grimace. It felt like I'd been in some dark faraway place for longer than a few seconds and I was on the verge of changing my mind about A&E. I could always get a taxi and not bother Karen. On the other hand, I didn't want to kick up a fuss and come across as a dreary hypochondriac. I was sure Karen would have taken me without hesitation if she'd thought there was any serious concern.

'So – tell me what you've been up to,' I asked with fake levity, 'What happened to Roland?'

'Roland? He's been and gone. That was a long time ago. I've no idea what he's up to now.'

'Anyone else on the scene?' Karen always had a man in tow.

'I'm taking a break,' she said unexpectedly. 'Don't you find relationships can be hard work sometimes?' I smiled, but didn't have enough experience to be able to share her sentiments. 'I've got someone lined up for when I get back,' she added. That sounded more like it.

'Where do you work? Where do you live?' I asked.

'Well – in the last few years, I've been working in West Hollywood as an au pair for a film star – did I tell you?'

'What? *The* Hollywood?'

'Yeah,' she pulled a funny self-congratulatory face. 'I met this amazing actor over there and things were going really well, but then,' she shrugged, 'I got pregnant.'

'Right.'

'He was too high-powered, you know,' she rolled her eyes, 'so I couldn't tell him.'

'Who was he? This actor. Would I know him? Tell me.'

She took her eyes away, ignoring my questions. 'It was only a fling for him and we split up. I wanted to keep the baby so I came back to Britain. After Melanie was born, I worked from home doing telesales and was a doorstep rep for a make-up company. Then I needed more flexibility, because Mel kept having to go to hospital. Things got really complicated when she was moved to Glasgow. I've been doing the odd bar shift near the hospital up to now.'

I wanted to ask why, with a first-class degree in Anatomy and Human Biology, she'd settled for doing au pair work in the first place, but I didn't want it to sound like a criticism.

'I know what you're thinking,' she said. 'I could have done a lot better for myself. But au pair work gave me the freedom to live my life. I didn't want to be stuck in an operating theatre with brown-nosing high-fliers – all that cut-throat rivalry.'

Except *that* was the Karen I knew in a nutshell – she

was ruthlessly competitive and always took the lead, out manoeuvring anyone who got in her way.

'You seemed so ambitious at Uni, talking about medical school and becoming a surgeon.'

She laughed, scoffing at her old dreams. 'I realised, in practice, it was going to be a long arduous slog to get that far.'

'But you were so keen – you couldn't get enough of dissection. I thought that was what you wanted – the challenge of learning…saving lives…'

'People change, Alice,' she said sweepingly. 'I'm glad I gave it up – now I've seen the daily grind inside a hospital rather too often, with Mel. Then there's all the funding cuts and pressure. I made the right choice.'

I dropped it. 'So, what made you decide to go to America?' I asked.

'Oh – there'll be plenty of time to tell you all that. It's pretty boring really.'

I was disappointed. She was fast-forwarding through all those missing years too soon. I wanted to be the judge of whether I found her life interesting or not. There was a hole – six years deep – since I'd last seen her and I wanted to find out what was inside it. What did she do? How had she changed? Maybe it was too early to go deeper. Like she said, there would be plenty of time to find out more. All the same, I had the feeling she was shutting me out.

At that moment a harsh wail broke through the baby monitor. Karen excused herself and went upstairs to check on her daughter. She crept back ten minutes later. 'Sorry about that,' she said. 'She's been waking up all the time. It's all so new – being outside the incubator at last and back in the real world.' She sank down beside me on the sofa. 'Where were we?' She spoke again before I could answer. 'I know. Jobs. What about you? What do you do?' she said.

I fiddled with my hair, tousled from my scramble under the sink. 'Oh – I just do office admin at the moment. At a college near St Pancras.' I glanced down.

There was a short gap before she spoke. 'Good for you. Sounds great. Do you enjoy it?'

I decided not to gloss over the truth. 'Not really. I'm looking for something new. I've been on self-development courses and had life-coaching. I've got goals now.' It came out sounding rather pompous.

She didn't seem to notice my self-righteousness. 'To do what?' She sat forward, looking impressed.

'I'm going to train to be a primary school teacher. I've got a place at college.'

'Hey – I can see you doing that. What a good idea.'

In spite of the bad head, I found myself sitting a little taller.

'So you're in Wandsworth?' she went on.

'Yeah.' I toyed with a loose thread on the arm of the sofa. 'With my parents,' I added, wishing straight away that I hadn't.

'O-k-a-y.'

'But, I'm moving out soon – they're driving me bonkers. They're so old-fashioned – more like grandparents. I'm going to share a flat or get a bedsit. How about you?'

'After these months up here, I'm going back to Brixton.' She didn't seem to want to elaborate.

'My parents expect me to be married by now,' I said, hoping to draw more from her. 'At Sunday lunch, Dad says things like: *Time's ticking on, Alice, you don't want to leave it too late before you settle down and start a family*, then he'll suddenly pitch to one side as Mum kicks him under the table.'

She laughed, but didn't offer me anything personal in return.

'Your parents were never the most broad-minded people,' she said.

I rolled my eyes. I'd had to fight to go to University; my parents saw it as a hot-bed of temptation that could only result in debauchery. Instead of a degree, they thought I'd emerge with twisted values; depraved and morally corrupt. Mum gave me 'the talk' several times before I went, but it turned out to be another in a long series of mixed messages. Apparently, boys between the ages of thirteen and thirty were 'dangerous and to be avoided' – so how I was expected to get married without meeting one was beyond me. Perhaps they thought I ought to marry an overseas pen-pal.

'Listen. Are you hungry?' Karen said.

'Well…' The nausea I'd felt when I came round was still bubbling at the back of my throat. 'I'm sure I'll manage something.' I tried standing up and shuffled behind her into the kitchen, trying not to move my head.

'I'll make supper – I don't want you to do a thing,' she said, realising I was having difficulty walking in a straight line. 'You sit here and talk to me.'

As she took two pieces of cod out of the fridge, I spotted the clock on the kitchen wall; it said the same time as the one in the sitting room. Later than I thought.

Karen set about frying the fish and I insisted on preparing the vegetables, but as I chopped the carrots, I kept having to stop and shut my eyes. I didn't say anything; I didn't want her to see how bad it was.

She asked me about boyfriends and I admitted there hadn't been a great deal of action in that regard. 'I met someone on a meditation course,' I told her, 'and we dated for a few weeks, but I think he was really looking for someone to take care of his children. There was a guy at work, but I found out he was married. And also a sweet guy at Dad's church, but he's moving to Spain to teach English.'

'Have you joined any dating agencies, gone online?'

'Yeah – I have. I'm sick of being single.'

'Go for it, Ally.' No one but Karen called me that. 'There's someone out there for you. I know there is.'

'I've still got the book,' I said, sensing she'd know exactly what I meant. In our first year at Uni, Karen and I had what was, for me, a risky and challenging chat about sex. I thought I was the only virgin in the entire place and trusted her with my mortifying secret. She bought me a tasteful 'manual' and shared her own experiences with me; explaining about condoms and foreplay and all the basics. She was never once condescending or patronising. It was one of the most wonderful things she ever did for me.

Another three months went by and I was able to tell her my good news: 'You'll be pleased to know I'm no longer as pure as the driven snow!'

She'd squealed and asked me for all the details. 'I'm

so proud of you – I knew everything would work out. You needed time, that's all.'

Karen had her back to me, browning the fish in the frying pan, turning round every so often as if checking I was still there. She licked the spoon and smiled, taking me back to yesterday evening, before I'd packed, when I dug out my photos from our Leeds days, eager to hold Karen's face clearly in my mind. In every photo she appeared in, she shone. Parties, barbecues, sunbathing, our trip to see the tennis at Wimbledon.

There was the weekend in the second year when we went to Brighton. She took me to my first comedy club (an eye-opener) and Salsa dancing (my hips *actually* had rhythm). It was during that weekend when we were on the beach and she was goading me to go into the water, that she found out I couldn't swim. So that became her project for the following term.

'You *will* float, Alice Flemming,' she said. 'Not only that, but you will glide through the water like a mermaid.'

One of the best things about Karen was that she believed in me.

She was right too. She became my dedicated personal trainer at the University pool and after seven weeks I was doing doggy paddle – it was splashy and uncoordinated, but I didn't go under. A few weeks after that I mastered breast stroke.

Without warning, Karen came over from the stove, wiped her fingers on her apron and gave me a broad hug. 'I'm so glad you've got all these plans and are doing so well.'

'A lot of it's down to you, you know.'

'Don't be silly.'

'It is. Honestly. You took me under your wing at Leeds and showed me what was possible.' I stopped there. I didn't want to embarrass her.

But there was something else.

She was saying all the right things, but none of it felt quite genuine. Karen had been my glorious vision of the person I dreamt of being and I wanted her to be that person again. The strong, intrepid woman who spoke her mind and relished a challenge. What wasn't she telling me?

When she dished up I tried to look pleased, but I wasn't the least bit hungry. I felt like someone was boring a pneumatic drill into my head and was still waiting for the tablets to kick in.

I glanced up at the clock again. One thing was clear. Karen had been mistaken about the time earlier – or maybe she hadn't wanted me to worry – but I hadn't been dazed for only a few seconds. I'd been out cold for at least twenty minutes.

Chapter 5

We're here and everything is set up. It's going to be a very lonely road from now on. I need to keep track of every detail. Mustn't stuff up.

Alice is so innocent and unaware. She has no idea why she's here. Quite sad, to be honest – she's clearly missed me heaps and is so keen and excited about being invited.

Had a near miss soon after we arrived, when she went and banged her head under the sink. Totally blacked out and I was in a real stew thinking I was going to have to rush her to A&E. I checked her pulse, of course, and made sure she wasn't having any weird kind of fit. She moaned a bit and when she finally came round I managed to convince her it wasn't that bad. Luckily, she trusts me. Really didn't want to risk her being kept in for observation or whatever – I need her right where I can see her, the whole time.

If only she knew why I've got her here. If it all goes smoothly she'll never know. I'm banking on her, hoping that she won't ask awkward questions. Or, if she does, she'll take my word for it and shut up when I tell her to.

She's come a long way emotionally by the sounds of it – trying to stand up for herself and be her own person. Good luck to her. She's trying at least. I don't mind a bit – as long as she doesn't get too big for her boots and mess everything up.

Chapter 6

When I woke the next morning, the world had changed. It was eerily quiet and still; as if all the sounds outside the cottage had been sucked away. I could tell from the quality of the shimmering grey light that there had been a fall of snow and I tugged at the curtains to see how deep it was.

Living in London again, I'd forgotten about the impact of a vast snowfall. Not just a dusting, but the dense accumulation that smothers everything in sight by dawn. I'd forgotten how it blanches the colours out of the air, smoothes over hard edges and creates new plump mysterious shapes.

I could see shades of white backed up for miles across the valley, over pine trees, crags and the occasional rooftop, but the scene was quickly closing in on itself. It felt as though the whole world had stopped and I'd stepped inside a black and white photograph. Nothing moved except the hands of the clock.

As soon as I turned round the headache hit me again. It was like being smacked by a blunt instrument. I knew the only reason I'd slept at all was because I'd taken a sleeping tablet.

Thank goodness I'd brought them. I'd grabbed them only as an after-thought, once my bags were packed and lined up by the front door. This was such a special opportunity and I didn't want to be so overexcited that I didn't get a wink of sleep. I'd never used the pills before. They were meant to be a last resort after I was mugged in September, but with the bang on my head yesterday, I don't think I'd have had a decent night without them.

I put the heater on and huddled under the covers. I waited and waited; the heater clicked and rattled, but it felt like the temperature was still hovering around zero degrees.

My mind drifted back to the day Karen and I met. We didn't share lectures or any of the same subjects. All we shared was a kitchen – known as B2 – with around twelve other students along the corridor. In fact, I didn't even belong there; my designated kitchen was at the other end, but for some reason the reception I got in mine was standoffish, verging on hostile.

With nothing to lose, I'd tried my luck in B2.

'I've not seen you before,' said Karen, introducing herself with a show-stopping smile as she skimmed past with a tray of beers. 'It's all-comers here. Grab a seat. Fancy some noodles?'

I felt like a valued customer in an exclusive restaurant. Everyone was chatting, sharing jokes and even toasting marshmallows on that first visit. I found out that, in the evenings, students gathered with instruments to form an impromptu band, drawing in an audience from other floors in the block. While the concerts were underway, another group would put together a huge pile of food – spaghetti bolognese or risotto – and share it with anyone who turned up. Karen,

I discovered, was the one who instigated this communal supper idea; her generosity was a revelation to me. She regularly handed round bottles of wine and pieces of cheesecake; she never seemed, like me, to buy any of those meals-for-one. I didn't hesitate. I shifted over my tins and jars from one locker to another and made 'B2' kitchen my new home.

I've thanked fate a thousand times for that encounter. It was as though my life really began that day.

I blew on my hands and, gritting my teeth, planted my feet inside my furry slippers and pulled on my bathrobe. I glanced at my reflection in the speckled mirror on the wall and caught the frown on my face. I was still mystified that at such a poignant, delicate time, Karen had chosen *me* to be here.

At University, Karen had throngs of friends and they all seemed to have more in common with her than I ever had. She'd made a point of befriending me, but I wasn't so naïve not to realise that there were plenty of others she was fond of. What about the friends she'd met since then, through her jobs or in Brixton? Why had she invited *me*?

Icicles had formed like dried glue on the inside of the window, but I didn't marvel at them for long. A knock at the front door shook me and I stood still to listen. I heard Karen hurtle down the stairs to answer it, as if she was expecting someone.

'Yay – they're here!' she squealed.

I ran out onto the landing.

'Who's here?' I called, hurriedly tying the belt of my bathrobe, my mouth wide open.

'The others…'

Others? Karen hadn't mentioned any others…

There were whoops and screams at the front door. Karen's arms were wrapped around a man's neck, dislodging his backpack. She was jumping up and down, circling around the two of them like a puppy. I didn't remember her face lighting up with such unbridled joy when I arrived on the doorstep.

'Didn't I say? You remember Jodie and Mark,' she cried. I tried to raise a smile as I tentatively descended the stairs. I was crestfallen. I thought it was just going to be the three of us.

I stood still on the bottom step. I *did* know Jodie and Mark – we'd been at Leeds together for three years, but they'd always been Karen's friends not mine.

'Hi,' I managed eventually, nodding in their direction.

Mark Leverton still looked about nineteen. He was tall and wiry like a bendy cartoon come to life. He'd created a stir with the female population at Uni – black shaggy hair, shifty eyes that made him appear inscrutable and out of reach. I'd never seen the attraction myself.

'Hey – how're you doing, Sugar?' he said to me. I'd forgotten what he sounded like. I'd expected a squeaky voice to match his body, but it was deep and rumbling, like thunder was on the way. It all came back: the way he used to call me after anything sugary – as if he could never remember my name.

Mark had always been a 'bad boy'; the dark, moody sort that girls seem to drool over. I remember asking Karen at the time why so many fell for blokes like him.

'Because they're exciting, I suppose,' she'd told me.

'You never know what they're going to do next. They're mysterious, intriguing. Women want to work out how they tick; they see dangerous men as a challenge.'

Mark invariably wore black back then; most of his t-shirts featured skull and crossbones or logos of indie bands he'd seen at Glastonbury. He'd been a talented drummer (his studies had suffered), and he'd lapped up the kudos of being in a band. Musicians were allowed to be glum, irritable and leave their dirty dishes about the place. I was pleased to see he'd ditched his trademark black eyeliner and his t-shirt was maroon, instead of black, and had an Armani label, with the logo of a US department store printed across the front. He still had three holes in one earlobe, sporting two studs and a silver scorpion.

Jodie Farringday had always been gorgeous; five foot ten, with thick frothy dark hair tied up into a ponytail and striking supermodel looks. Her legs were twice the length of mine and her typical facial expression was built around a plump pout; her lips enviably claret-red without the need for lipstick. She looked exactly as I remembered her – complete with kitten heels encrusted with snow – she hadn't changed a bit.

I felt a pang of inadequacy. I wasn't dressed and hadn't even brushed my hair. I was acutely aware of the bruise that now resembled a plum stuck to the side of my forehead. I hadn't had the chance to dab a blob of make-up over it.

'We've had a staggeringly awful journey,' Jodie moaned. 'We got here so late last night, we had to stay in Fort William.' She shrugged off her leather jacket in my direction. I caught it and hung it up. She did a double take as she saw the bruise on my temple. 'Why did you choose this godforsaken place?'

Jodie had been that odd mix of super-confident on the outside and insecure on the inside. She'd been obsessed with fashion and self-grooming, always washing her hair and making appointments at the tanning centre. She never went anywhere without a glossy magazine and even in company, she used to plonk one on the table to browse through in coffee shops, the pub, restaurants.

Mark did a circuit of the sitting room and emerged looking forlorn. 'There's no bloody telly! How am I going to survive without *Strictly*...?'

'He's not joking,' snorted Jodie.

Karen threw her eyes up in mock offence and took Jodie and Mark each by the hand. 'I'm making you both a bacon butty,' she declared, dragging them into the kitchen.

Karen turned to me as I lingered in the hall. 'It'll be *fun*, Alice. Come on – you'll see.'

I hurried upstairs to change and we settled in the sitting room with hot drinks and bacon sandwiches. Jodie had Melanie on her knee, but didn't seem to know what to do with her. The child didn't look too pleased to be there, either. She started whinging and flapping her hands in Jodie's face. Jodie couldn't wait to hand her back.

'She's a bit overwhelmed with all the new faces,' said Karen, picking her up and cooing.

'Does she have to have that mask on all the time?' asked Jodie, appalled.

'The doctors want me to wean her off it gradually, but she needs it most of the time, for now.'

Melanie still wasn't happy. Karen tipped a pile of toys onto the floor and tried to interest her in something. 'Look – how about we play with the shiny ball? Or the jolly truck?' Melanie reached out instead for the little playhouse Karen had made out of a large cardboard box.

It must have taken her ages to put together, to paint the brickwork blue on the outside, cut the four-pane window in the side and ruche the paisley curtains with string. There was a soft blanket and toys inside, so Melanie could explore her own little space. Karen set up the oxygen tank outside the box and lifted Melanie into the middle.

I played peek-a-boo at the window with her for a while before Karen insisted I stop to have a bacon sandwich. I took half a slice to join in, but I wasn't hungry. I was still in shock from this intrusion and still had a headache. Why hadn't Karen said anything? Why hadn't she warned me? Then, it suddenly clicked: she hadn't mentioned it because she must have known there was a chance I wouldn't have come if I'd known Jodie and Mark would be here. She wanted *all* of us – her own select reunion.

Karen got to her feet, poised for an announcement. 'I know it's not Christmas – but Santa got his dates mixed up this year and came early.' I looked on in horror as she produced immaculately wrapped gifts for everyone. There was a CD for Mark, a fitness DVD for Jodie and for me a thick book on photography. I felt terrible – I hadn't thought to bring any Christmas presents, not even for the baby.

Jodie prolonged the embarrassment by pulling out a parcel of her own from the bag at her feet. A delicate necklace with the letter 'M' on it for Karen. She turned to me. 'I'm sorry, I didn't know you were coming,' she said, 'but I've got these.'

She dipped into her handbag, gave me an unwrapped box and sat back to watch me open it. 'I made them on the train,' she added with pride. She reached over and held an earring up against my ear, at which point her face fell. 'Oh – you don't have pierced ears.'

'It's okay,' I said. 'I was thinking of getting them done.'

'I can do it for you if you like – we just need a sharp needle...' She looked like she was about to get to her feet to find one.

'No – it's fine,' I said hastily.

Even Mark had brought a gift for Melanie – a toy piano, which played a different tune with each key pressed.

An awkward silence followed the impromptu gift-giving ceremony. Jodie was looking at me – I was off the hook as far as she and Mark were concerned – but she was waiting for me to produce something for Karen and Melanie. I hadn't come up to scratch. I'd failed to grasp the unspoken etiquette. The odd one out. As per usual.

Karen saved me. 'Alice brought some lovely things for Mel.'

'Oh – what?' Jodie asked.

'They're upstairs. I'll show you later,' she said, without a blink.

I tried to thank Karen with my eyes, but she was watching Jodie, who had started telling some story about a friend at work. Unfortunately, Jodie was giggling so much I missed the punchline. As the others laughed, Mark was stabbing at burnt logs in the fire with the poker, sending sparks everywhere. A cluster of embers shot out on to the rug.

'Careful,' said Karen, touching his shoulder.

Jodie stood over a hole. 'Look - you've burnt it!' she said. 'Stop it – it smells like a dead sheep.'

'How would you know?' he retorted. He took hold of her ankle. 'Give me a kiss and shut up.' His Geordie accent made him sound friendlier than he really was. Jodie did as she was told, then the pair of them cuddled up together on the sofa.

When Karen took the plates into the kitchen, Jodie called over to me. 'I don't really like little kids, do you?' I noticed her hands were trembling.

I glanced over at Melanie. 'I haven't got a clue what to do with babies either, but I just follow what Karen does.'

Melanie was wearing a woolly hat indoors, because it was so cold. It made her look cute. 'She's adorable,' I said.

Jodie grimaced. 'I'm not doing any of that nappy stuff.'

Mark nibbled her ear and I took the mugs into the kitchen. From what I remembered of her, Jodie needed a lot of male attention and Mark was good at that.

Karen rolled her eyes as I joined her by the sink. 'They're just as soppy as they were at Leeds,' she said.

I leant against the fridge and folded my arms in silence. She spotted me staring into space and waved her hand in front of my face.

'I was just thinking back,' I said, lowering my voice. 'Do you remember at the end of our second year when Jodie told us that Mark wanted them to get engaged?'

'Vaguely.'

'She started looking for a platinum ring with an oval stone – do you remember?'

'Mmm…wishful thinking, I reckon. It certainly never happened.' She narrowed her eyes. 'Can't see him setting a date any time soon, can you?'

I pulled a face in response.

'You don't mind cooking tonight, do you?' she said, pointing to an open cookbook on the table. She'd left the relevant page pinned down with a potato. 'It shouldn't take long.' She draped the oven-gloves over my shoulder, playfully. 'We'll eat around eight o'clock.' Beside the recipe were all the ingredients for shepherd's pie.

'Of course not. It's my turn.' I grabbed her hand. 'Thanks, by the way – for earlier.'

'You owe me one,' she said, with a wry smile and left me to wash the dishes.

Chapter 7

We spent the next hour sharing banal anecdotes about 'the old days'. It didn't take long for the stories to get tedious. Then Mark insisted on a snowball fight in the front garden. I ended up on Jodie's team, but she was hopeless, dissolving into giggles and, leaving me to fend off a barrage of solid balls of ice. Karen was a demon. I should have remembered she'd be competitive even when we were supposed to be having fun.

My headache was still hanging around – Jodie's raucous laughter hadn't helped, a bit OTT if you asked me – and I was desperate to be on my own. All I wanted was to lie down in the warmth, but once again, Mark had other plans.

'Okay,' he declared. 'Lunch at the pub. Last one in the car is a slag.'

'That's not fair,' protested Karen, 'I've got to get baby gear.'

'Rules are rules,' he said emphatically, enjoying his moment of unjustifiable authority.

We all squashed into Karen's 2CV and rattled off to The Cart and Horses as though we were having a great time.

On the way back, Karen told us about the loch nearby.

'They have an archaic crossing system,' she explained, 'with two rowing boats tied at the shore on either side, so people can cross back and forth whenever they need to.'

'How long does it take to get across?' I asked.

'About an hour, apparently. There's a sign that says you must always leave at least one boat on each shore.'

'That's one little ritual I'd like to mess up,' said Mark. 'Let's go over there now and take to the water.'

Karen laughed. 'Not today,' she said. 'I need to get this little one back for a nap.'

'You're just chicken,' he said. He made a stupid clucking sound and Jodie tutted.

Mark fell asleep in front of the fire once we got back, while Jodie and Karen bathed Melanie. It wasn't a big deal to slice a few vegetables. I put the radio on and listened to a programme about fly fishing and gave them a call when it was ready.

Karen put Melanie to bed and the four of us sat around the small wobbly table and helped ourselves. The whole set-up felt staged and stilted, although it was hard to pinpoint exactly why. It was probably just me, feeling out of sorts.

Seeing them again had brought it all back, reminding me of how hard I'd found life at University, trying to be hip and cool like the other students. I'd done my best to fit in, but I was too withdrawn, prim and plain to do anything about it until Karen came along. I'd felt like I was walking round with the words *pitiful loser* stamped across my forehead.

To add insult to injury, somehow it got around that

my dad was an undertaker, instantly setting up a distasteful impression. I could see the reaction in their faces: *Woah – her dad works with DEAD people…!* No matter how much I tried to avoid the subject it always seemed to crop up and stain whatever credibility I had. It set me up as *weird* before I even opened my mouth.

Karen had rescued me back then and we'd become good friends, but I had no regrets about losing touch with Jodie and Mark. We'd rubbed along and I'd made an effort, because they were mates of Karen's, but there was no real love lost between the three of us.

Jodie had seemed glamorous at the time, but now I wondered about her hidden self. Was she happy? Something about her seemed forced. I was getting that feeling with Karen too – like she was playing at being upbeat, when she was really anything but.

Mark sat next to me and jiggled his elbow against mine in a playful way as I handed him the pepper. Had he changed, I wondered?

'What have you been up to, Honey?' he asked.

I wanted to sound impressive. 'Oh, I love London – I go to lots of photography exhibitions, concerts, films. I'm going to train as a primary school teacher.'

'Boyfriend?'

'No. Not at the moment…but you never know…' I added an optimistic smile for good measure.

Jodie didn't say a word to start with, taking tiny precise forkfuls of food at irregular intervals. When she finally spoke it was to ask a question.

'I'm really sorry, but is there anything else to eat?' She nudged a lump of carrot around the plate. 'This is a bit…mushy.'

'There's pudding,' said Karen helpfully. 'Alice made blackberry crumble and custard.'

'Or there's fruit,' I added, pointing to two navel oranges and a banana in a basket near the window.

Jodie winced as if we were offering her dead insects.

'You've done really well, Alice,' Karen said without a trace of condescension, chewing heartily.

'Very tasty,' reiterated Mark.

It didn't take long before the reminiscences resumed.

'Remember the time Karen managed to wangle tickets to see *U2*,' said Mark. 'She got those tickets just for you – I remember.' I waited for him to point his finger at me, but he prodded it against Jodie's chest, instead.

'Yeah – totally wicked,' said Jodie. Mark was wrong. Karen had told me she'd got those tickets especially for me, at the time. *U2* was *my* favourite band in 2005.

I was still silently smarting at Mark's mistake, when he turned to me. 'What's your favourite *U2* song, Alice?'

'I love *Where the Streets Have No Name*,' Jodie jumped in, which led to a heated debate about our greatest hits.

'Mine would have to be *I Still Haven't Found What I'm Looking For*,' I said.

'And have you, Alice?' Mark asked, over a fork piled high with mince and mash. 'Found what you're looking for, that is?'

'That's a big question.' I couldn't work out if he was trying to make fun of me or not.

'Come on – tell us. Have you found out what it's all about, since Leeds?'

'Well, to be honest, I feel like I'm only just starting out. I'm making serious plans for once, to decide what I really want. I'm going to explore loads of things; teaching, psychology, philosophy. I want to try archaeology, learn kick-boxing.' I took a breath and realised they were all looking at me. 'But isn't it more about the *journey* you go on, not just stuff you *do*? Isn't it about who you become on the way?'

No one made a sound.

'Nicely put,' he said eventually, a bit taken aback.

I smiled to myself. There was no way I'd ever have come out with a statement like that when I knew them at Uni. I realised something important. The 'Alice' I used to be felt like a long-lost acquaintance to me. Someone I'd felt compelled to leave behind at Uni, who would have held me back if I'd kept her in my life. Since then, not only did I no longer feel a failure, but I'd made friends with the new 'Alice'.

'You had that awful stammer back then,' said Jodie. 'You seem to have got over that now – thank goodness.'

Diplomacy wasn't Jodie's middle name. She had a tendency to speak before thinking – some might even say a honed talent for putting her foot in it. I found her an odd combination of sweet but insincere – earnest in many ways, but also thoughtless.

Karen brought out the crumble. Jodie slid a piece the size of a fig onto her plate. 'I haven't got much of an appetite,' she explained, 'since Mum died.'

'Oh, God – I'm so sorry,' I said.

Jodie hadn't shown any obvious signs of grief; although

49

perhaps that was why I sensed her frivolity was an act. She must have been covering up her feelings admirably.

'It was kind of expected,' she said. 'She'd been ill for ages.'

'Still,' said Karen with gravitas. 'It's a big thing to cope with.'

Jodie licked her lips and half-shrugged. 'I guess so.'

She didn't reflect for long. 'Do you remember that guy my textiles tutor hung around with…the one with the false leg?'

And so it went on. Meaningless banter. I had flashbacks of Karen, always the centre of attention, looking exquisite. At parties, she would work the room, making sure she shared a song with every individual – male, female, eligible, attractive, or not.

Somehow she managed to find out everyone's birthday and without fail she'd present them with flowers, a bottle of local ale or some other token on their big day. She was amazing like that – generous and giving of herself. She must have run up terrible debts by the time we left.

By the end of the meal Mark had drunk too much. His head was rolling forward like his neck had turned to rubber and his eyes kept closing. That didn't stop him reaching out to refill our glasses, but Karen said she needed a clear head for the baby and I put my hand over mine. He topped up Jodie's and his own, then went to the larder and helped himself to another bottle.

'We're on holiday!' he declared to quell any disapproval.

Jodie was knocking it back, too. Although she'd

claimed she *loved old rustic places*, she had clearly expected more home comforts: 'I thought there'd be radiators... There won't be any creepy-crawlies will there...? Anyone brought any fabric softener...? Where's the tumble dryer?'

She'd already made several complaints about the cold, having brought all the wrong gear: tops with low necks, capri pants, short sleeves. Even her slippers were open-toed, decorated with sequins and feathers. Karen offered to lend her a thick cardigan and I brought down a pair of thermal socks.

'I don't wear *socks*!' she said and wiggled her bare toenails, which were painted a lurid lime green.

Jodie had brought along various kits for making tiaras and hair combs. When I asked if she made them for a living she said she worked in the jewellery section of a major department store on Oxford Street, but was going to be opening up her own boutique in Notting Hill.

'Wow – that's brilliant,' I said.

'I've already started selling stuff online.' She held out a bracelet, jangling with charms; a tiny silver teapot, spoon, pair of scissors, saucepan, sieve. There were too many objects to see in one go.

'What she means is she sells costume jewellery on eBay and is *thinking* of getting a stall at Portobello Market, aren't you Jodie?' corrected Mark, slurring his words.

Although Mark and Jodie both spoke their minds, only Mark deliberately set out to provoke a response, whereas Jodie just opened her mouth. 'I *have* got a proper website...and the guy at the market office wants to interview me.' She turned on him. 'Why do you have to be so nasty?'

'Just telling the truth, that's all.'

'Since when were *you* so keen on the *truth*?' she growled. They exchanged a look that suggested they had a long and troubled history on that subject.

Jodie made no bones at University about falling for men who were possessive and controlling. She regarded it as the highest demonstration of true love; almost as though the feminist movement had never existed. I'd rather hoped she'd moved on from that and was surprised her relationship with Mark had lasted – although I was starting to get the sense it hadn't been a smooth ride.

'Look,' she exclaimed. 'I've got some business cards.' She delved into her high-shine Ted Baker handbag and handed them round. 'I wanted to see what they'd look like...'

'So – this is the boutique you're…going to open – but it isn't up and running yet?' I said tentatively.

'Not yet, but it's my ultimate goal.' Once again, I noticed a tremor in her fingers that seemed totally at odds with her glossy and immaculate long nails. 'What do you think of the name?'

'It's perfect,' I said, smiling at the words *Jodie's Gems* surrounded by a diamante heart.

'I said *Ditzy Dazzlers* would be better,' Mark contributed idly, looking at his watch. He'd done that more times than was polite since they'd arrived.

'Mark – it's not a joke.' She sounded wounded.

Six years ago, Jodie had come across as unrealistic

and immature. She meant well, but sadly didn't seem to have a clue. Since then, however, she seemed to have found her true passion. Only Mark wasn't exactly encouraging it.

Karen started clearing the dishes. I got up to help. Mark sat back, holding his mobile, and stared without focusing into space, while Jodie started giving him a shoulder massage. He hadn't been at the cottage long before I noticed him tapping on any available surface – the table, Jodie's back, the draining board – either with his fingers, a pencil or using cutlery as drumsticks. He was now making a living playing in a band, he told us, doing gigs around the country; Isle of Wight, Reading, Edinburgh that summer, as well as regular appearances in London pubs and clubs. He was obviously missing it.

Mark and Jodie were smokers and he'd already had three roll-ups during the meal. If the metallic odour was anything to go by, the roll-ups were stuffed with cannabis. At least Karen insisted they smoked outside the back door – which was something.

All in all, however, I was surprised at how different I felt being with them. I wasn't the 'downtrodden Alice with the stammer' they used to know. I could hold my own with them now. If anything, I felt sorry for Jodie – Mark seemed far too ready to put her down in public – and for Mark too – it was clear he was itching to be doing something else. I was glad to be standing in my own shoes for a change – and not craving to be in someone else's.

Chapter 8

Only early days, but everything is ticking along nicely. Alice seems happy to cook and clean without too much fuss and if she carries on like this, everything should be hunky dory. Hadn't told her about Mark and Jodie coming, because too high a probability it would have put her off.

So weird all being together again after so long. Mark is even more hyper than he used to be and Jodie still dotes on him. It's Alice who has moved on and I can't help thinking back to the early days when she first came on the scene at Uni.

I remember Jodie handled it pretty badly; Jodie could see I had a soft spot for Alice. She was very disparaging and put it about that Alice had gate-crashed our gang. 'She's hanging around like a little puppy,' she told people.

During supper tonight, Alice reminded us of the time I got tickets for U2. I'd bought them because I knew Jodie was into them, but stupidly left the tickets out in my room. Alice spotted them and she was over the moon, thinking there was one for her. Oops! I felt 'obliged' to let her have one, although Jodie tried to talk me out of it. Jodie gave in eventually, but she said she'd only go along with it on one condition – Alice had to earn it.

We'd put Alice to the test a couple of times already back then; easy stuff like ringing tutors to say we were sick and pinching ink cartridges from the Porter's Lodge, to save money printing out our essays.

Alice didn't like Jodie much – you could tell. She tolerated her, because Jodie was with me, but she never let down her guard around her. It's interesting to watch how she reacts to her now in such a different context. Ironically, it feels like Alice is the one who has grown-up and Jodie has been left behind.

Mark used to say Jodie was jealous of Alice. I remember Jodie once said, 'How could I be jealous of a no-hoper like that?' But for the first time, I actually think Mark might have been right.

Jodie was cruel during our time at Leeds, though. I knew she'd been going into Alice's room and taking stuff – pens, notepads, toothpaste, tampons, shoe polish – every so often when the mood took her. Alice was so trusting and hardly ever locked her door. Jodie never told me, because I reckon she knew she was going too far. Jodie could be a complete cow at times, but everyone has their uses. I had the feeling even then, that at some point Jodie would serve me well.

Chapter 9

As the evening wore on, I was looking for the earliest opportunity to escape. Once Karen and I had done the dishes, I let out an overblown yawn and went to bed. Shortly afterwards, I came back down for the glass of water I'd left on the draining board and I heard my name being spoken in hushed tones in the sitting room. I hovered by the connecting door and listened.

'Just be nice to her, that's all,' said Karen.

'But why did you invite her?' queried Jodie. 'You didn't say anything – I thought it was just going to be Melanie and the three of us.'

'Leave it, Babe – it's no problem – we'll look after her.'

'Just don't rock the boat, okay?' said Karen.

I heard a movement from within so I scooted back upstairs before I was caught.

I didn't get much sleep that night. I was worried about the snatch of conversation I'd overheard (what else had they said?), but mostly it was because of the racket above me from the attic conversion. Jodie and Mark weren't exactly discrete. Jodie wailed and moaned as the bedhead smacked repeatedly into the wall. The pitch and speed of her cries rose, until she hit a resounding climax. I didn't hear a sound from Mark, although, to be honest, I was trying my best not to listen.

By now, I was losing all faith in this holiday idea. Jodie and Mark's arrival had brought nothing but bad memories, and the four of us together didn't strike me as a good combination for an entire two weeks. We were all like radio-active chemicals that didn't mix and would begin to give off toxic fumes when left in the same room for too long. I couldn't help wondering which one of us would be the first to choke.

Chapter 10

There had been fresh snow overnight, so the landscape was pure and unsullied again.

As soon as I got downstairs I knew something was wrong. Karen had her coat on and was gathering together a tiny crocheted hat, anorak and mittens.

'Melanie's got a temperature – thirty-nine degrees – I'm really worried. I'm going to the hospital,' she said.

'Shall I come with you?'

'It's okay, Alice. We might be a while. Can you get the blanket from the sitting room?'

I waited with it in the hall as Karen went up for the bawling, red-faced bundle.

'I can come too, if you like?' I said again.

'That's very kind.' She brushed my cheek with her hand as she turned to go. 'You stay here. I don't want it to spoil your holiday.'

'But—' She was already padding through the snow and I was left holding the open door.

As far as I was concerned, the holiday was already spoilt. I thought this was going to be our opportunity to rekindle our special bond, to share everything and get back to how we used to be. There was so much I wanted to talk to her about, but she'd brought the others in before we'd had the chance to have one decent conversation. Now we were a group and everything had turned sour.

I watched her from the window as she used a plastic scraper to clear the windscreen and I waited to see if she could get the engine to start. To my surprise, the rickety boneshaker of a car revved into life first time and I watched it trundle down the track towards the lane.

The door to the sitting room was open and I spotted Jodie on the floor, sitting cross-legged on the carpet. She saw me and called me in.

'I've been thinking about my boutique,' she said, pointing to the sketches laid out by her feet. 'I thought it would be good to have the counters here...with the locked items in a glass cabinet, here...what do you think?'

The sketches looked professional. 'Sounds like you've got lots of ideas.'

'I dreamt about it last night. Can't stop thinking about it.'

Mark appeared at the kitchen door, clutching his mobile, and sniggered. 'Mark doesn't think it'll get off the ground, do you?' she said.

'Let's face it, Babe – you don't have the entrepreneurial know-how.'

'But I can talk to people who do – not everyone who's self-employed has a degree in business studies.'

'She wanders around Notting Hill when I go off to football at the weekends,' he said. 'It's like she's in training for Portobello Road.' He bent down and ruffled her hair. 'She's been watching that film with Hugh Grant – haven't you, Doll?'

'Don't call me Doll – I hate it.' Mark grunted and in spite of his slight build, picked her up in one sweep and she squealed with laughter.

I left them to it, made toast and coffee and took it upstairs. I huddled under the bedcovers, thinking about Melanie. Was it a serious relapse or something simple like an ear infection? True to form, Karen hadn't panicked and had everything under control. Typical, too, for Karen to refuse help and go it alone. She had a resilience I rarely saw in other people and certainly didn't have myself.

I heard Jodie calling me and went onto the landing. 'Want to have a go, Alice? I'm making earrings.'

As I went down, I nearly tripped over a hairbrush on the last stair. Jodie had left her mark around the place in other ways too. False eyelashes were lying next to the soap on the basin in the bathroom, her eye-shadow was left open on the toilet seat.

When I joined her, I had to mention that she'd forgotten to put her used wax strips in the bin.

'Oh, yeah, sorry,' she said. 'I'll clear them up in a minute. I'm just waiting for this glue to dry.' She was sticking lace around the edge of small box. The kitchen table had become a workbench, covered in tiny hooks, beads, clasps, wires, pincers and pliers. 'Want to make your own earrings? We can do some with a clasp,' she suggested.

'I'd love to. Thanks.'

Mark came in through the backdoor bringing a blast of icy air with him – he must have been out for another cigarette.

Jodie got up. 'We were going to put up decorations today,' she said, linking arms with him. She turned to me. 'Like a homecoming celebration for the baby.'

'Perhaps we should wait,' said Mark, 'given that—'

'I've got balloons to blow up and a Welcome Home banner I could attach over here,' she said, ignoring him. 'Or maybe over there…'

'I think Mark's right,' I said. 'Just in case. It would be awful if…' I bit my lip. Jodie looked disappointed and sat down again.

Mark started cutting slices of bread the thickness of a shelf. He slid them under the grill and folded his arms, looking at the floor.

Jodie showed me how to drop beads onto a wire and bend the wires. It was harder than it looked.

'Why don't we bake potatoes in the fire for supper tonight?' said Mark, leaning over her, smelling her hair. 'In foil, like they do in the Scouts.'

'They'll take ages,' scoffed Jodie.

'Or they'll burn to a crisp,' I added.

'Alright then – how about I go and get chestnuts. We can toast them, instead.'

Jodie faked a gag. 'Yagh – I hate chestnuts.'

I was faintly amused at the way Mark was treating the break like a camping holiday.

'Okay – well, let's stop being so bloody dreary and put some music on. There's a machine in our room.' He went upstairs and brought down a dusty portable CD player. 'It doesn't have a dock for an iPhone, but luckily – ta da – I've brought some CDs.' He tossed them on an empty chair.

Seconds later the walls were thudding to the beat of some raucous funk band I'd never heard of, using appalling language.

'This is bloody awful, Mark,' I said. He looked taken aback.

'You never used to swear, Alice,' said Jodie.

'I'm finally shaking off my puritanical background,' I replied cheerily, holding up the pair of misshapen earrings I'd just finished.

'Never mind,' she said, 'we can have another go.' The ones she'd made in the same amount of time looked exquisite.

As I twisted more wires, I wondered what Jodie was making of the person I'd become since Leeds. I'd turned up in Freshers' Week with no self-assurance whatsoever. I'd had no idea what to wear, what to say – all I'd known then was how to appear desperate. It seemed to me I was the only person in the world who felt that way and I spent most of those three years at Leeds faking my confidence; being chatty all the time to get people to like me, anything not to stand out like a sore thumb.

'She's right. It's too rowdy,' cried Jodie, her hands over her ears. 'Put on the Justin Timberlake, then we can dance.'

He huffed and tutted, but changed the CD.

'How about a dance, Alice?' he goaded as the music started. 'Going to show us what you're made of?'

'Yeah – okay, if you ask nicely.'

Jodie and Mark looked at each other as if I'd just beamed down from Mars. I led them into the sitting room, pushed the 'comfy' chairs aside and began by letting my body move with the rhythm. Fortunately, I knew some of the tracks. Mark joined me, finding it all very entertaining and Jodie twirled beside us, not quite sure what to make of the situation. I knew they'd expected me to bottle out, to make an excuse and run for cover. It was gratifying to be a different person from the one they remembered.

The CD ended and we all piled onto the sofa. It was made for two, so I ended up on Mark's lap. He dug his fingers into my ribs and I giggled helplessly and rolled onto the floor. The tickling match turned into a cushion fight until suddenly there was a flurry of white feathers everywhere.

'Oh, bugger!' shouted Mark.

'There's a snowstorm *inside*!' shrieked Jodie, batting the feathers with the palm of her hand as they fell.

I grabbed the cushion that had exploded and held it to my chest. 'Okay, guys – party's over. We've got to get this cleared up before Karen comes back.'

No one kicked up a fuss. Mark brought up the vacuum cleaner from the cellar, Jodie picked up what she could by hand from ledges and alcoves and I began stuffing handfuls back inside the cushion. Jodie had brought a sewing kit, so I threaded a needle and started mending the tear.

'No one will ever know,' I declared, pressing the sealed cushion back into the corner of the sofa.

'Why don't I go out and get fairy lights?' Mark suggested. 'We passed a shop that sells everything in the village.'

'What – in this weather?' said Jodie.

'I don't mind the walk – it's only three miles and I can probably thumb a lift.'

'Okay – I'll come with you,' said Jodie, getting up.

'No – there's no need for both of us to get frozen. You stay cosy by the fire.'

'He's been like this lately,' she said, addressing me as if he wasn't there. 'He can't settle. He's got so much energy, he can't sit still.'

She spoke about him like he was a toddler. Energy perhaps, I thought, but it looked to me more like nervous agitation. I'd seen it the previous night at supper. As if something was pursuing him and he was trying to escape.

He left and Jodie joined me in the kitchen while I washed up the breakfast dishes. She didn't offer, so I put a tea towel in her hand and told her where the crockery was stacked.

One of her false nails had split and I noticed her own underneath were bitten down to the quick. I didn't remember her biting her nails. Maybe she didn't think it mattered now she wore false ones all the time.

'You've changed, you know?' she said.

'I had a lot of growing up to do after University,' I replied. 'Still have.'

She took hold of my soapy hand and turned it over. 'No more eczema?'

'Good isn't it?' I said. 'I finally got rid of it after I started meditation, two years ago.' I'd had a severe case of it on my face and hands since the age of about three. I was one of those over-sensitive children; upset by loud noises and arguments, allergic to soaps and creams, nervous and delicate, made of matchsticks. Mum put it down to being a premature baby and Dad said I'd been born with a 'fragile disposition'. For me, it meant I was the one people stared at. As if I wasn't hampered enough at Uni, the crimson blotches made me feel like a leper.

I saw her glance at the clock and, with her back to me, she delved into her handbag on the table, snatching at a blister-pack of capsules. In the process, a pencil fell to the floor and rolled towards my slipper. As I handed it to her, I spotted the name on the foil. They were the same anti-depressants my GP had given me, together with the sleeping tablets, after I was mugged. I'd hated taking them – they made me feel spaced out and numb all the time. I'd stopped a few weeks ago and had refused to bring them with me.

I turned away like I hadn't seen.

Karen still hadn't returned when Mark came back, at lunchtime.

'Where are the lights?' Jodie called out from our cosy spot by the fire. He stood in the doorway, looking confused for a moment. 'Out of stock,' he said. He disappeared and returned waving a packet of fruit bannock at her. 'I got this instead.' He dropped it in her lap. 'We can toast it over the fire.'

Jodie didn't know what to do with it, so I took it into the kitchen and cut it into sections with the carving knife. We put pieces on forks and held them over the blaze. After about five seconds, Jodie dropped hers and the bannock went up in flames.

'I've burnt my bloody fingers!' she cried, blowing on them.

'We need longer prongs,' I said, but I knew there weren't any.

'You're both namby-pambies,' said Mark, easing his evenly toasted slice away from the heat. He looked pleased with himself, but something about his body language told me it was nothing to do with his fireside success. When I happened to go to the larder to check how many eggs were left, I knew for certain. The packet of bannock that had been there the day before had gone. Wherever Mark had been, it wasn't to the village shop.

Before long, Jodie and Mark were bickering about something. They went upstairs and, following a prolonged shouting match, it went quiet. Shortly after, the sounds carrying all the way down from the top of the house indicated they were getting along nicely, again, thank you very much.

I couldn't work the pair of them out. At Uni I hadn't questioned their relationship – they were just 'a couple' – but now, I wondered what was going on. It was clear Jodie wasn't happy and Mark was on edge all the time. Best to stay out of it.

Karen still wasn't back, so I saw my chance and left the cottage with my camera.

I was glad I did. It was incredibly fresh outside; a much needed escape from the cramped cottage with its low beams and musty atmosphere. I was wearing the wellington boots that belonged to the cottage, as they were easy to slip on at the door and I wasn't intending to go far.

The front garden was buried under the snow – a sheer coating like someone had tipped out skip-loads of sugar granules. The sun gave it a sheen of glitter. I watched the flakes as they speckled the grey sky, weaving in and out of each other, gliding and floating, before getting trapped in the elbows of trees. I tipped up my face and felt the sting as they fell on my skin. It was like a scene stolen from an old silent movie. It was invigorating and made me feel alive.

I gazed along the tyre marks that led from Karen's parking space, into the distance. She must have been out early as clusters of brown grit were scattered as far as the main gate. I tried not to think about Melanie; I didn't want to imagine how devastating it would be if Karen came back alone.

Instead, I thought about Karen and how life-changing meeting her had been for me. I'd had a handful of superficial friends growing up, but mostly they were underdogs and misfits, like me.

Every day at primary, then secondary school, I'd had to put up with kids sniggering that my skirt was too long, my socks never stayed up, my face was too sunken. There was always something to poke fun at. They crept up behind me and stuck chewing gum in my hair, dropped apples cores, used toilet paper and, once, a dead mouse in my satchel. They regularly stole my lunch box. Mum didn't understand. 'Just ignore them,' she said. 'You need to learn to stand up for yourself.' She was more upset about the missing lunch boxes than my welfare.

It was amazing, at Uni, to discover someone who was

not only decent to me for a change, but who actually showed an interest in me. I'd never experienced it before. To everyone else – kids at school, teachers, my parents, aunts and uncles – I was 'simple, plain old Alice'. I was to be ignored, a good for nothing. Karen was the first person to give me something, instead of taking it away.

I followed the parallel lines past the byre, until they curved at the end of the track towards the lane. Here, I took a path towards the woods with a view of the mountains to my right. It led to a small brook that gurgled beneath broken patches of ice and snow under a humpback bridge. I took a string of photos; it felt magical, like I was in Narnia.

I was too intrepid for my own good. Before long, I'd lost the trail as it disappeared under low branches and holly bushes. I stepped around thickets and over tussocks of coarse grass, regularly stumbling and losing my footing. It was heavy going and flakes began to drift down from the sky again.

After ten minutes of trudging, I brushed away a patch of snow on a wall and sat down. I listened. There were two layers of sound; the small birds skipping around nearby in the branches, sending short chirpy messages to each other and, in the distance, the caws and heartfelt cries from larger birds of prey. I closed my eyes and let the sounds wash over me.

When I opened them, I immediately spotted movement in the gorse bushes ahead. There was a rustling sound and then all was still. All the birds had gone – something had disturbed them. My heart fluttered – it was probably best to go back. I stood and took a look around. Movement again. Definitely. A solid figure in the trees to my left? The flash of binoculars?

Probably just a local birdwatcher or farmer. That's all, I persuaded myself. Why was I so jumpy? I began to retrace the trail of my footsteps back to the cottage, feeling the whole time as if I was being watched. I kept stopping and looking around, but saw nothing.

I plunged into the virgin snow again. From where I stood, I knew the cottage was within around half a mile, but in which direction? Nothing was marked out because of the snow. I came to a cluster of gorse bushes on one side and a spiky pyracantha on the other and took a route through the middle, instantly regretting it. I sank into a deep bed of snow and realised my foot was caught. I reached down and felt around to find out what was gripping me. It wasn't part of a tree trunk or tangled thorns – it was something sturdy and made of metal.

I followed through with my right foot, hoping that by stepping forward I would create enough momentum to break free, but I lost my balance and toppled over. My left ankle was still trapped against what felt like a metal blade in the ground and my right knee had crunched down into something hard under the snow. I heard my jeans rip as I sank down and waited for a surge of pain. I was twisted and wet, but didn't feel injured beyond a few bruises, unless the wound had been numbed by the snow.

I twisted around towards the leg that was jammed and tried to wriggle out of the boot, but everything below my knee felt like one solid block and I couldn't shift it. I called out, hoping I was near enough to civilisation for someone to hear me, but my voice tailed off hopelessly into the wind.

All of a sudden, the relief that I had no pain in my leg evaporated. It was snowing more heavily now and I was stuck out here – not a soul knew where I was.

I put the gloves back on and remained on all fours, propping myself up. The stabbing pain in my forehead kick-started itself into a regular throbbing again – like a stubborn child refusing to be ignored.

It could be ages before Karen returned to the cottage and even then, she'd be so preoccupied with the baby, she might not think to come looking for me. No one would be concerned until after dark – and by then I'd be frozen.

Chapter 11

My phone. Of course, why hadn't I thought of that?

I hadn't been using it at the cottage because there was no signal, but out here there should be, shouldn't there? For one horrible moment, I couldn't remember dropping it into my pocket before I left, but when I felt the back of my jeans, I found it.

I punched in Karen's number and waited. My teeth were chattering by now and the cold seemed to have crept inside every fold of my clothing. I couldn't feel my ankle at all – I didn't know if it was damaged or not – it was buried in snow which had pitched over the top of my boot and fallen inside.

There was no sound from my phone. I looked at the screen: no signal. I held it out as far as I could on all fours and waved it around. Nothing. It was dead.

Something heavy inside my stomach fell hard and fast, and my throat was burning. Visibility was quickly diminishing as the flakes of snow fell fatter and closer together. I was having trouble seeing – so how was anyone going to find me?

My wrists began to ache. I tried lowering myself down on to my elbows, but I couldn't endure it for more than a few seconds and had to force myself back onto my hands again. I was tempted to lower myself completely into the snow – give in to the soft pillow – but that put too much pressure on my leg. It occurred to me too that staying still probably wasn't a good idea. The bone-aching cold was eating deeply into my flesh by now. It coated my tongue with a bitter tang and made my lungs feel hollow. I was going to have to keep moving just to maintain my body heat.

I'd done two feeble press-ups when I heard a sound. A twig snapping not far to my right. 'Hello?' I called out.

I heard the swish of a waterproof jacket before I saw him. 'I'm stuck!' I cried out. 'I'm near some bushes caught in some kind of trap.'

There was a rustle and heavy breathing above me. 'What on earth's happened here?' came the voice.

'My ankle is jammed in some machinery, I think.'

'Okay – let's take a look.'

He had remained behind me, so I couldn't see his face, but he sounded neither youthful, nor elderly – somewhere in between. I heard him brush the snow aside with his gloves.

'Oh, yeah – it looks like a rusty old plough,' he said. 'Dangerous relic, left out here in the open.' He started jiggling the rods underneath me. His voice was posh and English, not Scottish. Most importantly, he sounded like he knew what he was doing.

'Ouch!' I cried.

'Sorry. Do you think it's broken?'

'No – it's just stuck,' I replied.

He came round to the front to inspect my other leg. 'How about this one?'

'Just a scratch, I think.'

'Part of the frame is twisted,' he said. 'I reckon the best thing is if I press on the blade here, and you try to twist your foot out. Try to get it ninety degrees this way. How does that sound?'

I blew out a nervous breath, my face close to his. 'Okay – let's try it,' I said. He was wearing a green wax jacket and a tweed cap, looking like a typical upper-crust landowner. In spite of the state I was in, I couldn't help noticing how distinguished he was; with sweeping curves beneath his cheekbones and a narrow nose.

'Okay, let your weight rest against me and let's get you into an upright position.' I did as I was told, leaning into him. He smelt of bracken with warm peppery undertones. 'Now, keep hanging on to me while I push.' He looked earnest and determined. 'Trust me?'

'Yes…' I said. I didn't have much choice.

My heart was battering away inside my chest. Screwing up my eyes and fists, I waited for the agonising jolt as I tried to pull away. The space opened out – and I didn't feel a thing.

'It's free,' he said. 'Your foot's out.' I had to look down to be certain. Sure enough my boot was resting on the edge of the tangle of metal, not buried beneath it. I pressed my face into his jacket for a second, overwhelmed with gratitude. I wasn't going to be trapped here all night and die of hypothermia after all.

I thanked him, my lip trembling.

He helped me climb out of the contraption onto solid ground. The snow was tumbling down like breadcrumbs now. 'I'm staying in a cottage near here,' I told him. 'But to be honest, I got a bit lost.'

'What's the name of the cottage?' He was still very close to me; his body heat continuing to envelop me.

'The name? Sorry, my mind's gone blank. It's owned by…Mrs Elling…ford…or something.'

'Ellington. It must be McBride's Cottage. I'm renting the next one along.'

'There are others? I didn't know.'

'You could be forgiven for not realising you had neighbours,' he admitted. 'Mine's a good ten minutes further west.' He held me up under my arms and I looked straight into his sequin-grey eyes. 'Can you make it back, do you think?'

'Yes, it doesn't hurt.' I said it too soon. My ankle was stiff and cold, but I could have made more of the situation; affected a little pain so I could hang on to him for longer.

'Husband staying with you?' he enquired.

'I'm with friends.'

We made our way back to the cottage. It was hardly any distance at all. I didn't know how I could possibly have lost my way. I felt stupid by the time he guided me into a chair by the fireplace.

'I'm fine, honestly,' I said.

'I'll light this for you,' he said, scooping up Karen's lighter from the hearth and getting the fire going. 'Where are your friends?'

It was nearly three o'clock. 'Karen's stuck at the hospital – her daughter's unwell. The other two – are upstairs, I think. Or maybe they've gone out,' I said, hoping they weren't still in bed.

He propped my leg on a stool and took a look at my ankle.

'It doesn't look swollen.' He stripped off the sock and put his palm against the sole of my foot. 'Can you push against my hand?'

No problem. He moved it gently side to side. 'And this?'

'Honestly – it doesn't hurt.'

'How long are you staying?' he asked.

'Until a week on Friday or Saturday, I think,' I said. 'Are you a doctor?'

'No – but my father is.' He smiled warmly.

I rolled down the leg of my jeans. 'Listen, I don't even know your name.'

'Stuart,' he said, swinging the cap off his head and bending forward into a ludicrous bow. 'Stuart Wishart at your service, Madam.'

I laughed. 'I'm Alice Flemming.' We shook hands in an awkward fashion. I noticed his eyes lingering on my face and then felt my cheeks heat up from the inside.

He put his cap back on and adjusted it, then zipped up his jacket, clipping the poppers into place.

'Well – I'll leave you to rest. Have you got painkillers?'

'Yes – thank you.'

'Right then…' He slapped his pockets, seeming reluctant to go.

'You'll come back, won't you?' I said, craning my neck as he moved away. 'I feel like I haven't thanked you properly at all.'

'Sure.' He sent me a glowing smile that made me feel like I'd been kissed – and left.

*

'What happened to you?' said Mark, creeping towards me shortly afterwards, as though afraid he might catch something. He was holding his mobile.

'Hurt my ankle – that's all. I'm fine.'

'You need a stiff brandy. Have we got any?'

'No, I don't and no, we haven't,' I said playfully.

'Are you able to get a signal on your phone?' he asked, serious for once. His phone had been glued to his hand since he arrived.

'You have to go down the track to get any reception. Even then, if the weather's bad, it doesn't work. I've tried to ring home, but I haven't been able to reach them yet.'

'Bloody nuisance,' he said.

I heard the putter of Karen's car and Mark helped me to my feet. She came in with Melanie asleep in her arms. 'False alarm,' she whispered.

'Thank God,' I whispered back, squeezing Karen's arm.

Melanie gurgled and Karen took her straight upstairs. 'Freezing out there…'

Karen settled Melanie in the cot and joined us by the fire. 'She's had another thorough check over and it turns out she's got a slight throat infection, but it's nothing serious.' She sank back into the cushion that had erupted earlier. 'I'm knackered – waiting around in hospital is such a trial.'

I moved over to sit beside her and she noticed my limp.

'It's nothing – just slipped in the snow,' I said.

She looked at her hands, as if trying to figure out

what to say next and, for a second, I had an edgy feeling that she was playing a character on stage and that none of this was real.

She rubbed my back and I made the thought go away.

Mark cracked open a can of lager and pushed a *Pink* CD into the player. He put his feet up on the rocking chair, his trainers dripping pools of slush from standing on the back step to smoke his latest cigarette. I reached over to turn the music down. 'Melanie's asleep,' I said.

Karen barely seemed to register; she was resting her elbow on the arm of the sofa, watching the fire.

'Yeah, yeah,' he grunted. I hobbled over to the pile of newspaper by the hearth, beckoned to him to lift up his trainers and slipped a sheet underneath to soak up the mess. 'You've turned into a proper bossy boots,' he said sniggering, but nevertheless he leant forward to unlace them and left them on the tiles.

'I'll make some tea,' I said, as Karen went upstairs again. As I brought in the pot, Mark looked like he'd fallen asleep. Echoey voices came through the monitor on the sideboard.

'...I know – you were a long time at the hospital,' said Jodie. She must have met Karen on the stairs. I heard a door closing, then Karen spoke.

'I'm going to be such a paranoid mother.'

'Of course you are. That's only natural. But it's a good thing. It'll make you extra careful with her so you don't put her at risk.'

'Is her breathing regular do you think? I can't tell anymore.'

Silence. 'It sounds okay to me. Let's just leave her be.'

I could hardly believe Jodie was uttering such wise words for a change. When Mark wasn't with her she seemed to be a nicer person.

Chapter 12

It's all moving so fast. Can hardly believe it. I'm still desperately nervous about it all. I have to keep going over what I need to do to see if I've left anything out and make sure I don't make any mistakes.

Alice is her usual clumsy self – she took a tumble in the snow, but she seems fine. I'm relying on her loyalty to hold everything together. She was never one to break rank and I'm hoping she's still under my spell – enough to stick by me if there's any trouble. I need her to vouch for me when the time comes.

Dear Alice has always had illusions about our relationship. Felt sorry for her back then – did what I could to help her out, but never thought of her as a friend. It was more like looking after an injured animal; you have to take it in, you can't leave it by the roadside. Of course, I'd never tell her that – it would break her heart.

When I think back to those early days and how gooey and grateful Alice was, I feel a bit crap actually. But my 'affection' for her wasn't entirely phoney. My sisterly instinct kept kicking in; she was so lost and helpless, but my main motive was to make sure she did what we wanted.

No one else I know would have worked as well in this current situation – my real friends are too smart. That's why Jodie and Mark are good, too – they're too self-obsessed to see what's really going on. We all have our parts to play.

Chapter 13

We'd settled into a routine by now, where I was the one who did most of the cooking, which didn't seem quite fair under the circumstances. I'd agreed to it when there were only two of us; now there were four. So, I drew up a three-day rota with Mark and Jodie's names on it and Blu-tacked it to the fridge. I waited for a big showdown, but the backlash from Jodie and Mark was minimal.

'I see you're taking it in turns,' Karen said to me, later, when I began preparing the veg for that night's chicken risotto. 'I hope that's going to work.' Her tone was clipped and she made me feel like I was the hired help. She must have been overtired. I looked the part, standing at the kitchen sink with my rubber gloves on and my hair scraped back. It seemed like any chance of sharing any special time together was rapidly evaporating.

Without warning, my blinding headache was back, like a thick metal band squeezing my temples and I reached into my pocket for another painkiller.

After supper, I bumped into Mark at the bottom of the stairs, putting his jacket on as I came down from the bathroom.

'We're going to the pub,' he said. 'That wailing kid is doing my head in. You can come if you like. Karen said we can use her car.'

'Thanks – but I need a cocoa more than anything.'

Jodie flapped her mittened hand at me by way of a goodbye, and they disappeared into the night.

I checked the fire was safely dying, made two hot chocolates and took them upstairs.

Karen was lifting a bawling Melanie out of her cot in the half-light as I eased open the door. 'Can you pop into their room upstairs and bring another towel down from the linen cupboard? One of the soft white ones? She's just been sick.'

'Go into their room?' I asked. 'Shouldn't we—?' I glanced downstairs. I'd already heard the car leave.

'It's okay,' she said. 'They know I need access – they're fine with it. It's the thin white cupboard in the far corner.'

I felt highly uncomfortable invading Jodie and Mark's private space. When I pushed open the door, the room was a shambles. How could they have made that much mess in such a short amount of time? Clothes were plastered over the bed, shoes littered across the floor and there were open jars of potions and creams left out on the dressing table, the chair, the window ledge.

I snapped open the cupboard in the corner and scanned the shelves. There were sheets and pillowcases near the bottom, a squashed up counterpane, spare pillows, and at the top, under a canvas sports bag, the spare towels. I tried to drag one out without dislodging the bag, but it came down too, landing with a thud at my feet. There was a ripping sound as it fell and I stopped to inspect it, concerned I'd damaged it. I discovered it was only the zip that had made a sound – it had opened at one side and the contents were spilling out.

There were CDs, a tatty paperback, aerosol cans. Then I took a sharp breath and stood back.

Poking out at the bottom was a wad of fifty-pound notes.

Chapter 14

I'd rarely seen a fifty-pound note before and gave the bundle a closer inspection, tracing the silver line inside the top two. Curiosity got the better of me and in one swift yank I whizzed the zip open along its full length and took a good look inside. Salmon-coloured fifty-pound notes – a *lot* of them. Five batches, maybe forty notes to each one, held together with elastic bands. I worked it out in my head. Crikey – that was a heck of a lot of money – ten thousand pounds! Surely not. What the hell was anyone doing carrying that amount of cash around in a holdall?

I closed the bag and flung it back over the towels on the top shelf, backing out of the room. I held the towel I'd taken comfortingly against my face.

I tapped on Karen's door and she called to me. 'Can you leave it in the bathroom, Alice?'

'Sure…need a hand?'

'No, I'm fine. Don't worry.'

I draped the towel over the edge of the bath and left the mug by the sink so she'd see it. Melanie was wailing now and I could hear Karen trying to sooth her. 'It's okay, sweetheart – we just need to get you cleaned up a bit.'

I didn't relish Karen's task of re-establishing the bond

between them after so many interruptions. I sat on my bed with the door open and drank my cocoa, waiting for her to finish so I could tell her what I'd found.

Karen eventually appeared in the doorway with a sleepy Melanie tucked into her breast. Karen seemed fraught, her sleeves rolled up, barely looking at me.

'Thanks for the drink. I'm shattered. G'night.'

I beckoned her inside, but I was too late. She'd gone.

Chapter 15

The front door knocker rapped just as I was thinking of having an early night. The others wouldn't be back this soon. I answered it. A firework ignited inside my chest. It was Stuart.

'Hello again...' I said. I thought he was just being polite earlier, when he said he'd come back; I didn't expect to see him again.

'I wondered how the patient was getting on.'

I waved him into the warm. 'I didn't even come down with pneumonia,' I said. 'But, I don't know what I'd have done if you hadn't turned up when you did.' He followed me into the kitchen. 'Thank you again, for getting me back here safely.' I held up a mug in one hand and an empty wine glass in the other. 'Which one?'

'Actually – I came over to see if you fancied the local pub,' he said.

There was a tiny flash between us. 'I'd love to.' The blanket of tiredness that had been wrapped tightly around me slid to the floor.

Stuart looked pleased with himself. I scribbled a note and left it under the sugar bowl on the kitchen table.

A khaki Land Rover was parked where Karen's 2CV had been. It looked like an old army-style model with thick tread on the tyres and a spare wheel clipped onto the bonnet. We bundled inside and chugged down the track, onto the lane. It was a bumpy ride, the clanks and thuds made it noisy, but made me laugh, too. It was like being thrown around on the mechanical bull at the funfair. I was glad of the seatbelt.

The Cart and Horses was surprisingly busy. There must have been dozens of landowners, farmers and holidaymakers from little hamlets, tucked away from the main roads. This wasn't simply a rustic country pub; it looked as though it acted as a kind of community centre. There was a group of men in tweed caps playing chess, another playing Trivial Pursuit and a game of darts was well underway at the far side. Best of all, it had a raging log fire. I expected to see Mark and Jodie, but they must have gone somewhere else.

I was going to stick to apple juice because of all the painkillers I'd had during the day – then thought *what the hell* – and chose a brandy instead. Stuart had the same and we swilled the drinks around in our glasses in unison. We had the whole cavernous hearth to ourselves, so I took off my boots and put my feet up on a padded stool. No one batted an eyelid.

I felt a shiver of emancipation. No one knew me here; I was just another tourist-stranger. I could even afford to reinvent myself a little – try out a bolder Alice; one who wasn't frightened to close her eyes at night for fear of reliving the trauma she'd been through in September.

'It's my birthday, tomorrow,' I announced.

'Ah – so *that's* why you're on holiday at this time of year. Doing anything special?'

'Very low key, I think,' I said. I was anticipating the contrary, but didn't want to get my hopes up. Karen wouldn't make a point of highlighting my birthday then forget all about it, would she? I swiftly shunted the conversation on to other subjects. 'So what brought you to this particular area? Do you know people here? Have you been here before?'

'No,' he said simply. 'I came across it browsing online. I wanted somewhere remote and quiet – mainly to try birdwatching.' I didn't tell him about my mother's interest in wild birds; I didn't want to bring my parents into the discussion, just in case I let slip that I hadn't yet left home.

Stuart asked what I did for a living. I skipped the bit about being an administrator. 'I'm starting a teacher-training course soon.'

'Ah.' He looked pleased. 'I'm in teaching too.'

He told me he lived on his own in a crescent of Georgian houses near Edinburgh railway station and worked at the University as a lecturer in Classics and Archaeology.

'It's revision week for students right now, followed by exam week, so I've been able to sneak away. I usually spend this period with my brother or take off somewhere warm, but I fancied a change.'

He was probably in his forties and dressed like a TV 'lord of the manor', but he was affable and charming. More to the point, he was disarming. It made me realise that even though we were all getting on at the cottage, I found myself walking on eggshells a lot of the time, partly because Melanie wasn't yet stable, but also because Mark was so changeable. It was a relief to let my guard down a little.

As we spoke, I began to sense something else; I could

only describe it as an aura of sadness around him. It came from the lines around his eyes, the way his mouth flickered into a smile and then died quickly. From time to time I caught him looking into the distance, squinting, as if he was looking for someone.

'How long are you staying for?' he asked. I'd told him this already, I noted, when he'd found me in the snow.

'Until a week on Saturday at the latest.'

I took it as a good sign that he was keen to confirm how long I'd be around for.

'Well, then – if you're stuck for things to do, we can always team up together and go for walks.' He stopped himself. 'That's if – you know – you haven't already made plans with your friends or—'

'No…thank you. I'd like that. I've brought my camera and was hoping to take plenty of pictures. I'm not very good – but I do love trying to capture a moment, an atmosphere.'

'You've come to the right spot.'

A few feet away, a man tripped over someone's rucksack and my mind flitted back to the money I'd found in the holdall. Stuart seemed like someone I could trust, but it felt like an odd thing to bring into the conversation when we'd only just met.

Stuart asked me whether I went to art exhibitions in London and we chatted about an odd combination of subjects: the O_2 arena, escalators, crinkle-cut crisps, the pros and cons of electric blankets. By then it was getting late and we stood to go.

As I got up I spotted a local paper folded over on the table behind us. There was a photograph of a man staring out at me. He'd been arrested for shoplifting and was wearing a hoodie. The same kind of hoodie that had plagued my nightmares. He looked older and broader than the man at the centre of that dreadful day, but I knew in an instant that I hadn't beaten back the demons he'd left me with. They were still alive and kicking under the surface, waiting to climb out and terrorise me when I was least expecting it.

*

Three months earlier
It had been raining. Mum had sent me over to East Street Market to buy net curtain material and I was minding my own business, heading back to the bus stop when I saw what I thought was someone in pain down an alleyway. I thought he was hurt, doubled over next to two industrial-sized wheelie bins, clutching his stomach.

I called out to him; I couldn't see his face. I thought perhaps he'd been mugged or a gang had beaten him up. Then I thought perhaps he'd been stabbed. I should have alerted other people; I should never have drifted down there on my own.

He didn't seem to see me when I got closer, he was still holding his stomach and moaning. I tapped him gently on his shoulder and asked if he was okay. Then it all happened so quickly. One moment he was bent double, the next my umbrella went flying and he dragged me behind the bins, his arm was around my neck. He'd tricked me.

I'd been partly right; there *was* a knife, but it was in

89

his grip at my neck. I could feel the point of it pressing against my skin as he pulled me further back into the shadows – we were invisible from the street. He told me in a deliberately rough voice to hand over my purse. I dropped my bag trying to do as he said and at that moment a dog came trotting into the alley.

I've asked myself the same question over and over since it happened. What if the dog hadn't come along at that precise moment? What if my attacker hadn't freaked out, thinking the owner was right behind it?

He spotted the dog, grabbed my purse and bolted.

I picked up my wet handbag, followed by the bundle of soggy fabric, and ran back to the busy street – my sole aim being to blend in and disappear, just in case he came after me. What if he thought I'd seen his face? What if he decided to find me and finish the job?

I went through the first open door I could find – an off-licence – and feigned interest in Chilean wines, waiting for my heartbeat to subside.

Only it didn't.

I ran out, knowing I was in difficulty, my breathing all over the place. I couldn't swallow. There was a brick lodged in my throat, jagged, crushing. Then the anxiety gathered steam and developed into a full-blown attack. I didn't know what it was at the time. All of a sudden the light was too bright, the pavement was sliding away from me.

I was in the middle of the market, green and white striped awnings flapping everywhere. My legs didn't belong to me anymore, but I couldn't afford to collapse in front of all these strangers; I had to get away, get home, get help.

The street before me suddenly dipped sharply to the right and I reached out for something to grab hold of. I felt my arms close around a wastepaper bin. My mind was rapidly filling up with sand, my focus chipped and fragmented, like I was looking at the world through a smashed windscreen. A cyclist became a post-box, a car blended into a tree. I hadn't a clue how I was supposed to deal with what was happening to me. I held on to the black bin and felt the street lurch the other way.

I felt a touch on my arm and shot round, thinking it was him. A black woman in her fifties was saying something to me. Her face came and went, backwards and forward as if she was on a swing. A mustard-coloured hat, torn gloves, the tassels on a scarf. I couldn't put her words together.

'Bus stop…darlin'…alright…?'

Then she was gone.

I tried to get a grip. *Everything's okay now. He's got your purse – that's all – you can cancel your cards, no one's hurt.*

I wanted to run, but my feet were embedded into the pavement. I watched women at the stalls press their thumbs into mangos and weigh out shallots with their eyes. They made life look so ordinary. So safe. I didn't know what to do. I patted my pocket. I still had the Oyster card – thank God. It was fine. Everything was fine. *Just breathe. Wait for the world to straighten itself out again.*

I joined the queue at the bus stop, my head down against the internal blizzard, trusting I would find my way out. I waited.

The roar of the outdoors hit me when I got off the bus, but I knew I'd done it. Got away. Now all I had to do was find my way home. I heard my heels hit the pavement, so I knew I must be moving. Click, clack, click, clack. I turned a corner and the road ahead looked vaguely familiar. I hung on to a telegraph pole, but didn't want to stop. A corner shop, the deli – *yes, this looks right*. The white gate, the black gate – then I was there.

I fell inside the hall and let myself sink to the floor, clutching the front-door key to my chest. Exhausted, but triumphant.

Thank goodness Mum and Dad were both out. I didn't want anyone to see me like this. I got to my knees and grabbed hold of the newel post, waiting for my breathing to settle to a regular judder. Inch by inch, I pulled myself up to my feet, still wobbly and disoriented. My head was throbbing, but it felt more like a severe headache than anything else. Normal. I could cope with that.

I felt my way into the kitchen, opened a drawer beside the sink and took out three paracetamols. Cupping my hand under the cold tap, I took several sips and washed them down.

Mum came back soon afterwards having given a talk at the local library, rattling on about how much sugar should go into a vat of jam. I let her talk. She asked for the curtain material. She asked why it was soaking wet. Then she realised something was wrong. I told her. Only the details about the mugging, though, not about the panic attack that followed. I've never mentioned those to anyone except my GP and therapist.

Mum's reaction was to get onto the police straight away. It all had to go through the official channels, she said. I knew we had to report him, but also that it was hopeless.

I told the police everything I could, but the mugger had been bent over when I first heard him crying out, then suddenly he was behind me with the knife at my neck, so I didn't see his face. His hood was up, so I wasn't even sure of the colour of his hair. All I could tell them was that he was white – and a man. I wouldn't have been able to pick him out in a line-up even if the police had gone that far.

Dad came back from a chess game later to prepare for his prayer group. I didn't want to tell him – I didn't want to worry him – but Mum insisted. His immediate reaction was to fling his arms around me. He'd hardly ever done that before and it made me burst into tears.

'My dearest Pumpkin – what a terrible nightmare it must have been for you. My poor little girl.'

I withdrew, trying to contain two conflicting emotions. Gratitude, that Dad actually seemed to care about me, but disappointed that he'd ended up making me feel so pathetic. That's how Dad – and everyone else always saw me. Hapless, wretched, pitiable.

Chapter 16

Alice seems to have a man in tow!

I heard a car engine chugging outside my bedroom window, just after I got into bed and wondered who on earth it was. I peeped out and a guy was coming to the door, looking dapper and sophisticated. Then they both went out together. Very chummy. I didn't see this one coming!

When Alice first came along at Uni, she reminded me of the girls at boarding school. Immature, gullible and eager to please.

My days at St Cecilia's were a great training ground for my future. It was so easy to get girls like that to do what I wanted. They were all lost causes desperate for someone to look up to, someone to protect them. Being pretty and smart helped, of course, but I learnt how to turn on the sweetness and light to get my own way.

I get better and better at it! Why not? You have to use whatever you can to get on in this world – if my dad taught me anything, it was that.

Jodie used to be so naff at hiding how she felt about Alice at Leeds; she seems less nasty with her now. I remember I had to keep telling her, back then, that she mustn't make it obvious that we were using her, but Jodie couldn't bear her.

Alice wasn't that bad. She was terribly appreciative and sincere. Only problem with her being so clingy was that I could never be sure she wasn't lurking around the next corner waiting for me. Dicey or what?! Didn't want to give her any ammunition that could have caused havoc. A girl needs to have secrets, after all. Just like now.

I must hold my nerve for the next step.

Chapter 17

Stuart pulled up behind Karen's car – the others were back – and walked me right to the door.

'Thank you,' I said, turning to him.

'You were quiet on the drive home,' he said. 'Are you okay?'

'I'm fine. Just tired,' I said, refusing to allow the memory to suck me under. I had to remember that what happened in September was merely a blip in my mission towards becoming a more self-assured and impressive woman. I'd done a lot of work to shake off that old skin and I wouldn't let an incident like that drag me down. 'I really enjoyed the drink,' I added, giving him my best smile.

'Me, too – you're very good company.' He took in the whole of my face like he was appraising a portrait. 'I hope they've got something exciting lined up for you, tomorrow.'

Karen, Mark and Jodie were all in the kitchen drinking coffee when I went down the following morning. Karen was joking with Mark; she sounded in high spirits, so I dared to ask the obvious question.

'Is Melanie alright?'

'Yes,' she said. 'I'm just going to change her, then I'll

bring her down. Come up if you want.'

I nodded and followed her upstairs.

Once we were out of earshot of the others, I asked the question that had been bugging me. 'Everything in the linen cupboard belongs to the cottage, does it?' I'd gone for as innocent a tone as I could manage.

She thought for a moment. Karen tended to keep her room dark, so I waited in the doorway as she snapped the poppers of Melanie's fleecy all-in-one over the fresh nappy and picked her up, wrapping her in a blanket.

'I brought extra towels for Mel, but most of the stuff is Mrs Ellington's,' she said.

'You haven't got anything else of yours in there? Like luggage, or anything?'

'No – why?' she eyed me quizzically, straightening up.

A sound alerted me. Jodie was standing in the doorway. 'I'm not interrupting am I?'

Karen shook her head.

'Only I wanted to try holding her again,' said Jodie.

'Wanna cuddle from Jodie?' Karen asked Melanie in a sing-song voice, rubbing her nose against the child's. Melanie stuck her arm out and Karen passed her over.

'She looks just like you,' said Jodie, stroking the girl's cheek. It was hard to see how she could make that assessment, given that the pink hat had slipped down over Melanie's eyes and the blanket was pulled up almost to her nose.

'Everyone always says that,' Mark chipped in from the landing. 'It's bullshit.'

'Mark!' snapped Jodie. 'Don't be so rude.'

'Well, it's true. All babies look the same.' He came

into the room and shrugged at Karen. 'Sorry – no offense.'

Melanie called out a word that sounded like 'dada' and we all laughed.

'Dada ain't here, Babe,' said Mark cuttingly, holding out his finger so Melanie could squeeze it. Jodie told him to shut up. 'By the way, someone's at the door, for Alice,' he added. I eased past them and went downstairs.

Stuart was standing in the hall. He was holding a bunch of roses.

'Happy birthday!' he said, handing them over. 'Just a little something – I know it's early, but I wanted to catch you before you went off somewhere.' Once more there was a moment between us; the air expanding then shrinking back again.

The others had appeared at the top of the stairs.

'Thank you,' I exclaimed, burying my face in the petals. I gave him a brief, self-conscious hug. 'What a lovely thought. Come and join us.'

I took Stuart's wax jacket and hung it in the hall, pressing his gloves into his pockets. One by one we all trooped into the kitchen. Karen put Melanie in the highchair.

'Who's Stuart?' grunted Mark rudely, as he opened the back door, a roll-up between his fingers. He glanced over at us, then shut the door behind him without waiting for a reply.

'Indeed – and flowers already?' said Jodie coyly, looking Stuart up and down. 'Alice must have made quite an impression on you.' I took a breath that swelled to fill the room.

Stuart looked as relaxed as ever. He winked at her, 'You're right there.'

'We met when I was out for my walk,' I said pulling out a chair for him. 'He was the one who rescued me yesterday when my ankle got stuck.'

Karen emerged from the scullery with a huge cake smothered in glossy chocolate and flaming candles. The message on the icing read *Happy Birthday, Alice*. I sucked in a gasp.

'I know it's not even elevenses,' she said, 'but, as we're all here...' She put the cake down in the centre of the table and led the others in a rendition of the birthday song. Mark came back in, covered in specks of snow, shivering, looking like he was afraid he might be missing something.

'I'm Jodie and that's Mark.' Jodie nodded towards Mark as he shuffled his weight from one foot to the other.

'Happy birthday,' said Jodie, reaching over and giving me an air-kiss.

'And there's this,' said Karen, handing over an envelope. I pulled out a silver-edged card.

'A one-day spa experience in Mayfair...wow, thank you,' I stuttered, folding my arms around her.

Karen introduced herself to Stuart. She lifted Melanie out of her highchair and held out her hand so Stuart could take it. 'This is my daughter, Melanie.'

'Alice told me,' he said with sympathy. 'I hope everything is going well.'

I blew out the candles to a raucous cheer. 'I hope no one has had breakfast,' I said as I cut the cake. 'You didn't make this yourself did you, Karen?' I handed round thick sumptuous slices.

She looked bashful. 'I did, actually – the day before we arrived. I'm sorry the icing's a bit wonky – it got bashed about a bit in the car.'

'It's perfect,' I whispered, a tremble creeping into my voice. No one had ever made a cake for me like this before. When I was little, Mum used to buy a plain Victoria sponge and pin a silver plastic cake-topper with *Happy Birthday* on to it, but the ritual stopped suddenly when I was sixteen. No one had ever gone as far as icing a cake with my name on it.

Not only that, it was delicious. How come she was amazing at *everything*? I watched Karen as she dipped her little finger into the chocolate coating and let Melanie have a taste. She was going to be a brilliant mother – so thoughtful and competent.

'Did you hear the news?' said Stuart eventually, licking his lips.

'We haven't had the radio on today,' I replied. 'What's happened?'

'Perhaps I shouldn't say – I don't want to spoil your special day.'

'You can't do that,' said Mark. 'Half say it, then bottle out.'

'Don't mind Mark,' said Karen. 'He's a bit forward.' Deep down I admired his upfront approach – it was refreshing when the timing was right.

Stuart wiped his fingers on the napkin. 'I probably should tell you, actually. It's a local thing – a little boy has been abducted. From near here, just over the other side of the Loch.'

'Really?' said Karen. 'When?'

'Yesterday – early evening, apparently. The police are making house-to-house enquiries. You need to expect them – I'm sure they'll cover all the holiday cottages.'

'How awful…' I said.

Karen had her hand over her mouth, looking like the world had just come to an end.

Chapter 18

'How did you find out about the boy?' I asked.

'The village store,' said Stuart. 'The police were there this morning.'

Stuart and I went for a short walk after the breakfast celebrations. The news of the abduction had somewhat flattened the birthday mood, but he'd been right to tell us.

'Do you know what happened exactly?'

'There's a group of cottages over the other side of Loch Tierney in a hamlet called Ockley.' He pointed across the trees. 'See the chimney smoke just through there?'

I was forced to stand close to him to follow the line of his arm and didn't want to move away. I spotted a tiny waft of grey smoke blending into the skyline. 'There's a farmer, Harry Minter, who lives at Cleve Cottage with his family. He was out securing the barns at sundown and his wife was preparing the evening meal. Someone must have got in through the back door and snatched the child. No one saw a thing.'

'His poor mother must be beside herself,' I said.

'The child actually lives next door; the kids have always been in and out of each other's houses and there's never been a problem before. The woman was just babysitting.'

'Mrs Minter must feel terrible that someone else's child went missing on her watch.'

He sank his hands into his pockets.

'We should go back, really,' I said. 'Be ready when the police turn up.'

I tripped over a rock disguised by the snow and Stuart offered me his arm. I refused to let go all the way back and he didn't find a reason to pull away. I felt torn. He seemed such a gentle and kind man and yet his life was established at the opposite end of the country from mine. If something *did* happen between us – and that was a big if – we'd only have to say goodbye in a week or so's time and I'd be left with heartache.

A whirlwind romance had been the last thing on my mind when I came here, yet the idea of being close to Stuart thrilled me. Was this merely holiday chivalry or did our meeting mean more to him? I didn't know if he was genuinely attracted to me, but there was something about him that made me want to make the most of every moment I spent with him.

Karen was playing with Melanie in the sitting room when we got back. Melanie was dressed in cute pink dungarees, putting coloured bricks into a plastic bucket and then tipping them out onto the floor. She chuckled behind the clumsy oxygen mask as the bricks clustered on the carpet and my heart quivered. Karen looked like she was in seventh heaven, but it wasn't long before the child was grizzling. Stuart and I crept out as Karen tried to placate her.

The sounds of doors and cupboards slamming shut came from Jodie and Mark's room. Then Mark came down for a cigarette. He gave us a passing grunt as he came through. After that, he buttered several slices of white bread and smothered them with jam, before disappearing upstairs with them. He hadn't said a word.

The unsettled atmosphere he left behind him triggered a memory that I'd completely forgotten from our first year at Uni. I'd gone to the communal bathroom one evening before bed. The lock didn't slide across on my cubicle, but I'd used the loo anyway and was just about to leave when I heard Karen's voice.

'Have you ever had the feeling when you meet someone and just know you loath them right from the start?' she said. She must have thought the place was empty. I stayed still, not making a sound.

'Yeah, it's a psychological thing, I've read stuff about it – it happens because you're too similar to the other person.' Karen was talking to Natalie, one of her 'inner circle'. 'You kind of become instant rivals, because you're "twins"', she added.

'Is that so?' Karen didn't sound convinced. 'I've never ever felt like this with anyone before now,' she went on. 'There's a guy in our kitchen and as soon as he walks in, he makes my skin crawl. He doesn't even have to do anything or open his mouth – it's just his entire being.'

'Mark Leverton, you mean?'

'Ssh – yes – how did you know?'

'I've seen the way you glare at him.'

'I know, I must stop being so obvious,' she giggled.

'Don't say anything, will you? He literally makes me feel sick. He's the bolshy, silent type – but weak as hell underneath.'

I'd forgotten all about this little revelation, mainly because Karen always appeared to be civil to Mark. She must have felt differently about him now, otherwise it was considerably two-faced to invite him here.

But what if Karen still felt like that? Was she playing out this big chummy act for a reason?

Karen called out from the sitting room and I put the memory out of my mind. I popped my head around the door.

'You couldn't get her dummy from upstairs, could you? It's on the dressing table – I forgot to bring it down.'

'Yes, of course.'

I left Stuart rinsing a couple of dishes and went into Karen's room without a second thought.

Except, I wasn't the only one in there. Mark shot round as I stepped inside. He put his finger to his lips straight away and made a hissing noise.

'What are you doing?' I whispered. In the split second that I'd seen him, he'd been leaning over Karen's half-empty suitcase on the floor. It was obvious to me that he was looking for something.

'None of your business,' he said. 'Me and Karen have an understanding. Don't stick your nose in.'

I grabbed the dummy from the dressing table and backed out without another word.

*

I was showing Stuart my camera when a police car pulled up behind his Land Rover. We all gathered in the kitchen and two officers, male and female, introduced themselves and told us more or less what we already knew. They took down our names and asked if there were any others staying with us. Stuart explained he was renting out the McGann Cottage up the lane.

'The child who has gone missing is Brody Holland,' said Sergeant Mallory. 'He's eight and a half months old and was being looked after by Mrs Minter that afternoon. She definitely had all five children with her at five o'clock.' She tapped her pen against her notebook. 'Mrs Minter has three young kids of her own and was also looking after Brody and his sister, Danielle, who is three and a half.'

'Unreliable witnesses,' said Mark unnecessarily, chewing the end of a plastic baby spoon.

'What happened?' I asked.

'Mrs Minter went into the utility room and when she came back, the back door was open and Brody had gone.' Sergeant Harris cleared his throat. 'We have to ask where you all were yesterday afternoon. Around five o'clock…'

We all looked at each other. Jodie went first. 'We were all here – apart from Stuart.'

'Karen came back from Glasgow with the baby, mid-afternoon,' I said.

'What time exactly?' the sergeant asked.

'About half-past three?' I said.

Karen nodded. 'Yeah, about then.'

'I'll second that,' said Jodie.

'We flopped in front of the fire for the rest of the afternoon,' I said.

'Yeah – then I helped Alice chop veg,' chipped in Jodie, 'while Mark listened to music in the sitting room. Karen was in and out of the kitchen, looking after Melanie.'

'None of you went out before six?' asked the sergeant.

'No,' we said in chorus.

'Then we all had supper,' I said, 'at about seven-thirty.'

'And Mark and I went to the pub about…what? Eight-thirty?' said Jodie. She turned to Mark.

'Yeah. We took Karen's car. Back at around eleven.' Both officers were scribbling down the details.

'I left here shortly after three and went back to my cottage,' said Stuart.

'He came back at about 9.30pm and we went to the pub,' I said. 'The Cart and Horses – got back about 11.30. Everyone was in by then.'

Sergeant Harris turned to Stuart. 'Can anyone vouch for your whereabouts after you left here at around three o'clock, Mr Wishart?'

His tongue darted around inside his mouth. 'I don't think they can, no. I'm staying on my own at the cottage and I don't know if anyone saw me return.'

Mark stared at him, intrigued.

The female officer held up a coloured photograph of the little boy. He had thick blond curls and was beaming, sitting in a highchair wearing a Donald-Duck bib. 'Does anyone recognise him?' she said. 'Did you see him around here any time yesterday afternoon?'

We passed the picture round and shook our heads in turn.

'Have any of you witnessed anything unusual in the last few days? Anyone hanging around? Vehicles standing at the roadside?'

I was tempted to say I'd found ten thousand pounds in Mark's sports bag, but managed to hold my tongue. I couldn't see how it was related.

Sergeant Harris pointed to the baby buggy in the hall. 'Can we see the child, please?'

'Yes, of course,' said Karen. As if on cue, the baby-monitor let out a loud wail. 'She's not been well, I'm afraid,' she said, her foot on the first stair. 'She's a bit grouchy. You'd better come up. '

'And we'd like to take a look around the property, if no one has any objections?' announced Sergeant Harris as they followed Karen.

We all muttered our assent.

I overheard Sergeant Mallory asking Karen to undress the child, so they could see her in full. The officers then tramped into each of the rooms in turn – I could hear them opening cupboards and drawers. They checked the cellar, then went outside to the byre along the track.

'I wonder where the poor mite is?' asked Jodie, her fingers toying with her bottom lip.

'In this terribly cold weather…' I added, looking out of the window. The last of the day's sun had lit an invisible touchpaper and begun to scorch the sky. It would be dark in an hour. The child had already been missing for around twenty-four hours.

Five minutes later, they came back inside and I overheard the officers' parting words; a warning to Karen to be particularly vigilant with the baby.

'No worries there,' muttered Mark. 'She's all over the kid.'

After they'd gone, I remembered my feeling yesterday morning that someone had been lurking in the woods. Except, there wasn't anything to go on. A possible figure, but I hadn't seen if it was male or female. Perhaps it had been Stuart, before he found me, but it could easily have been a black bin liner blowing about in the wind.

Stuart slipped on his jacket as I began putting together the evening meal. I invited him to stay, but he said he'd already taken lamb chops out of the freezer for that evening.

'I'll give you a ring tomorrow, if that's okay. The reception isn't great here. Do you have a landline?'

'No...' I hadn't seen a phone anywhere and assumed there wasn't one, but decided to double check. 'I'll ask Karen.'

I swung my head around the door and opened my mouth to speak.

'No, 'fraid not,' came her reply; she'd been listening to our conversation.

'That's a shame.' He wiped his feet on the mat as if he was coming in rather than going out. 'See you soon, then.' He left with his shoulders hunched, looking troubled.

'Someone doesn't have an alibi,' said Mark, watching me from the kitchen.

'Oh, shut up,' I said, scuttling back to the warmth of the oven.

He echoed my words in a high-pitched whiney voice and disappeared into the scullery. Within seconds, I heard the cork pop from yet another of bottle of wine.

During the meal, Karen was uncharacteristically withdrawn and left half of her food. My birthday seemed long forgotten by everyone.

It was Mark and Jodie's turn to wash up, so I followed Karen when she drifted into the sitting room. She paced up and down in front of the fire, rubbing her arms.

'Are you okay?' I asked, patting the sofa seat beside me. 'Is it the news about this awful abduction?'

'Makes you think, doesn't it?' she said, perching on the edge of the seat. 'Especially when I've got a little tot of my own.'

She shuddered and I put my arm around her; her body was stiff and full of corners. 'I'm sorry your birthday has fallen rather flat,' she said.

'It's not your fault. You made the cake – and gave me the lovely voucher – it's far more than I ever expected.'

The others joined us and Karen handed over a pile of activity leaflets she'd collected. 'Didn't know if you wanted to have a go at something sporty,' she said in a vacant tone.

Mark flicked through a few and held one up about the Gleneagles Pursuits Centre. 'Ah, man – they do snowboarding and rock-climbing and all sorts...'

Jodie snatched the leaflet and skimmed through it. 'It says here, you need to have experience.'

'Yeah, well, I *have*, remember? When we went to Innsbruck. You went shopping and I went to the beginners' camp. How about it, Babe? Come on – let's pack.'

'Pack? What – now?' Jodie turned to Karen and me. 'Sorry about this,' she said, getting up to follow him. 'He's been itching to get out and "do something", as he puts it, since the moment we got here.'

Mark came back with a backpack slung over his shoulder. Jodie was right. Mark did seem keen to grab hold of any excuse to leave the cottage. He was grinning and breathless, as if someone had pressed a 'supercharge' button inside him. It was followed by the announcement that the two of them were going to a pub they'd heard about called The Bull.

'We'll spend the night in Fort William,' he said, 'and tomorrow, we'll head off to have a go at snowboarding and stuff. Looks like it's about thirty miles away, so might be back tomorrow…might not.' He tipped his hand to demonstrate the uncertainty. 'I'll go down the lane to get a signal and call a cab.'

'No, it's okay,' said Karen, getting to her feet. 'I'll take you both – to the pub at least – if you tell me where it is.'

'You sure?'

'I thought you might want to go out for a drink again. I was going to offer to drop you at the pub, anyway,' she said.

'What about the kid?'

111

'I can keep an eye on her,' I interjected.

'It's fine, Alice. Mel's restless – a ride in the car might lull her to sleep. It always used to when she was tiny and it did the trick on the way back from the hospital.'

'Ah, brilliant,' said Mark. 'The Bull's not far.'

'You going to join them at the pub?' Karen asked me.

I heard Mark utter a barely perceptible groan, before wiping his hand over his mouth, pretending it was a burp.

'No – it's okay. I'll stay here,' I said. No way was I going to be the gooseberry. 'Got a bit of a headache.'

As if on cue, a loud wailing came through the baby monitor beside us. Karen shrugged. 'I'll get her ready.'

Jodie came down the stairs and dumped a rucksack by the front door. 'Mark's always got itchy feet,' she said apologetically.

I wasn't sorry they were going; it would be a relief to wave goodbye to the squabbling and backhanded remarks for a while – not to mention the racket from the top floor.

Karen came down with Melanie shortly afterwards. 'Right,' she said. 'Keys, torch, cell phone.' She patted her pockets. I'd noticed a couple of times before that she'd used American words: eggplant instead of aubergine, cookie for biscuit. She didn't have an accent, but the time she'd spent in LA had rubbed off on her, nevertheless. 'We'll see you later. Don't wait up if you're tired.'

I opened the door and they all set off into the night.

I'd been sitting in front of the fire reading a book and must have dozed off. It was the clink of glasses that woke me. Karen was above me holding one inches from my face, half-full with red wine.

'A final nightcap,' she said, handing it over. She sat in the rocking chair sliding her feet beneath her. 'I've just put Mel to bed – she's fast asleep.' She crossed her fingers and we both stared at the silent baby monitor.

I lifted the glass. 'Thanks – I shouldn't really.' I was aware that my head had been throbbing on and off since lunchtime and I'd taken several doses of painkillers. I discretely touched the spot above my temple where I'd whacked it under the sink; it was tender and felt like the top of a hard-boiled egg.

'Come on. It's your birthday,' she said leaning over to tap her glass against mine.

I took a long sip. 'Here's to you and Mel and your new life back together again.'

Karen looked down and smiled, but it didn't light up her face. 'It's going to be tougher than I thought,' she said.

I cleared my throat, thinking back to a few hours before. It seemed only right to mention it.

'Karen? You know when you asked me to get Mel's dummy earlier?' she waited for me to go on. 'Well, I found Mark snooping about in your room.'

She straightened up. 'Really? What was he doing?'

'I'm not sure. Looking in your suitcase.' I said. 'I'll show you.' She frowned as I led the way upstairs.

Inside her room, I stood where Mark had been, with his feet touching her opened suitcase on the floor. Karen quietly rifled through the baby clothes inside.

'I don't think anything's missing,' she whispered not wanting to wake Mel.

She ushered me out onto the landing. 'What would he want?' I asked.

'Perhaps he came in to borrow a hot-water bottle…'

'There's something else,' I said. 'You know when you asked me to go into their room yesterday and get the towel?' She stood with her arms folded, her head on one side. 'There was a bag on the top shelf and it fell out…and some of the contents sort of spilled out…and I found about ten thousand pounds in cash…'

She did a double-take. 'You what?'

We went up another flight. I flipped the light on in their room and opened the cupboard in the corner. Karen looked awkward, holding back on the threshold. The bag was sitting on the towels as it had been before. I lifted it down.

I should have known straight away; it was lighter. I put it on the bed and unzipped it, rummaging through the cans of deodorant and CDs.

'It's gone,' I said.

Karen sank down onto the bed. 'Are you sure about this?'

'Definitely, absolutely,' I said. 'Batches of fifty-pound notes.' I looked more carefully at the contents this time and pulled out an aerosol. 'Look – it's shaving foam.' There was a packet of razor blades and a pair of dirty men's socks. 'The bag must be Mark's.'

'Bloody hell,' she said, inhaling the words.

'I know…'

Our faces were mirrors of each other as we chewed our bottom lips in unison.

'Why would he need that amount of money on him?' I said.

'Who knows?' she whispered.

She ushered me out and closed the door. 'Maybe he's buying a car,' she added, without conviction.

'Yeah – maybe…' I said, wanting it to be that simple.

Chapter 19

I woke far too early, with one of those jolts that shook me instantly from deep sleep to super-alert, as though someone beside my pillow had called my name.

I slid the curtain to one side, not sure what to expect. There had been no further snow, but what had already fallen looked solid, like immovable blocks of ice. I picked at the frozen condensation inside the window, staring distractedly into space and reached down to switch on the heater.

Then I saw him. Lying, face down on the floor. His left arm was squashed underneath him, his right splayed out to the side. He was wearing a brown leather bomber jacket and his jeans were hanging low, the waistband lying across his buttocks. The skin on his back was meringue white. He looked like a half-dressed mannequin. It looked like Mark.

I made a whimpering sound, my hands over my face, staring at him, not knowing what to do. One leg was hitched up like he was trying to drag himself across the carpet. Except he was perfectly still. I stood on the spot waiting for him to move – then I rushed out of the room and hammered on Karen's door.

She opened the door a fraction, her eyes screwed up. 'Hush – you'll wake her,' she hissed. 'It's not even seven, yet.'

'Something's happened,' I said, reaching out for her wrist. 'You've got to come – right now!'

I dragged her, barefoot in her flimsy chemise, into my room. She stopped abruptly, her toes inches from his boot.

'What happened,' she whispered, looking down to him and then up at me repeatedly.

'I don't know. I just found him here…'

Karen went to the window and pulled the curtains right back. Under the man's head a pool of blood the size of a dinner plate had made its way across the floor.

'Shit – how long has he…?

She was far braver than me and bent down, placing her fingers against his neck.

'Try his pulse,' she instructed. I stretched out my fingers and let them hover above his limp wrist. I didn't know how to do it. She nudged me aside and did it herself, shifting her fingers around, trying to find the right place. She looked up.

'Well – he's dead,' she whispered.

'Oh, God…' I said.

I stood up. 'We mustn't touch anything.' I swallowed a taste like rotting slug inside my mouth. 'It's Mark, isn't it?'

Karen got down on her knees, then slowly pulled on his shoulder to turn him over.

'You shouldn't have done that,' I spluttered. 'You're disturbing a crime scene!'

His eyes were open but gluey like egg white, the colour already draining from his lips. I hovered by the doorway, not wanting to take a closer look.

117

'It's not Mark,' she said.

I stepped forward. 'Oh, God – it isn't,' I spluttered. 'Who the hell is it then?'

'No idea…'

She stood up. I was looking at the door, the rug, the bed, attempting to work out what could have happened.

'How come you didn't hear him?' said Karen. 'He must have made one hell of a crash when he fell.'

I shook my head. 'I didn't hear a thing. I didn't even hear him come in…'

'He must have tripped over the mat and hit his head on the corner of the bedstead.' We both honed our gaze onto the solid iron balls on the top of the bedframe. I tried to remember. There was something about what Karen was saying that sounded familiar, but it was like a dream I'd once had where only fragments remained, floating around in the wrong order.

'Maybe it was so quick he didn't make a sound,' I suggested. 'But – what was he doing *here* – in my room?'

I stared in astonishment at the weight of him, the size of him, unable to see how it could be true. 'How could I not have heard him?' I muttered.

Karen walked over to my bedside cabinet and held up the bottle of sleeping tablets, rattling them. 'I think these might have something to do with that.'

I reached over to reclaim them. 'I hardly ever use them,' I protested.

She put the bottle back. 'We'll talk about it later,' she said.

'We should call the police.' I grabbed my phone from the pocket of my bathrobe and punched in 999. Nothing happened. I looked down at it, then pressed it to my ear. There was no tone. I checked the bars on the screen. Of course, no signal.

'We're out of range,' said Karen. 'I'll get changed and go down the lane – see if I can get a connection. I'll drive if I have to. You stay with Mel.'

'We should roll him back to how we found him.'

Karen leant down and gave his shoulder a push so he slumped back against the floor.

I grabbed a bundle of clothes – I had to get out of the room as quickly as possible – and stumbled into the bathroom. I got to the toilet just in time. Three surges of vomit spattered against the sides. I sat on the floor holding the bowl, shaking. What the hell had happened?

Edging my way out, I dropped my clothes and patted the wall beside me as if I was blind. I gripped the windowsill on the landing and made myself focus. Outside, Karen was running along the track, stopping, then waving her phone around. Then she held it to her face and I saw her lips move. Thank God, she'd got through. I rested my head against the wall and breathed heavily.

I reached out with both hands and grabbed on to the bannister. I don't know how I got down the stairs without falling. My legs were like sticks of cooked spaghetti and there was a snowstorm behind my eyes.

Karen came inside and sat with me at the bottom of the stairs. 'They're coming,' she said, 'but it could be a while.'

'Who is he?' I said.

'I told you. I've no idea.'

'Why would he turn up like this? How did he get in?'

She grabbed my hand and we went from room to room together, checking for any signs of intrusion. We spotted it straight away; the kitchen window was open. Blasts of cold air were bursting through. Karen reached out to shut it, but I caught her arm.

'We mustn't touch anything,' I said.

'It's freezing,' she said, nudging it almost closed with her elbow.

I pointed to a single wet boot-print on the window ledge. 'That's his,' I said stupidly, my mouth hanging open.

'Looks like he was on his own,' said Karen.

'Was he trying to rob us? Is this connected to Mark – and all that money I found?' I was chuntering on, mostly to myself, trying to fill the space with words so I could block out the dead man's image.

I went through to the fireplace and resorted to pacing back and forth. My heart was thudding away under my ribcage, my palms sweating even though I was shivering at the same time. The hand on the clock face shifted to quarter-past, then half-past.

'Where are the police?' I said, taking hold of the bookshelf for balance.

'I told you. They might take a while.' Her hand was shaking as she took my arm. She was more perturbed than she sounded. 'Why don't you get dressed? You're freezing.'

The thought of the man lying at the foot of my bed kept me rooted to the spot. I'd had my clothes in my hand a minute ago, where were they now? Seeing the stupefied look on my face, Karen went upstairs. She came back with my jeans and jumper. I pulled them on over my pyjamas without thinking.

'I'll light the fire,' she said. 'It'll give me something to do.' Her face was puckered into a confused frown, her shoulders sagging. 'How's your head been, by the way?'

'Oh,' I instinctively put my hand up to the bump. It was the last thing on my mind right now. 'It comes and goes.'

'I can't see anything missing. We should have a check around.'

'Is Mel okay?'

'She's fine. Still asleep.'

I didn't like the idea of the baby being so close to the man in my bedroom, but he wasn't going to do anything, he wasn't going to hurt her. Not now.

I watched Karen get the fire started, feeling I should be doing something, but my brain was too busy firing questions like ping-pong balls in every direction. I got up and stood by the window in the hall so I could see the track, while Karen went around checking for signs of disturbance. I just wanted the police to come and take the body away.

No sign of them. It looked like it had rained and re-frozen overnight; everything was covered in shards of glass. The roads would be treacherous.

'Come back to the fire, Alice,' Karen called to me, 'there's nothing we can do.'

I stared at the flames, then the clock, then the window in turn as the minutes ticked by. Just before 10am, a sharp rap of the knocker made me jump and

Karen leapt to answer the door. *At last – the police.* I felt too wobbly to get up – by that stage my headache was scorching a hole through my temple.

After a few seconds, I turned to listen, expecting Karen to show them through at any moment. I could hear low voices, but they weren't getting any closer. Then there was nothing. Karen came back in on her own.

'Just Mrs Ellington,' she said. 'Wanting to know if we had enough blankets.'

'Did you tell her?' My eyes were wide in a frantic stare.

'Of course not!'

I was taken aback. 'Why ever not?'

'She would only have panicked – why upset her like that? The police will deal with it.'

'But where are they?' I sank back down again gripping the chair arm, watching the clock on the mantelpiece like it was a bomb about to go off.

'The police aren't coming, are they? We need to ring again.' My phone was in my bedroom and I wasn't going to retrieve it unless it was a last resort.

'You're right,' said Karen, backing out of the room. 'I'll try again.'

Chapter 20

It was lunchtime and still the police hadn't arrived. Karen fed Mel and ate a sandwich herself, but I couldn't touch anything.

'They should have been here by now,' I said confused.

'Maybe I didn't get through properly,' she said simply.

'I thought you spoke to someone.'

'I did…it was a very bad line…maybe I was cut off…'

'I'm worried someone will come looking for him,' I said, plucking at the skin under my chin.

'Stop fussing,' she snapped. 'I'll put Mel down for a nap and try them again – see what's going on.'

It was snowing heavily when Karen enveloped herself in her thickest coat to brace the elements again. I lost her in the blizzard as I watched from the hall window. White flakes had stuck to the fur around her hood and she shook them off when she got back inside.

'No good,' she said, shuddering with the cold. 'I reckon the atmospherics are playing havoc with the signal. It's dreadful underfoot, too – I don't fancy driving unless I have to. I'll try later.'

I stood at the bottom of the stairs. 'I can't bear this.' I stamped my foot on the verge of hysteria.

'Okay – come on.' She took my hand and put her foot on the first stair, but I pulled away.

'Come on – where?' I said, backing off.

'We should find out who he is. It might tell us why he came here.'

'No – I don't…I can't…'

'Let's just see if there's anything in his pockets.'

I let her open my bedroom door. I tried not to breathe in; there was already a bad smell, a cross between Mel's nappy and cat food that had gone off. I noticed a dark stain in the seat of his jeans this time and put my hand over my mouth.

Karen was already beside him on the floor. She felt his pockets and pulled out a wallet from the inside of his bomber jacket. She began fingering through it. My body was stiff with terror.

'Okay – it says here he's called Charles Smith and he's twenty-three years old.'

'Smith?'

'You don't think that's his real name?' She pulled out a piece of card. 'There's a train ticket – for tomorrow – from Glasgow to London.'

'What else?'

'Looks like there's also an open train ticket to Europe.' She sank back on her heels. 'It's okay, he's a backpacker.'

'What do you mean, *It's okay*? It's hardly okay, is it? He's dead.'

'He's a free spirit.'

'But won't someone come looking for him? Wouldn't he have told someone where he was going?'

She flipped through the rest of his wallet; I saw a few notes, but no credit cards.

'There are no photos of a girlfriend – no photos of kids. I reckon he was on his own.' She peered up and down the body. 'Look at him – he's been living rough, he's a drifter. He was about to leave the country. No one's going to miss him.'

I sent my eyes across the floor, everywhere but the spot where his body lay. 'If he's a backpacker where's his rucksack?'

'Let's look outside,' she suggested. I followed – any excuse to get away.

We stuffed our feet into our boots at the front door and hurried out. Karen checked the hedges at the front and I followed the wall round the cottage to the back.

'Got it,' I called out. A tall rucksack had been left under the same window where the intruder had let himself in. Karen joined me.

'He obviously wasn't planning on staying long,' she said. 'Quick in and out – then he was heading off to Europe with his rich pickings.'

'Just an opportunist thief, you think?' I asked her. 'Trying his luck with the holiday cottages?'

'Maybe.' She pointed to the window. 'It was pretty easy to break in – he probably just levered it open with a penknife.'

She was unzipping his rucksack before I could stop her. 'Not much here,' she said. 'A paperback, a few maps – oh, look – a passport,' she said, flipping it open. 'Yeah – Charles Smith.' She started putting things back.

'Shall we bring it inside?'

'No – better leave it here. The police need to know where we found it.'

I looked down at her bare hands. 'You've touched things, Karen. Your fingerprints are going to be all over his wallet, his bag, his clothes...'

She straightened up, shrugging me off and we went inside. 'At least we know,' she said, blowing into her hands in the hall.

It did little to set my mind at rest. All we really knew was that our cottage was exceedingly easy to break into and we'd contaminated a murder scene. We didn't know how he'd died and we didn't know why he'd broken in.

'Why don't you have a bath? You look frozen,' suggested Karen. 'I'll try the police again. If I can't get through, I'll risk the drive to the village and find a public phone.'

'There's one in the pub,' I replied. 'And there's a phone box on the village green.'

'There you are – I'll go once you've had your bath if I can't get a signal.'

As soon as I stepped onto the bathmat, I knew I had a problem. I felt the floor sliding away from me. *Oh, no. Not here. Not now.* I buried my face in the towel, hoping I could wipe this crazy seizure away. *It's okay. Breathe. In. Out. Steady.* But it wasn't okay. Another earthquake was coming on inside my head, just like the other time.

As I tried to make my thoughts follow a straight line, my vision began to go patchy; large white holes started appearing where the floor should have been, where the door should have been. It was back; the same terrifying episode I'd had in London after I'd been mugged. I thought I'd left it behind.

I couldn't get my brain to work at all; an intense vertigo had claimed me. Next thing, I was lying in a heap on the wet lino holding the base of the sink, blinking slowly in big pronounced swipes but seeing only fractured shapes. I could feel the panic hissing behind my teeth. I kept seeing the man's body as if he was right next to me – feel his skin, his hair brushing my naked leg, his cold stiff hand on my arm. *Get him off me! Someone – take him away!*

I couldn't think straight, whatever was taking over felt loud and angry and was heading straight towards me. I lay there, my mouth hanging open, waiting for whatever this was to pass.

There was a loud rapping on the bathroom door and when there was no reply, someone came in.

'What the—?' cried Karen, cradling my head. 'Speak to me, Ally. What happened?'

She must have heard me. I didn't know I'd cried out.

More than anything, I was ashamed. I was better than this. I'd done a lot of work on myself in the last six years. I'd stopped being weak, stopped giving in to negativity, but what happened three months ago – and now this dead body – had done more damage than I could handle.

My mouth wouldn't work anymore. There was no moisture inside, only grit. But I knew who Karen was. A good sign. I was coming back. She half shook, half cradled me, repeating my name. Eventually, I could feel sensation in my fingers. I could smell her coffee breath over my mouth, feel the hard floor pressing into my bare backside and the pain in my head. I stirred and tried to sit up.

'Shit, Alice – what the hell happened?'

I tried to form words but they came out sounding nothing like I wanted them to. 'Imffnnnn…'

'What?'

'Imffnnnn…'

She hauled me towards the bath and leant me against it while she grabbed something in the sink. The next thing I knew she was dabbing a cold wet flannel over my face. She squeezed a few drops of it into my gaping mouth. It tasted soapy and I coughed, trying to spit it out.

She wrapped a towel around me and tried to rub sense back into me.

I lost track of what happened next until I could feel my eyes being peeled open with damp fingers. I was lying flat on something soft. I blinked, then kept my eyes open, my vision pulling items back into focus again.

'Alice – what the hell happened? Are you okay? Have you had a stroke?'

I checked the carpet quickly, wanting to know which room I was in. It was Karen's.

'I slipped, that's all,' my mouth was dry and clacky. 'I lost my balance…'

She rolled her tongue over her lips and stared at me. I could tell she didn't believe me. She held my hand for a second or two, then let it fall on the bedspread. 'You'd better rest,' she said. 'I'll bring up some tea.'

As she set the mug down beside me I decided to

explain everything – the mugging in September, the subsequent panic attack.

'Why didn't you tell me this before?' she said.

'I would have done,' I insisted, 'only the others turned up and you were worried about the baby…and …'

'Getting mugged at knifepoint is a big deal, Alice. No wonder you've had panic attacks.'

'Only one…before this. They're like seizures,' I explained, 'parts of my brain burn themselves out. That's the only way to describe it. I've never experienced anything like it before. I thought I wouldn't have any more…I don't have the tablets…'

She took hold of my hand. 'You're going to be fine, Ally. You've had one nasty shock after another. Finding someone dead on the floor…can't have…well…' She didn't need to go on.

'I didn't want you to think I was a head case,' I admitted.

'Don't be silly. A mugging can happen to anyone. And this…you were in the wrong place at the wrong time – that's all.'

'Thanks…' Everything she said reminded me of why I liked her so much. Attentive, caring, no shred of disapproval.

'You're a tough cookie now,' she said. 'You'll get through this.' She grabbed my shoulders, gripping me firmly. 'We both will.'

I nipped my lips together, cursing the fact that she'd caught me like this. I was desperate she shouldn't feel sorry for me. I wanted to be her equal, not the fragile, hopeless one who still needed looking after. 'What time is it?' I said, trying to sit up. 'No sign of the police?'

'I tried again just now,' she said. 'There's still no signal and the car won't start. I must have forgotten to top up the anti-freeze – she's normally incredibly reliable. We'll wait until the morning. The police will take it in their stride, I'm sure.'

She had more faith in their understanding than I had. Once the police knew how long it had taken us to inform them – and the fact that we'd interfered with the body and his belongings – I was convinced they'd be waving their fists in our faces.

'One of us should walk to the village,' I said.

'Well, you can't go like this,' she stated. 'And Mel isn't too great – she's been coughing – so I'm staying put.'

'Has Stuart been round?' I asked.

'No.' She smoothed out the pillow beside my head. 'Try to get some sleep.'

A tidal wave of exhaustion claimed me before she left the room.

I woke to cooking smells rising up from downstairs, but they made me feel sick. I kept thinking of what was lying behind my closed bedroom door. What if the others came back?

Karen had brought my clothes back from the bathroom and left them neatly folded on a chair, so I pulled them on, ready to join her. I had to make myself eat something; I was feeling light-headed.

I plumped up the pillows so they'd feel fresh for Karen that night and tidied up the bedspread. Simple, normal, familiar actions to ground me. I put the lamp on beside her bed and glanced down into the suitcase Mark had been hovering over when I'd caught him.

It looked full of baby clothes; that's all. I lifted out a pink sleepsuit, a pullover, a pair of leggings. They had all been well worn, the colours fading, the surface slightly pilled through many turns in a washing machine.

A batch of baby clothes – nothing could be more innocent – and yet, there was something that struck me as not quite right. It was then, I noticed. The label on the vest I was holding read 9-12 months. I picked up a coat with a hood, which read: 12-18 months. Mel struck me as a fairly small child, not surprising, given she'd been so ill – these items were bigger yet they had been worn.

I heard a footstep and snapped round. Karen was standing right behind me.

'What are you doing?'

'I'm sorry – they looked…so soft and cute…'

'You're not getting broody now, are you, Alice Flemming?'

I laughed. 'No – I…'

'She's going to grow, you know,' she said, taking the coat from my hand and folding it. 'I've been stocking up. Kids go through things at such a rate – it costs a fortune.'

She was absolutely right, of course, but Karen had never been the sort to buy second-hand clothes. I remembered her making fun of me once, when I'd turned up to a party in a Laura Ashley dress I'd found in a charity shop.

Karen must have changed a lot since then.

There was so much I didn't know about her.

Over supper we both acted like the body upstairs wasn't there. It was the only way to get through it. With continuing brutal weather, no signal and the car refusing to start, we couldn't get the message through by any other means. There were no police on their way. We asked each other superficial questions about life after University, killing time until we were tired enough to go to bed.

I didn't refer to the period straight after we graduated, when we'd spent a couple of days – just the two of us – at her parent's place in Bristol.

I could tell instantly from the size and interior of their huge property that they were rolling in money. Karen's father owned a record label and was fiercely ambitious. I'm sure Karen learnt how to win people over from him.

He had a way of making you think you'd made a decision of your own, when in fact you'd only gone along with one of his – just like she did.

Her mother, too, was a high-flier; a senior editor for an antiques magazine, if I recall correctly. She oozed grace and allure, chatting with me and asking my opinion as if I was a trusted friend. I could see where Karen got her ability to make people feel special.

That stay hadn't worked out too well. She was seeing Roland at the time – he was a mechanic and her parents didn't approve. It only dawned on me some time later that I'd been brought in purely to cover for her. The two of us would stroll down to the harbour and then Roland would turn up – *Oh, what a coincidence!* – and she'd ask me to disappear for a few hours, but not tell her parents about it once we got back. I'd had nothing better to do at the time; I ate ice creams, went to a couple of art-house films at the quayside and got through a novel. With hindsight, I could see she'd used me. The memory brought back uncomfortable reminders of the old me – the one who was too eager to please and didn't expect any better. I didn't want to dwell on either of those unpalatable aspects of myself.

'In the year after Leeds, what happened then?' I asked. 'You didn't jet straight off to America?'

She pushed the rest of her cauliflower to the edge of her plate. I'd barely touched mine.

'I stayed in Bristol with my parents for a while. I needed to make some money. I'd spent everything my parents had given me to tide me over at Leeds.'

'So, you got a job?'

'I worked in a lab for a few months for a pharmaceutical company, researching metabolic diseases. My father suggested it. I loathed everything about it – setting the alarm, getting on the bus every morning, meetings, rules. Within about six weeks it had driven me mad.'

Wasn't that what life was like once you stopped being a student? Didn't people in the real world have to set their alarm, live to other peoples' schedules and work within corporate systems? Didn't you just knuckle down and grin and bear it?

'You left?'

'I couldn't do it anymore. It was making me ill. I couldn't breathe.'

'And your parents let you swan off to America to be an au pair – just like that?'

I knew they'd ploughed lots of money into Karen's education. They clearly expected great things for her future.

'They made a hell of a fuss,' she said, casting her eyes upwards, 'as you can imagine. They wanted better for their brainy daughter, but they didn't understand. I just wanted time to let my hair down and live a little.'

'And you were an au pair, letting your hair down for, what…nearly five years?'

She laughed, her mouth full. 'You disapprove.'

'I'm just surprised that's all. You seemed so motivated at University. I always saw you as go-getting and, well, a bit ruthless, to be honest…'

'Life in LA was so easy,' she said. 'I was living way above my means in a rich family home. I realised I didn't have to climb a career ladder to be happy – there were easier ways to earn money.' She smiled as she said it, but her words didn't ring true. I knew more than ever now that she was hiding something from me.

I winced as I turned my head.

'Headache again?' she asked.

I put my hand out. 'Honestly – there's nothing wrong with me. An intruder is dead at the end of my bed – I think that's enough to give anyone a funny turn.'

'Yeah, you're right,' she conceded.

At bedtime, Karen wound some wire she'd found in one of the drawers around the arm of the kitchen window, so it couldn't be opened. All the other ground-floor windows were too small for anyone over about six years old to get through.

We went upstairs. There was nothing else for it. The police wouldn't be coming until the morning, so Karen brought a clean white sheet from the attic room and we covered the body with it. It was the best we could do to afford him some dignity.

'Sofa or top room?' suggested Karen.

My preference would have been to sleep on the floor in Karen's room, but there wasn't space. Karen helped me change the sheets in Jodie and Mark's room and, reluctantly, I took a deep breath and settled down in there, hoping they wouldn't come back.

I had to take another sleeping tablet or else I wouldn't have slept at all. I had no option, but I wasn't pleased with myself. I could picture Dr Winslow's face.

'Absolute last resort,' he'd said. 'These are to be used once in a blue moon, okay?'

During the night I had vivid dreams of wandering around the house. I floated like a ghost in and out of every room. I started in the top bedroom, opening the drawers and cupboards, finding odd things – like a pair of wire-cutters and a box of lollipops. Did they belong to the cottage or to Mark and Jodie? At one point I had visions of leaning over the dead man, peeling the sheet away from his face, and then backing away because of the smell; putrid offal with a sickly sweet overtone. After that, I was in the sitting room trailing my fingers over the books in the bookcase. I remember it being cold. A cruel, gnawing cold that ate into my bones. I looked down and my bare feet were buried in snow.

The next thing I knew I was in the kitchen. Karen

was slapping my face.

It was 3am and I was holding a knife.

Chapter 21

I wasn't dreaming anymore. Karen really was slapping my face and I really did have a knife in my hand, holding it in front of me like a sword. I dropped it as soon as I realised what it was, then I flopped into Karen's arms.

'What are you doing down here?' she hissed. She put the frying pan she'd been wielding on the floor. 'I heard a noise. It's the middle of the night.'

It was hard to focus; the table, the fridge, the floor all seemed to be covered in a grey fog. 'I'm not sure – I'm a bit confused.' I knew my words were slurring one into the next; the sleeping tablet tugging me towards oblivion.

'Alice – you had a carving knife in your hand.' She was leading me towards the stairs.

'Did I? I don't remember.'

She must have taken me back to the attic room and put me to bed. I didn't remember a thing.

Karen was on her own when I went down for breakfast.

'Where's Mel?' I asked.

'Still asleep.' It was early. I hadn't heard a peep out of her.

Karen poured me a cup of coffee and handed me a plate with two slices of toast. She stood over me waiting to see what I had to say; whether I'd remember last night.

'I've…I've never done that before,' I said, my voice small, dropping away.

'What do you remember?' she sat down, leaning forward, her chin cupped in her hand.

'Not much. I think I was wandering about the place; going into different rooms.'

'Did you take a sleeping tablet last night?'

'Yes.' I didn't look at her.

'You had a knife, Alice. You were holding it up when I came towards you. I was scared.'

I didn't believe her at first. 'I can't have…' Then the picture crystallised inside my mind. She was telling the truth; I remembered the blade clattering onto the flagstones. 'What was I doing with a *carving knife*…?'

'You'd been outside,' she said.

'Had I?'

'The back door was open. You were frozen.'

'Like I said – nothing like this has ever happened before. I can't understand it.'

Karen spread a layer of thick strawberry jam on her toast. For a second it looked congealed and obscene.

'My brother used to sleepwalk,' she said, getting straight to the point. 'The GP put it down to his sleeping tablets, because he only started doing it once he was taking them. They swapped him to a different type.' She licked her lips. 'Perhaps you should try that.'

I was shaking, not sure if it was from the cold or the shock. I wrapped my hands tightly around my waist.

'Yes, yes, perhaps I should…' I said in a half-whisper.

I put the toast to one side; I couldn't cope with anything solid just now.

'You hear of people attacking their nearest and dearest in their sleep, sometimes,' she said. 'Even *killing* them – when they're actually sleepwalking. I remember a case when we were at Uni. A bloke stabbed his mother-in-law and the defence tried to claim it was diminished responsibility. He was sent down, though – the jury didn't believe a word of it.'

'Oh, God – don't say that,' I burst out. I wasn't sure what she was implying. 'You don't think I…'

There was a silence and Karen didn't close up the yawning gap fast enough. I got up, my chair scraping across the floor like nails on a blackboard. 'It can't have been me,' I cried. 'I wouldn't do anything like that.'

'Look – we'd better try the police again,' said Karen. 'I can't stand this much longer.'

She picked up her phone and went to find her boots in the hall. 'Wait…' I said. 'I'm really terrified.'

'I know – we both are.'

'No – what I mean is…wait…I need to...'

I left her at the bottom of the stairs and went up to the landing outside my bedroom, my hand on the doorknob. I held it there, feeling the sweat build up for half a minute, before I dared turn it. I knew the smell would be getting worse by now. I squeezed my eyes shut and stepped inside. And came straight back out again. I heaved and ran for the bathroom, but nothing came up.

I had to do this. I had to go back in.

I took a deep breath and hurried back inside. Karen had left a window open – or maybe it wasn't Karen, maybe it had been me, last night – I couldn't be sure anymore. My sense of reality was buckling at the edges.

It was a bizarre scene, like a shot from a television crime drama. I had to know if it was possible. I had to double check.

I made myself think it through, starting with the intruder creeping up the stairs and coming into my room. Could he have tripped on the rug? I glanced at the sheet covering him. I'd have to move it to be certain.

I lifted it away from his body, using two outstretched fingers, squeezing my nostrils together with the other hand. I gazed down at his boots. Did he look like he'd slipped? The rag rug was rumpled under his legs, but maybe that had happened when he fell.

I looked at his head. There was definitely a wound on the top near the crown. Karen's theory about him hitting his head on the bedstead was plausible, surely. I scrutinised both of the iron balls on the frame at the foot of the bed. I couldn't tell if there was any blood on them; in any case, it would have dried by now. I didn't want to touch them. We'd already touched enough.

I thought about the police. Was Karen really calling them as I carried out my amateur re-enactment? I turned to the door. She was standing on the threshold with her phone in her hand, waiting.

'I'm trying to work out if I could have killed him,' I said, my voice breaking.

'You'd had a sleeping tablet then, too, hadn't you?'

I nodded, not looking at her.

'You think you might have hit him with something and not realised?'

I dissolved into tears, dropping my head. 'I don't know. After last night…'

Karen side-stepped the body and gave me a brief hug. I looked around the room; there was nothing there I could have used to hit him – the washstand was too heavy, the lamps were built into the wall. The weapon must have come from somewhere else.

Then I realised the flaw in our thinking.

'If I *had* hit him – why wasn't the weapon right here, when we found him?' I ducked down to check under the bed, then ran my eye under the cupboards. Nothing had rolled underneath, out of sight. I stood up straight. 'Unless, I got rid of it – or hid it, or…'

Karen made a smacking sound with her lips and didn't contradict me.

'What about the police?' I said.

Karen looked down at her phone. She'd already put her boots on, ready to go outside to get a signal. 'What do you want me to do?'

I couldn't think straight. I might have done something outrageous, unthinkable, without even knowing it – but equally, I might not have done it. My fingerprints would be on a weapon, my DNA would give me away. Forensic techniques were ingenious, these days, once the police got here they'd tear the place apart.

Karen was offering me a choice.

'I need time…to think,' I said.

I didn't have anything concrete to go on – nothing

but an all-consuming panic and dread whirling into a tornado inside my head. I could see the blue light flashing in my mind's eye, police officers pulling me away, feel the snap of the handcuffs around my wrists.

Karen was still waiting, holding up her phone.

'Don't call them,' I said, my words barely audible. I knew it was wrong; against everything I believed in and had been brought up to abide by. But terror was billowing inside me over what I might have done. I couldn't see straight, never mind think straight. I cupped my forehead. 'Just until I can think it through.'

'Okay.' She lowered the phone. 'I won't – for now.'

'Really? You'll do that for me?' I rushed over and clung to her, but she pulled away.

'Let's just agree it was a complete accident and he fell,' she said. 'Don't beat yourself up about it. It's over with.'

'It's not really, though – is it? What if…it *was* me? That means…'

I couldn't bring myself to put into words what it would mean.

She tugged at my sleeve. 'Let's go down to the kitchen – away from him.'

We sat at the table and I waited for her to speak. To do the Karen-thing and take control. All I could hear was my breath coming in and out in tiny snatches.

'Right,' she said, finally. 'If anyone comes back – Jodie and Mark or that man of yours – they'll know straight away from the smell that something's badly wrong. We can't avoid it any longer.'

I gaped at her, waiting for her to make everything right again.

'Let me think.' She stared at the grain of the wood in the rustic table, her finger trailing over her upper lip. 'Okay – I know what we should do. The main thing is to stay calm and be rational.'

I said nothing.

'This random stranger, Charlie whatever, broke in,' she went on, 'and there was a freak accident. It serves him right. No one is going to come looking for him. The damage has been done. He's dead. It's over. Let's clear him away before the others get back – then we can think about what to do next.'

'Clear him away?' It sounded so heartless, so callous.

'Alice,' she snapped, 'there are two outcomes at the moment – either we tell the police or Mark and Jodie come back and all hell breaks loose – which one do you want?'

I couldn't remember what had happened on the night he died. I couldn't remember last night either, but I knew I'd been sleepwalking, because I'd been found with a knife in my hand. If I'd killed the intruder, the police were going to work it all out. What kind of a defence would I have?

The alternative was that Karen was going to help me. Together, we could make it all go away. It wasn't right, but it was what I wanted more than anything. I'd only just started living my life after twenty-seven years. I wasn't a bad person. In my right mind, I'd never dream of hurting anyone. I couldn't lose everything now.

'Okay,' I whispered.

I'd have to pull myself together and go along with whatever her plan was.

'Right,' she said. 'Just do what I say. Let's go.'

We worked quickly and in bursts, to focus all our energy. Even though there were two of us, and the man had a slight build, he was heavy and the stairs were narrow.

We'd started calling him Charlie now – somehow it made the situation seem less dreadful. We sat him on the top step and had to bump him down each one, wrapped in the sheet like a big sack of luggage. It kept coming loose and every so often I'd see the buckle on his belt, a shoelace, the stubble on his chin and remember he was a real person.

Dragging him down was horrible; even though he was dead, it seemed cruel – disrespectful – to be putting him through that. I'll never forget that sound; the thud as his shoulders humped down to the next step. Thirteen of them in all; they were interminable. I winced at every single one, thinking his body was going to split apart with the impact.

When we reached the kitchen, we left Charlie on the floor, tightly bound in the bedsheet, leaning against the fridge.

'We'll just have to pray it's too early for the others to come back,' said Karen, fully geared up for the task.

I couldn't believe I was doing this. My brain, my gut, my conscience were all telling me to stop. I wanted to yell at Karen and make her see that moving the body – and hiding him – was *so wrong*. We *had* to tell the police and brace ourselves for the consequences. Then I

144

remembered Karen's face when she found me sleepwalking and imagined myself being led to a cell for the rest of my life – and I lost my nerve.

Karen turned and dragged my hands away from my crumpled face. 'Come on, Alice. There's no room for pussy-footing around. We've got to do this as fast as we can.' She opened the door and a blast of freezing air made me snatch a breath.

'Byre, first,' she said.

Once outside, the bleak chill of morning was a blessing. Its rawness brought me to my senses. Ahead of us, the sun was sliding slowly upwards behind the black spindled fingers of the trees. The snow had done its job of covering everything and the sky was heavy with more to come.

Karen's car had melted into the landscape in one dome-shaped blob; all paths were gone, boulders and shrubs were hidden. The detail was disguised. It was going to be our best friend.

Because of our position, I could see mountains, dips and swathes of land, valley after valley unfolding in white for miles. The scene would have been enchanting if we hadn't had a body to dispose of.

Once inside the byre I'd been expecting abandoned stalls, buckets on their sides and piles of rotting hay, but the place was being refurbished into a studio. Instead of the ammonia-rife stench of manure, emulsion caught in my nostrils. There was a series of modern recessed down-lights in the beams and radiators leaning against the walls ready to be installed. Apart from a spot in the roof where snow must have recently broken through, the conversion was well underway.

Karen tracked down a rusty wheelbarrow leaning up against an old cow stall. 'Look for something thick to cover him with,' she said.

I found a tatty tarpaulin squashed into a metal bathtub and we made slow progress back to the cottage, Karen trundling the barrow with difficulty into the drifts ahead of us. At least the snow was muffling all the sounds we made.

'We've got to get him in without any faffing about,' she instructed, opening the back door. 'Imagine he's a heavy sack of potatoes, okay? Don't drop him.'

On the count of three we dragged him outside and heaved him into the wheelbarrow, laying the tarpaulin over him. We tucked it in at the sides, but there must have been a gap, as one of his arms flopped out onto the snow. Karen dared to squash it under the sheet. It was at least thirty-two hours since he'd died and the rigor mortis was starting to wear off.

'What's that on his wrist?' I asked. A line of black ran around the spot where his hand joined his arm.

'It's just an elastic band, I think,' she said. 'People use them to help give up bad habits.'

I'd heard of the idea. You ping the elastic when you're tempted to eat chocolate or have a cigarette. Charlie wouldn't need to worry about that anymore.

Karen wiped her nose with her glove. 'Perhaps he was trying to give up breaking and entering.'

I hoped she didn't expect me to laugh.

The snow meant we made slow progress back to the

byre. His weight was slumped to the left and his feet bobbed up and down over the edge, as we went. Once we reached the track, I kept looking up thinking I heard the sound of a car engine – Stuart in his Land Rover or Jodie and Mark coming back in a taxi.

Karen sent me to get his rucksack, which we'd left leaning against the wall next to the sloping grit bin, under the kitchen window. It was now transformed into a snowman.

Karen had manoeuvred the wheelbarrow under the hole in the roof when I reached her. A white cascade had tumbled through the broken tiles, spilling out over the surrounding concrete.

'We'll leave him here – just until we work out what to do with him.' she said. 'We can bury him under all this snow.'

I sniffed and picked up a shovel.

'Wait – we'll need thicker sheets to cover him properly first,' she added.

I found a green pond liner and laid it over the tarpaulin so nothing – his clothes, his skin – was visible. I used a spade while Karen tipped the snow over him. In the end, he looked like a heap of bricks or compost covered in snow that had come in through the hole in the roof.

We returned the wheelbarrow to the corner, hung up the tools and turned to go. Had I not been so petrified by the whole process, I would have been impressed. We made a good team.

'Can we lock it?' I asked.

'Yes – there's a padlock for the main and side doors.

The keys are on my key ring for the cottage.'

As soon as we got back to the cottage the backlash of emotional upset and exhaustion took its toll. I sat holding my head in my hands at the kitchen table, feeling as if every ounce of energy had been sucked out of me. All I could say was we were extremely lucky no one saw us.

Mel was wanting attention by now, so Karen went to her. Moments later, a waft of lemon air-freshener pervaded the whole house. Karen really had thought of everything.

I set the fire going for something to do and waited for Karen to come down with the baby.

'She's fed and changed.' Karen put her down on the mat in front of the fireguard and tipped a few toys out for her to play with.

'You know it's too late to report it now, don't you?' she said seriously. 'There's going to be DNA from both of us all over everything.'

I nodded.

'We're in this together – you and me,' she said conspiratorially. 'We've got to look out for each other and make sure our stories match up.' She ran through what we needed to be clear on: *no, we hadn't seen anyone hanging around; yes, we were out this morning enjoying the snow and we'd been using the air-freshener because Mel had been sick.*

'Got it?'

It was just as well she knew I was good at following instructions. 'Yes. Fine,' I said, gnawing at my broken nails. The reality of what we'd done was beginning to sink in. We'd interfered with a crime scene right at the start. In fact, we'd gone past the point of no return some time ago, but moving him – *hiding* him – truly sealed our position. We'd committed a crime.

But that wasn't the worst of it for me. I had to live with the knowledge that it could have been me who'd killed him.

Chapter 22

I needed to get out of the cottage after what had happened. I needed to walk away – even though I knew I would have to come back to it again.

First, however, I had to make sure my room looked normal. I pulled on rubber gloves, dropped the rag rug Charlie had been lying on into the bath and ran cold water over it. The stain dissolved into red-brown liquid and I frantically helped it on its way towards the plughole, swooshing the water with my hands, squeezing dollops of disinfectant onto the flow. I scrubbed the rug like my life depended on it, rinsed and scrubbed again. I squeezed out as much water as I could and hung the rug in the lean-to, because I couldn't bear to have it near me.

We agreed to tell the others that I'd spilt coffee on it.

I set out after that, desperate to get away from our crime and all signs of it. Nothing Karen could say now could pacify me; I had to wrestle with my own conscience on this one. I knew what we were doing was terribly wrong, but I couldn't see any other way.

I'd taken a well-worn leaflet that had a map of a short circular walk from the pile on the dresser. It was the only one I could find that was less than three miles and included the words 'well sign-posted' in the description. Otherwise, I risked getting lost again.

I made sure I had my phone, as well as the camera, and stomped my way through the snow, following the route which led to a farm, on to a small tarn, then off across open fields. Towards the end, just when the landscape was starting to get familiar, I turned a corner and there was the loch.

I had to shake my head at the wonder of it. So still and expansive. It was how I wanted my internal world to be, but that was way out of my reach for the time being.

From the moment I set out, I'd been running a never-ending series of mind-videos through my head about what might have happened to Charlie. How had he died? Had I really hit him with something? Would we ever know?

Then my questions turned to darker fears: Would Karen and I get away with it? Would one of us slip up and give ourselves away? What was the next step in our plan? We couldn't leave Charlie in the byre.

And Karen? She'd stepped in demonstrating an allegiance towards me that went far beyond friendship. She was risking serious trouble to protect me. I didn't know how I could possibly repay her.

'You look cold,' came a voice to my right. I jumped and the woman put her hand on my arm and apologised. 'I thought you'd seen me,' she said.

'Sorry – I was miles away.'

'Well – that's a good thing, eh?' She turned to share my view. 'Gorgeous, isn't it?'

I smiled at her misunderstanding.

'You live around here?' she asked. Her chin was buried inside a thick scarf that wrapped around her neck several times. She had kind eyes; the sort that seemed to listen to you, as well as look.

'No – I'm in one of the holiday cottages, just over there,' I pointed to a bank of trees to the east.

'Ah – we're on holiday too, my husband and I – over the other side of the loch.'

We found ourselves walking down towards the water's edge together. 'It's like another world here,' she said. 'I live in the centre of Dunfermline – and I'd forgotten what it's like to slow down.'

She brushed a tuft of snow away from my shoulder that had fallen from a branch above. It was the sort of thing Karen would have done.

'Fancy a walk around to the other side?' she said. 'It's a fair distance, but I can make you a hot chocolate and there's lemon meringue pie, too.'

The chance for a bracing walk without getting lost ticked all the right boxes. 'Sounds good,' I said, my forced tone sounding rather flat.

She must have picked up that I wasn't in the best of spirits. 'Malcolm can take you back later, if you like – he's out painting just now.'

'Isn't it too cold to stand still?'

She chuckled. 'He's a hardy soul. He takes a flask of coffee with him and every half an hour or so he retreats to the car and listens to the radio.'

I laughed. 'Nice.'

'Come on,' she said, pointing towards a stile at the corner of the field. 'I'm Nina.' I gave her my name and gloved hand in return.

I couldn't believe I was acting as if the horrors of that

morning had never taken place. It was as if I'd shifted into autopilot, being polite and interested, when the grave sin I'd just committed should have brought me to my knees.

My energy was flagging by the time we arrived at Nina's cottage. It was grander than ours. The walls and fences were intact; the garden tended to. This was what our cottage might have looked like, if it had been higher up the list of Mrs Ellington's renovations.

Once indoors, I could sense the radiating warmth of that blissful combination of central heating and double-glazing. I removed my boots and she showed me through to a conservatory in the sun at the back, overlooking a long sloping lawn.

'Ours belongs to Mrs Ellington,' I said.

The conservatory was bigger than our sitting room and decorated in dusky blue with Wedgwood dishes on the walls, a cross-stitched sampler beside a chunky Welsh dresser.

'Yes, she owns this one too. She runs about six of them, I think.' Now that she'd peeled off her outdoor clothes I could see Nina was in her forties, with grey roots already creeping though her dark brown hair. She looked slim and fit, with the poise and apparent unflappability I always associated with someone who practised yoga on a regular basis.

'Ours is a lot more basic,' I said. 'We don't even have a landline.'

'Oh – they all have telephones – I'm sure of it. There's free wifi here, too. Not that we're using it much. Malcolm insisted on bringing the laptop, but I keep telling him off every time he opens it. I'll get the drinks.'

She padded off in her sheepskin slippers as I stood in the bay of the window looking out towards the horizon. A movement caught my eye and a tall stag came into my line of sight in the distance. It stopped and stood alert and elegant, as if it was staring straight at me. We were locked in a moment together, neither moving a muscle.

It both unnerved and thrilled me. The deer stood there, like it was accusing me, like it knew what I'd done. I shuddered and turned to grab my camera, but by the time I'd pulled it from the case, the deer had gone.

Nina came back with the hot chocolate and pie she'd promised. I was surprised to find myself hungry. Perhaps it was because I'd been swept up into this serene world, a million miles from the one I'd walked away from.

The chocolate had a thick froth on the top. It was creamy – warming and calming me as it went down. I really needed this. It was such a relief to be with someone who didn't know about what had happened. Someone welcoming and open, who made me feel at home.

Then I thought about Stuart. I really liked him. I wanted nothing more than the chance to take things further with him.

I'd only eaten one mouthful of lemon meringue pie when Nina noticed my camera on the stool.

'That looks a good one,' she said.

'It's my hobby,' I said, picking it up and showing it to her. 'I do landscapes mostly.'

'Fancy that? I've just started a beginners' evening

class in photography.'

'My uncle was a keen photographer – just amateur.' She was wide-eyed so I carried on. 'He was highly commended in the *Wildlife Photographer of the Year* competition a couple of years ago.'

'I went down to London to see that, last year – at the Natural History Museum. It was amazing. Your uncle must have been extremely good. Which category?'

'Botanical – like me, he loved trees with unusual backlighting – and close-ups of insects, too.' I grimaced, 'I'm not much into those, personally.'

I asked about the type of camera she used and she went to fetch it – a Nikon P600, probably worth about four hundred pounds. 'Malcolm says I should wait and see if I've got any talent before we splash out on a better one.'

I held mine out for her. It cost about twice as much, before you started adding on the extras, like lenses and tripods. The same uncle had left me money in his will, unexpectedly – it was my only indulgence. Even my parents approved. 'Do you want to have a go?'

We spent the next twenty minutes sizing up potential shots from the conservatory and then went outside. We tried to fix my camera to her tripod, but my Fujifilm was too big, so we continued with handheld frames.

'Now, wait,' I told her, 'until that cloud starts to shift so the sun doesn't flood the whole scene. I'll tell you when.' She curled her tongue as she concentrated. 'Now…' She pressed the shutter release and there was a satisfying click.

'Wow,' she said, it's so slick to use.

'With any camera, it's the quality of light that makes all the difference,' I explained. 'It's best to shoot early in the morning or late afternoon when the sun is lower, with less contrast. You'll get more subtle moody shades.'

I explained a few other basic ideas she hadn't yet covered on her course.

'Thanks for the tips,' she said.

It was satisfying to feel I could make a difference. I thought again about the idea of teaching and it felt a good fit.

We scuttled back inside to get warm and sat by the fire in the sitting room to finish our pies.

'Fancy a tipple?' she said, leaning over and whispering as if we weren't alone. 'I know it's early, but Malcolm found this amazing single malt over at the Lors Valley.' She nudged my arm. 'Go on!'

'I'd love one,' I said, not being a whisky person at all, but thinking it might do me good.

As she poured, I pictured the decanter Dad kept in a small cabinet in our dining room at home. It was the only alcohol he allowed himself and one bottle lasted him the whole year. I remembered trying it once when I was about fifteen. It burned my throat and made me cough and mum came rushing in, catching me red-handed. She slapped me hard and made me save my meagre pocket money for months to buy Dad a new bottle, even though I'd only taken a spoonful. I'd never touched whisky since.

As Nina handed over the glass, the fumes reached me and I wished I'd asked for coffee instead.

She asked what I did for a living and whether I had

children. I told her about my decision to try teaching and, like Stuart, she sounded sincerely interested. 'You should speak to my sister; she's just started teaching five-year-olds at a school in Peckham. She's in Malta, just now, on a dig for amateur archaeologists.'

'I'd love to do something like that,' I said, tipping the drink to my mouth, but keeping my lips nipped shut. 'Take time out to discover relics and bones from the past.' I dry swallowed, suddenly remembering the little tomb Karen and I had made only that morning. An intense wave of giddiness passed through my head.

'What about you?' I asked, trying to blink the spinning sensation away.

'I teach at Edinburgh University. English Department.'

'Oh – do you know Stuart Wishart? I've just met him. He's in one of the other cottages. He lectures in Classics and Archaeology.'

Uncertainty hovered in her eyebrows as she ran the name through her internal directory. 'It doesn't ring a bell, but the University is a big place.'

'Yes, of course.'

She looked engrossed in the changing shapes in the fire as the flames sizzled, then she inhaled sharply. 'Did you hear about the little boy who was abducted on Monday afternoon? It wasn't far from us at all. Look...' She got up and led me through to the kitchen. The sunlight caught the backs of copper pans and pots, lined up in rows of ascending size as we walked past, making me think of a Gamelan orchestra.

She pointed out of the back window towards a group

of buildings in the distance to the right.

'Cleve Cottage,' she said. 'The Minters are sheep farmers, apparently. Brody Holland was whisked away while Mrs Minter's back was turned for half a minute. He lives in the next cottage along – you can't see it from here.'

'The police came to question us,' I said.

'It's dreadful, isn't it? We come away to a remote, tranquil part of the world to escape from city life and something like this happens on our doorstep.' She blew her nose on a handkerchief. 'That's crime for you – wherever there are people, it's just around the corner.'

We wandered back to the fire. 'I've been tuning in to the local news, but I haven't heard anything.'

She wrung her hands together. 'No – they haven't found him. Not yet. We joined the search on Tuesday and again yesterday – but the snow is so thick.'

Why hadn't I thought of that? I should have been out there, like any other decent human being, helping the police find him. Then I remembered why. We'd been preoccupied with the dead body that had appeared overnight at the end of my bed.

The daylight was fading fast when Malcolm returned. After brief introductions, I said I needed to head back. Malcolm offered to take me over to the cottage and I accepted gladly.

'Nice to meet you,' said Nina, squeezing my hand. 'Give me a call if you're at a loose end.' She handed me a slip of paper with her mobile and cottage phone numbers.

I thanked her and followed Malcolm round to his jeep. He was probably about the same age as Stuart, but by no means as attractive. He had a block-like head that melted into his shoulders without the apparent need for a neck. His thinning mousy-to-grey hair had already given way to a glistening bald spot on his crown. But, he was cheerful and kind to me, which was what mattered.

It wasn't far and Malcolm chatted all the way. On the main road we passed a police car. My heart-rate doubled. Had they been back to the cottage? They'd already checked over the byre searching for the missing boy – they wouldn't want to check again, would they?

'You must have heard about the boy who's been taken,' said Malcolm.

I cleared my throat. 'Yes.'

'We're going out again tomorrow,' he said. 'I forgot to tell Nina.'

'When?' I said. 'I'd like to come.'

'Early – as soon as it's light. We're all meeting at The Cart and Horses at 8.30. Shall we pick you up?'

'Yes, please.'

We drove up the track and the lights of our cottage came into view. It was the last place on earth I wanted to be.

Malcolm came to a halt behind Karen's car. 'Great – we'll see you tomorrow. Come to the end of the track – we'll pick you up there. We've already been over the local fields with dogs and drawn a blank, but we have to keep looking. He might have been moved. We've had the police round to our place several times,' he said, his hands still on the steering wheel. 'They have a good idea who they're looking for.'

'They know who did it?'

'Not exactly, but they've got a decent description. Nina thinks she saw who took him – didn't she tell you?'

Chapter 23

'Stop the bus!' came Jodie's voice from the sitting room.

'Nah – you're cheating,' Mark retorted, laughing.

They were back, playing cards by the sound of it. I envied them, with nothing more serious to worry about other than getting a score of thirty-one.

I couldn't face their high spirits just yet, so I went straight upstairs. I hesitated outside my bedroom, still carrying visions in my head of what had been lying so recently on the floor. *He's gone*, I told myself.

I eased the door open. I could smell nothing but residual air-freshener. The carpet was unstained and felt dry under my palm. The rug was probably still wet in the lean-to, but we had a reasonable excuse for that. Everything had the pretence of being back to normal.

I tapped on Karen's door. She answered, dragging the belt of her bathrobe around her middle. The curtains were closed and she looked bedraggled and annoyed.

'What is it?' she snapped.

'Sorry,' I said. 'I was going to make hot drinks. I didn't know you were asleep.'

'Well, I am. I was.'

'I saw a police car – they didn't call back did they?'

'No.' She dragged me inside. 'Look – you're going to have to stop asking questions and looking so bloody guilty all the time. Just be normal, for fuck's sake.'

I bit my lip, ready to leave. She'd never sworn at me before.

'Sorry, Alice…' She let go of my sleeve. 'I'm just tired.' She beckoned with her head towards the cot.

'How's she doing?'

'She's crying a lot,' Karen said, sinking her fingers into her hair and pulling at it. 'I had to ring the doctor, but she said there's nothing to worry about. Mel's teething and not used to being outside the ward. The doctor said it's just a matter of time before she settles down.'

Mel was fast asleep, a cute frilly mop cap framing her face. I watched her body rise and fall in the dim light, envious of her oblivion.

'And how are you?' I asked. We'd both been pushed to the brink emotionally in the last few days. 'It's been tough.' I took a step forward for a comforting hug, but she lifted up her arm like a barrier.

'Yep – look, I need some sleep. I'll catch you later.' She hustled me back out of the door and shut it, without looking up.

Jodie was alone in the kitchen when I went down.

'Good time at the Gleneagles Centre?' I asked.

'Brill,' she said. 'Well – Mark went snowboarding and I bought these.' She carefully tipped a bag of trinkets on to the kitchen table. A glittering collection of diamanté brooches and pendants.

'They're for my stall – aren't they lovely? I found them at a place in Fort William. Managed to haggle the guy down to a fiver for the lot.'

They weren't my thing – too bling for me – but I could imagine plenty of women would pay a good price for them. I picked up a hairclip in the shape of a swan. Jodie certainly had a good eye. 'You've got your heart set on getting this market stall up and running, haven't you?' I said.

She nodded seriously and sat down, resting her chin in her palm. 'Mark is always having a go at me for having "crazy" dreams, but this is what I want. The stall is only the first step. He thinks I should stay in the department store because it's a steady income. He says we shouldn't both be self-employed. But I *really* want this. He doesn't know, but I've got it all worked out. I've got a five-year business plan, a loan arranged, a financial advisor – the whole thing mapped out.'

'You haven't told Mark all this?'

She sighed. 'Sometimes I think he doesn't want me to do well. I've carried on being the dizzy, hapless, silly young thing he knew at Leeds. He wants me that way, but I'm not that person anymore.'

For a moment, I almost liked her. 'Go on.'

'I play along…that's all. But it's not me.' She threw me a shamefaced look, keeping her voice down. 'Don't say anything, will you?'

'Of course not.' Jodie had never confided in me before. I was touched. 'How would he react if you got your act together and you really started to shine?'

'He'd hate it. I know he would. Every time I suggest something, he pooh-poohs it.'

'Why do you think that is?' I was thrown by their relationship; I couldn't get a handle on it.

She trailed her index finger idly through a pile of spilt sugar. 'I'm not sure. It's like he doesn't want me to have much say in things. He wants to be in charge the whole time.'

I knew so little about the dynamics of relationships, but this felt like some kind of oppression. They were all lovey-dovey with each other and clearly had an active sex-life, yet he was so mean to her. Why did she put up with it? He constantly stepped in to make decisions for her, snuffing out her plans before they were even fully formed. I couldn't understand why she didn't fight back.

'And are you happy with that?' I said.

'I used to be. I loved having this all-powerful macho guy protecting me, leading the way, but...' She sat back. 'I've grown up a bit – like you.' She dropped her voice even further. 'Thing is, I'm scared of losing him. If I change and start making decisions on my own, he'll dump me. I know he will. I couldn't bear that.'

So, Mark was only interested if Jodie was under his thumb. She wanted to grow and Mark didn't seem to want to let her. She was keeping up a pretence all the time; playing the part of a brainless piece of arm-candy.

She was about to say something else when Mark strode in.

'Where's my beer?' He saw me and lifted his hand. 'Hey, Candyfloss – what've ya been up to?' He swung a chair around and sat on it backwards. He seemed to be a different person each time I saw him – chummy one minute, cold, distant or playful the next. Was it the cannabis? I remembered he'd offered me some at a party once at Uni and I'd politely declined. He'd never offered again.

'I took a walk down to Loch Tierney and met a couple staying over in a cottage on the other side,' I said. Jodie was whispering something to Mark and I realised halfway through my sentence that they clearly weren't listening to me. I carried on, anyway. 'We're going out tomorrow to join the search for that missing baby. Did you want to come?'

'What?' said Mark.

'How about it? Help find the little boy?'

'Um. Nah. We're probably going off somewhere,' he muttered, pulling a packet of tobacco from his pocket and rolling up his next joint.

'That's news to me,' said Jodie. 'Where are we going?'

'I don't know yet,' he said, leaning over and giving her a sloppy French kiss.

I looked away.

'Want any help with supper?' I offered, getting up. Anything to take my mind off things. It was Mark's turn, but I knew Jodie would end up doing it. She and I went into the larder to see what was left. There were sprouts, parsnips and a swede on the shelf. I remembered there was a piece of pork shoulder, defrosting, in the fridge.

'What can I make with these?' she said, faltering.

'A hotpot?' I suggested.

'You'll have to show me,' she said.

I patted her arm. I knew she was struggling with the rustic farmhouse food; it certainly wasn't what she was used to. She probably lived off a macrobiotic diet at home – from the size of her, it certainly wasn't meat and two veg.

An hour later, Karen joined us and Mark sloped in, reluctantly slapping the cutlery on the table. Karen's skin tone had drained to grey and her hair hung like sprigs of parched wheatgrass on her shoulders.

She didn't even try being jovial. She chuckled once, but her laughter was flat and she kept squeezing her eyes shut as if she was in pain. Jodie and Mark probably put it down to Mel being a handful and were undemanding as a result.

Not engaging in the usual throwaway conversation made me uncomfortable, but I couldn't think of anything light-hearted to say. Eventually, Jodie broke the oppressive silence, pointing to my neck with a smile. 'You kept that chain we got you years ago, Alice.'

I reached inside my collar and pulled out the locket.

'Of course. That was in our first year. I don't know how you knew it was what I wanted. It was perfect.'

Karen looked up and let out a soft murmur of recognition.

I wrapped my fingers around the warm oval shape, remembering my glee and amazement when I'd peeled open the tissue paper and found it inside.

The very next day, of course, I'd done something for them I wasn't exactly proud of, but it felt like it was for a good cause at the time. I sighed at the memory of our time at Leeds. What I wouldn't have given to be back there, instead of here.

As I went over to the sink for a glass of water, I screwed my face up at the irony involved. Back then, having someone like Karen in my life meant everything to me. And for Karen and me to actually share something – just the two of us – I would have seen it as the ultimate triumph.

Well, I'd finally got my wish. It just happened that in the end, all we shared was a vile secret.

Chapter 24

Shit! A massive spanner in the works has knocked me sideways. I'm trying to keep up a calm front, but underneath I'm frantic as hell. I've got to block it out of my mind and carry on. There's so much to sort out. I must keep focusing on one step at a time and ride the storm.

I'm going to have to keep an eye on Alice – I hope she's not going to ruin everything.

Over supper, she reminded us of the time we got her a silver locket for her birthday at Leeds. What she didn't know was that Jodie had been snooping around in her room and had got hold of Alice's diary. There wasn't much there of any interest, apparently – just a lot of rubbish about how hard she was finding the course, but how brilliant it was to have 'real' friends.

Jodie did, however, hit on something useful. Alice had written down what she would have loved to get for her birthday – some jewellery. What she'd wanted more than anything was a silver necklace. Jodie decided straight away that we could use it as a bribe to win her over for our next little task.

The day after we gave it to her, Alice did exactly what we agreed and got hold of the fashion design paper for the end of term exams. Frankly, how was Jodie going to get into her second year without it? It was too big a job to hack into the computer system, so we had to wait until the papers had been printed out. We knew they'd be in the locked filing cabinet in the main office, but Jodie managed to 'borrow' the keys from Freddie while she entertained him.

All Alice had to do was get in, find the right paper, copy it, put it back and get out – without being seen.

Thinking about it, it was a pretty tall order. Alice isn't a natural when it comes to breaking the rules, but we got her to agree that if anything went wrong she'd never mention our names – ever.

Somehow, I can't see that kind of tactic working with Alice, anymore. She seems to have developed a mind of her own in the last few years and I get the feeling she won't be so easy to buy off. Pity. I'm going to have to tread very carefully.

Chapter 25

After supper, Stuart turned up at the door – all grins and good humour.

'Fancy a drink?' he said.

I almost fell into his arms. I needed to get away for a while; Karen's oppressive mood was dragging me further and further down just when we needed to be strong for each other.

The Cart and Horses was extra busy and we didn't manage to sit near the fire. We settled for a bronze table with a hammered top in a cramped corner by the Gents' loo. The couple behind us were playing backgammon and a few feet away there was a rowdy group celebrating someone's birthday. A woman kept taking unsteady steps backwards and I held my elbow out to make sure she didn't end up sitting on our table.

'So – feeling better?' Stuart asked. He was casually sitting astride a stool, his thick hair tossed charmingly askew by the wind. He was at the opposite end of the stress spectrum compared with how I felt.

My hand trembled as I reached for my glass. 'Feeling better?'

'Karen said you'd banged your head the day you got here and you'd been having headaches.'

'Did she?' I felt my forehead crumple into a frown.

'When did she tell you that?'

'When I popped over.' He saw the bewildered look on my face. 'Yesterday morning. She said you weren't feeling too well, so I didn't disturb you.'

'Oh…' I backtracked to the hours when we were waiting for the police. Someone had come to the door, but Karen said it was Mrs Ellington. Had I got things mixed up?

He dismissed it with a shake of his head. 'Anyway, what else have you been up to, apart from recovering?'

What *had* I been doing since we last met? I ran the words through in my mind in answer to his question; *Well, Stuart, only hours ago, I helped move a dead body from my bedroom to the byre…and before that, I woke up in the middle of the night with a knife in my hand. I might have killed the guy. Not sure. Anyway, how about you?*

I felt the skin under my eye twitch and hoped he hadn't noticed. I had to hold my nerve. I told him about meeting Nina near the loch. I told him she'd seen who the abductor was.

'Really? Did she give you a description?'

'No – not yet. Her husband mentioned it.' Another thought – a question – presented itself. 'By the way – where's the landline in your cottage – you said you had one?'

'Yeah,' he said. 'In the sitting room.' He studied his beer, swilled it around. 'What's troubling you?'

'Nothing,' I said too sharply.

I'd been considering the fact that if there'd been a phone in our cottage, the police would have found out all about Charlie minutes after we'd found him. They'd have taken him away shortly afterwards. And perhaps taken me away too, by now.

'Heard any more about the boy?' I asked, not wanting to dwell on what might have been.

He shook his head. 'The police wanted to speak to me again – I don't have an alibi for the time the boy went missing – but everything's fine. They're not about to arrest me.' He laughed and I did too, but the noise I made sounded forced.

'That poor little boy. I'm joining the search tomorrow morning. I should have thought of it before. Did you want to come?'

'I'm already booked in for the 8.30 start.' He reached down to pull up his sock. 'We went out yesterday afternoon. I warn you – it's not very pleasant. Every time you see a little mound of snow against a wall or catch sight of a fragment of loose rag or sack, you think: *This is it*.'

'Are they assuming he's dead by now?'

'The police are double-checking sheds, outhouses, cellars – but it's so cold and the snow is doing a great job of smothering everything and hindering the operation. It really depends on the reasons for the abduction. He could already be miles from here. Might even have left the country.'

'It sounds well-planned doesn't it? Someone waits outside a cottage where they know there are children and then swoops. It's not like Brody got lost in a shopping mall or wandered off on his own.'

He stroked the side of his glass. 'I don't know if that makes it better or worse.' He had a line of froth on his top lip and I had visions of leaning over and kissing him. 'The friends you're staying with – do you know them well?'

'Yes and no. I know them from University – especially Karen, but I've not seen them since. Karen was in LA for about five years, looking after rich people's kids. It's been a bit of a U-turn for her to be honest. I can't believe she's not working in medicine – it was more or less set in stone, but…'

I was thinking back to when I'd looked Karen up online after she'd contacted me. I'd found no trace of her on Facebook, Twitter or any other online network. It seemed incongruous that someone who was so outgoing with friends galore wouldn't have a presence on social media. Perhaps I hadn't looked hard enough. I arched my hand up to my hairline, rubbing my forehead.

'Head injuries can be a serious business, you know,' he said firmly. 'Had any blurred vision?'

I shook my head. Now he mentioned it, there had been one or two times when I'd moved quickly and seen two of everything. Is that what he meant?

'You should get it checked out – you mustn't be flippant.'

'I know. I will.' I smiled at his concern. 'As soon as I get back to London.'

There was a moment when he looked like he was going to say something else, but he smiled at me instead.

'You look lovely, by the way. I should have said earlier. That turquoise skirt really suits you.' He let his eyes trail from my chin right down to my boots. He'd noticed.

He ran his fingers across his jaw and I wondered how prickly his stubble would be against my skin. 'I'm glad I came across you in the snow,' he said.

I grinned, daring to let my gaze linger on his cheeky, probing, mother-of-pearl eyes and silently thanked him from the bottom of my heart. I'd felt barely human, never mind feminine, these past few months.

The next couple of hours rolled by more easily than I could have imagined. As long as we talked about the past or future, I could think in a straight line.

I listened to the thick velvety tones of his voice, let his words sink into me along with the brandy. For a few minutes at a time I managed to shift Charlie's body from centre-stage in my mind and move him to the wings. It was as if Stuart switched a light on inside me whenever I was with him. I liked him. I really did. But our time was running out. I didn't want to do anything rash to spoil it, but if something didn't happen soon, I'd be waving goodbye to him and would never see him again.

It was late and he got up to find my anorak. I was wide awake now and didn't want our cosy connection to come to an end, but I could hardly ask him back to the cottage. I couldn't invite him into my bedroom – I just couldn't, after what had happened there – and trying to engage in intimate conversation downstairs with Mark and Jodie popping in all the time, was out of the question. We'd probably all end up playing Monopoly. It didn't seem right, either, to invite myself over 'for coffee' to his.

I got up at the last minute to go to the loo and on the way back, I saw him standing in the corridor, my coat slung over his arm. He had his back to me and was hunched over his mobile as if he was finding it hard to hear the caller. I was about to tap him on the shoulder to let him know I was there when he spoke into the phone.

'No – not yet,' he said, 'but I'm certain it's him.'

I turned quickly and hurried back to the bar area, hoping he hadn't been aware of me behind him.

On the journey back, we chatted about food we liked, films we'd seen, places we wanted to visit, but I was distracted by the tiny snippet of phone call I'd overheard.

He'd told me he didn't know anyone in this area, but it sounded like he was looking for someone. I opened my mouth to ask, but stopped myself. I was getting paranoid. He could have been talking about something on TV, or been referring to a friend or neighbour at home – anything.

'See you tomorrow, first thing,' he said, bobbing down to let me out of the Land Rover. I was disappointed he hadn't walked me to the door this time. Perhaps I'd misjudged his interest. I waved and watched the Land Rover disappear into the lane, wondering if I was wasting my time hoping for anything more.

I was surprised to find the kettle on the stove had already boiled early the following morning. Karen was outside when I set off to meet Malcolm at the end of the track. She had a fire going in a metal cage not far from the byre. As I came towards her, she had her hands on her hips and didn't look particularly welcoming.

'Is everything alright?' I asked, looking from the fire

up to the byre door and back.

'Yeah.' She said it curtly in a way that suggested, *Why wouldn't it be?*

'Where's Mel?' I asked, looking around for the buggy.

'She's fast asleep.'

I hoped nothing was wrong, but Karen didn't look concerned, so I left it. She was heaping flattened cardboard boxes onto the fire and I caught a glimpse of what was underneath them.

'A stool?' I said, crouching down. 'You're burning a stool?'

'It was broken and getting on my nerves.'

I remembered the one – it was small and three-legged, like an old milking stool. It had been in the corner on the landing. 'But you can't just burn it – it belongs to the cottage, to the landlady.'

'She's not going to miss it.' She rocked on to one hip, staring at me. 'And you're not going to tell her, are you?'

I shook my head, waiting for her to smile and cut through the bogus animosity, but it didn't happen.

'I'll leave you to it,' I said, rubbing my arms, wanting to be on the move. 'I'm going out to help look for the boy.'

She was prodding the burning pyre with a garden fork. 'Good luck,' she said, without looking up.

Just as Stuart warned, the search was demoralising. We started in the field next to Nina's cottage and combed everywhere for the next two hours, checking sheep pens, drinking troughs, sheds, lean-tos – everything – on the way. We found a dead sheep, a man's slipper and a rabbit that looked like it had been savaged by a fox. No little boy.

Stuart said hello, but when he saw I'd arrived with other people, he joined up with a police officer, telling me he'd see me later.

The police thanked us and a new team of volunteers gathered by the next gate, ready to trawl through the adjacent hamlet for the next two-hour search. Nina invited me back to the cottage for a warm by the fire and a hot chocolate.

'Malcolm said you might have seen the person who took him,' I said.

'Yes – a man – mid to late twenties, I'd say – I should have mentioned it, yesterday.' She invited me to look out from the kitchen window. 'It was getting dark and I was shutting the curtains at the back. He fled across that patch of land – there – and stopped to get over the stile. He was a rough-looking chap.'

What she said next sent a dribble of sweat down my spine. She'd seen something quite specific.

'He was wearing what looked like a brown bomber jacket. He seemed to be holding something against his stomach. Of course, it was only afterwards that I realised it was probably Brody he was carrying.'

I was inwardly buzzing over the words *brown bomber jacket*.

She was speaking again. 'He had a blue or black woolly hat with a white stripe around the rim.'

'It sounds like you got a really good look at him,' I said huskily.

'He went over the brow of the hill after that and I lost him. The police have been over the whole area to try and find out where he came from – and where he went – but that's all I saw of him'.

Malcolm appeared in the doorway. 'It's okay,' he said, touching her cheek. 'You did your best.'

I found it hard to keep my attention on the conversation after that. I couldn't stop thinking about the man Nina had described. Could it have been Charlie? The bomber jacket sounded a bit too much of a coincidence.

I was keen to leave after that and, thankfully, Malcolm saved me the long trek back and gave me a lift. There was something urgent I needed to check – then I'd know for certain.

Chapter 26

On my return, I hovered on the landing, listening to the gurgles and splashes coming from the bathroom as Karen bathed Mel.

Mark and Jodie were up in their room, so I snuck my head around Karen's door and spotted her keys on her bedside cabinet. I removed the ones for the byre, just in case she needed the others in the meantime, and left. I intended to tell her what I was doing anyway, as soon as I was sure.

I had no desire to go anywhere near Charlie's festering body, but Nina's description of the hat felt too important to ignore. We'd already checked Charlie's pockets, so I knew the only place to check now was his backpack – only Karen had rifled through that. We'd left it tucked next to his body under the layers of plastic in the byre.

I slid the smallest key into the padlock and it snapped open. The door moaned as I nudged it ajar and I slipped inside. As I crossed the concrete floor, something small darted away from the pile of snow and scurried into a recess at the back. A rat. I stood still, determined not to scream. Another one headed the same way. I turned around. I couldn't do this – I had to get out. But, I didn't hurry towards the door, instead I leant against a bench waiting for my breathing to stabilise, talking to myself. *It's okay. Nancy Templar used to keep a pet rat at home, remember? A cute little white one. You were fine with it. This is just the same. It won't hurt you.*

I straightened up, my hand pressed against my breast bone. I forced myself to move it down to my belly. My therapist had taught me a technique to control any panic attacks: to breathe from the abdomen in the way that mothers are told to when they're about to give birth. It was a good idea in theory, but so far, when the attacks had struck I'd found it hard to put into practice. They'd happened so fast, it felt like someone else had taken over the control panels to my body. The trick was getting to my body before the panic attack got there first and firing off a few techniques to fend off the 'beast' before it could take hold.

In – out – nice and slow. You can do this. You'll be out of here in less than five minutes. Then it'll all be over. In – out. You can do this.

I picked up an empty tin from the bench and tossed it towards the mound of snow. There was another rustle and scuffle, then silence.

I walked right up to our makeshift icy tomb; the snow had in turn melted a little, then re-frozen, creating a ridge of ice around the edge. Wearing my gloves and pull my scarf over my mouth, I found the rim of the cover and gingerly peeled it away from the floor. Due to the hole in the roof, the light was good enough, but all I could see was Charlie's sleeve. I had three goes, shifting position, before I saw what I was looking for: the grey canvas of his rucksack. I pulled it towards me and opened the buckles on the top. *Focus on the rucksack – just look inside.*

I pulled out a thin book about Rome, local maps, his passport and a bottle of water. Then it was in my hand. I'd found it. Charlie's hat. Exactly how Nina had described it; woolly, dark blue, with a white stripe round the edge. Exactly the same.

I was about to stuff it back inside, when I decided to check further to see if there might be details about where Charlie might have been staying or who he could have been working with. There was no mobile phone, no notebook, no scraps of paper with names or numbers on them. I flicked through the guidebook, looked for markings on the maps: nothing. He had certainly covered his tracks.

Only now did it occur to me that, for someone heading off to Europe, there wasn't much in is backpack. It was mostly empty – no clothes, toiletries. He must have been going somewhere else first.

I fastened the bundle, before thrusting it back under the plastic sheet. Blood was pumping into my throat like a resounding drum and my hands were hot and slippery inside my gloves. I felt waves of vertigo, but had to focus. I needed to get this job done and not make any stupid mistakes.

I'd dislodged ridges of snow in the process, so I found the spade we'd used before and scooped the snow back over the pile, hiding the liner as far as possible.

Then I left the spade where I'd found it and ran.

Karen was in her bedroom with Mel, but it didn't matter – I'd already decided to come clean about the keys, especially as it gave us some useful new information. I tapped and waited.

'Just hold on,' came Karen's voice.

She opened the door a fraction as if she had no idea who might be on the other side. Her expression said that whoever it was, they weren't welcome.

'It's only me,' I said. Her expression didn't change. 'Can I come in? It's a bit delicate.'

She stood back letting me in, vexation in her laboured movement. 'What's delicate?'

'I went to the byre again.'

She pressed her fingers into her browbone. 'And what made you do that?'

'Nina – a woman I met – she's staying at the far side of the lake. She saw the guy – she thinks – who kidnapped the little boy. Her description was…well, it fits Charlie exactly.'

'She cut me off with a loud, '*Shush* – keep your voice down.'

I shifted from one foot to the other. 'She described him,' I went on in a whisper, 'his build, his bomber jacket and she mentioned he was wearing a hat. Well, I went back to his rucksack to check – and there it was – the same one, matching her description precisely. It was him. Charlie took the baby.'

I was waiting for an expression of astonishment to flood her face, but she snorted.

'Just because he was wearing a bomber jacket and a hat…'

'But she said the hat was blue or black – woolly – with a white stripe around the rim – and Charlie's is *exactly* like that. It's too much of a coincidence. He must have taken the child. But the issue is where is little Brody now?'

'Stop using the boy's name – like you know him.'

I was smarting at her rebukes. Karen was stressed and knackered, because her baby wouldn't settle. I understood that, but this was important and I was making sense.

'Charlie might have taken him somewhere, *hidden* him somewhere – in another byre, a pig sty, a hut – wherever – but he isn't around now to take care of the baby anymore, is he?'

The words came gushing out as the realisation that we might have played a part not only in ending Charlie's life, but also the life of an innocent infant began to hit home.

'Who's looking after him now?' I tried to stop my words rising in pitch and volume. 'Did Charlie take the boy, hide him and never go back for him?'

She hissed at me, prodding her finger into my shoulder. 'Keep your bloody voice down, will you? And think this through.' She pulled me down beside her on the bed. 'If Charlie *was* the one who took the child, he would have passed the kid on in a matter of hours and certainly before the end of the day. These people don't hang around. He broke into our place during the night on Tuesday. If Charlie took the child on Monday at 5pm – I can't see him sticking around with a small infant, changing nappies, feeding him, singing sweet lullabies for longer than he needed to. Can you?'

I thought about it. 'I suppose not. People are going to

notice a baby crying – and the police have checked everywhere around here.'

She softened and cupped her hand over mine. 'The family I was with in LA were paranoid about this sort of thing happening to them. They used to follow stories of abductions in the news and got a clear idea of how it worked. Charlie wouldn't have been snatching the baby for himself – you just needed to look at him to see that – he would have been one link in an organised chain.

'Someone arranges everything, another finds the target, someone else – Charlie – makes the grab for the child and then passes him on to another person, who gets the child out of the country. Brody was probably a million miles away by Tuesday evening, being transported to a couple in the States who are rich and infertile.'

That's what Stuart had said.

'You're right,' I concluded. 'He had a ticket to go to Europe, but there was no baby passport in his bag. No baby gear. From what we saw of him he didn't look like the settling down type.'

'He was a loner out to make a fast buck,' she said. She put her arm around me and pulled me close. I could smell baby milk on her collar. 'You can't say *anything* about this,' she went on. 'We'll both be in big trouble if you do – the police will know what we…you…did.'

'What if the snow thaws?' I said, snatching a breath. 'What if the temperature rises and the snow covering his body…melts and…'

A vision of Charlie's decomposing body emerging from his crude tomb, for all to see, flooded my mind.

'We'll deal with it,' she said dismissively.

'Why do you think Charlie came to the cottage?' I asked.

She tried to cover a sigh. 'We don't know, do we? Maybe he needed money for a taxi, maybe he was on the lookout for jewellery, perhaps he'd got the wrong cottage, or he could have left something behind here and was coming back for it – who knows? It doesn't change anything – we can speculate all we like, but we have no idea why he was here.'

'Maybe he knew about the money Mark had, somehow.'

'Except that had gone by the time he broke in.'

'Ah – yeah…' It was all a complete muddle.

'Why were you burning the stool?' I asked again, trying to make my voice sound light.

'I told you why – it was broken and annoying me.'

It had been on the landing by the bathroom – near my bedroom door. It was small and compact and just the kind of thing you might reach for if you were caught by surprise and needed to defend yourself. Was I the one who had lifted it up and swung it at the back of Charlie's head?

'Was there blood on it, is that why you were getting rid of it?'

I could picture fragments of the scene – me in bed in my penguin pyjamas, the splintering sound of my door as it slid open. A shadow in the doorway, me startled out of my wits, searching desperately for something to keep him away from me, the stool in my grip. I could see the snapshots in my mind, but they weren't memories – I was sure they weren't.

In any case, the stool was on the landing – how could I have reached for it when I was in bed and it was behind him?

I kept coming back to the same gnawing, sick place. Perhaps I wasn't in bed when he came in. Perhaps I wasn't even in the room. It all hung on whether I'd been sleepwalking again. I *had* taken a tablet on Tuesday night – it *was* possible.

She laughed. 'You're overreacting, Alice. Don't you believe me?'

She was lying. It was obvious now I considered it. There was no doubt that Karen looked shifty when I caught her over the bonfire – like she had a job to do that she didn't want anyone else to know about. She probably hadn't expected me – or anyone else – to be up and about so early. The stool could easily have been the murder weapon. But who was she protecting – me or herself?

'I know you've been anxious and you've had awful panic attacks, but don't become a liability.' Her voice was sharp.

'A liability? When have I ever been a liability?'

She softened. 'You haven't – you've always been completely reliable.'

Reliable. It sounded so business-like – not what friendships were made of.

Another thought came to mind. 'Why didn't you tell me when Stuart came to see me on Wednesday?' I said, keeping my voice even. 'Why didn't you let him in?'

'You don't really know Stuart, Alice. None of us do.

We don't really know why he's hanging around here so much. I was just trying to protect you – protect us all.'

I wanted to remind her that he was *hanging around* because of me, but I didn't think it would have made much difference. 'You think Stuart is involved somehow?'

'We don't know – do we?' She pulled me towards her. It was a tender gesture, but it felt forced. 'Besides – you were upset – we were waiting for the police at that point – we didn't want him interfering.'

I retreated to my own room after that. Karen was being cautious about Stuart, but she should still have told me.

What she said about the abduction made sense, but I was still uneasy. Karen was trying to convince me that Brody was miles away, but we didn't know for certain. Charlie had been 'an intruder' until Nina told me about the hat. Now he was involved in the snatching of the boy. By not speaking up, we were withholding evidence and we could be putting the missing boy at risk.

I lay down on the bed and stared at the crazy-paving cracks that crawled across the ceiling, meeting at the light fitting in the centre. What was I going to do?

I glanced at my suitcase sitting on top of the wardrobe. I could leave. I could leave right now and in a couple of hours I'd be far away from this dreadful situation. On the heels of that thought came another. I couldn't just slope out. I'd be leaving Karen with Charlie – the police would find him as soon as the snow melted and they'd be after me in a shot.

I sat up and looked out at the unrelenting white sheet spread across the landscape outside. After only a few days, I was fed up with it. I longed for the snow to be gone and to see velvet green fields in its place. Snow felt like part of an ending and all I wanted was a beginning.

I had another option, but it meant defying Karen and throwing myself to the wolves. I could tell the police about Charlie and face the consequences.

Chapter 27

My conscience had got the better of me by lunchtime and I had an idea about how to handle the situation. I hastily put together a ham sandwich, put a note saying *Gone for a walk,* on the table and left the cottage before I bumped into anyone.

I walked the three miles to Duncaird and caught the number one bus, which took an hour to reach Fort William. Ideally, I should have gone as far as Glasgow, but that was nearly a hundred miles away. With my hood up and my head down to avoid the CCTV cameras, I strolled around and found the busiest area; the shopping centre on the High Street – and ducked into a phone box. From there I rang the police.

I left an anonymous message in the best Scottish accent I could muster, saying that the man who had taken the boy in Ockley on Monday was called Charles Smith. He'd been wearing a brown leather bomber jacket and blue woolly hat with a white stripe – a twenty-three-year-old backpacker with a passport in his bag.

The voice at the other end demanded my name and more details, but I hung up. They might think I was a crank caller, but they'd probably at least look into it. Of course, I didn't want them to look too far – just far enough to pick up any trail on Brody. As far as the missing boy was concerned, I'd told the police everything I knew. I didn't have any details about where Brody was or where, when and who Charlie had passed the child on to.

When I got back, I was greeted with the smell of steaming wool. Jodie was forever washing out her clothes by hand and leaving them on the wooden rack by the fire – only nothing ever dried and any day now she was going to run out of things to wear.

She was in the kitchen painting her false nails. When she wasn't gluing lace or studs to her pockets or belts, she was adding glitter to her eyelids or plucking her eyebrows. Self-grooming was a full-time hobby for Jodie.

Mark was hunting for something to eat in the larder and Mel was snug against Karen's chest in a baby sling. 'Nice walk?' Karen asked brightly. Close up, her skin looked like dry pastry and her eyes were rippled with broken blood vessels.

'Yeah – thanks,' I said. She poured me a cup of coffee from the pot on the stove and pointed to a plate of scones.

'Taken many photos?' Jodie asked without looking up. My camera was where I'd left it the previous day, on the dresser in the sitting room.

'Not today – the light isn't right,' I said. 'Maybe tomorrow.'

'We should have some group photos,' said Jodie, her eyes lighting up. 'And what about some mother and daughter portraits – have you taken many of those, yet?'

'No – we must do that,' I said. 'Portraits aren't my forte, but the camera's very good. How about it, Karen?'

'My hair's a mess,' she said wearily. 'We'll do it another time.'

Jodie blew on her final sparkly green nail and showed the full set to me. 'I've got a spare pack with me – I can put them on for one of you, if you like?' Karen and I both declined. 'How about we do something with your hair, Alice – pretty you up a bit? It's such a dull brown, all flat and going nowhere.'

'It's okay, thanks,' I said, struggling to hide a smile.

Several years ago, I would have been practically destroyed by a comment like that. Now I could see it was just Jodie's way.

'Tell us about Mel,' Jodie asked Karen. 'What went wrong?'

Karen waggled the child's foot, gently. 'She was originally diagnosed with bronchiolitis, but when they found out she had a lung condition – something called bronchopulmonary dysplasia – the doctors thought it best to take her to the specialist children's unit in Glasgow,' she explained. 'BD is the abnormal development of lung tissue. It can be fatal. You can see why I was terrified.'

'Absolutely,' agreed Jodie.

Her sympathy didn't last long. 'You fell off the radar, you pig – what happened? Mark and I didn't hear from you for ages. Did you forget about us?'

'Of course not. If you must know, I didn't keep in touch with anyone from Leeds, not really.'

So, it wasn't just me.

Karen wiped a dribble from Mel's chin with her thumb. 'I feel very bad about it, I can tell you. I don't have any decent excuses. I was just a crap friend.'

Mark stepped in. 'It's just what happens – people move on.'

'*Guys* do,' Jodie pointed out, 'but women are usually better at keeping in touch.'

Mark tutted, turning away.

'You must tell us about America,' Jodie exclaimed starry-eyed. 'Hollywood, for crying out loud! That must have been incredible!'

'Yeah, well – all in good time.'

'And the father? Who is he – this famous Hollywood actor?' she pressed.

'I can't say.'

'Why not? Come on, give us a clue – we're hardly going to get on the phone to him.'

'I can't.' Karen was serious. 'I haven't told a soul.'

Jodie asked another of the questions that was on my own mental list. 'Did you plan the baby?'

'No – actually.'

A silence was suspended in the air. I cut it short and turned to Jodie. 'When you have children, would you want a boy or a girl?'

'Urgh – neither,' she said. 'Don't want kids. Ever. Do we?' She glanced at Mark who was drinking milk directly from the carton and didn't appear to be listening. 'I've got too many things I want to do. I couldn't have a kid holding me back. No offence intended,' she said, holding up her hands. 'We'll get married though, won't we?' She turned to him again, but he had his head inside the fridge.

I remembered asking Karen once, in our final year, about what it was she saw in Jodie. She'd claimed she found Jodie funny (especially when she was tipsy), scatty and harmless. 'I like the way she always tells it how it is,' she'd explained.

I thought about those words – *funny, scatty and harmless* – they were hardly grounds for a particularly close relationship. Again, it made me think – why invite her?

It was as if Karen had failed to fill me in on a key part of this arrangement, just like she'd failed to tell me Jodie and Mark were turning up at all. What *were* we all doing here?

Jodie picked up a half of scone from the plate on the kitchen table, took a bite, then put it back. She turned to Karen. 'What about your pictures from Hollywood, Kaz? You must have loads.'

'I didn't get the chance to take many.'

'You were there for half a decade, girl – how can you *not* have photos? I love that sign on the hill that says "Hollywood". Did you take a selfie with that? And any of the family you were with?'

Karen got up reluctantly and came back with a thin yellow envelope.

'Is that it?' complained Jodie.

'I've got piles at home,' said Karen. 'I wasn't going to cart them all up here.'

She handed Jodie the snaps. Jodie glanced at each one, then passed it on to me. 'Is this their kitchen?' she asked. 'It's not very big.'

'That was just the one I used on the top floor.' Karen seemed reluctant to elaborate, as if her time there was best forgotten.

'What about the pool? You said there was a swimming pool in the grounds.'

'I haven't got any pictures of that.'

'What about the kids, then?'

'Okay, this one is Zena – she's about four in that picture.' She pointed to a child on a swing.

'That's a nice one of you,' said Jodie, gratified at last. 'I like your hair parted on the side, like that. When was it taken?' She turned it over hoping for a date.

'I don't know,' said Karen, scrutinising the picture. 'Two years ago, maybe?'

'And none of the gorgeous superstar you fell in love with?' Jodie asked coyly.

'No.' Karen's face was still, giving nothing away.

'Oh, come on – you must have some!'

'I do – of course, I do – but I didn't *bring* them, because I knew you'd pester me and you'd recognise him straight away and then…'

'Then what, Kaz?' Jodie's tone was less playful. 'Me and my big mouth would blab to the press and Mr Blockbuster would be named and shamed?'

Mark spoke. I'd almost forgotten he was there. 'Something like that, Jodie,' he said. 'You know what you're like.' Jodie reached across and gave him a playful slap on the knee.

'I don't gossip…I'm just interested in people,' she said, lifting crumbs scattered on the table with the pad of her finger. 'Tell us more about Hollywood,' she went on, 'the people, the life-style, the weather – transport me there – I want to know every last detail of what it was like.'

'What can I say? You've seen it on TV. It's hot – there are palm trees everywhere. There are hundreds of places to eat – bars and cafés.' She dusted the remains of flour from her hands. 'I was in West Hollywood in a seven-bedroomed place. It had huge grounds with a fountain. I used to take the children out every day. We'd go to the local park, swim, play tennis, ice-skate in the winter.'

'There was Zena and who else?'

'Fabio and Lola. They were seven and eleven when I started with them. The girls were cute, but real prima-donnas. Fabio was a nightmare; he was sly and never did as he was told. It was hard work, I can tell you.

'The first family I was with – they didn't stipulate exactly how many hours I was due to work – and I ended up on my feet practically all day, every day. I left after three months and moved on to a new place with a great family. Judy was a frazzled mother of three. She was a bit detached, but friendly enough and I did what they call light housekeeping – laundry, ironing, vacuuming, as well as helping the kids with homework. Zena was only small when I started.'

'Was it like playing at Mary Poppins the whole time?' I chipped in, trying to figure out how she found meaning in her work there, when she was capable of so much more.

'I liked lying in the sun. They had a pool in the grounds and, on my mornings off, I used to lounge around with a book, have a dip, soak it all up...'

'Did they give you time off?'

'One morning a month – and sometimes Sunday

afternoons.'

My chin shot forward. 'Is that all?'

'It was a job, not a holiday, Alice,' she said.

'Tinsel Town,' I mused. I couldn't think of many situations more awful. Looking after someone else's spoilt children, scrubbing kitchen floors and not having a minute to yourself. 'What else did you do?' There was a rap at the door before she could answer.

It was Stuart. My world shifted out of the clouds and into full sunshine.

'We're just having scones,' I said as he stomped the snow off his boots onto the front doormat. 'Fancy afternoon tea?'

'Ooh, how very English,' he chuckled. I reached over to give him a discrete peck. He'd brought in the chill. 'Sorry to call unannounced. I tried your mobile, but it didn't connect. Are you sure there isn't a phone here?' His eyes surveyed the skirting boards in search of a socket on his way into the kitchen.

'Tea?' said Karen, pointing to the kettle.

'Hi – yes, please,' he said, shaking off his wax jacket. He hung it over the back of a chair.

'We were just talking about Hollywood,' I said patting the seat.

'Ah – the joys of Sunset Boulevard and the Comedy Store.'

'You've been there?' I said.

'For a while – when I was a student.'

I gave him a two-sentence version of what Karen had already told us to save her covering the same ground.

'So, you were near Santa Monica Boulevard?' he said, between sups of tea.

'Yeah – just your average leafy suburb in West Hollywood.'

'Were you anywhere near Plummer Park?'

'Er…probably…there were so many parks.' She skimmed her fingers down her hair. 'I've forgotten half of them already.'

'I played tennis there once.'

'Really?'

'Where were you based, exactly?'

'West Hollywood.'

'I meant the road.'

'Craven Avenue.'

'Ah, yes, I know…near Fountain Avenue…' said Stuart.

Her shoulders give a narrow shudder. 'I'm not sure – I was at the house a lot.'

'So, Hollywood-Highland Station would have been the nearest Metro?'

'Yeah – that's right.'

'The Orange line?'

Karen smiled with a slight nod and scooped the last of the jam from her spoon before sucking her finger. Her answers were clipped and to the point. I could see no trace of nostalgia.

'So – you headed back once you knew you were pregnant with Mel?' said Jodie.

'Shortly after – yes.'

'Do you miss it?' I said.

'In a way…' She shrugged. 'I miss the guy I met.'

'Five years is a long time,' I said. 'You haven't picked up an American accent.'

She laughed. 'I'm too British for that.'

Mel woke up and started making a fuss. I could only see her nose and dribbling mouth poking out from the oversized hat.

'Here we go…' moaned Mark. Jodie elbowed him roughly.

'Okay, little one,' she cooed, stroking Mel as she yawned and kicked in the sling. 'Sorry, guys, nature calls,' she said. 'See you in a bit.'

'Shall I come and help?' I offered.

'Not this time,' she said, leaving me behind. 'She's got a stomach upset…'

'Aw – gross!' said Mark, making a puking sound.

'Anyway. Stuart's here.' she said, raising an eyebrow.

I sat back down again.

Jodie and Mark looked at each other, then at me. 'We'll leave you and Stuart to have a nice *chat*,' said Mark, taking Jodie's hand and pulling her upstairs.

I was about to invite Stuart through to the fire, when he looked at his watch. 'I can't stop,' he said.

'Oh. Did you want to meet for a drink later?'

'Er – not this evening, I'm afraid.'

His tone had changed; he sounded formal, like we were work colleagues. I made light of it and took him to the door. He barely acknowledged me as he left, narrowing his eyes as he stared out into the moribund afternoon. My world shrank as I closed the door.

I took a quick bath, then tuned in to the local radio in my room. The weather dominated the broadcast; more heavy snow was on its way. There was no more news about Brody – no mention that they had a name for the abductor. They must either still be looking into it or have dismissed me as a crank caller.

I went to the window and watched as tiny flecks of white began spilling from the sky. Flakes landed on the glass inches from my face clinging on in single star shapes. I thanked each one, willing it to stay there; more snow meant Charlie would remain hidden and we were safe – for now.

I must have entered the kitchen without making a sound, because it was a few seconds before either of them registered my presence. At first, I thought Mark was leaning, hip to hip against Jodie at the sink, but when they whisked around, I saw it was Karen. She had a towelling turban on her head so I couldn't see any of her hair.

They broke apart awkwardly and I was tempted to apologise, only doing so would have highlighted the fact that something had been going on between them. They both looked daggers at me. I wasn't sure if I'd caught them in the middle of a steamy argument or in a moment of forbidden passion. Either way, it left me unnerved.

'I'm getting supper ready,' I said, walking purposefully towards the larder.

'I had an idea, didn't I?' said Mark. Karen gave him a blank look. 'I thought I'd go over to Duncaird to get a takeaway from the pub,' he went on. 'They do burgers and chips to go, apparently. I've checked the lane and it's passable. Save you the bother tonight, Alice.'

'Oh. Great. Thanks.'

Karen walked past me to the fire and I joined her. She was sitting with her knees up against her chin. She had let her hair down – it was still wet and hung like solid spikes over her eyes. Underneath, her pupils caught the flickering of the flames and glowed like black beetles.

I tilted the rocking chair towards the fire and sat down. I heard Mark's voice in the hall then the door-knocker rapped twice. There were more voices – a female voice, jovial, light-hearted and Mark's sullen tones in reply. Then I heard him call Jodie and the door slammed.

After that, it went quiet.

The silence between Karen and I opened into a frosty chasm and I hugged myself, instinctively, as I built myself up to asking the burning question.

'Karen? Why did you invite me here?'

She didn't move, kept her gaze on the mercurial flames.

'Karen?' I repeated.

She slowly turned to face me. 'You've changed a lot since Uni, haven't you? You were so innocent and, dare I say, easily led, back then.'

'I know. I was more like thirteen, instead of eighteen,' I admitted.

Karen pursed her lips. 'I asked you as a way of saying sorry. I should have kept in touch and I failed miserably.' Her gaze went back to the fire and I waited, but she added nothing else.

I wanted to ask about Charlie, but the others could return and barge in at any moment.

I was getting increasingly jittery about the fact that

we'd simply left him in the byre, lying there, 'waiting'. Waiting for us to decide his fate. We were going to have to do *something* with him one of these days – he couldn't stay where he was for ever. And we'd have to act soon, because every time the temperature crept above freezing his body was sinking into increasingly foul states of decay.

I left Karen and went through to the kitchen, just as the others came back. Mark dropped a white plastic bag on the table and we tipped the burgers out onto our plates. I gathered cutlery and Jodie found tomato sauce. Karen sat down and didn't say a word.

'Stuart was in the pub,' said Jodie, without any preamble. She was picking out the small chips and adding the larger ones to Mark's plate.

'Oh,' I said. 'On his own?'

'I knew you were going to ask that,' Mark said. 'He was with a stunning red-head and they left arm in arm.'

'No – he wasn't!' interjected Jodie. 'He was talking to some other guy.'

'They looked a bit shifty, actually – seriously,' added Mark. 'They were poring over a map – very intense. Then Stuart handed him an envelope.'

'You're right,' said Jodie, nodding. 'It did look dodgy. Stuart kept looking up – you know the way people do when they're checking to see if anyone's watching them. A bit of a giveaway if you ask me.'

Stuart had told me he didn't know anyone around here. I didn't know what to think.

*

We were all mucking in with the washing up, later, when Karen idly asked Mark who had been at the door before they went out for the takeaway.

'The biddy who owns the place, I think. Mrs Eller...'

'Ellington,' Karen corrected.

'Yeah – that's it.' He opened the back door with his roll-up nipped between his fingers, ready to light up. A blast of freezing air made me take a step back. 'I dunno what she wanted – something about needing to get into the barn – the byre – whatever it's called.'

I shot round, a dirty plate in my hand. Karen stood perfectly still.

'When...when does she need to get in?' she asked.

'It's no big deal. She said she has a key – it was just a courtesy call in case we saw any strange blokes down the track. She's got re-fitters or decorators coming.'

'When?' I said.

'Who are you two? Bill and Ben?' He stared at his grubby trainers. 'Tomorrow...lunchtime? I dunno. I wasn't really listening.'

Karen's eyes flashed at me as I dropped the plate into the soapy water.

'I'm going to fix my nails,' Jodie called out to Mark and anyone else who was interested. I gave her a weak smile and watched her go. With Mark outside, Karen nudged the back door with her foot, so it was nearly closed, and dragged me into the sitting room.

My throat had shrunk to the diameter of a straw. 'Oh shit, oh shit,' I chanted, turning in little circles.

She pulled at my arm. 'Stop it,' she hissed. 'Stop this

right now!'

I made myself stand still in front of the low flames and watched them spit and crackle, then break open one after another.

'It's too dark to do anything now,' Karen whispered. 'We'll have to do it early tomorrow morning.'

'Do WHAT?! What are we going to do with him?'

'Do with who?' said Mark, easing open the connecting door.

'None of your business,' snarled Karen. 'Go away.' He sniggered and backed up in jerky robot steps, pulling the door towards him.

All the while, there was a latent curdling in my stomach. Somehow we had to find a way out of this impossible mess we'd created for ourselves.

'I don't know yet,' she said, twisting her lip to one side. 'Meet me in the morning at seven-thirty on the dot.' She turned at the sound of the wailing baby monitor and left the room.

I closed my eyes and fought the urge to take in too much air. *Slow and easy breaths. Slow and easy.* I couldn't afford to have a panic attack now. I needed to conserve all my energy so I didn't fall apart.

My head felt like it was trapped inside a spin dryer by the time I got into bed. The sleepwalking incident had pointed the finger at me, but as time went on, I was having more and more doubts. A thought suddenly occurred to me. What if Karen wanted to let me carry on believing it was *me*, when in fact *she* was the one who'd killed him? It made sense logistically. Once Charlie had got into my room, *she* could have hit him from behind.

I reached for my bottle of sleeping tablets. How else was I meant to sleep at night with all this turmoil going on in my head? Not only that, but by tomorrow morning we needed to come up with one hell of a magnificent plan for getting rid of Charlie. And I didn't have a clue.

Chapter 28

Dawn was still off-stage, hovering in the wings when my alarm went off. I opened the curtains and brought my hand to my mouth. I'd never seen a snowfall like this; tall drifts were banked up against the trees, the walls, blocking up all the gates and fences. Icicles hung like tubular bells from the edge of the bird table. Such a dramatic transformation had taken place in silence, overnight.

As I reluctantly peeled off my bathrobe, I felt a blast of cold, as though I'd thrown open the window.

I crept downstairs and pulled on my coat and boots at the front door. When I tried to open it, nothing happened. I couldn't even get the key into the lock; icicles must have formed over the keyhole. I went from room to room – every windowpane was splintered with frost, an L-shaped frill on the outside like a Christmas card.

Shit.

I heard a door open upstairs and Karen crept down to join me, holding her finger to her mouth.

'Kitchen,' she whispered.

I followed her to the back door. This one did open, but with an odd creak. We were greeted with a thick wall of snow reaching to a foot below the top of the door frame. It was shoulder height; I couldn't believe it.

'What are we going to do?' I whispered, the powdery tufts blowing into my face. 'We can't get out.'

Her frown softened. 'No one can get in, either. That's good. No one can reach *us*.'

'Yeah, but that won't put off workmen who live around here. They must deal with these conditions all the time.'

'Okay – but it'll take them longer than normal to get through to us. The snow against the house is only a drift – over there it's about a foot high at the most. We'll just have to be quick.'

'There's a shovel in the scullery,' I said, louder than I meant to.

'Keep the bloody noise down,' she hissed, flapping her gloved hands at me as she headed, instead, for the cellar door in the hall.

'What if Mel wakes up?' I whispered, when she came back, a spade in her hand.

'She won't.'

Time slipped by as we chipped and chipped, hacking at the white mound that had tried to seal us in.

'It's going to take us ages,' I said, stopping and leaning against the cupboard inside the door. We hadn't even made it outside yet.

'Stop moaning and get on with it,' she instructed without stopping.

When we finally crossed the threshold, having built waist-high banks of snow on either side of us, I was exhausted. The chill bit into my fingers and turned our breath into clouds of fog.

A gnawing, icy wind came at us in repeated harsh bursts. It was a spiteful and vindictive cold – that made you want to do only one thing – turn back.

'Right, now we make a path,' said Karen getting on with it.

I began scooping away the snow with the shovel, carving out a groove towards the track. The scene before me melted into a blur as my eyes watered with the cold.

Karen was right, by the time we reached the track, the level of snow had dropped and only reached our knees. She stood upright and rubbed sweat from her forehead with her scarf. I turned around and stared at the bank of snow that had come crashing against the walls of the cottage like a freak frozen wave.

'Bloody hell…'

'Good,' said Karen, ignoring me. 'It's barely light – there won't be anybody about.'

We managed to scramble through the snow from then on. I pulled up my hood and kept my head down against the gusts. An even fiercer wind was brewing and it was snowing again, coming down in large flakes. Clusters of them caught on my eyelashes and blinded me for a second. I brushed them away impatiently.

'Are you going to tell me what the plan is?' I demanded, catching up with her.

'Tell me your ideas, first,' she deflected.

Before I'd been sucked down into sleep by my sleeping tablet last night, I'd run through all the murder plots I could think of, from films and police dramas.

'We could make it look like he fell in the byre. There's already a hole in the roof – we could make it look like a beam came down on top of him…'

'Stage an "accident"?'

'Yeah. It would explain why he was covered in snow.'

'We can't risk it – the wound on his head wouldn't match. And where are we going to get a massive wooden beam big enough to have fallen down and killed him?' I pictured the byre. She had a point; there'd been nothing that big lying around. 'In any case, anyone who comes to the byre will know the hole has been there a while. It didn't just happen overnight. Mrs Ellington wouldn't be fooled.'

'Yeah – but maybe with a fresh fall of heavy snow, like we had last night…it would have taken more of the roof down…' I was clutching at straws. I knew we wouldn't get away with it that way.

I was wheezing by the time we got there. While Karen unlocked the padlock on the side door, I leant against a stack of wooden pallets to get my breath back. I glanced out at the horizon. I could see that dawn was already on our heels keen to catch up with us; the sky splashed with blood red streaks.

'Perhaps we could leave him by the roadside,' I said. 'Make it look like he was hit by a car.'

Karen put her hands on her hips. 'It's the same problem – his injuries won't be consistent.'

'Mmm – how about we move the body again,' I suggested wearily, 'hide him in the woods?' I was fed up by now; I was the only one coming up with all the ideas and Karen was shooting them down, one by one.

'Bury him?' She thought about it, but not for long. We were standing by the icy mound by now, like relatives in a cemetery visiting a new grave. 'The ground will be rock solid. No – we have to get rid of him for good.'

As if we hadn't done enough already, the idea of getting rid of his body *for ever* felt like an unforgiveable sin. Until now, there had always been the potential to come clean and tell the police the truth. Once the body was gone that door would be closed. My gut was telling me, however, that it was all we could do.

By now, following my phone call, the police would be out looking for him. We'd gone too far – there were no other options, if we were going to stay out of prison. Nevertheless, I knew, once we'd disposed of him for good, it would eat away at me for the rest of my life. I'd brought my phone with me and glanced down at the number nine on the keypad. I was tempted to press it.

Karen saw what I was doing and swung me round, roughly. 'Don't even think about it,' she growled, pressing a torch into my other hand. 'Come on, we've got a job to do. We've got to clear away all this snow and get him back into the wheelbarrow.'

I did as I was told from then on, moving like a zombie, following instructions, trying not to look, trying not to think about what we were doing. Charlie was floppy when we got to him, but bloated and stinking like no other smell I'd ever come across, the snow having melted and refrozen in stages. I had to squeeze my nostrils shut as we stood over him. I was glad I'd not eaten any breakfast, but still I wretched, bringing up liquid.

'For fuck's sake, Alice. Get something to clear that up.'

I rummaged around in the boxes near the newly

installed sink at the back and managed to find a full bottle of disinfectant. I inhaled long and hard on opening it, sniffing the rich antiseptic fumes in an attempt to drown out the putrefying stink that was following me around.

I drizzled the neat liquid over the mess and used an old-fashioned mop, dipped in snow, to clear it away. Karen waited for me, her arms folded.

'Okay – on the count of three…' She grabbed Charlie's shoulders, I took his ankles and we swung him into the barrow. We stuffed the tarpaulin around him, covering him as quickly as we could. Karen lifted the handles and started to push the barrow round to the side door. I was struggling to keep it from tipping over with one hand, training the torch beam on the floor with the other. Thank goodness he had a small frame.

A sudden shudder of hysteria made me want to laugh. We probably looked farcical, like a scene from Laurel and Hardy; two hapless creatures struggling with an unwieldy body in a wheelbarrow. It might have been funny had it not been so abhorrent.

I held on to my forehead, suddenly too hot, stars starting to sparkle in front of my eyes. I steadied myself against the wall.

'What are you doing? Come on – let's go,' said Karen, and we steered him out into the breaking daylight. The near distance was clear and snowbound, the far distance pure mist. I couldn't see the outline of any trees or mountains. That was good – one factor in our favour.

'What if someone sees us?' I said, switching off the torch and dropping it into my pocket.

'They won't. Just keep moving.'

'What about his rucksack?' It was still lying on the floor under the pond liner.

'We'll burn it later.'

It was hard going at first, ploughing against the snowdrifts; awkward mounds had swollen in our path like carbuncles. We took it in turns to push the wheelbarrow, then tried for a bit with a handle each.

I knew straight away where we were going. It was the obvious place. With every minute that passed, the mist grew thinner and before long we could see for miles. Thankfully, the clouds remained and the sun didn't break through, as we trundled with our burden through stretches of wasteland. It was wild and hostile – everything I was feeling inside at the disgrace of this terrible wrongdoing.

The path opened out and we had to cross the corner of a field to get down to the water's edge. Overnight, the loch had been transformed, giving the false appearance of a steaming cauldron. I could barely see the water; I tried to locate landmarks on the horizon, but could only guess at the expanse of it. At this spot, the temperature seemed to dip below freezing and wasn't about to get any warmer. Flecks of snow were turning my cheeks to ice.

We stood back on the bank with Charlie in front of us like a child in a pram.

'Now what?' I said.

Karen was searching along the water's edge. Of course; the boats – Karen had told us that at least one was always left on each side. We both scoured the shore, batting away the reeds with our gloved hands. Then I spotted one, half-hidden, wrapped up in the curling mist like an Impressionist painting. It appeared to be floating away, but I soon realised the boat was still and it was the mist that was moving.

We dragged it onto the bank and, after several ugly attempts, managed to tip Charlie inside. Karen got into the boat while I followed her instructions and found rocks for his pockets. I dropped them into the boat and got in.

We took an oar each, although it was clear early on that Karen was stronger. She kept tutting and waiting for me to straighten the boat up. We kept going until we could see the far side of the lake with the same degree of haziness as we could see the place we'd come from.

'This is probably about the middle,' she said. 'Start filling every pocket you can find.'

I'd forgotten we'd have to touch him like this. She started with his jacket pockets and I couldn't help turning away. She nudged my elbow and pushed a stone into my hand. Silent tears came as I made myself press it into the back of his jeans. Then another. She tucked in his t-shirt and dropped a bundle down the front and back, against his torso. I was glad of the tears; they turned his limbs before me into indeterminate blobs.

I couldn't believe Karen was being so matter of fact about it. She tugged him across the edge of the boat so his head was almost touching the water.

'Wait,' I said, outrage catching my throat. 'Shouldn't we say something – a prayer or something?'

'Do what you like – I'm getting him in.'

She huffed and puffed and managed to tip his whole body overboard without my help. The splash sounded loud and lasted too long in my ears. I looked up, scanning the horizon. We were exposed in the boat. If the mist cleared, as it was doing in patches, we'd be spotted straight away.

'Right,' said Karen. 'Row with all you've got, back the way we came. We need to mess up our tracks.'

We sploshed and splashed furiously in an attempt to turn the boat and get back to the bank as quickly as possible. I was nearly sick with fatigue, my head on fire, by the time we reached the shore.

'There will be DNA in the boat,' I said, staring into its shell.

'Let's smash it up and sink it,' she said, grabbing a sharp boulder from the edge of the water. I looked up – knowing we were going to be making a noise. I saw movement to my right.

'There's someone there,' I said in a loud whisper, my breath in snatches. 'We've been seen.'

I felt sweat prickle under my arms. I was starting to feel trapped. Everything was collapsing. What we were doing was terribly wrong. It had been wrong from the start. If only Karen had been able to get through to the police when she'd made that first call. If only there had been a landline in the cottage.

Karen brought the rock down on to the ribs of the boat. 'Just get on with it,' she said. 'Anyone will think the noise is someone chopping firewood.'

We battered the boat with all the energy we had left and gradually it splintered and several planks gave way.

We set it off into the water with a brusque shove and then threw more stones at it, willing it to sink. It rocked and floated, rocked and still floated.

'Nothing's happening,' I wailed. It was too late to reach out for it, the rope had sunk and the boat itself was too far away, bobbing innocently on the surface.

We stared at it and slowly the boat listed to one side, then steadily – barely perceptibly – it tipped all the way in.

I'd been holding my breath. I let it out in one grateful sigh. *Thank God.*

Still – our job was far from finished. Karen snapped off branches and fronds of ferns and we swished at all our footprints and, more particularly, the line the wheel of the barrow had made in the snow.

We carried the barrow between us, so it wouldn't leave a trail, using the branches to brush snow over our footsteps. Our tracks wouldn't be fully covered, but they'd be transformed into smudges by the time we got back to the cottage.

It was snowing more heavily now. I looked up at the sky and thanked it for aiding and abetting us.

Chapter 29

I kept a lookout while Karen built a fire in the metal cage near the byre. She dropped in all the contents of Charlie's backpack – his passport, the woolly hat, the book, maps – the wallet from his pockets, then the rucksack itself. We watched it shrivel and buck in the heat, like it was alive.

'Get the rug from the lean-to,' Karen instructed. 'It's evidence, even though you've washed it.' It smoked with the damp at first, but gradually disintegrated.

She used a garden fork to shift the remains around so the flames ate up every inch, turning every bit to grey cinders. The fire died down and there was nothing left, apart from the charred buckle of a belt. Karen raked it out, tossed it into the snow to cool it down and put it in a plastic bag. She raked out all the ash too and tipped it in a bag. She always wore gloves and seemed a real expert when it came to covering our tracks.

We were just about to set off back, when my phone rang. It was a shock as we'd all been having such difficulty with the signal. Karen headed off to the back door and left me outside on the track, where I could keep the connection.

It was Stuart. 'Hi – I'm outside – you were lucky to catch me.' I tried to sound light and airy.

'Sorry I had to rush off yesterday. Glad I caught you. Are you free this evening for a drink?'

I hesitated, thinking about what Mark and Jodie had said about spotting him in the pub. He spoke again, his tone conspiratorial. 'Listen…are you alone?'

I looked up and saw Karen entering the cottage. 'Yes, why?'

'I don't want to worry you, but how well do you know Karen?'

'Karen? Like I told you – we were friends at Leeds about six years ago, we lost touch but this holiday is a kind of reunion.'

'It's just – I'll come straight to the point – I've been thinking about it and her description of her time in Hollywood doesn't ring true.'

'Stuart – what is this? Are you a private detective?'

He laughed. 'No. I'm not…' He laughed again. He seemed to find the idea extremely amusing.

'What's going on?' I said, wishing he was there in front of me so I could read his face.

'I think you should be careful. I'm not sure she's been telling you the truth.'

'Just because she was a bit vague about LA? It's over a year since she was there.'

'But she said she was there for nearly five years. She must have got to know the area – the road names, the Metro lines – pretty well in that time.'

'Yeah – I suppose.'

'And yet – she got something totally wrong.'

'What?'

'The Hollywood-Highland Metro line – the closest

one to where she was living – on all the maps it's coloured red, not orange.'

'You were trying to catch her out?'

'She agreed it was orange. It's a big mistake to make – that's all. It's like living in London for five years and calling the Central Line the blue one.'

'Maybe she didn't use the Metro that much.'

'In five years?' He expelled a loud breath. 'It's the only line that serves that district – you can't confuse it with any other.'

'You know the area better than you let me believe.'

'Sorry, I don't mean to make trouble.'

'No. You're right. It's odd. The whole *thing* is odd – Karen being an au pair for five years… it doesn't fit with her at all.'

'You think she's making it up?'

'Why would she?'

I thought about the handful of photographs we'd looked at earlier. 'Actually there was something else…' I said. He waited and I started walking around to keep warm. 'There was a photo of her with the youngest child she was looking after and she said the girl was four, but the picture was only taken two years ago. That must have been towards the end of her stay…'

'What are you getting at?'

'Well – she said the child was there when she got arrived – but the dates don't add up, if she was only four, she wouldn't have been born when Karen started with them.'

'Ah…' he said. 'You see?'

'Mmm…' I murmured. 'It could explain why she's

been so unforthcoming about it all.'

'Can you get hold of those photos so I can have a look at them? I'll collect you later.'

I was taken aback. 'Why? Why are you so interested in her?'

His voice dropped to a hush. 'I can't say right now. I don't want to frighten you – but I think you should be very careful.'

'Around Karen?'

'Yes,' he said emphatically. 'She's not what she seems.'

Chapter 30

Major panic about Charlie has taken over everything, but I think I've managed to get it under control. Still…snags seem to be cropping up all over the place. I'm going to struggle to hold it all together. It's awful having no one here I can talk to about it – I've got so much bottled up inside.

It's Alice I'm worried about now. I've changed my mind about her, but it's too bloody late! She's more sure of herself, more independent in her thinking – so different. I can't afford for her to be like this. She needs to be my acolyte, to back up everything I say and do. My plan depends on it. Why else would I have asked her?!

Alice used to be simple, straightforward and naïve – everyone trusted her. She wasn't practised at spotting lies, either, she used to go along with everything. Now I'm not so sure. I don't want her thinking too much, putting the pieces together and complicating things.

I can't believe I might actually be the cause of this – it's probably my *fault that she's punching above her weight! I taught her to come out of herself, to spread her wings and cherish her strengths. Now, she's read self-help books, been to assertiveness classes, even had life-coaching, The result is she's not as pliable as she once was. I'm worried now. I'm not sure I can trust her to keep in line anymore.*

Chapter 31

Karen was in the bath when I got back indoors. I, too, wanted nothing more than to scrub away the thick layers of shame after what we'd done, but I knew no matter how hard I scoured my body, I'd never scrub out the disgust buried beneath my skin.

Now I had something else to worry about. More and more, Karen seemed to be turning into the enemy, snapping and being short with me. I didn't dare imagine what was going on inside her head, but an increasingly terrified part of me wanted to be anywhere, but here.

I made myself a coffee while I waited to use the bathroom and Jodie joined me by the stove, unexpectedly. She was huddled over in her bathrobe, her long hair screwed up as if the contents of a mangled knitting basket had been tipped over her head.

'It's early for you,' I remarked.

'Tell me about it – Mark wants a coffee,' she groaned, reaching for the kettle.

'It's just boiled,' I said.

She held onto the edge of the draining board as if she might collapse without its support. I stood behind her, wondering if she knew anything about the ten thousand pounds I'd found in Mark's bag. I cringed at the thought of it.

She shuffled out without another word.

Chapter 32

I rinsed my mug and went upstairs. Karen was still in the bath; I could hear more running water. Jodie had disappeared and Mel was whining in Karen's room.

If I was quick, I might be able to do it in time.

I slipped inside; the curtains were still drawn so I flicked on the bedside light, hoping not to startle Mel. She looked over. She was standing in her cot, holding on to the side, looking rather lost.

'Hello, sweetheart…' I said. I went over to her and stroked her hair. She was in shadow, but nevertheless I was able to see the purple patches under her eyes. Her cheeks were puffy like she'd had no sleep at all and there was a rash near her ears.

'Mama,' she said and her face crumpled.

'Mummy won't be long, darling – she'll be here in a minute.'

Mel banged the side of the cot with her fist and, losing her balance, flopped down on her backside. That set off a new round of blubbing.

'Shush, now,' I said. I was torn about picking her up. I wanted to soothe her, but I didn't want to get caught in Karen's room.

I scanned the surfaces, looking for the yellow envelope with the photos from LA. I couldn't see it, so I checked the suitcase on the floor and a plastic bag near the bed. It was full of dirty washing. I opened the bedside cabinet, looked on the floor. Then her handbag. *Yes* – I found them.

'What are you doing?' said Karen.

I had my back to the door and hurriedly shoved the photographs up my jumper.

'Mel was upset,' I said. 'I wanted to give her a cuddle.'

She pushed past me, her hair sopping wet and reached down for the child. Mel clawed at her face. 'Mama…' she cried, again, babbling other sounds that weren't real words. 'Gaba…nada…waah…'

'Did you know she's got a rash? I wasn't sure if—'

'Thank you, Alice. She's fine,' Karen said abruptly, and I backed out of the door.

Later that morning, I went along the lane to find a signal and rang Nina.

'I hoped you'd call,' she said. 'Malcolm is out painting as usual. It's a fabulous day. D'you fancy a stroll?'

I'd barely registered that following the misty start, the sun had finally broken through and blessed the day with light, a vestige of warmth and, best of all, the promise of a thaw.

'I'd love to,' I replied.

'I'll pick you up,' she said. 'Malcolm went off on foot today.'

She collected me from the end of the track shortly afterwards, a map on her knees.

'Where do you want to go?' she asked. 'Mountains, valleys, lochs?'

'Anywhere away from here,' I said, before I'd been able to filter my response. I qualified it. 'With the boy – and everything.'

'Let's head for Stonaton,' she said. 'There's a lovely pub that overlooks the river. We can get lunch there.'

We wound along narrow country lanes, leaving the cursed cottage, the byre, the loch far behind.

The sun was bright and it was wonderful to be forced to half-close my eyes as we drove into it. We stopped in a car park on the edge of a hamlet and set off towards the river, passing a small Norman church and adjoining graveyard. We skirted a tiny village green surrounded by a white picket fence with an old red telephone box on the corner. It felt idyllic; peaceful and untouched, with chocolate-box charm.

We followed the path down to the river, clambering over rocks and through sheets of ice and slushy mud until we arrived at a magnificent waterfall. It was around ten metres high, hollering with a great thudding noise as tons of water came tumbling over the top.

Nina had to shout so I could hear her. 'Isn't it spectacular?' she said, beckoning me closer. I nodded, but stayed where I was, not wanting her to see the tears in my eyes. I felt unable to move, transfixed by the turbulent power of it, wanting to be consumed by it; to let the thunder deafen me so I'd no longer have to listen to the perpetual round of questions and fears that batted around inside my head.

For a moment, I wished I could die right there and then, swept up inside the cleansing command of the water, pummelled by the crushing weight of it. Then I'd be washed away like a broken twig. I took half a step forward.

Suddenly Nina's arm was around me. She didn't say anything; she just wanted me to know she was there.

A couple of boys ran screaming on to the bank at the far side, throwing stones at chunks of ice and broke the spell.

We walked on, her arm linked into mine until the narrowing path forced us into single file. I followed behind until we reached the Old Forge Inn. Painted white, with black window frames, it stood next to a humpback bridge.

We settled near the fire, with two halves of real ale and a plate each of fish and chips. I asked how Malcolm was getting on with his pictures.

'Three finished and one on its way,' she said. 'A guest in one of the holiday cottages wants to buy one of them.'

'Already?'

'It happens every time. It's such a novel idea to take an original watercolour home with you, instead of a few snaps on your smartphone – *if* you had a jolly time, that is.' We shared a knowing look. 'You heard any more about the missing boy?' she asked, collecting the empty sachets of sauce and salt we'd used and leaving them on her empty plate.

'Not a thing – you?'

'The police think he's either a long way away by now – or that he's…you know…'

I let out a prolonged sigh.

On the way back, we stopped off at a small lake, set in a ring of pine trees. The thaw had continued; it was a relief to see the solid earth pushing through, restoring itself again. Walking back to the car we took a detour and found ourselves in a group of abandoned farm buildings. Nina had to refer to her map.

'Sorry,' she said. 'I think we should have stayed on the track back there.' She traced a line across the page. 'If we turn right, here, we should be okay.'

We followed a tumbling wall along the edge of a path and threaded our way through a pile of old railway sleepers. A trailing rope caught my eye; swinging from the branch of a tree with a thick piece of wood on the end and several knots above it.

'The boys at my school used to call them "Tarzies" when I was growing up, after Tarzan,' I told Nina, pointing it out.

'What's that?' she said, pointing to a cream coloured shape behind a clump of trees. We walked towards it. It was a caravan right in the middle of nowhere.

'It looks really old,' I said. 'Abandoned by the looks of it.'

'The door's slightly open – shall we have a quick look?'

I stood still. I wasn't sure I was in an intrepid mood; all I wanted was for everything to be ordinary, safe and straightforward. But she'd already eased open the door.

'There's no one here,' she called brightly.

I stood on the metal step outside while she looked around. From the doorway, it looked like kids might have been using it, with no one to clear up after them.

'Someone's been here recently,' she called out. I stood on the mat inside the door. There was an empty carton of milk on a counter amongst a pile of crisp packets, empty foil containers from take-aways, cans of lager and a newspaper. She read out the date. 'December

2nd, this year – the milk says sell-by December 4th.'

'The second of December? Wasn't that the day the boy was taken?'

'I'm calling the police,' she said. 'They need to know about this.' She pulled out her phone, but couldn't get a signal. She stepped outside to get a connection.

I found myself giving the place a visual once-over, being careful not to touch anything. It smelt like my dad's damp shed with an additional rising current of stale urine.

All the surfaces were covered in unopened packets of food and tins, as if someone had tipped out a bag full of provisions instead of putting them away in the cupboards. Unwashed dishes and two pans caked in sauce from a tin of baked beans were stacked in the sink.

One bunk had been used; there was a sleeping bag and blanket on it, tossed aside. There were no clothes, no other belongings. It looked like only one person had been there, but going by the remaining provisions, they'd had every intention of coming back.

I could hear Nina taking instructions over the phone. 'Right, okay…no…I understand…of course.'

She came inside. 'They already know about it,' she said, sounding disappointed. 'Forensics have been over it and they think the boy was here at some stage.'

'Really…?'

She tentatively opened the cupboards under the sink; the drawers between the bunks. She saw my disapproving look. 'So – it doesn't matter if we touch things,' she said.

'What are you looking for?' I asked.

'I don't know. Anything.'

We were about to go, when Nina jumped. 'Argh – there's a mouse!' she cried. She stuck out her tongue and patted her chest.

I gave a light-hearted laugh, but my mind was on something else. I'd sent my eyes instinctively down to the point on the floor where she'd seen the movement and spotted a small loop. A thick black rubber band. I wouldn't have thought anything of it, had I not seen one just like it on Charlie's wrist. Had Charlie been here with the missing boy?

The police couldn't have seen it or maybe they'd overlooked it – it wasn't anything personal, after all. They wouldn't have known it had any significance.

I didn't tell Nina and we turned to go. As she referred again to the map, I spotted scraps of torn blue police tape discarded in the bushes, flapping in the wind like trapped birds.

Nina's phone rang as soon as we found the car. 'When? Is he okay? Of course. Where was he? Oh. Thanks. I'll see you soon.'

'That was Malcolm,' she said, pulling on to the road again. 'He's been speaking to one of the police officers and they've had a sighting of the missing boy.'

'Really? When?'

'Someone's only just contacted them to say they saw him being put into a car on Monday evening. Malcolm knows more – he's got quite chummy with the local bobby. Do you want to come back to the cottage and get all the details?'

Chapter 33

The next half an hour trawled on as I ached to find out more about the boy. Driving back seemed to take an inordinately long time. Finally, the three of us settled with hot drinks, and Malcolm gave us the full story.

'I'm not sure how much closer it gets the police,' he said, 'but they think Brody was handed over to someone near Craigleven on Monday evening around nine-fifteen. The driver took off, but the witness didn't register the make or colour of the car – it was too dark. The witness was a man in his sixties, apparently he heard the baby crying and a car door shutting, but he didn't think anything of it until he came back from Glasgow last night and heard the news.'

'Did they find any evidence, though?' asked Nina.

'Yes, the police found a small yellow bootie nearby. Mrs Holland identified it as Brody's. And there were tyre tracks they'll want to examine.'

'Isn't Craigleven near where we got lost?' I said. 'Near the caravan?'

Nina was about to answer when Malcolm spoke again. 'The sergeant mentioned a caravan. They said Brody had definitely been there and they're still running forensic tests. They've got various items of adult clothing and found a selection of photographs – all different babies. There was also a hand-drawn map of the local area marking out the cottage where Brody was taken. Oh, and scribbled at the side was "9.15pm", so that links in with the witness.'

'The handover time?' I asked.

'Looks like it. Whoever had him wasn't exactly smart,' Malcolm added, tutting. 'Leaving obvious evidence around like that…'

Malcolm didn't know Charlie had never made it back to the caravan; he'd probably planned a major clear up before he took off for Europe.

'So they still don't know if Brody is alive or not?' said Nina, her fingers fiddling around her mouth.

'No,' he said, softly. He put an arm round her. 'But it sounds like it was planned and money probably changed hands and, if that's the case, Brody had a value and it wouldn't make sense to harm him.'

'That's what I need to know,' she whispered. 'It's my fault they didn't start looking for him sooner.'

Malcolm pulled her to him. 'It's *not* your fault. You weren't to know.'

'The police told you a lot,' I said, surprised at how detailed his information was.

He chuckled. 'I managed to catch Tom – Sergeant Harris – at the pub. He was knackered – they're all doing shifts around the clock and he let his guard down probably more than he should have done.'

It sounded like a party was in full swing when Nina dropped me back at the cottage. It was mid-afternoon, but a blast of alcohol fumes hit me as soon as I got through the door.

'Here she is – the lonely wanderer,' said Mark as I put my head around the sitting room door.

'Come-on-in,' said Jodie, slurring her words so they came out as one. She was sitting cross-legged on the floor waving a bottle of wine.

'It's a bit early,' I said. 'I'll join you later.'

Mark muttered something I didn't hear and Jodie sniggered.

'Join us for a cup of tea, then,' said Karen. She was sitting apart from them with a mug at her side.

'It's okay,' I said, backing out. 'I'll be upstairs.'

'I'll bring one up in a bit,' she insisted. I shut the door without a sound and went to my room.

I'd been trying to read my novel and had fallen asleep on the bed, when I heard the door open. There was a thud as someone tripped over the ruckled carpet just inside the door. I woke and turned over. Karen took hold of the iron bedstead to steady herself.

'Only me,' she said, trying to stop the tea from spilling. 'See how easy it is to slip on these floors? No wonder Char—'

'Don't,' I said. 'Please don't.' I sat upright taking the mug.

'Can I sit?' she said and perched on the edge of the counterpane without waiting for a reply. 'Remember when I used to come to your room at Uni?'

'I think it was me who used to come to you,' I said dryly.

She didn't acknowledge her mistake. 'We talked about the boys you fancied and worked out little schemes and plans in order to get them to notice you.'

229

I remembered. 'It paid off in the end,' I said. 'Sort of.' I looked at her, wishing we could wipe out the last few days altogether. 'You helped me a lot.'

Her eyelids drooped and her head drifted to one side as if it was too heavy for her to keep upright. There was no sparkle in her eyes, no soft sheen to her skin. Without the smile, she looked like someone who'd battled with life and lost – it was her smile, I realised, that kept her face alive.

I'd changed in the time we'd been apart, but so had she. There were rough edges to her now that I'd never seen before and a brutal calculation in her eyes that unnerved me. I wanted to put it down to the business over Charlie – but it was more than that. I felt like I barely knew her at all.

'There's some good news,' I said brightly. 'I heard that Charlie had passed the boy on to someone…like you said.'

'I told you.'

'It means we weren't to blame…you know…with Charlie out of the picture. The boy had already been taken somewhere else by then.'

'Have they found the boy?'

I looked down at the bedspread, tugged at one of the candlewick tufts. 'No.'

I waited for her to say something reassuring or supportive, but she simply stared blankly ahead. I changed the subject.

'Do you keep in touch with Mel's father?'

'Not really. It's complicated.'

'Do you really miss that life – in Los Angeles?'

'Yes and no,' she said, noncommittally.

I took a breath. 'Does Mark owe you money? Is that why he's here? Does that explain the ten-thousand pounds I found?'

She shot upright as if someone had thrown cold water in her face. 'Don't be silly.' She lurched towards me. I thought she was going to slap me. 'You don't know what you're talking about. You don't understand any of it, Alice – so just leave it.'

I straightened up, pressing my hands flat down on the bedspread. 'Who killed Charlie, Karen? Who killed him?'

Her stare set my eyes on fire. She swung round and kicked the door shut with her foot, turned back to me and snatched my arms, pulling me up from the bed to face her.

Her words were clear and precise. 'You *know* who killed him.' Then she shook me so violently that my teeth rattled. 'Don't you start going all flaky on me, okay?' I'd rarely seen her this angry. 'STOP asking questions and nosing around. You'll make people suspicious and you'll say something stupid.'

Her thumbs were making divots in my arms. 'You're hurting me!' I said, trying to pull away. She was way too strong for me. I'd never faced her in this way before. When had she become so aggressive? She had muscles of steel and could have overpowered me in an instant if she'd wanted to.

She dropped my arms and left the room without saying another word.

Stuart picked me up at 8pm and I felt I could finally breathe again. 'You're quiet,' he said as we drove into the lane at the end of the track.

'Been a long day,' I said.

It had, but there was so little about it I could tell him. I couldn't mention Karen's behaviour – he'd want to know why she was so upset. I found the two things that were on reasonably safe ground: the latest news from Malcolm and finding the caravan.

'And the police think Brody had been held there?' he asked.

'Yes. Not for long. It was abandoned and it didn't look like anyone was going back.'

'Did you take a look around?'

'Yes – the door was open.'

'And? What did you find?' There was an urgency in his tone that didn't fit with simple curiosity.

'Nothing. It was a mess. Tatty, dirty – like someone had made use of it for a few days and then taken off.' His shoulders climbed an inch. Was he testing me? 'Stuart, do you know something?'

He looked startled and took his eyes off the road for a little too long. 'About the boy? No…'

I pointed urgently at the road ahead, he swerved to correct our position and slowed down.

'We've…stepped right into the middle of something, here,' he muttered.

An odd thing to say, I thought, but I didn't answer him; I wanted to get to the pub in once piece.

It was a rowdy Saturday night and I was glad. I wanted to lose myself in the boisterous trivialities of ordinary people living ordinary lives. We found a table set apart in an archway and I bought the first round.

'What did you mean… "stepped right into the middle of something?"' I asked.

He took a long sip of Guinness. 'Did you manage to get the photos?'

I put them on the table between us.

'Well done.' He took them out one by one and scrutinised them. I dotted my finger in the froth inside my glass, waiting for him to say something. 'These could have been taken anywhere – there's nothing about LA stamped on them.' He looked closer. 'In fact, this one wasn't taken in America at all.'

I leaned forward. 'Why? How can you tell?'

It was the one with Karen in a kitchen, wearing shorts, with a child holding her hand. 'Look at the packets on the shelves.'

'What am I looking for?'

'See the box that says "cornflour" on the side? In the US, they don't call it cornflour, they call it corn*starch*.'

I considered it. 'Maybe she…brought it with her from the UK.' He gave me a cynical look.

'And there's this,' he continued. See here, the blue box of clingfilm on the counter – they call it *plastic wrap* over there.'

'Really?' He looked thoughtful, flapping the photo against his palm. 'You know a lot about it,' I said disconcerted.

He looked at the others. 'She's lying,' he said, a misty look in his eyes. 'These pictures weren't taken in America.'

I looked down at my drink, about to take a sip, then spoke instead. 'But why would she lie? Being an au pair over there isn't exactly impressive – it's not exactly enviable.'

'But it's credible,' he said. 'Also, a bit fanciful and glamorous from what you've described. A famous actor who fathered her child, but she won't tell you who it is? Hard to check up on.'

'Okay,' I conceded. 'Maybe it's because she's spent the last six years doing some run-of-the-mill office job. Maybe she's embarrassed and made up the story about being in Hollywood.'

He put the photos back in the envelope. 'She's gone to great lengths to hide the truth, don't you think? She must have brought the photos with her specially, maybe even staged them, because she knew you'd ask. None of you questioned them, did you?'

'That's true.' I nipped my lips together.

Stuart was far away, following his own train of thought and I lost him for a while. He finished his drink and plonked the empty glass down on the beer mat. 'Mmm – it's all falling into place.'

'Falling into place? What do you mean?'

His eyes flew to mine, as if he hadn't meant to say those last words out loud. 'It's complicated,' he said.

I always hated it when people said that. It means they didn't trust you. I looked at my watch, but he was already on his feet ready to order another drink.

I must have been quiet for a while after he came back, because he asked me if I was feeling unwell.

'Sorry,' I said. 'Just thinking that our holiday is half over.'

Perhaps he was overly shy or a proper gentleman –

but time was running out between us. Was he married or gay, or just not interested in that way? I didn't know – but he was shutting me out and I was starting to give up on him. I wondered again about his questions about Karen.

'Why the interest in Karen's past, Stuart? What are you looking for?'

He paused and ran his finger around the rim of his glass. 'I don't like to see people getting messed about,' he said slowly.

'Me – you mean?'

'Anybody.'

I didn't understand exactly what he meant, but I could see from the set look on his face that I wasn't going to get any further.

'Are you looking forward to getting back to the University – to Edinburgh?' I asked.

He stretched before he answered. 'Not to the unruly students, but I've missed home comforts – my books, my bread-maker and the cat,' he said. He pointed towards the nearest window. 'But how could you not love this landscape – it's so rich and slow. Oh, I meant to ask, have you taken many photos?'

Taking pictures had been the last thing on my mind. 'Not as many as I should have,' I said. 'By the way, how good are your binoculars? Could I have a look at them?'

I'd been considering going down the loch to check the view of the water from different vantage points. I wanted to know how likely it was that Karen and I could have been spotted in the boat.

'Binoculars?'

'For birdwatching. Isn't that why you are here – to look for birds?'

'Oh – right. Yes, of course.' He cleared his throat. 'I don't have them in the Land Rover. I'll have to show you another time.'

The catch in his voice gave him away. He blinked a couple of times and looked into his glass. I shivered, but felt a burning heat inside my forehead.

I bit the bullet. 'What's this all about, Stuart?'

He tried to look innocent.

I carried on. 'Something really weird is going on and it's making me very uneasy.'

He scratched his ear. 'Okay. Listen, I haven't told you the whole picture.'

I laughed. 'I think I can see that! Spill.'

'I'm going through a divorce. Not my idea. It's nearly over now.'

I stared down at my boots. 'Oh…I'm sorry.' It explained a lot; his reticence, his tendency to take one step towards me, then two more away from me.

'I've also been going through a difficult time with my family. A few years ago, my brother was seriously injured in an armed robbery.' I could hear the tremor in his shallow breaths. 'Tony had to have his leg amputated.' He focussed on my face. 'He won't go out; he's turned into a recluse.'

'How awful…'

'It's hard for me to know what to do. I feel so powerless.'

He told me more, revealing his torment and guilt, knowing his brother was in such a bad way. I followed his words intently. They weren't the kinds of emotional details you'd share with just anyone.

He blinked. 'Sorry – you don't want to hear all this.'

I hooked a loose strand of hair behind my ear. The time had come to own up. After his brother's suffering, what I'd been through didn't seem like such a big deal.

'I need to tell you something, too.' My voice wavered and I wondered if I was going to get it all out without melting into tears. 'I was…attacked…at knifepoint a few months ago,' I said.

His mouth fell open, his eyes fixed on mine.

'It shook my sense of everything in my life. I've had…a couple of panic attacks.'

His head shook a little as if taking in what I'd said, before he spontaneously reached out his hand. He folded it over mine, enclosing it completely. His understanding pressed into my skin through his warm fingers. I felt tears prickle at the corner of my eyes with instant relief, but I didn't want to cry.

'Alice…how terrible…'

'It was a mugging in a busy market – he fooled me into thinking he was in difficulty and I went into a blind alleyway. It was stupid, but I was trying to help. I didn't think.' I sniffed, not wanting to pull away from him to reach for my tissue.

'From that day on – everything was different. The world became a dangerous, unpredictable place. I couldn't trust people. I couldn't even trust myself. I took tablets for a while…I'm getting proper therapy now…' My little testament fizzled out. It wasn't a success story – like his brother, it didn't have a happy ending.

Without warning he was on his feet and in a clumsy movement – with me still sitting and him leaning over me – he threw his arms around me. I hid my face in his collar, feeling a combination of embarrassment – because people were staring at us – and utter emancipation.

He pressed his face against mine, rocking me lightly. Finally, with his arm still around my waist, he sank down next to me. We didn't say anything for a while, then he asked me if I wanted to talk about how the therapy was going.

'I *will* do, but not just now – I'm suddenly really exhausted.'

By the time we stood up together, everything had shifted. No words on the matter had been exchanged, but I knew our relationship had altered. We were no longer acquaintances. I didn't know enough about this kind of thing, but it was as if something was sealed between us, an invisible pact. I could feel it as he held my hand on the way out. Stuart and I were no longer 'just friends'.

Chapter 34

Stuart pulled up at the cottage behind the 2CV and switched off the engine. 'Come over to my cottage for a meal tomorrow evening,' he said as I turned to him to say goodnight.

His eyes were trained on mine and then drifted down to my lips. 'I'm fairly inept in the kitchen, but I can take your mind off it with some decent wine. Prepared to risk it?'

'That would be wonderful,' I said. I'd barely known him five minutes, but I felt capable around him. So many times in my life I'd been invisible, but he made me feel solid and whole.

'I can't let you go without another kiss.' He'd already given me six – I'd been counting – since we'd climbed into the Land Rover. He put his arms around my neck and for a short while his lips took away the cold, the anxiety about Karen, all the frenzy over Charlie. If only I could have stayed locked inside this precious cocoon.

My dreamy encounter came to an abrupt end when I got inside. There were squeals of laughter coming from the sitting room as loud music thudded through the floor. I tried to hang on to my final parting with Stuart, but the sitting room door burst open and Karen threw herself at me.

'Nice night?' she said, grabbing my wrist and dragging me in. I stood like a lemon in the middle of the room. There were piles of empty cans and bottles scattered everywhere, crisps crushed into the carpet, wet patches of spilt alcohol.

'Have you screwed him yet?' said Mark.

He was wearing camouflage combat trousers and a Newcastle United top. He never seemed to need extra layers like the rest of us. *That's because you're a cold-blooded creature,* I said, spitefully, to myself.

'Shut up, Mark,' said Karen. She handed me a glass spilling over with white wine. 'Come and join us. No excuses.'

She cleared a space on the sofa, tossing magazines and empty bags of crisps to the floor, and pushed down on my shoulder so I was forced to sit. What were they doing making all this noise? Wouldn't they wake Mel?

All I wanted was to go to bed and reflect on the delicious end to my evening – now it was all being spoilt.

'We're talking about the future, Alice,' said Karen. She looked tired, she'd tied her hair back into a ponytail, but it seemed grey, not blonde in the firelight. 'What are you going to do with *your* life, Alice?'

'Let's all name one big dream we're aiming for,' said Jodie excitedly. She looked fabulous in one of Karen's pale pink mohair jumpers, its cowl neck revealing an inch of bare flesh at the base of her throat. She was kneeling by the hearth and Mark was playing with her feet. 'You go first, Karen.'

'Mine's easy,' she said, swinging her glass around. 'I want to spread my wings. I want to explore the world, to live in different places.'

'And how are you going to fund this round-the-world trip?' asked Mark.

'It would be linked to my job – I'll get a job where I travel around as an executive.'

'Haven't you been out of the loop a bit too long – looking after others people's kids?' queried Jodie.

'Yeah – I'd need a top-up – an MA, maybe.'

'In what?' I asked.

'IT,' she said definitively. 'That's where the money is these days. I'll get a job in Google or Apple and go back to America with Mel...then Australia...Europe maybe.'

She stared into the fire and seemed to have ground to a halt.

'Okay, Mark,' said Jodie, 'your turn.'

'This is a stupid idea. Girlie twaddle.'

'What's girlie about having goals for the future?' asked Karen.

'Oh, come on,' whined Jodie. 'It's just for fun.'

'I want to enjoy life, man. Just have a good time. Go to Vegas. Play the tables...' His eye glassed over at the thought of it. 'Make shit-loads of money. Do gigs all over the world and come back to my penthouse flat in Soho.'

'What about me?' chipped in Jodie. 'You haven't mentioned me.'

'Yeah, yeah – of course – with you.' He patted her on the head as if she was a dog.

'Okay – my turn,' she said. 'I'm going to get my stall, then my boutique in Notting Hill, and run my own business in fashion. And Mark and me will carry on being together and...' her voice flagged a little, 'get married.'

'Not yet,' he protested.

'No – not yet – obviously, but eventually.' She couldn't disguise the flicker of disappointment in her voice.

The three of them turned to me. It was my go. 'I'm going to train to be a teacher – I told you. Get my own flat, meet Mr Right…'

'That's not very exciting,' said Mark. 'What else?'

'Take more photos – have an exhibition, maybe.'

Mark snorted. 'Push the bloody boat out or what…'

'Okay,' I said, my voice loud and firm. 'I'm going to be the kind of person who doesn't stand for your putdowns, Mr Mark Leverton. I'm going to take some risks, be more daring – fly a plane, maybe, join a steel band, take a course as a stand-up comedian…'

Karen laughed and clapped, almost tipping over the full glass balanced on the chair arm.

'That's more like it,' chuckled Mark.

'Bloody hell – you have come on, Alice,' said Jodie. She hiccupped and her head slumped forward. 'I wasn't very nice to you, was I, at Leeds?' she grimaced. 'I think Karen and I took advantage of you, especially me – I owe you an apology.'

She stood up and threw herself on me in an inelegant embrace. 'I'm sorry, Alice, I was a cow.'

I didn't know what to say. This had come completely out of the blue, largely fuelled by alcohol. She would have forgotten all about it by the morning.

'Right – now we're all friends again, I think it's time to say good night,' said Mark.

'Noooo,' groaned Jodie, flopping down between

Mark's open legs as he tried to get up. 'Let's talk more.'

'I don't think so,' said Mark, his eyelids blinking in slow motion with the effects of the drink.

'Come on – let's talk about where we wanna be in five years' time. We could support each other, make a pact...you know – like mentoring.'

Mark got up, shooting a look at Jodie. 'You're off your effing trolley,' he said and stormed off upstairs.

Jodie's eyes followed him. 'Why? Wha'd-I-say?'

She stayed where she was and sulked, rubbing her feet as though Mark had injured them. It took me back to the first time Jodie had cajoled me into following Mark. I'd forgotten all about it until now and it made me realise how selective my memories had been from Leeds.

Seeing the three of them again, it was obvious that my mind had chosen to hang on to the more favourable aspects and not how it really was at all. I had conveniently forgotten that both Karen and Jodie took advantage of me more times than I'd like to admit.

This particular unsavoury memory was from the start of our second year, when we were still in halls. Jodie had been edgy and paranoid at the end of the first year, thinking Mark might have been seeing someone else, but it had all blown over.

Now Jodie was panicking again and yours truly was called upon to spy. I tried my hardest to talk my way out of it – said I was too busy with course work – but Karen pleaded with me to follow him just a couple of times to put Jodie's mind at rest.

She bribed me with promises to spend time together; a trip, just the two of us, to Knowsley Safari Park in

Merseyside or any film I fancied at the cinema – and I caved in and agreed.

Jodie wanted to know where Mark went and who he saw when they weren't together, so I tailed him a few times after our evening meal.

'Tell me,' Jodie whispered, as I went to her room the following morning.

'There's nothing to tell,' I said, holding my palms out to her. 'He didn't do anything.'

'So, where did he go?'

'He was in the bar, playing on the fruit machines.'

'On his own?'

'Yeah. For ages. He kept winning and putting all the money back in again.'

'Then what?'

'He went for a swim.'

'At ten o'clock at night?'

'He must have borrowed a key – he was a bit drunk, I think?'

'Was he on his own?'

'Yes. He did loads of lengths in the dark – I waited. He was on his own the whole time.'

'Then what?'

'He had a shower, got changed and at about ten forty-five he went back to his room.'

'On his own?'

'Yeah.'

'You're sure – you'd better not be lying to me? Because I'll find out.'

'I know. I'm not lying.'

But I was.

Chapter 35

I hadn't been able to relax that evening, chatting with the others, knowing I had to return the photos without being caught.

I found a moment shortly after Mark went up to bed, leaving Karen and Jodie engaged in an inebriated conversation about feminism and fashion magazines.

I collected the envelope from my bag in the hall and put the photos back where I'd found them, in Karen's room.

Mel had been asleep in her cot. I bent over to check on her. Her little hands were pressed into tight fists and dribble formed a gluey string from her open mouth onto the bedclothes, glistening in the moonlight. I stood waiting to see the covers rise and fall in a regular rhythm.

She twitched and her foot broke out from the cover of the blanket. I reached down to carefully tuck it back into the warmth and my hand rubbed against something hard down the edge of the cot. I pulled it out thinking it was a buried toy, but it was a brown bottle of tablets.

I took it over to the window; the curtains weren't drawn and the moonlight created enough light to read by. The label said '*Promelegan*', but it was handwritten and there was no date or information about the dosage. I tipped a few tablets out – they had all been broken in half. I dropped them back in the bottle and hastily put it back where I'd found it. As I went to my room, I chanted the name to myself over and over then scribbled it down on a scrap of paper.

I sat on the bed – was Karen giving Mel something she shouldn't?

I yawned and flopped back onto the pillow. I was too exhausted for once to think about that now. It would have to wait. Instead, I could let sleep carry me away and wrap me up in sweet dreams of Stuart. It didn't look like I'd need a tablet tonight.

Ever since the night I found myself in the kitchen at 3am, I'd been wrapping a scarf around my door handle and attaching it to my clunky alarm clock. It was a precautionary measure, just in case my body took it upon itself to take off sleepwalking.

I'd brought the clock from home – I loved the bells on the top which jingled in a high trill when it went off. I'd been leaving it close to the edge of the chest of drawers, relying on it to crash down and wake me if I tried to leave the room.

Before I got undressed, I set it up again, just in case – although so far, I hadn't attempted any more nocturnal wanderings.

Karen and Mel joined me in the kitchen the following morning just as I was wiping up my cereal bowl.

'You look perky,' she said.

'Slept *really* well,' I told her. I noticed the slim tank in the corner, disconnected.

'No oxygen?'

246

'I know, isn't it great?' said Karen. Mel was fixed into her highchair wearing a frilly mop cap a couple of sizes too large.

'Are the others up?'

'They seem to have had a bit of a row,' she said.

At that moment Jodie burst in, snivelling and red-eyed. Her mascara was smudged copiously, as though someone had trampled over her face with dirty shoes.

'Mark's being a complete pig,' she wailed. 'He's disappeared down the track again. I don't know what's wrong with him.'

Karen gave me a stare behind Jodie's back that said *don't ask*.

It reminded me again of that night when I'd followed Mark. He hadn't gone straight back to his room after he'd been to the swimming pool like I'd told Jodie.

Mark had been drunk, that bit was true, but he'd gone to the music practice rooms after his swim. I followed him past the gym and the oldest hall of residence until we reached a small quadrangle. He looked at his watch and unlocked the store cupboard. He went there most days to get his drums, but not usually at that time of night. Live music wasn't allowed after 11pm.

Recalling this now, I felt disgusted at myself for what I did. It seemed I was prepared to do more or less anything for Karen and Jodie in order to be accepted.

I followed him through the arch and stood a few metres away, hiding in the shadows under cover of the entrance to the concert hall. It was windy and scraps of cigarette and crisp packets swirled and gathered around my ankles. I bent down to scoop them away and heard footsteps – a woman's high heels. I pressed my back against the glass panel out of sight and the clipped rhythm stopped.

'I didn't think you'd come,' said Mark.

'I can't stay long,' said the female voice. I dared to lean out a little so I could see her face. I recognised her straight away; Lena Arzano, known as *the* desirable minx in our block. She wore a short red dress that fitted like a tight bandage, showing off her heavy boobs and vase-handle hips. Mark shoved her against the wall and ran his hands along the inside of her thigh.

'Rough tonight – is it?' she giggled, pushing her tongue into his ear.

'Whatever you want,' he muttered.

'Not here,' she whispered.

Mark ushered her into the storeroom and closed the door. I'd seen enough. I went back to my block and found Karen.

'You can't say anything,' she insisted. 'It would break Jodie's heart.'

'But he's fooling around with someone else. She should know.'

'Leave it, okay. It's what Mark does.'

'He's done it before?'

'Of course.'

'Why did you push me to spy on him, if you knew?'

'Better you than someone else,' she said. 'That way she doesn't have to know the truth.'

She made me run through my account of the events time after time, making sure it ended once Mark had left the pool. I realised I'd never been any good at making things up. 'Just explain what you saw, but miss out the bit at the end,' Karen said sounding exasperated. 'That's all you have to do.'

Lying obviously came a lot easier to her than to me. 'Tell Jodie you saw Mark go to take a shower and then go back to his room,' she said deliberately.

'But…'

'Do this for me, Alice – will you?'

She said something surprising after that. 'This could be useful one day – never give up leverage easily, Alice.' I didn't really know what she meant at the time.

The next day, neither of us mentioned it. Nor the day after that, and so it went on. Jodie continued to ask me to check up on Mark, every few months or so – right through until the end of our course. I hated it. And Karen was right – it wasn't the only time. Mark was the stereotypical two-faced cheat, claiming he was devoted to Jodie and seeing a string of other women on the side.

What was more interesting was Karen's face that day – she seemed more excited than distressed about Jodie's predicament. Only now, did it occur to me that she wanted to hold back Mark's secret – so she could make use of it one day.

Karen dropped a spoon as she prepared some mushy cereal for Mel, bringing me abruptly back to the present.

'She's slept for hours these last few days,' she said. 'It seems to have really done her good.'

Mel didn't look a hundred per cent to me. Her eyelids seemed swollen and her cheeks paler than when she'd first come out of hospital. I thought about the tablets I'd found stuffed down the side of the cot. There must have been a reason why they weren't in a properly prescribed bottle. A simple explanation? Nevertheless, I found myself wanting to know more about them. After Stuart's comments, I was questioning Karen's actions a lot more than I had before. It occurred to me that Nina's laptop might be useful.

Karen filled the kettle and waved it at Jodie, but she shook her head and left us. Karen turned to me.

'You're seeing a lot of this man.' Her voice was cool, but there was a sting in her words.

'Stuart? Yes – he's really sweet.'

'Married?'

'Getting a divorce.'

She laughed. 'Be careful, Alice. Make sure you find out more about him before you get too attached. Rebound relationships and all that.'

She sounded like my mother. 'It's okay,' I said. 'I know what I'm doing.'

'And you must be very careful not to let your guard down.' She leant over me, her hands flat and wide on the table.

'I won't. I know what I'm doing.'

'It's a bit of a cliché, isn't it? "Younger woman, older man" syndrome.' She turned up her nose. 'You're not jumping at the first guy who steps in as your protector are you? Women have moved on from all that, darling.'

'He's the first man I've found in ages I actually like!'

'Well, he's not going to like you very much if he finds out you killed someone, covered it up – and dropped the body in the lake,' she smirked.

I got to my feet, my arms stiff at my sides. 'I think we

should leave the cottage.' The words shot out of my mouth.

Her eyes gave away how startled she was, but she quickly recovered and smiled.

'I know. Me too,' she agreed casually. She shook a pile of granola into her dish. 'But it would look suspicious. It would look like we had something to hide.'

The holiday had been such a good idea, it had started out with such promise – now all I wanted to do was go home. I was miles from anywhere and without any immediate means of escape.

There was a mounting catalogue of horrors: I'd been plagued with headaches and tormented by what we'd done to Charlie. Mark was agitated and high on drugs all day. Jodie seemed to have regressed to a forlorn teenager and Karen wasn't the bright, enviable role-model I had always thought she was. She was sharp with me and not always fun to be around. On top of all that, it seemed she'd been lying to us all about America.

I didn't know what was real anymore. The situation might have made a good TV sitcom but right now – living it – it felt like hell.

I took a dustpan and brush and began cleaning up last night's mess in the sitting room. As soon as I got started, I realised my tools weren't up to the job and brought up the vacuum cleaner from the cellar. It had a short lead and the socket by the fire only allowed me to cover half the room, so I searched the skirting boards for another one.

I shifted chairs and pulled cupboards away from the wall, but couldn't find one. Then when I moved a small bookcase, I saw the edge of a socket poking out from behind the French dresser. I heaved at the monstrous piece of solid oak and after four goes managed to drag it away from the wall by about two inches, breaking my fingernail in the process. It was just enough.

As I slid the plug in, I froze. Beside the electrical socket was another one. A small white plastic box with a slot in the middle. A phone socket.

There *had* been a landline here all along. I pulled open the drawers in the dresser and checked the cupboards. They were full of spare cutlery and glasses that smelt of buttery tea towels; there was no handset.

I went into the kitchen and watched Karen carefully as I asked my question: 'There's a phone socket in the sitting room, did you know about it?'

'Where…?' Her expression suitably lopsided with disbelief.

'I'll show you.' I led her through and pointed to the wall.

'Well – there you go. Where's the phone?'

'I don't know. Maybe in the cellar?' I said.

'Maybe it doesn't work. Perhaps that's why it was removed.'

Or maybe you disconnected it and pulled the dresser across before I arrived, I queried, within the safety of my own head.

Had Karen deliberately cut us off from the outside world? Why would she do that? If she had known about the phone, we could have called the police straight away when we found Charlie.

A new thought whiplashed into my mind. Was Stuart

right? Did I need to be afraid of Karen?

Once I'd cleaned up, I returned the vacuum cleaner to the cellar and took the opportunity to root around with the torch. There were all kinds of things down there; a dartboard, an outdoor basketball hoop, a skateboard, as well as various tools hanging on the wall – a mallet, wrench, hacksaw, hammer.

In the boxes were old domestic items: damaged lampshades, cans of spray paint, rolled-up curtains, an old iron. I checked the final box and found it; an old green handset with a dial, wrapped up inside a plastic bag. I couldn't help thinking it looked deliberately hidden. I opened out the plastic bag; it had *Your M&S* written on it. It certainly wasn't from the same era as the rest of the stuff down there, besides Marks and Spencer was hardly a local store.

I took the phone into the sitting room and plugged it in. The dialling tone purred straight away, so I rang Nina's mobile number. She answered after three rings.

'It's you,' she said, chuckling. 'I didn't recognise the number.'

'There *is* a phone here, after all – you were right.'

'I knew it…'

I asked if she was free later that day and she invited me over after lunch.

I was about to go through into the kitchen to tell Karen that the phone was working when I heard Mark's voice. I stopped short of the door. It was clear they were in the middle of an argument and I didn't want to intrude.

'That's *not* what we agreed,' Karen claimed.

'Things change – I need it.'

'Well – it's too late.'

'I told you, I need it.'

'For your little secret, Mark? Does Jodie know just how bad it's got? I'm not stupid. I know you've been finding every excuse to get out of here and back to civilisation. When she went shopping, I bet you didn't go snowboarding at all.'

'Don't you *dare* say anything,' he hissed.

I didn't want to risk getting caught, so I left by the door to the hall and went to my room. I threw myself down on the bed, squashing my hands over my ears. What was going on? Were they talking about the ten thousand pounds?

I tugged at the bedcovers and slid under them, pulling them down over my head, trying to cut everything out. This whole situation was an illusion – a lie. I saw images of the phone, the stool, the wads of money, Charlie's hat, the wheelbarrow – all tripping over each other inside my head. I'd been drawn into some sort of conspiracy without my knowledge – I was convinced of it.

Am I safe? Am I really safe here? Or were things about to get even worse?

Chapter 36

It was a relief to get outdoors after lunch. Tufts of green and sandy paving stones were emerging again with the thaw, the snow turning into grey clumps like polystyrene boulders by the roadside. The layer of frost sprinkled on the verge appeared to be merely masquerading as snow. Nothing was as it seemed.

I walked over to Nina's cottage fighting the urge to let panic get the better of me. I took deep breaths and tried to allow the colours, the air, the endless vista, to pull me out of myself.

Once again, there'd been nothing on the news about the missing boy or the man who took him. I wondered if Malcolm had managed to find out any more from the local police.

There was chuckling in the background when Nina opened the door – she already had guests. She looked like the kind of person who held regular Sunday lunches, dinner parties and sparkling cocktail evenings. I could imagine her as a supreme and effortless host – flitting through the room like a long silk ribbon, offering drinks and nibbles, keeping everyone happy.

'Sorry, Alice,' she whispered as she took my coat. 'I wasn't expecting them.'

'It's fine. It's nice,' I said hoping I didn't sound disappointed.

She led me into the drawing room and introduced me to Ted, Mandy and their young son, Laurence, who were staying in another holiday cottage along the lane.

'We're near the loch – Loch Tierney,' said Ted. 'How about you?'

I didn't answer straight away. *How near the loch?*

I felt saliva from the back of my throat bolt down in a hurry. I gave him vague directions to our cottage.

'We're like a little English ex-pat group,' tittered Mandy. Malcolm gave a polite chuckle and she laughed louder, exposing teeth that were too big for her face and looked like they belonged to someone else. Ted had doggy brown eyes and thin hair. It was obviously dyed in one flat chestnut colour and was coated in gel that made it lie in flat brittle slices. I found it hard to stop scrutinising it.

Nina pointed to the decanters and I asked for brandy this time. She pressed the glass into my hand and we all made excruciating small talk for around twenty minutes. *Where are you from? What's your line of work? Oh, how nice – you take photographs?* The inane questions grated on me and I was beginning to wish I hadn't come. As each day passed and the string of appalling events multiplied, it was becoming more of an effort to put on a brave face and appear normal. I felt nothing like normal inside.

'Well – we'd better make a move,' said Ted. 'I promised Lorrie we'd go fishing before it gets dark.' They collected their coats from the hall and Nina started the round of courteous farewells. *How nice to meet you.*

Glad you could come over. We must meet up again before you go. I hung around in the doorway, aching for them to be gone.

'We saw a boat, didn't we, Daddy?' said Lorrie as his mum helped him into his puffa jacket.

'Very early it was, yesterday morning; we were walking the dog. Someone was out on the loch,' said Ted. He put his boots on at the front door and straightened up.

'Really...' I said. It came out too high, like I was playing a fairy in a school play.

'The locals use it to cross the loch, apparently,' said Nina, 'there's always at least one left on the bank.'

'Old custom,' confirmed Malcolm.

'There was a big splash, wasn't there?' said Lorrie. There was an odd silence and I could hear the boy's eager breathing. 'I want to have a go on the boat. Can we have a go on the boat, Daddy?'

'We'll see,' he said, ushering the boy towards the door.

What had they seen exactly? Had they told the police? I didn't dare ask. If I mentioned the police, it would look like there was reason to involve them and their little tale had sounded innocent enough. It had no taint of suspicion wrapped around it.

I collapsed on the sofa once they'd gone. Nina put my relief down to them leaving, not knowing it was the turn of conversation that had unnerved me.

Malcolm sensed we wanted to chat alone, but before he went I asked if he'd heard any more inside details through the sergeant he'd spoken to before, but there was nothing further.

'You look frazzled,' Nina said. 'Another brandy?'

'Yes, please.'

I told her about the others in the cottage. How volatile everything had become.

'It's not the calm relaxing break you were expecting, then?' she queried.

'I don't know what I expected, after six years. Mark and Jodie seem to have a skewed relationship. Jodie seems hooked on him even though he's publicly nasty to her. Jodie wants to move on in her career – but she's being held back, playing at being helpless and silly, when actually she's a lot smarter than that.'

'Strange, isn't it – how some people stay in a dreadful relationship, because the idea of being on their own seems worse?' She shrugged and looked mystified. 'And Karen? You said she used to be your best friend.'

'She's changed,' I said quietly. 'Or maybe I'm just seeing her without the rose-tinted glasses. She used to be so undefensive and appreciative – now she's harder, more judgemental.'

'Well – people do change – especially in their twenties, I think. I know I did. I was loud and bossy at twenty-one. I thought I was immensely funny and entertaining – but then I quietened down, became more introspective. More sensible and thoughtful, I hope.' She smiled.

I took a long sip of warming brandy, felt it charge like electricity through my veins. 'Can I ask a favour?'

'Of course.'

'Could we use your laptop – you said you'd brought one – just to check something?' I pulled the slip of paper out of my pocket.

She was on her feet, keen to help, before I'd stopped speaking. She came back with the computer and set it up on the coffee table. 'We get a reasonable signal here,' she said.

I explained about the tablets I'd found. She did a double-take. 'And you think she's giving them to the child? That is worrying.'

She tapped a few keys then angled the laptop towards me so I could use the keyboard. I typed *Promelegan,* into the search engine. The NHS site described the drug as an antihistamine, used for hay fever and travel sickness. I read on:

Promelegan also has a sedative effect. It may be taken (for a few days only) to help promote sleep. It is available on prescription, or you can buy it without a prescription at pharmacies. It is not suitable for children under 2.

'That's interesting,' I said, pointing out the last line. 'Melanie is only nine months old.' I looked down and chewed my nail. 'Mmm, now I think of it, the baby does seem to be sleepy a lot of the time. Every time I go past her room, she's in her cot. Is that normal for a child of nine months?'

'Maybe the tablets have been specially prescribed,' Nina suggested. 'You said the baby had been in hospital for a long time. It could be something the doctors have advised her to use – completely above board.'

'True…except it isn't in its original packaging. Don't you think that's a bit odd? The name of the drug has been written on the bottle. It's Karen's writing.'

Nina eyes went wide, then shrank back again. 'Maybe the box got crushed. I don't know. It doesn't sound right, though,' she concluded.

'It looks like the tablets have been broken in half, so she's giving Mel half the dose…but still…'

'But what can you do about it?'

'Ask her about it, I suppose.' My heart leap-frogged at the thought of it. At the moment, Karen and criticism went together like a spark and gunpowder.

Between the tinkle of pots and dishes I could hear Malcolm whistling in the kitchen. 'Could we look up one more thing?' I asked. 'Could you access Edinburgh University and check a name for me?'

She put the laptop on the coffee table so we could both see. A pattering at the window made us both look up as sleet threw itself against the glass. Malcolm must have heard it too and let out a groan.

'Stuart Wishart,' I said slowly. 'Classics and archaeology.'

'Undergrad or postgrad?'

'Not sure.'

She used the keyboard, pressed enter and sat back.

No records found.

'I'll just put his name in – are you sure about the spelling?'

'Try Stewart with a 'w' – and Wisheart with an 'e''

We tried every combination we could think of in the degree courses and post-grad tutors. It turned into a bit of a game – briefly – as we tried to imagine the most obscure spellings.

'I'll try *my* name, just in case there's something wrong with the system.' She typed in Nina Ford and instantly a photograph and full CV came up.

We were both serious again. I didn't like this one bit.

Stuart wasn't listed at Edinburgh University at all.

Not surprisingly, dinner with Stuart that evening was smothered under a blanket of awkwardness.

He hugged me when we got inside his front door and tried to press a kiss against my mouth, but I wriggled away using my dropped scarf as an excuse. He stroked my face instead. I hoped he'd think it was the shift in our relationship that was making me nervous.

'Come through into the warm,' he said.

He'd made a tremendous effort. The table in the dining room was laid out with a lacy tablecloth with pretty willow-patterned plates, a silver candelabra in the centre and there was a Chopin nocturne playing in the background.

He was affectionate and sweet from the start, asking about my panic attacks, checking I was warm enough. I sat at the table and he brought through a steaming casserole dish.

I felt myself saying all the right things, but it was like I was sitting behind a glass partition, separated from him. A bewildered look crossed his eyes from time to time and I felt I had to apologise for my reticence, blaming it on a bad night's sleep and recurring headaches.

'You must get yourself checked out as soon as you can,' he said. He studied my troubled face. 'The pains are really bothering you, aren't they? I can run you to the nearest hospital if you like – it's no trouble.'

'That's very kind, thank you. I'll wait until I get back.'

'Head injuries can lead to strange behaviours, you know,' he said, half-jokingly, passing me the salad bowl. I thought about the sleepwalking and chewed on my lip. I'd assumed the sleeping tablets had brought it on, but maybe it was more complicated than that.

I didn't want to dwell on it now. If I added yet another concern to my ever-increasing heap I might end up being crushed by the weight of it. I took another forkful of casserole and made an appreciative sound.

'This is delicious,' I said. 'You were obviously fibbing when you said you couldn't cook.'

'It's true – I can't. This is the one and only dish I can do presentably. Nothing else. If you'd asked for ravioli or ratatouille, I'd have been flummoxed.'

It was hard to match up Stuart's warmth and generosity with the fact that he must have lied about working at the University. A layer of trust between us had been shattered, no matter how much I wanted to push it to one side. Our relationship had been deepening and I'd finally got what I'd been waiting for; an intimacy that took us beyond 'friends' – but now I felt the need to backtrack.

Was he expecting me to stay tonight? Isn't that what I had originally wanted before discovering he was some sort of fraud? My quandary did nothing to help the evening along and I became more jittery as time passed.

Once the meal was over, we moved to the sofa and sipped wine, staring into the flames of the fire. He put his arm around me. I wished I hadn't asked Nina to look him up. How different this evening would have been!

'Penny for your thoughts,' said Stuart, his voice disconcertingly loud.

I was going to bluff and claim I was miles away simply enjoying the fire, but that was the old me – the new me had to pluck up the courage to say something.

'Are you really a lecturer at Edinburgh University?' I asked.

He stiffened. 'You don't believe me?'

'Only, someone in one of the other cottages works there and…well, we looked you up on the computer.' I looked at the floor, my stomach shrinking.

'And I'm not in the system?' he said, a frown folding into his forehead. He took his arm away, shifting to the front of the sofa. 'I can assure you I'm telling you the truth.'

'It threw me, that's all. What with all your questions before about Karen and the terrible business about the boy…'

He shot to his feet. 'You think I'm involved?'

I took too long to answer. In that tiny gap, everything was spoilt.

'You think I had something to do with that little boy's abduction?' he repeated.

He didn't wait for me to answer, moving out into the hall – for my coat, I presumed. Was Stuart somehow involved in this – with Charlie? He had no alibi for the time the boy was taken. Had he been playing me along to see how much I knew?

'I'm sorry,' I said. 'I don't know what to think. So many weird and awful things have been happening, I don't know who to trust.'

He came back with his own jacket, not mine. He pulled out his wallet and handed me a credit card.

263

'This is me – Stuart Wishart,' he said. He slipped out a card for Edinburgh central library, again with his name on it. 'Look. And here's my driving licence,' he said, 'with my address in Edinburgh on it. I'm afraid I don't have any ID from the University on me – but I can give you a couple of names of history tutors I work with: Gerry Holding – he teaches post-grads…let me see…Liz Weatherby, she covers the Tudors…'

'Okay…'

He laughed and flopped down into the sofa. 'It still doesn't prove to you I'm not a child-snatcher, does it?' I wasn't sure if he was expecting a response.

He rubbed his jaw and there was a prickly silence. 'I think, perhaps, we should call it a day, don't you?'

He left the room and this time he did bring back my coat.

'Stuart?' I blurted out. 'Look – it's not that I'm accusing you of anything.' I took the coat, but let it fall over the arm of the sofa. 'I'm confused – all those questions about whether Karen was in LA or not – I can't see why it would matter to you.'

'Is that what you're worried about?'

I dropped my eyes to the carpet. 'You pop up out of the blue – my knight in shining armour, so lovely and attentive – and I suppose it feels a bit too good to be true – like there must be another reason why you're coming round to the cottage all the time.'

He looked genuinely hurt. 'How I feel…about you…is totally real. Honestly. I really love your company – you're warm, gracious, sincere.' He ignored the hand I put out trying to stop him. 'It's true.'

He withdrew his hands into his hips, shaking his head. 'But, okay. There is something. Something I haven't told you.' He reached for my arm and pulled me back to the sofa. 'I've told you part of it already.' *He had? Which bit?*

His expression looked pained. 'I told you my brother had been injured during an armed robbery...'

'Yes – but, what's that got to do with this?'

'It's a long story. Last year my brother, Tony, and his wife split up – and their grown-up son disappeared.'

'I still don't—'

He lifted his hand to shush me. 'The lad always had a turbulent relationship with his mother and when they broke up – it hit him hard. Tony was going downhill by then and I don't think his son could cope with any more emotional distress. He walked out one night in March, this year. There's been no word from him since.

'He seemed to slip off the edge of the earth – he closed down his bank account, stopped using his phone... My brother wants nothing more than to have him back, but he was in no fit state to go looking for him. So – for the last few months, between teaching commitments, I've been trying to find him.'

My eyes were glued to his face, wondering where all this was going.

He went on, 'I was hopeless on my own – I was certain my nephew had changed his name – so I hired a private detective.' He broke into a smile. 'That's why I laughed when you asked me if *I* was a detective – I'm such an amateur at this kind of thing.'

'Go on…'

'Anyway, two weeks ago he contacted me to say he'd tracked down a young man he thought was Charles.'

'Charles?' I sat upright, gripping the arm of the sofa.

'Yeah. His real name is Charles Wishart, but apparently, he changed his surname to Smith.' He rolled his eyes.

A faint buzzing sound started inside my head.

'Jim followed his trail to Glasgow and managed to find out – from chatting to some of Charlie's tipsy mates in the pub – that he was heading this way. It was the best lead we'd had, so I booked a cottage, thinking I could stay in the area and look for him. It was a bit of a long shot, but I had to try.' His eyes met mine. 'I'm not here for birdwatching – I think you saw through that – sorry.'

The buzzing was getting louder. 'Did you…f-find him?' I stammered, 'This…Charles?'

'I thought I spotted him leaving The Cart and Horses the night before you arrived, but when I got outside, I lost him.

'Then the police were talking about the little boy being snatched and they had a description of the man seen running across the field that day. I had to tell them I thought it sounded like Charlie. He'd been wearing a brown leather bomber jacket when I saw him in the pub.

'He'd never been in trouble with the police before, but Jim told me the guys in the pub said he was planning on doing some kind of "job" and then taking off to Europe.'

The sound inside my head had escalated to a thunderous drilling.

'It's not looking good for him,' he added.

No, it's not.

The words were all there – bursting to come out. *It's not looking good for him at all, because I found your nephew, Stuart – and he's dead…*

A new image flashed into my mind. Stuart must have been within yards of Charlie's body, festering by then in the byre, when he'd visited me at the cottage. *You can stop looking, Stuart. I know exactly where Charlie is now. He's in the lake. Karen and I threw him in there yesterday morning.*

Shame polluted every cell of my being. Stuart wasn't the bad guy in all this – the person with something to hide. That was *me*.

I couldn't bear any more. I didn't feel at all well. I ran for the door and bolted upstairs to the bathroom. The next moment, the entire meal that Stuart had prepared so beautifully was ejected into the toilet bowl. I sat on the floor, coughing and trying to breathe, as Stuart's footsteps came closer up the stairs. 'Alice? Alice are you okay? Alice?'

He tapped on the door. I splashed water on my face and called out the only word I could think of, 'Sorry…'

I opened the door and fell into him. 'Sorry…' I said, again.

'Are you alright?'

I held on to him, unable to say anything. Right there, right then – this experience felt like the most dreadful thing in the whole world. But I couldn't say anything. How could I?

'I've poisoned you,' he said, straightening up, biting

his lip. 'I told you I'm a terrible cook. I'm so sorry.'

I held my stomach. 'Maybe I'm allergic to something…'
I wiped a band of sweat from my forehead with my fingers,
hating myself for letting him think this was his fault.

'Let me get you home,' he said urgently. 'Will you be
okay in the Land Rover?'

I took hold of the doorframe with my free hand. For a
fleeting moment, I thought I might be swallowed up in a
panic attack, but it passed. 'Yeah…I think so… thanks…'

We went downstairs, slowly and deliberately, and he
held my coat for me.

'Thank you,' I said. 'You went to such a lot of trouble. I
really appreciate it.'

We barely said a word on the way back to the cottage.
When he pulled up, I unfastened the seatbelt and turned to
get straight out so there was no awkward moment over
whether or not we should kiss. I felt desperately ashamed
of myself.

He took me right to the door, more or less holding me
up.

'Thanks for…'

'You get yourself better and we'll talk some more. I
haven't told you the whole story.'

I stumbled going up the steps and he caught me.
'There's more?'

'Not now,' he said. 'I'm not sure of my facts yet. I don't
want to make a mistake. I've got some calls to make. We'll
speak tomorrow, okay?' He stroked my arm. 'But, be
careful,' he said, his voice hushed. 'Especially where Karen
is concerned.'

*

It was unnervingly quiet when I got inside. The place felt deserted and for a moment I wondered if they'd all left. As quietly as I could, I lifted the latch to the sitting room and peered around the door. There was no light on, just the flickering of candles. Two had already dripped solid trails of wax down the Welsh dresser, two more were creating a conspicuous fire hazard standing in saucers on the carpet. A strong waft of pot hit me.

The three of them were lying on the rug in front of the fire like corpses. They were all stoned. Karen made an attempt to raise her head, but flopped down again.

'It's-you,' she said, as one word. It sounded like a sneeze.

Mark rolled onto his back. 'She's back,' he groaned. Jodie put out an arm to thump him, but missed.

I could hear Mel faintly whining through the baby monitor, but Karen had her hands over her ears, blocking out the noise. In a matter of days, she had sunk from being attentive and devoted to careless and irresponsible. What was she playing at?

Without a word, I left them to it and crept into Karen's room. Mel was quiet now as I stood over the cot to take a look at her. Her little belly was rising and falling gently and evenly under the blanket, her arms spread out above her head. The woolly hat had slightly dragged down over one eye, but I didn't dare touch it in case I woke her.

I slipped out before I could get caught; I knew there'd be hell to pay if I was found intruding.

Chapter 37

I woke the next morning and, for the briefest nano-second, I thought I was back in my room at home in Wandsworth. Then I felt the rough tufts of the candlewick bedspread under my fingers and it all came back.

With a shudder of despondency, I missed Mum and Dad's bland, run-of-the-mill company, the delicate wisteria pattern of the wallpaper, the home-embroidered pillowcases. Everything there suddenly seemed cosy. In comparison, everything here felt coarse and threatening. I never thought I'd ever feel that way about our antiquated little home, but I ached to be back there.

I looked at the bottle of sleeping tablets beside me. I'd had to take another one last night after Stuart's shocking disclosure. I'd already taken more than I'd wanted to this holiday. I knew I mustn't have any more.

As I got dressed, Stuart's revelation about his connection to Charlie rattled around inside my head like a silver ball inside a pinball machine. He could hardly have had a more innocent and honourable explanation for his mysterious behaviour. Now, I needed to know the rest of the story and what part Karen had to play in it.

I glanced down out of the window as I pulled up my

jeans, my entire body shivering in great spasms. The thing about cold is it makes you crave cosiness – fires, hot drinks, the warmth of others. Yet, everything in the house had an extra layer of hostility – not just because of the chilly living space, but the lack of genuine connection between us. We were all separate – like strangers – without any real allegiance to each other. It made the temperature drop even further.

Karen was in the kitchen, sitting alone at the table, holding her head up with difficulty. Her chin was squashed into her palm and her eyes were barely open. I whispered a polite, 'Good morning.'

She grunted.

'Can I get you anything?' I asked, waving the kettle in the air.

'I'm going for a bath,' she said, heaving herself to her feet. 'Can you keep an eye on Mel? She's out of her cot in my room.' She grimaced. 'But leave the curtains closed, okay? Everything's too bright...'

'Yeah. Sure.' I hurriedly made a coffee and took it upstairs with me. Karen crossed in front of me, clutching a towel, walking towards the bathroom like a ghost. I remembered from our college days that she didn't handle the aftermath of cannabis too well.

I switched on the dim lamp beside Karen's bed and rooted around in the toy box. Mel was sitting on the floor in the shadows playing with a paper bag.

'Now – let's see what we've got here,' I said. 'Do we want to play with bricks or rings?'

'Ger-ger,' she spluttered, flapping her arms.

'Come and choose,' I said.

She crawled over to the box and I held her steady as she looked inside. She picked up a plastic dinosaur and flung it away, pulled out a fluffy dog and let it fall, then chose a small ball that tinkled as it moved.

'We've got a bit more energy this morning, haven't we?' I said. 'That's nice.' I was really thinking, that's *normal* – certainly much more what you'd expect from a nine-month-old baby. It occurred to me that maybe Karen had been too high last night to remember to give Mel a sedative.

Mel sat down on the carpet in her all-in-one babygrow and put the ball in her mouth.

'No, let's not eat it – let's play with it.' I sat a couple of feet away from her and rolled the ball to her legs. She felt for it and threw it back. 'Wow – that's it – good girl.' She jiggled around on her backside, chuckling.

Repetition was the key to keeping her interested – so we went back and forth, back and forth as she squealed with delight. Then she sent it back slightly to one side and it rolled all the way under the chest of drawers.

I had to lie flat on my stomach to find it. I groped into the darkness, trying not to think of the legacy of dead insects that had been accumulating under there over the years. My fingers came across something, but it wasn't the ball.

It crackled as I touched it and felt like a crumpled plastic bag. I pulled it out and glanced behind me at the closed door; I didn't want to find Karen standing over me wondering what I was doing. I opened it; inside was a rolled-up pair of stained rubber gloves.

I heard the click of the bathroom door opening.

I squashed the gloves into the plastic bag and rammed it back under the chest of drawers. I had just picked up the ball again when Karen walked into the room.

'Why the guilty look?' she asked, rubbing her hair with the towel. I wished she couldn't read me so well.

'Just, she's crying again – and I'm meant to be entertaining her.'

Karen knelt down and picked up the ball. 'Don't worry about it. She's a bit out of sorts – aren't you?' She waved the ball at Mel, then ran it across the floor to her. Mel repeated the last trick she'd learnt and threw it under the chest of drawers.

'Oops – it's gone the wrong way,' I said, letting Karen reach for it. Karen made a *humph* sound I couldn't interpret.

'Listen, I don't want to interfere,' I said apologetically, 'but she's been really sleepy lately.'

'Yeah – she's still on medication – will be for a while. The tablets keep her calm, but it means she's drowsy. I can't do much about it.'

'Right.' I got up. 'I'll let you get changed,' I said.

'Oh, Alice…'

I swallowed hard and turned back.

'Thanks…'

I waved her words away. 'No problem. Any time.'

After breakfast, I needed to get outside. The cottage continued to feel like a place where bad things happened. Corruption had seeped into the walls and carpet and I felt it leeching into my skin like noxious rays. I grabbed an extra fleece from my room and made sure I'd turned the heater off.

I glanced at my slippers on the mat by the bed and seeing them there, huddled together, brought another wave of homesickness. I sat down for a second to control this sudden sense of abandonment.

I didn't want to think about how many miles from home I was, how I didn't have an immediate means of transport and, even if I did, the weather was cutting cottages like ours off from the rest of the world at regular intervals. Both inside and outside was forbidding – nowhere felt safe.

Outside, it was deathly quiet; the snow had gone completely and the landscape appeared innocent and unscathed, like the icy weather had never been there. But it felt like a trick, a test set to lure me into another dangerous situation.

I thought about the stained rubber gloves I'd found under the chest of drawers. Had Karen hidden them? Or had they been tucked under there for months?

As I wandered past the byre, my phone chirped. It was Nina.

'Listen – I have what I think is good news,' she said.

'Tell me.' My voice sounded desperate.

'Are you okay? Where are you? I tried your landline but they said you'd gone.'

'I'm just outside the cottage. I'm…alright.'

'I know you're concerned about Stuart claiming to work at Edinburgh University.'

I felt a shiver trail over my skin. 'And?'

'I made some calls and a tutor by the name of Stuart

Wishart *is* working at Edinburgh University as a *locum*. He was brought in to the History Department at the start of the Autumn term and admin haven't added his name to the staff list, because they don't know how long he's staying.'

In an instant the doubts melted. I had to stop myself from punching the air. 'So, it's all above board!'

'I thought you'd be pleased!'

'Thank you, Nina, for taking such trouble.'

I didn't know whether to fill her in on Stuart's connection with the man she'd spotted running across the field. I didn't want to talk about Charlie.

'What are you up to today?'

'Not entirely sure. I think I'm catching up with Stuart.' I decided to tell her a fragment of the background just in case she found out some other way then wondered why I'd not said anything. 'I saw him last night. Apparently, he's in this area looking for his nephew. He's been missing for ten months. Stuart's searching for him to help his brother.'

'Oh – that's sad. Is he making any progress?'

I felt my cheeks go hot. 'I don't think so.'

'Well – let me know if you get any free time and want to hook up.'

'I will. Thank you.'

It occurred to me that had I met Nina at Leeds University, I might have looked up to her in the same way I'd latched on to Karen. Nina was generous, warm and showed an interest in me – those same qualities had bewitched me with Karen when I was younger. Only now it didn't occur to me to suck up to Nina or put her on a pedestal. It was good to know those days were in the past. I didn't need to feel inferior to anyone any more.

I ended the call and noticed I had a missed call from Stuart. A burst of adrenalin fizzled in my chest; I didn't need to be wary about him now. I was about to press *connect call* when his Land Rover pulled onto the track. I waved and he drew up beside me, the window open, the engine running.

'How are you feeling this morning? You look a lot better.'

'I am,' I said, reaching over and kissing his cheek. He put his hand on my neck and pulled me to him, so our foreheads touched. 'I'm sure it wasn't your meal,' I said, kicking at the tufts of grass near the front tyre. 'And I'm the one who owes you a big apology. I feel terrible about doubting you.' I told him what Nina had found out.

He switched off the engine and the chugging stopped. 'No – you did the right thing to check up on me. I could have been anyone – weaving a web of lies to deceive you.'

'Well – it happens,' I said, straightening up, nipping my lips together. 'There are a lot of con men out there.'

'Of course, I wasn't thinking,' he said. 'I should have understood that you'd need to be more cautious with people. Sorry.'

'Let's stop saying sorry, shall we?' I said lightly.

'It's a deal.' He gave me a high-five and I laughed.

'I know it's still early,' he went on, 'but I thought you might like to risk lunch with me?'

He patted the passenger seat. 'I promise I won't cook. I wondered if you fancied a drive over to Ebersley

276

– it's about fifteen miles – there's a lovely restaurant over there, does simple home-cooked food, apparently.'

He tapped his stomach. 'You could just have something light, if you're not feeling a hundred per cent.'

His hair looked thick and freshly washed. Within the space of twenty seconds, he'd touched my shoulder, squeezed my hand and given me a spine-tingling smile. This man had a magic ingredient that won me over in an instant.

'I'd love to,' I said and walked round to the passenger door.

We chatted on the drive over as if we'd known each other for years, stopping at several spots to admire the view. I felt I could give in to his enchantment now, certain that his allure wasn't that of a siren, leading me onto the rocks.

We pulled into the car park. 'Can I ask you something?' he said, sounding more serious.

I sat up straight. 'Okay.'

'Well – I'd like to tell you something first and then ask you my question.' He switched off the engine and we both unfastened our seat belts, so we could face each other. 'Right – here's what I want to say.'

His mouth twisted to one side as if he knew he had to get this right. 'I think you're a gentle, kind, thoughtful and basically irresistible woman.' I swallowed hard. 'I'm in the middle of a grim divorce – not instigated by me, but I came here in the hope of getting my head clear about a few things as well as trying to find Charlie.'

He didn't take his eyes off mine. 'This wild place has been exactly what I needed to help me see that…my wife is right…we *have* drifted apart over the years and we're not made for each other anymore – probably never were.'

He peeled off his driving gloves and put them on the dashboard. 'What has helped me see the wood for the trees – is you. Because I feel something for you I've never felt for her.

'It's hard to explain, but Sandy is a forthright woman. Now, that's good – of course it is – she's strong and assertive and knows her own mind, but what I see now, since I've met you, is that she's selfish. I've spent most of my life trying to placate her and fit in with the way she wanted everything to be.'

He rubbed his hands over his knees. 'The point is, I don't think Sandy and I ever brought out the best in each other. I think we were rivals – or she certainly felt that way about me. Our marriage was a power struggle to her and she had to win every time. I let her win – but that meant giving up a part of myself.'

I thought briefly of Jodie and Mark.

'Go on…'

'I gave up honesty, the truth. I gave up integrity. I gave up my point of view. It applied to small things – like choosing which plants we had on the patio, but also big decisions – like having children. Sandy never wanted them – and I did. I tried to fight my corner so many times, but she either stormed out of the house or dissolved into tears. In the end, I stopped asking.'

I put my hand on his. 'I'm so sorry.'

'Maybe that's why I feel safe with you. I can talk to you, be open and not fear that you're going to judge me. If you disagree – that's fine – that's no problem, but it's

278

your manner that I find so heart-warming. It's something to do with respect. How can I put it?' He leant his elbow on the steering wheel, looking at me. 'I think you're a beautiful person – on the inside as well as the outside.'

I didn't know where to look. 'That's probably the nicest thing anyone has ever said to me.'

'You see?' He held up his palms as if to say *I rest my case,* then put a fingertip on my cheek. 'And now I've made you cry.'

I didn't know a tear had escaped. 'Sorry,' I said.

'No – don't apologise.'

I managed a crooked smile. I could barely believe what I'd just heard. 'You said there was also a question?'

'Ah, yes. It follows on, really. I wanted to ask if you thought there might be a possibility you could feel something similar. It's early days, I know, and things are messy my end – and we live at opposite ends of the earth – but am I…you know, in with a chance, do you think?'

I gave him an answer without hesitation 'Yes,' I said. 'I think you might be...'

He reached across to me, searching my face. He must have found what he was looking for and sank his mouth into mine. I closed my eyes and in that instant, images of Charlie and the lake dissipated into oblivion.

I don't know how many minutes passed as we remained locked together in one long, sumptuous embrace. It was the voices of young children approaching that forced us to separate.

'Let's go in,' I suggested, reaching for the door

handle. 'We can continue this particular conversation later…' I turned and gave him a coy smile.

'Why not?' he patted his pockets, collecting himself. 'Don't think I've ever had such a meaningful discussion in a car park.'

As Stuart had promised, the lunch was delicious and my appetite was gradually tiptoeing back. The restaurant specialised in organic, local produce and I managed nearly half of probably the best winter pheasant stew I'd ever tasted. Stuart had a sticky-toffee pudding all to himself and we moved to a comfy sofa by the log fire.

I thought of how far we'd come since the doubts and unspoken accusations of yesterday evening, but hanging around in the back of my mind I knew there were parts of his story he hadn't yet told me. I hated the idea of pulling our romantic moment into darker waters, but I needed to know the rest of it.

'You said there was more to tell about your nephew and…Karen…'

He turned to me and took both my hands, pressing them together between his. 'How's it going at the cottage?' he asked.

'Karen's worrying me. She's been good to me in the past, but she's not the fun-loving, bright spark I remember.'

It was true – and not just since the terrible business with Charlie. Karen had seemed different; she'd been distant and tense from the start.

'She's got her daughter back after a long life-threatening illness and you'd think she'd be over the moon. But she doesn't seem happy. It's as if she's had her good qualities – the vibrant colours of her personality – washed out of her.'

'Why do you think that is?'

'I've no idea. I had no contact at all with her for about six years. I don't know anything about her life now – a lot must have happened during that time. You reckon she's lied about those years since Uni, don't you – popping up out of nowhere with what now looks like a made-up story about being in Hollywood…?'

He bowed his head. 'Has she done anything else to make you distrust her?'

The muscles in my neck had gone rigid. 'Tell me what's going on,' I said.

'Okay.' He leant closer and lowered his voice. 'This is going to be hard,' he warned. I kept perfectly still. 'Jim Cohen, the private detective I told you about, has done a lot of background work trying to track Charlie down. Charlie doesn't have a criminal record, but seems to have friends on the wrong side of the law and Jim came up with a bunch of names in connection with his search. Karen Morley is one of them.'

'O-kay,' I said slowly. 'What does that mean?'

'Jim followed as many avenues as he could to try to find a link to Charlie – he's costing me a fortune, but he's doing a thorough job. Apparently, Charlie is pally with Don Rees; he's married to Pamela Rees, who was in Holloway prison until earlier this year.'

My hand was gripping his as if we were about to topple over the edge of a cliff.

'This is where it gets interesting,' he said. 'Pamela's cell-mate was none other than Karen Morley.'

Chapter 38

Suddenly I was terribly hot, as if an inferno had ignited inside my stomach.

I stared at him, my mouth gaping. 'Karen's been in prison?' I was astounded. 'It can't be the same person – not *my* Karen.' I'd raised my voice and people in the restaurant were turning their heads.

'It's definitely her,' he said, patting my knees. 'Jim has only just confirmed it. That's why I couldn't say anything before now. I still haven't got the details.'

'What did she do? Why was she put away?'

'Like I say – we don't have the full facts yet. He's working on it.'

'I can't…not Karen…what could she have done...?'

An image of Karen standing in the snow beside the bonfire, burning the stool, came into my mind. I thought about how methodical she'd been about getting rid of Charlie, how in control she'd been the whole time. I thought about how she'd appeared to call the police straight after we found the body and they hadn't come. About the car that wouldn't start. The phone socket in the sitting room she said she knew nothing about…

'You're in shock,' he said, a look of concern darkening his face. 'Do you want to get out of here?'

'No…' I was staring into space, trying to figure it all

out. Did she know Charlie? Did she know why he had come to the cottage?

For the first time, the idea that Karen *had* killed him solidified in my mind. I hadn't dared let it take full hold before, but with everything else – and her subsequent actions – it made sense.

'She didn't want the police involved,' I muttered, not realising I'd said it out loud.

'What?' he said.

'Nothing…I don't know…'

He held me close and I hid my face inside his jacket. Everything seemed to be flashing; shapes in the room, pictures in my head. I closed my eyes hoping it would stop, but it only got worse.

He gently shook my arm. He'd been speaking to me and I hadn't heard him. 'I said, do you want a coffee?'

'Oh…a brandy, I think…'

He disappeared for a while and returned with two glasses – a double shot for me and a soda and lime for him, as he was driving.

'When will you know more?' I asked him, gulping down half of my glass in one go.

'Jim will be in touch later today. I'll let you know as soon as I hear from him,' he promised.

'Thank you.'

He settled back, one ankle on the other knee, his arm around me. It felt so natural to be cuddling up against him. Suddenly my life split into two parts – before Stuart and now; this chance of a new beginning with such a compelling man at my side. If only…

At that point he mentioned the police. 'Did you hear?

283

They're sending divers down into the lake – Loch Tierney.'

I tried not to stiffen. 'Why?'

'At least two families say they saw something early on Saturday morning. A boat in the lake, something dropping into the water – sounds very dodgy.'

I knew this beautiful encounter with Stuart was too good to be true. The reality of the situation came flooding back over me again. Everything *wasn't* going to be alright. Karen and I had been seen.

I kept my gaze on him, tried to keep my hands still. Now the police were going to find Charlie and start asking yet more questions. Stuart would be beside himself. I couldn't face a round of enquiries, omissions and lies. I'd break – I knew I would.

'Did the police say what they'd seen?' my voice had weakened to a hoarse whisper.

'I don't know. It was just a short update on the local news.'

Nina might know more. I made an excuse to go to the Ladies' and gave her a call. I told her I'd heard a boat was seen at the loch and asked whether she could tell me any more.

'Not really. Ted and Lorrie – do you remember? They saw something. And a couple in the cottage further down, closer to the water. They spotted the boat right in the centre of the loch very early on Saturday morning, apparently. The sun had barely come up and they were out at the crack of dawn looking for wildlife with their binoculars.'

I shuddered at her last word.

'Did they…see what happened?'

'Only that there were two figures in the boat – and they threw something over the side. Something heavy. The police think it's the boy.'

'Oh – they think it's Brody?'

'Yeah – they're sending divers down today. I didn't really want to go and look, but if you— '

'No, no, no,' I said. 'I'm just…you know…interested. Obviously, I want the police to find him – but it might not…' I stopped before I gave myself away.

'Malcolm and I are going out shortly – I've got my camera and he's got his paints, but if you wanted to meet up later, I could come and collect you?'

I didn't know if I could face it. The police would have found the body by then – I dreaded to think what state he'd be in – but one thing was for sure, they'd know it wasn't Brody.

Nina would want to tell me all about it and I didn't know if I could keep up with the mock surprise, *They found a man, not the boy*? I told her I'd call her later and thanked her for the offer.

As Stuart and I walked back to the Land Rover, I felt completely disconnected from myself. I felt dangerous, on the edge. I didn't trust myself to say anything, because I couldn't guarantee that my words wouldn't run away with me and my mouth wouldn't spill out all kinds of revelations about my misdemeanours in the last nine days. Was it only nine days since I'd got here and my life had become one long surreal nightmare?

Stuart took me on a scenic route back to the cottage. It was starting to snow again, as I knew it would. I sat back and let everything wash over me; his idle chatter, the bare trees and patchwork fields, the vacant road winding ahead of us. I coiled in on myself, thinking and thinking about what was going to happen next. Stuart took it that I was horrified and confused with the revelation about Karen and didn't appear to expect any conversation in return.

The divers would find Charlie. The police would go round all the cottages asking about him. They'd check the byre again. They'd look through the remains of the bonfire. They'd find something. Someone might identify Karen or me from the boat.

I needed to warn her. This was happening right now and we had to deal with it – regardless of what Karen had done in the past. We needed to run through our story again. I needed her steely resolve, because I could feel mine unravelling.

I gave Stuart a firm hug at the front door, but didn't invite him in. I felt appalling guilt for keeping from him the one thing he was here to find out.

'I just need…you know…to let things sink in…' I said. Part of me wanted to tell him the truth, but somehow the words refused to form. I had too much to lose.

He seemed to expect nothing more. He brushed my cheek with his hand and said he'd call later.

The three of them were in the sitting room. Mel was in the sling, tucked against Karen's body, asleep.

'Come and play cards,' Mark called out. 'Small stakes, nothing too risky.'

'It's okay, thanks,' I said wearily. 'Karen…?'

'What?' She looked up, holding her cards in a fan in front of her. I barely dared to look at her – unable to square the intelligent, poised and captivating woman I had known with someone who had apparently been tried, convicted and spent time in jail.

'Can you come…a minute?'

'What is it now?' she huffed, standing up, trying not to disturb the baby.

I led her upstairs, out of earshot of the others and told her the news.

'They're going to find him…they're going to find him…' I chanted. Everything was collapsing.

'Keep your voice down,' she snapped.

'Shit – the police will check for blood. They use special lights and it comes up blue.'

'Shush – calm down. We burnt the rug.'

'What about underneath it?' Panic was bolting up to the surface. 'The blood could have soaked through.'

'It was dry, clean. Honestly.'

'But, we'll have left traces on the carpet when we dragged him down the stairs, won't we?' We couldn't burn the stair carpet.

She sighed heavily as if I was overreacting. 'They have no idea he was here,' she said. 'Just wipe that whole story from your mind – finding him, moving him to the byre, taking him to the lake. We don't know his name. We don't know a thing, okay? He was never here.'

If only it was that easy. I didn't want to tell her Stuart was looking for him – I didn't think that would go down too well.

'What if they find something – his shoe might have

slipped off, or—'

She cut me off. 'They *won't* find anything.' She took a step towards me. I flinched, expecting her to grab me again. 'Don't let me down on this, alright? Don't cock it up!'

At that moment Jodie called up the stairs shouting, 'Your turn, Kaz,' and I lost her.

That evening I was glad to have the distraction of cooking supper. I was on autopilot from the start; chopping carrots, peeling potatoes, slicing cauliflower, dicing onions. I called it Lancashire Hotpot, but I simply threw in a random mix of ingredients without thinking. The only thing you could say about it for certain was that it was hot.

I'd called Stuart three times by then, but he hadn't yet heard from Jim.

The atmosphere around the table was unexpectedly subdued and I suspected something had happened – another row between Jodie and Mark, a telling off from Karen, an ultimatum from Mark? I scrutinised each of their faces to see if I could work out who the injured party was, but they all seemed equally downcast, barely communicating, only looking up to pass the salt.

Jodie and Mark offered to do the dishes without any prompting and, while Karen was upstairs settling Mel, I tried the landline again. Jim had called Stuart, but he had only a handful of details about Karen. She'd ended a sentence in May, but he didn't yet know her crime, or how long she'd served.

By the time I put the phone down, I was overwhelmed with exhaustion. There was nothing for it, but to go to bed.

Chapter 39

I didn't take a sleeping tablet that night; I wanted to stay alert – apart from anything, I was concerned for my own safety.

I spent most of the night tossing and turning, working out my next move and waiting for dawn to rescue me. I turned to my clock, but it was only 4am. By 4.05, I'd made my decision.

My bags were packed within ten minutes. As soon as it was morning, I was leaving.

The brave thing to do would be to ask Karen what was going on, of course, but I was afraid of what she might do to me. There was now an alleged prison sentence to factor in and, while that still seemed preposterous, Karen had Mark and Jodie to call on. If I caused any trouble, they would be at her side in the blink of an eye. It would be three against one.

Everything felt slippery and insecure. I no longer had a handle on the truth; the landscape was shifting drastically at regular intervals within these four walls, just as it was outside.

What *was* the truth about the night Charlie died? In my gut, I felt certain it had been Karen who'd hit him over the head with the stool. It must have been self-defence, but why didn't she just come out and admit it? I would have protected her – after all she'd done for me – she must have known that.

Would the divers find him in the loch? There was no way I could hold it all together if they did. Every waking hour I was on full alert, expecting a police officer in the doorway at any time.

As soon as my alarm went off at 7.30, I scurried to the bathroom and grabbed my toothbrush and final toiletries without making a sound, then I crept down the stairs with my bags. I did a final check to make sure I hadn't left anything, unlocked the front door and stepped out into freedom.

Outside, the night was still refusing to let the light take hold, but the dense snowfall from yesterday was beginning to thaw. I wished the weather would make up its mind.

I hurried down the track, not daring to look back. The landscape was like a vintage postcard, completely still, apart from tiny silvery white chunks that dropped from branches on the edges of my peripheral vision. Always just to one side or behind me. I turned each time but not quickly enough. Bit by bit the world was crumbling around me.

At the end of the track, I took the path towards the village. There was a phone box at the far side of the green, where I could ring for a taxi to get to Fort William. I'd make calls to Stuart and Nina once I was there.

Stuart could then decide if he wanted to collect me, but I had my sights set on Edinburgh or London – I didn't want to stay anywhere near Duncaird. I couldn't spend one more hour in this place. I'd send a text to Karen as soon as I was far enough away that she couldn't come and find me.

A tractor clattered past me, kicking up brown slush. There was no other traffic. I'd considered going straight to Stuart's cottage, but I was starting to doubt whether I could be with him when I wasn't able tell him the truth about his nephew. Besides, I hadn't paid attention when we'd driven over and there was no way I'd find my way.

It occurred to me how inhospitable it was up here, how cut off I was from civilisation. Anything could happen to me and no one would know.

It was quicker to stick to the lanes; from past experience out here it was too risky to head through the undergrowth, especially before the sun came up fully.

I had reached the second crossroads when I had the strange sensation I was being followed. There were sounds around me all the time – creaking trees, the rush of the wind, the rattling of faraway freight trains – but they were mostly sporadic. There was a more regular sound, hard to pinpoint and muffled because of the remaining snow. Every time I stopped and turned, it stopped too, so it was difficult to track it down. After a while I decided it must be the fabric of my anorak catching as I walked.

I had to put all my effort into not slipping over in the crunchy banks of dirty snow at the side of the road. I thought again about the duplicity of snow; hiding things, but also revealing what was normally invisible – footprints, for example. I thought back to the trail we'd made getting Charlie's body to the lake in the wheelbarrow and wondered if the thaw would throw up fresh clues that would link us to Charlie's death.

There was another sound behind me now, like a small tractor. I came to a standstill to swap my suitcase from one hand to the other and as I turned I saw two headlights, like beasts' eyes, in the road. It was a Land Rover.

Stuart wound down the window and called out, trailing alongside me as I started walking again. 'I've found you – what are you doing?'

'I was going to ring you as soon as I was on the train.'

'Train to where?'

'Fort William to start with.'

'What – without saying goodbye? What's happened?'

I stopped and dropped my bags. 'It's time for me to go, that's all.'

He rubbed his forehead, dislodging his cap. 'What's going on? Are you hurt? Was it Karen?'

I pulled myself up tall. 'I'm okay – I just can't carry on here anymore.'

'I can't let you go like this – this is awful.' He pulled over onto the verge and got out to bundle my bags in the back. He wrapped his arms around me. 'Come on…' He opened the passenger door.

I climbed in, my body inert. 'I didn't want to leave you behind, but I didn't feel I had much choice,' I said.

'You could come to mine,' he said. 'You don't have to stay with them.'

'I don't want to be anywhere near here,' I said.

'But you'll be safe with me at my cottage.'

I hesitated. 'What are you doing out at this hour? How did you know I was here?'

'Karen rang me.'

'*Karen* rang you? How did she get your number?'

'She rang the cottage...maybe the owner gave it to her. Karen said you'd gone and she was worried about you.'

Stuart switched up the heater and I dropped my head back against the headrest. I didn't have the energy to insist on getting to Fort William. He was hunched over the wheel, giving me a sideways look every few yards with concern in his eyes and deep grooves in his brow.

'What did Karen say exactly?'

'That you had a kind of seizure in the bathroom.'

Bloody Karen. 'That you've been sleepwalking and doing strange things during the night,' he went on. 'Is this true – is she telling lies again?'

I shut my eyes. She'd taken it upon herself to tell him about the sleepwalking. She was making me sound like I was completely off my rocker. 'You know I've been having the occasional panic attack,' I said, too tired not to sound defensive. 'Well, I had one in the bathroom that's all.'

'She said you completely blacked out – she thought you'd had a stroke.'

'She's exaggerating,' I huffed. 'What did she tell you about the sleepwalking?'

'That she'd found you in the kitchen in the middle of the night...that you'd been taking sleeping tablets...acting out of character.'

'*Out of character!* Oh, great!' I banged my fist on the dashboard, then realised it only confirmed any suggestion that I was unstable.

'She said you're still troubled by the headaches,' he added. 'More than you let on. Is that true?'

'I've had a few headaches,' I admitted. 'But, *you're* the one who told me Karen has a criminal record and isn't to be trusted – why are you paying so much attention to her all of a sudden?'

'Because I'm worried about *you* – because you haven't denied what she told me.'

'I'm fine. I've just had enough – that's all.'

He pulled away from the next junction with a squeal of the wheels. 'We'll get a decent breakfast inside you and talk this thing through properly. Then we'll decide.'

I didn't appear to have a great deal of choice, short of throwing myself out of a moving vehicle. I said nothing further until we got to his cottage. I was angry that he'd intervened but also touched that he cared enough to rush out and find me.

We left the bags in the car and he unlocked his front door. The sun had come up by now, splitting open the sky like a wide yawn.

'Bacon and eggs, or cereal?' he offered.

'Just coffee, please,' I said, as he led me through to the kitchen.

He switched on the oven, unhooked an apron from the kitchen door and tied it around his waist.

'Help yourself,' he said a few minutes later, putting a pot of coffee, orange juice, granola, muesli, cornflakes and a plate of hot croissants between us on the table. The aroma of buttery pastry won me over and I took a croissant and scooped a teaspoon of black cherry jam on to the side of my plate.

'Thanks for this,' I said.

Stuart sat back looking at me, his eyes wrapping me in a glowing warmth as I ate.

This was what true attachment felt like and it came to me then that our little group – Karen, Jodie, Mark and I – were connected only through a volatile tangle of secrets, bribery and deception.

'I can see how people get taken in by Karen,' he said, as if reading my mind. 'She's very charismatic.'

'When I first knew her she was like a warm apple pie giving off an aroma that drew people towards her before they had any inkling as to what was happening.'

'And how do you feel about her now?' he said.

'Regardless of what you find out about her,' I said. 'I don't feel the same way anymore.'

I was still beholden to her because of what she'd done at Uni, that was true. But the adoration was over. Since being here, I'd seen things afresh. Our association wasn't really a friendship at all; it was a trade-off, based on a series of subversive errands I'd felt coerced into running, because I thought it was the only way to be accepted. I'd been a performing monkey in her little troupe of followers.

I tried to explain. 'Coming to the cottage has been like a time-travelling exercise,' I said. 'Throwing the four of us in the ring together: Mark, the cocky layabout, Jodie, the insecure wannabe, Karen, the shining light, and me. I used to be everyone's puppet, but not anymore. The dynamics have shifted.'

Mark didn't scare me anymore – I could send putdowns straight back to him and he had nothing more substantial in his arsenal. Jodie was taking anti-depressants, trapped in a subservient role with Mark. And Karen? I was no longer under her spell – she wasn't enviable to me anymore. She seemed unhappy and there was an undercurrent of aggression and manipulation about her. She was little more than a bully.

'I'm not sure there's any genuine friendship left,' I went on. 'It's all an odd kind of barter system.'

I thought about the ten thousand pounds I'd found in the attic room. Surely it must play a part in this too? I recalled Karen's words: *leverage – never give up leverage easily, Alice*, she'd said.

I wondered if blackmail was involved. Perhaps Karen was making Mark pay in order to keep secret other misdemeanours I knew nothing about.

Stuart's phone rang at that point and he took the call. 'It's Jim,' he said.

I cleared the dishes, catching snippets of his end of the conversation. I knew they were talking about Karen; I heard certain key words, *sentence…Holloway…guilty*. When he ended the call and turned to me, he looked concerned.

'Sit down,' he said. 'You need to hear this.'

I dropped heavily into the chair, staring at his face.

He hesitated. 'Tell me,' I said. 'What did she do?'

'In February 2008, Karen gave birth to a baby girl. The child cried a lot and…when she was nine months old, Karen shook the child to make her stop. She shook her so violently that she died.'

I felt like I'd wandered blindly out of a safe dugout onto the frontline, with bullets flying at me from all sides. 'Oh, my God – she killed her own baby?'

Stuart's words kept coming at me. 'It used to be called "shaken baby syndrome"; now it's known as "non-accidental head injury". She was sent to Holloway prison in 2009. She came out in May, this year.'

Now it made sense. Of course Karen had changed. She was completely removed from her former self. It was suffering I'd seen. That's what it was – suffering – dragging at her face. Now I knew why. In the years I'd not seen her, she'd been locked away behind bars. All that guilt. She'd had all the softness hammered out of her.

I couldn't stop staring. 'Why didn't I hear about it?'

'Her case was overshadowed on the news at the time by another big story – remember the Arvon Bank data scandal in 2009?' It vaguely rang a bell. 'Jim said that computer discs containing bank details and National Insurance numbers went missing. It left millions of households susceptible to identity theft. Karen's case didn't even hit the local London news.'

'Are you sure it's her? I mean – her child is that kind of age *now*...and she's called Melanie. I don't understand...'

'Well – it's her alright. Convicted, fair and square in 2009.'

'I still can't see it – I can't imagine her wanting to...harm her own child. I've seen her with Mel – she's been amazing, making special things for her, doting on her – going to see her all those months when she was ill.'

Admittedly, she'd been sharp with me, lately. More than that – rough and mean, at times. But shaking a child to death…she seemed so sweet with Mel.

'You hear about it all the time,' he said. 'Often parents of young babies don't realise how tender the neck muscles are. I remember my father telling me he came across far more cases than he wanted to believe. A baby cries, the adult has had enough and wants it to stop – one shake is sometimes all it takes.'

Chapter 40

'D'you think Mel is safe?' I said, chewing my thumbnail, pacing about in Stuart's kitchen.

What he'd told me had thrown everything up in the air. I thought about how often the baby had been sleeping – and when she was awake, how often she was crying. Was she at risk? 'I've got to go back,' I said.

'Are you sure?'

'I need to talk to Karen – see Mel – make sure she's okay.'

He got our coats and reluctantly led me back to the Land Rover. Stuart could see I was nervous; I sat during the drive with my head down and my gloved hands squeezed between my thighs.

'I'll stay with you from now on,' he said. 'I won't let you out of my sight, I promise.'

I gave him a bleak smile. My mind was racing about all over the place. All I knew for certain was that I was heading back into the lion's den.

Karen's car wasn't there when we came to the top of the track.

'Looks like she's gone out,' I said.

'At least it gives us time to think about what to do,' he said. 'Come on – deep breath.'

'You're back,' she said. It was Karen who let us in.

The other two must have taken the car. She didn't sound pleased, merely stating a fact. 'I was worried about you,' she conceded. 'Thanks Stuart.' She nodded at him.

'I'm fine,' I said churlishly. 'And I'm not about to do anything *out of character.*'

Karen laughed and rubbed my back, but I pulled away. I was looking over her shoulder into the kitchen. Mel was sitting in her highchair having breakfast.

I tipped my head so Stuart would get the message to go into the sitting room and I joined Karen in the kitchen.

'Where are the others?' I said, scrutinising Mel for any signs of distress. I couldn't see much of her face under the hat, but she seemed bright and perky.

'Mark insisted on borrowing my car. I don't know where he's gone. Jodie is still in bed.'

Karen tried Mel with a spoonful of porridge, but she threw out her arm and sent it flying over to the fridge. Karen laughed. 'Okay – enough porridge, eh?'

I remained standing as she brushed past me and shut the door to the hall.

'You didn't say goodbye,' she said flatly.

'I was going to phone.'

She glanced at the connecting door to the sitting room and brought her voice down to a whisper. 'What's going on? I thought we were in this together?'

'Karen…' I didn't know where to start. I closed my eyes briefly and decided to jump right in. 'I know you were in prison. I know there was no job in Hollywood.'

Her face hardened. 'How did you find out?'

'Stuart told me.'

'Right,' she said noncommittally. She leant against the fridge and folded her arms.

'I know what you did,' I said in a hushed breath.

'No – you don't,' she hissed, her eyes blazing. 'I lost my baby. I was falsely accused.'

I shook my head in dismay.

'Let me explain,' she said. 'It wasn't my fault.'

'What? Someone else did it?'

'No – what I mean is – it was never conclusive.'

'I think you need to explain,' I said.

'Sit down,' she instructed. I stayed standing where I was, but she dropped into the nearest chair.

'I'm going to get a bit technical, but it's the easiest way to explain it. When shaken baby syndrome is suspected, pathologists look for three signs – swelling of the brain, bleeding between the skull and the brain, and bleeding in the retina – known collectively as the triad. If all three are present then a conviction is likely.'

'And that's what they found in your case?'

'Yes – but a growing number of doctors believe that relying on the triad alone is no longer enough. During my sentence I did all the research I could. I found out that in a small number of cases, injuries associated with the triad can occur naturally and are not always the result of trauma.' Her eyes were bright and wild. 'I've got people fighting for me, now.'

'And no one supported you at the time?'

She shook her head. 'But these exceptions are so significant that experts *now* believe that at least half of those brought to trial in the past for this kind of injury have been wrongly convicted.' Her voice tailed off into a croak. 'I was too late to get my conviction overturned.'

'So – you didn't do it?'

Her head dropped. 'She was choking on baby food. I was trying to get her to breathe, to get rid of the blockage…'

'Why didn't you tell me? Why all the lies about America?'

She slapped her hand down and laughed. 'Would you have kept in touch with me if you'd known? Would you have wanted to be associated with…a child-murderer?'

'I would have wanted to hear your side of the story,' I insisted. 'I might even have been able to help.'

'Thanks – Alice.' Her expression was sceptical. 'You only have my word that I was wrongly accused – but everyone – the medical profession, the courts – found me guilty. I'm not sure you would have found it an easy ride.'

'It would have been nice to have had the choice,' I said.

'I've got stacks of paperwork at home with all my findings, if you're interested,' she said. 'I should have a PhD in it by now. Ironic, isn't it? You were right. Medicine *was* going to be my grand illustrious career. I was going to go right to the top, once I'd taken a year out to travel, but I got pregnant…and after that everything fell apart.' She gave a chilly laugh.

'Nevertheless, I've spent *hours* scrutinising reports, statistics, other cases. You can see it all – back in Brixton – if you like. My lawyer is filing an appeal for miscarriage of justice at this very moment. I'm determined to clear my name.' She was back to the old Karen; fiery, single-minded, invincible.

'What about your parents? Did they stand by you?'

Her hands snapped into fists. 'Did they hell! They disowned me. Completely.'

I dropped my head. 'Oh…'

'It wasn't just me. I never told you that my brother went off the rails when he was in his teens, did I? He did the total drugs-drink-crime rebellion thing. Serves them right. My dad is a conniving swine. I found out he's been fleecing his mates out of money for years, reneged on deals, cheated and lied. He *uses* people.'

I looked at her. Like father, like daughter.

The door opened and Jodie came in looking flustered.

'You okay?' said Karen.

She threw herself into a chair. 'I don't know. Mark has been so bloody weird, lately. It's like he can't stand my company for more than about half an hour, anymore.'

'Where's he gone?' I asked.

'How the hell would I know?' she snapped. 'I mean – what is there that's urgent – out here? We're on holiday for fuck's sake. What's wrong with him?'

'Maybe it's not you that's the problem,' said Karen.

'What do you mean?' Jodie asked. She snatched the packet of capsules from her bag and threw a tablet into her mouth before taking a long swig of orange juice.

'Maybe Mel is driving him mad,' Karen suggested.

Jodie didn't look convinced. Karen seemed about to speak again – as if she knew something – but then she shrugged. 'Perhaps he can't stand being cooped up. Being cut off like this isn't everyone's cup of tea.'

'Yeah, well – he's driving me mad.' She laid her head

on her folded arms on the table. 'Any coffee going?'

Karen pointed to the fresh pot on the stove.

'I don't want to speak out of turn,' I said, 'but is he using too much dope these days, Jodie? Has it got out of hand?'

She shook her head adamantly. 'He uses the same as he always did – we both do.'

Karen twisted her mouth to one side.

'There is one thing,' said Jodie. She propped her head in her hands. 'I shouldn't be telling you this – but I don't know what to do. He's in a lot of debt and I've lent him piles of money.' Her chin started to wobble. 'It's getting really bad...'

Karen pulled up the chair next to her and put her arm around her. 'Oh, dear,' she said with a sigh.

Jodie buried her face into Karen's neck and spoke in short bursts between blubs. 'I'm scared...he's cleaning me out...I've got nothing left...he doesn't pay me back.' She looked up in horror. 'He's even started stealing from my bag.'

At that moment, the door slammed and there were footsteps in the hall. Mark breezed in as if he was the long-awaited special guest at a party.

'What's happening, guys?' he said.

'Jodie's upset,' Karen said, giving him a stern look.

'What's wrong, Babe?' he crouched down beside her, holding her hand. 'Is it about losing your mum?'

She pulled away. 'No, it's not.'

I left them to it at that point, aware that Stuart had been sitting patiently in the other room.

'Sorry,' I said, joining him on the sofa.

'That sounded melodramatic – are you okay?'

'Yeah. Did you hear any of it?'

'I got the gist,' he whispered. 'Karen claims she's innocent.'

'Come on – let's get some fresh air,' I said, pulling him up.

There was sleet in the breeze as we set out. Once again nature couldn't decide whether to rain, thaw or snow. This apparent indecision matched my confused situation perfectly. We pulled up our hoods and walked in silence against the wind, linking arms, our free hands in our pockets.

'There's a brook down this way with a cute humpback bridge,' he said. 'Let's go there. If we get too cold we can come back for the Land Rover.'

I made a brave attempt at a smile and merely followed him. I didn't know what to think. I didn't know what to believe.

It was the same spot I'd found before. I wanted to sit on the bridge but it was too wet. Stuart pulled a tangle of dead leaves from a branch above him. His thoughts must have been somewhere else, because his next words came out of the blue. 'Has anything odd happened at the cottage?'

My stomach lurched to one side. I had to be selective about what I told him. I hated it; having to hide information from him about his own nephew, but I could see no alternative. Karen was right. How would Stuart react if he found out we'd covered up Charlie's death and dropped his body in the lake?

My mind leapt to the police divers. I'd heard nothing on the local news about the search. Surely, they'd have given up looking by now. Or maybe they'd found him and were still trying to identify the body, before releasing any information.

Whatever the outcome, I still couldn't believe I'd gone along with it – Karen had been so clever making me doubt myself – making me think it could have been me who killed him. She made it look like she was doing me a favour, when really it was the other way round.

'I found ten thousand pounds,' I said. 'It was in Mark's room and then it disappeared.'

He whistled. 'What's that all about?'

'I've no idea. It went soon after I discovered it. Maybe you heard Jodie say just now, that Mark was heavily in debt.'

He frowned.

'Do you think it could be connected to the boy who was abducted?' I said, not looking at him.

'According to the police, the boy was handed over to someone in a car near Craigleven on Monday evening,' he said. 'Where was Mark at around nine-fifteen that night?'

I thought about it. 'Mark and Jodie had taken Karen's car sometime after eight o'clock...' I scanned my memories. 'Karen was with me at the cottage. She went to bed early, before you picked me up to go for a drink, at around nine-thirty.'

'So Mark and Jodie were out at nine-fifteen?'

'Yeah...they *said* they went to a pub...although I didn't see them at The Cart and Horses.'

'Do you think Mark could have been hiding the boy somewhere?'

'Bloody hell…' I exhaled loudly at the idea of it. 'I can't believe Jodie would go along with something like that,' I said, running my finger in the snow along the edge of the bridge, 'but Mark does keep finding any excuse to leave the cottage.'

'Maybe Jodie doesn't know,' he suggested.

It wouldn't be the first time Mark had kept secrets from her, I mused.

The air was thick with a number of things that didn't add up. 'What about Karen?' he said. 'Now you know about her past, has anything struck you as suspicious?'

'She's barely left the cottage since we've been here – apart from going to the hospital – she's been too busy with Mel.'

'And the child's been fine?'

I frowned. 'Karen's been giving her sedatives, but she said the doctors prescribed them as part of her recovery.'

An unwelcome thought caught me unawares. 'There is another thing. Karen grabbed me and…'

'And what?'

'Well – she took hold of me by my arms – she was cross about something – and shook me pretty hard, as it happens.'

'She *shook* you?'

'It doesn't mean—'

I could see him chewing the inside of his cheek. 'I'm not going to leave you alone with her,' he said.

Supper was uneventful. Stuart and I didn't betray Karen's Holloway secret. Mark barely said a word, Jodie spent the entire time snuffling into a tissue and Karen kept up some semblance of appearances by asking Stuart questions about Edinburgh University.

307

I saw glimmers of the old Karen – the one who could make a person feel special and important – but my sense of wonder only lasted a few minutes. More than anything, I felt sad. I'd lost her for good. We wouldn't be keeping in touch after this holiday. I didn't know who she was anymore and what I did see of her no longer held any allure. I gripped Stuart's hand under the table. He was the one I wanted in my future.

We all helped out with the dishes, making small talk about the weather, then Mark and Jodie sloped off to bed. Karen made herself a hot drink and followed them.

Stuart said he'd stay the night and tried the sofa for size.

'Are you sure about this?' I asked. 'I'm not sure it's going to be all that comfy.'

'I'm not going anywhere,' he said. He'd offered to sleep on the floor in my room, but the thought of him lying on the same spot as Charlie – his own flesh and blood – was just too gruesome.

I brought two blankets down to the sitting room from my chest of drawers. I opened them out. They were musty, infused with the camphor smell of mothballs.

'Will you be warm enough?'

'Sure,' he said. 'I can pull this over me if I'm chilly.' He'd hung his wax jacket over the back of a chair.

'We should plan what we're going to do tomorrow,' I said, my fingers fiddling with my lip.

'The police will have checked us all out on their national records after they interviewed us, so they'll know about Karen's conviction. At the moment Melanie seems fine – do you agree?' I nodded.

He went on, 'Did the officers say anything in particular when they came over the day after Brody went missing?'

I backtracked to their visit. 'Karen went upstairs with them – do you remember? So they could see Mel. They were up there a few minutes checking her over and taking a look around. I don't think the officers said anything when they came down.'

'Maybe there were being discrete – she's served her sentence after all. It's not their place to tell everyone about her criminal history. It will be Social Services' job to keep an eye on the child – they should be aware of everything.'

'We should ask Karen about that tomorrow,' I said. 'She ought to be having visits from them. Perhaps we should contact them ourselves, to be sure?'

'Good idea.'

He looked down at his feet, that familiar searching look in his eyes.

'What about your nephew?' I asked tentatively, feeling like the worst possible Judas, but it would have seemed odd not to ask.

'Jim has completely lost him again. There's no trace of him anywhere. Probably best I let him go – stop the search. If Charlie is involved in the boy's abduction the police will track him down. I don't want to go back to Tony having played a part in that kind of news.'

He stroked my hand. 'I'll go back to Edinburgh. You could come with me for a few days.'

'I'd love to,' I said. He pulled me to him and held me

firmly. We were locked together, solid, like a sculpture made from one piece of stone and I didn't want to let go.

'So – we'll leave tomorrow, shall we?' I asked, cheek to cheek.

'Let's make sure Melanie is safe and Social Services are fully aware of the situation. Then – yes – let's go to Edinburgh and get you to a doctor to see about these headaches.'

'Oh – okay.' I was getting used to them by now; they'd become a natural part of every day.

'My father knows people – we can get you looked over, before you get proper tests done in London.'

'Thank you – that would be good.'

'Sleep well,' he said, before giving me a tender kiss. 'See you in the morning.' He said, tweaking my nose like my grandfather used to do. 'Mine's a strong black coffee by the way.'

I had to force myself to break away. I wanted nothing more than to spend the night with him in one long embrace, but it wasn't the right time or place.

I planted one final kiss on his lips. 'I'm glad you're staying.'

He squeezed my hand. 'Me too. I'll be right here. Sleep tight.'

I climbed the stairs. *Sleep tight.* What chance did I have of sleeping tight tonight after all the revelations about Karen?' Sleep tight (fists with white knuckles)? Sleep tight (body screwed up into a ball)?

I passed her room; the thin slice of light under the door bled onto the landing. Was I right to be concerned for Mel? Was she in danger? Had Karen been wrongly convicted, or was she bluffing about her anticipated pardon?

Before I clambered into bed, I propped a wooden chair under the door handle so no one could get in. Then I reached into the drawer for the little bottle of tablets. I knew I shouldn't have any more, but I couldn't bear to spend the darkest hours of the night ahead in a frenzied panic.

I quickly swallowed one with a sip of water and drew the covers over me. Just one more night. *Stuart was with me now – he wouldn't let anything happen to me.* We were leaving tomorrow and as long as Charlie stayed hidden at the bottom of the lake, this would all be over.

Chapter 41

Snow had claimed the ground again overnight. Furthermore, the dazzling sunshine had sucked away all the grey. It was a perfect scene, like the inside of a Christmas snow-globe, crystals twinkling on the window ledge as they caught the light.

It took my breath away and brought a fresh perspective. Stuart and I were leaving today.

In a hurry, I bundled up my pyjamas and squashed them into my suitcase, slipping into the same jeans and thick sweater from yesterday. I couldn't find my bathrobe, it was probably still at the bottom of my backpack.

I hadn't bothered to unpack my gear since returning yesterday, not even my clunky alarm clock – that was still nestling inside my case. No matter what we discovered, I didn't want to hang around any longer than we had to. Stuart and I were going to make a swift getaway – as soon as we could.

I went to the bathroom and splashed water on my face. Then scuttled down to the kitchen to make strong 'wake-up' cups of coffee for Stuart and me.

Our three housemates were already up and about. Karen was pouring orange juice into a glass, Mark was finishing off a cigarette – one foot outside the back door

– and Jodie was taking the manic curls out of her hair with straightening irons. The atmosphere was that of a dentists' waiting room with the aura of past pain, current pain and the anticipation of further pain filling every molecule of air. It was ripe for a showdown.

I went through the connecting door into the sitting room. Stuart's bedding was folded up neatly on the arm of the sofa.

'Where is he?' I asked.

'Stuart, you mean?' said Karen. 'He left early. He said he had something important to do and he'd call you.'

No – how could he? He wasn't supposed to disappear. He said he wasn't going to leave me. I needed him now more than ever. Then another thought crept in and my stomach clenched – maybe he'd got news about Charlie.

Karen put four pieces of fresh toast on the kitchen table and scooped up a jar of marmalade from behind the butter. It made a *plunk* sound as she opened it.

Everything looked so frigidly normal. I took a seat and dared to glance at her face. It came to me then that she must have had a hellish time in prison. Karen couldn't cope with rules and routine; she broke them like a lumberjack snaps branches. She was a leader, not a follower; I couldn't envisage her in a queue waiting to use the payphone, or the shower, or trouping in a line carrying a plastic tray, with individual compartments for her meat and two veg, to a Formica table.

Karen was renowned for going further than anyone else, pushing the limits. Surely, that attitude didn't go down too well with the prison wardens. She'd have had a return quip for every barbed comment that came her way – I bet that had cost her dearly inside, with the authorities as well as the other inmates.

Holloway – ha, so close to the sound of 'Hollywood' – Karen's little ironic twist.

I helped myself to cereal, then sat back; I wasn't hungry. Karen started clearing the table.

'What you doing today, Sugarlump?' said Mark, blowing out his last lungful of smoke and rubbing his hands together.

'A walk, some photos, lunch at the pub – not sure…' I didn't want to tell them I was leaving until I'd spoken to Karen.

'Don't you wish you weren't so predictable?' he said.

'Why do you have to be so rude?' said Jodie.

'I'm only teasing – can't people take a joke?'

Karen broke in. 'Actually – she isn't.'

'She *isn't* predictable?' Mark retorted. 'Safe, stuck in a rut old Alice – how can you say she's *not* predictable?' '

'You might find out.' She turned to me. 'You're not the least bit predictable are you?'

I opened my mouth with no idea what I was going to say. What was she getting at?

Jodie scrutinised the bruise which was now turning yellow near my eye. Since we'd been here, it had gone from flame red to purple, then green and now this. 'I can put some make-up over that for you, if you like. I meant to offer before. Is it bothering you?'

'No – it's fine,' I said dismissively. Actually, it wasn't fine. My injury might have happened days ago, but it was still sending shock waves through my forehead whenever I turned quickly or bent over.

'Anyone fancy a game of Truth or Dare?' said Mark.

I looked up. 'At *this* time in morning?' I gave Karen a nervous stare.

'Not sure that's such a good idea,' she said, slotting the final soapy plate into the draining rack.

Mark was clattering the latch of the wooden door – up and down, up and down – making a racket. 'A game of Truth or Dare will do *me* good,' he said.

'Do we have to…?' Jodie groaned, sounding about eight years old. If only she would stop behaving like a little girl. Now I'd seen a different side to her, I could see how creative she was; she had so much going for her.

'Let's do it.' He went over to Jodie's chair and dragged her to her feet.

'Don't spoil everything,' warned Karen.

'Why will he spoil everything?' came Jodie's voice, high-pitched and innocent.

Jodie really didn't have a clue. I felt sorry for her – it wasn't the first time.

We went into the sitting room and sat cross-legged in a circle in front of the fire. Mark had put fresh logs on, too many for my liking, and it was crackling and popping like Guy Fawkes' night.

He leant back to take a bottle from the pile of empties by the fire. 'We'll spin it to see who starts,' he said. He laid it flat between us and swung it round. It ended up pointing straight at me.

'Ah – it's Alice. Truth or Dare?'

I didn't trust that Mark's dare wouldn't involve crippling humiliation, so I said 'Truth' knowing I always had the option of telling a lie.

'Let me see,' he tapped his lip. 'What are you most afraid of?'

Jodie groaned.

I ignored her. I wanted my turn to be over with. I wanted Stuart to come back so we could plan our escape. 'Afraid of? Right now?'

'Yeah – what are you most scared of?'

I glanced at Karen but she had her eyes fixed on the volatile flames. I braced myself. 'Living half a life,' I said, picking at the tufts in the rug.

He looked confused. 'What? You mean dying young or something?'

'No – I mean living my life as only half a person – being only half the person I can be.'

Jodie clapped her hands. '*Great* answer, Alice – well done.'

Mark grimaced and sent his eyes to the ceiling. 'Woah – that's a bit too deep for me, Honey-pie.'

'I thought you'd say giant spiders or being stabbed in the night, or something,' said Jodie.

I wished she hadn't used those words.

'Your turn to spin the bottle, Alice,' Karen said, nudging my elbow. She looked, like me, as though she wanted this over with.

The bottle blurred into a green circle and stopped at Mark.

'Oh – my turn,' he said in a silly high voice. 'I choose truth.'

Damn – now I had to think of a question. 'Okay.' I tried to think of something that would make them laugh, but was essentially harmless. 'What is Jodie's most irritating habit?'

'That's a crap question – we'll be here all morning,' he snorted.

Jodie slapped his knee in mock disgust. 'Think of a better question, Alice,' she demanded.

'Um – right. Okay – what are *your* worst habits?'

Mark slapped the carpet. 'Oh – for fuck's sake, Alice.'

Karen took hold of my hand. 'Don't be such a bastard, Mark. You never have anything nice to say about anyone.'

'Thank you,' chipped in Jodie. 'He's been such a miserable git this holiday, spoiling it for everyone.'

Mark laughed and trailed a finger slowly across the carpet. 'Why don't you ask about my deepest and darkest secret, Alice...?'

Silence sucked the four walls that bit closer together. I shuffled on my backside, aching to get up and walk away. What was he doing?

'Why would we want to know about that?' cautioned Karen, giving him a stern stare.

'Come on, I think we've had enough,' said Jodie, getting up, sensing trouble was brewing. 'Let's call it a day.'

Mark was in a dangerous mood. His eyes were bloodshot in the firelight, smouldering with the effects of the dope. He was about to fling a pile of mud and someone was going to get hurt. I just knew it.

'I had an affair at the end of our third year,' he announced. 'I was seeing someone – a tutor – and we had...a kid together – a girl.'

I was half expecting to hear rumbling under the floorboards and the entire place to start crumbling around our ears.

Jodie was stunned into uttering only single syllables. 'Hold on…a…*child*? When? Did…who…?' She didn't seem to know which question she needed an answer to first.

Mark leant back on both arms, his chest swelling. 'Siena Trovato was her name – the maths tutor – May 2007,' he said clinically.

Jodie had her hand to her mouth. 'But we were…'

'Yes – we were…'

'How long?' Jodie slowly got to her feet, looking down at him with loathing, as though he was gradually transforming into an ugly beast before her eyes.

He shrugged as if it wasn't important. 'Two months, three maybe – I can't remember exactly.'

'And you got her *pregnant*?' Jodie was leaning over him, swaying slightly in her bare feet. He picked at a remnant of breakfast trapped between his teeth.

'Where do you think I go on Saturdays?'

'Football…' said Jodie pathetically.

He laughed. 'Not always. I admit I'm not the greatest dad, but I get over to see Scarlett now and again – she's nearly six years old now. I can show you a photo of her, if you like.'

Jodie looked shell-shocked. She stared at the fire as if it was calling to her.

'So you cheated. You *were* seeing someone.' She turned away from Mark and shot a dagger's stare at me instead. 'See – I was right. I *told* you. You little shit. Did you know?'

I got to my feet and perched on the edge of the sofa, shaking my head.

'You liar. You knew all along. You were supposed to find out. You were supposed to tell me.' She came at me, raising her hand ready to strike. I threw my head to one side, but half braced myself for the slap. Karen, however, stepped in front of her and grabbed her arm.

'Leave her alone. This has *nothing* to do with Alice!'

Karen held both her arms up out of harm's way as Jodie dissolved into tears. 'But she was supposed to spy on him – she was supposed to tell me what he did.' Jodie sank into the chair beside the sofa, snivelling.

Mark laughed. 'Ha – Alice Flemming – Inspector Morse in disguise!'

'It's not Alice's fault.'

Jodie's eyes went back to Mark as if suddenly realising who the true culprit was.

'I can't believe you did this to me. I thought you loved me.'

'You might want to hear the rest,' he said. His eyes were bright with a madness I'd never seen before. 'It's confession time.' He said it with an American accent.

Mark was still sitting on the floor – the only one, now – swinging back and forward on his backside, holding his knees.

'The rest? There's more?!' Jodie put her hands over her ears, but slid them down as soon as he started speaking.

As if what he'd said wasn't enough, he went on to detonate more sticks of dynamite in an already decimated corner of the room. 'I've been seeing other women all along, right from the start. I even had an affair with madam – over there.'

Karen and Mark? None of us moved as this next shock wave hit home.

Beside me on the sofa Karen let out a little moan; her forehead sunk into her hand and she was gripping her temples. 'A brief, but enjoyable, fling at the end of our first year,' he said.

'Why are you doing this?' I said. All I could think was: *He doesn't care. He really doesn't care about Jodie at all.*

Jodie looked down and mucus from her nostrils dribbled into her mouth. She wiped it away with the heel of her hand.

'Mark?' I pleaded. 'She's just lost her mum, for crying out loud.'

Mark acted as if he hadn't heard. He was good at that. 'It's all over,' he declared. 'I've had enough.'

'What do you mean?' cried Jodie.

'I'm calling it a day. We're done, Babe. Can't do it anymore.'

I sat still, trying to be invisible, uncertain about which way this was going to go.

A spark from the fire cracked and made me jump.

Karen finally said something. 'Mark's got problems – haven't you Mark? He's not in his right mind.'

'Yes, I am. I know exactly what I'm doing,' he said absently, flicking bits of ash that had fallen on the rug. 'I should have ended it ages ago – it was just so easy to carry on as things were.'

'But why now? After all these years together?' I said.

He threw his eyes over to Jodie. 'Because she's been banging on and on about settling down and it's driving me nuts.'

'YOU were the one who first mentioned marriage,' Jodie screamed, glaring at him. 'At Uni, remember?'

He ran his hand through his hair. 'That was pillow talk… I wasn't…you know…' He turned to face Karen. 'You have no hold over me anymore, so I'll have it back, if that's alright with you.' He got to his feet and held out his palm. 'We can end this stupid little farce right now.'

'I told you – I haven't got it. We had an agreement.'

He rubbed his stubble, shaking his head. Jodie looked like she'd just come up for air after a longer than comfortable period underwater. Her hair was all over the place, her cheeks wet, her eyes puffy and she was panting heavily. Shock and outrage had claimed every muscle in her body.

'Karen's been doing something pretty nasty,' said Mark. 'She's been blackmailing me over my little affairs. Why do you think I agreed to come here? It certainly wasn't for the sun, sea and sand.'

He'd given her the ten thousand pounds and now he wanted it back, hence the time I caught him snooping around in her room.

'You didn't tell Jodie, did you, Mark?' said Karen in a superior tone.

'Tell me what?' she sniffled.

'Mark won twenty grand in a game of blackjack a few months ago,' she said breezily.

Mark sank down on the sofa arm with a loud sigh.

'What are you talking about?' Jodie whined. 'He's been *borrowing* money from me all the time. He hasn't got any.'

'Jodie, I hate to tell you this,' said Karen. 'But Mark has a serious gambling problem. It's not just fruit machines anymore, is it Mark? I take it you didn't know.'

Jodie's face said everything; she looked completely blank.

'That's why he keeps slipping away,' Karen said. 'He's got no Internet connection here so all his online gambling sites are out of reach.'

Jodie turned to him, disbelief twisting her face, waiting for him to challenge what Karen had said. Nothing happened.

Suddenly Jodie was on her feet. 'I don't care about the money. I care about what you two DID!'

She looked like she was going to throw a punch at Mark, then spun round to Karen. 'You were my friend. You've played me for a fool all this time – you bitch!'

She grabbed something from a plate in the hearth and flung herself at Karen. The prongs of a fork sank into Karen's bare arm and she squealed. I pushed Jodie away and she fell into Mark, almost toppling him over. He got up to keep her at bay.

The fork hung out of Karen's arm at a right angle and for a second she stared at the blood trickling down in four thin lines. Then it fell to the floor.

'You crazy bitch!' yelled Mark shaking Jodie.

I ran for a tea towel and soaked it in cold water. I nudged Mark out of the way and gently held it against Karen's wound.

Where the hell was Stuart? Why wasn't he here beside me, like he said he'd be?

Mark shot his arm out and jabbed his finger at Jodie. 'You. Upstairs. Now. Pack your bags.'

He turned to me. 'Alice. Ring for a taxi. I want her out of here. And one for me. We're both leaving.'

I was happy to do as I was told. As it happened, it was exactly what I wanted too.

Within the next hour, the dynamics at the cottage changed dramatically. A taxi arrived and Jodie left for good. In a flash, Mark was gone too.

It was just the two of us – and Mel – again.

Karen joined me by the fire once Mark's taxi had driven away. Silence billowed out across the room. Mel had managed to sleep the entire time. Karen must have dosed her up with sedatives again. The quiet after the ferocious storm was like a soothing, but prickly, blanket. A false sense of security.

'I thought you might have gone too,' she hissed through gritted teeth, cradling her arm. I'd bandaged it while we waited for the taxis.

'I'm waiting for Stuart.'

I didn't tell her I was also still here because I had questions – sack-loads of them – I needed answering. 'How's the arm?' I said.

She stroked the bandage with care. 'Nothing that won't heal.'

'What a morning,' I said, lying back, my hands over my eyes.

'Mark really takes the biscuit. I can't believe he came out with everything,' she said.

'Was he telling the truth?'

'About having a child with the math's tutor?' She sniffed. 'Oh, yeah. I knew about that alright. Saw them scurrying around together plenty of times. I knew she was pregnant, too.'

I sat up. 'And you and him?'

'I wasn't sure if you knew,' she smiled. 'You were Jodie's chief spy, after all.'

'Not a very good one.'

'I don't think being deceitful comes naturally to you, Alice.' She threw me a ravishing smile. I swallowed, filled with sadness for the friendship that never truly existed.

'I can't believe he did that to Jodie,' I said softly.

She folded her arms, then realised it was too uncomfortable.

'He needs some serious help,' she said. 'The compulsive gambling has made him a nightmare to be around.' She wrinkled up her nose. 'He got seriously hooked soon after we left Leeds, I reckon. He's really gone downhill. Become aggressive, rude – turned into a complete tosser, don't you agree?'

She was skirting around the issue.

'Totally, but what about cheating on Jodie?' I said. 'Right from the start he's been a complete sleazebag…all those years…and *you*…'

She didn't say anything, wouldn't engage.

The air between us chilled a fraction. 'We should have said something. *I* should have said something,' I corrected.

'Jodie could only be blind and stupid not to know he's always fooled around. She didn't want to see it, that's all.'

'How did you know about his gambling problem?' I asked.

'You get to learn a lot in prison. I recognised the

signs. I didn't say before, but I was in touch with him when I came out; it was just after he had a big win at blackjack. I bumped into him in Soho. He let slip that he was on a "winning streak" and was heading for the local casino. He was trying to impress me, I think.'

She laughed. 'That's when I decided he owed me and put forward my demand for the ten thousand quid. I was skint after prison. I threatened to tell Jodie everything – the affairs, his secret love-child and the gambling too.

'At the time he was terrified, but he knew I meant business. He handed it over once he got here. But, obviously, he seems to have changed his mind about Jodie, after all this time together. He decided he wanted his money back and didn't care about what she knew, anymore.' She sent her eyes up. 'That's what the truth or dare charade was all about.'

'Why have you been friends with Jodie all this time?' I asked her. 'Did you use her, too?'

She winced with the pain in her arm and sat forward. 'Had a soft spot for her, that's all. She's smart in her own way, if you cut through the silly girly façade. She's much better when she's not with Mark.'

'Does she know where you were in the last few years? Does she know you were in jail?'

For some reason it was important to me. She glanced down at her hands. 'No – no one knew – we didn't keep in touch after Uni. I only saw Mark again, by accident.'

I was gratified; they weren't *really* friends, then.

'I need to feed Mel,' she said, getting up.

'Can I do it? Can I help?'

'You can come up if you want.' She moved gingerly,

her shoulders rounded, looking like her whole body had taken a battering.

Mel didn't move as Karen approached the cot. Her eyes were almost glued together with yellow crusts of sleep. I didn't say anything, but it obviously wasn't normal. Karen picked her up and her head flopped to one side. I snatched a breath. 'Is she okay?'

How much had she given her?

'She's just sleepy from the medication,' Karen said.

We went down to the kitchen and while Karen prepared Mel's milk, I tried to wake her up, rolling toys across the table to her highchair, tickling her in an attempt to bring her back to life. Even though her legs were kicking and her arms were flapping about, her focus continued to waver, as if following an invisible insect around the room.

'So, Mel is your second child. You gave her the same name...' It felt a bit morbid, somehow.

Karen didn't respond.

'Do you get visits from social services?' I asked innocently, 'after...what happened.'

She looked up at me warily. 'Yeah. I went to see them on the way back from the hospital last week. They're coming tomorrow for a visit.'

I hesitated. Was this another lie?

'I'll give you their card and you can ring them, if you don't believe me,' she added, her tongue hooked under her tooth. 'It's upstairs.'

'Stuart and I...are going to leave today. I'm going to get myself checked over by a doctor...'

'Okay,' she said blankly.

I shrugged. There would be time later for the awkward goodbyes – we didn't need to have any now.

After Mel had been fed, Karen started running a bath. I went up after her.

'I can do it, if you like – you've only got one arm.'

'No – it's fine,' she said firmly, putting a clean nappy on the wooden chair. She gathered a couple of towels and squirted bubble bath into the flow of the water. The froth multiplied quickly, foaming up into a cauldron.

I went down to the sitting room and tried ringing Stuart. The landline rang and rang, then his mobile went to voicemail.

'Where are you?' I said. 'Call me – as soon as you get this.'

I'd just put the phone down when it rang, making me jump. 'What's happened?' I said, without waiting for his voice. There was a silence at the other end before a woman asked to speak to Karen.

'Oh, sorry – who's calling?'

'Mrs Ellington – I own the cottage – it's quite important.'

I left the receiver on the French dresser and ran up the stairs. Karen had the radio on in the bathroom and was singing along with Mel to an old song by *Wham*. I called out. No reply. There was a sharp glug and the water starting gurgling down the plughole. I called again, then tapped and opened the bathroom door a fraction. Karen was sitting on the edge of the bath, a towel on her knees. Mel was sitting facing me, naked.

My mouth fell open.

Chapter 42

I stared at the baby and then up at Karen's startled face. There was no doubt about it. The child was a boy.

I made my mouth form the words. 'There's a call for you,' I said, barely audibly, as though in a trance. 'It's Mrs Ellington...'

Karen didn't say a word. She carefully wrapped the boy in a towel and took him downstairs. I stood on the landing, blinking fast, aware of her voice in the distance on the phone.

She came back to the bathroom and carried on as if I wasn't there, wrapping the infant's nakedness inside the towel and rubbing him down. 'Mrs Ellington wants the rest of the payment for the cottage,' she said with a yawn. 'I'll drop it round for her.'

I picked up a wet flannel that had fallen to the floor and held it out like a gift.

'It's Brody, isn't it?' I said aghast.

No wonder he was crying a lot when he was awake. Karen was a complete stranger. He wanted his mother.

I stared at her. She was like an apparition emerging from the billowy steam. A phantom. Several pieces of the jigsaw began to float into the spaces around me.

I'd never seen her baby's face clearly the *whole* time; the hat the child always wore, the oxygen mask, the drawn curtains, the sedatives so she would sleep for long periods – all designed so we wouldn't see her properly. The stained rubber gloves – of course, Brody's hair had been blond – the rash around his hairline.

I frowned in confusion. The police had examined 'Melanie' after the boy went missing. At some point she must have made a switch; Brody for Mel.

I left the flannel on the edge of the sink, backed out of the room and closed the door.

I had to call the police.

And what about Stuart? Why wasn't he answering?

I went to the window in the stupid way people do when they're waiting for someone who isn't due back for hours. I thought I might see his Land Rover pulling up, or see him walking towards the cottage.

Except, to my horror, the Land Rover was still there. I swung open the front door and, still in my slippers, I ran towards it. I slapped my hand on the bonnet; the engine was cold and the vehicle was empty. Stuart's cap was lying on the seat where he'd left it, yesterday.

Why hadn't I checked for the car, earlier? Where on earth would he go on foot? Did Karen know more about his departure than she'd told me?

I came back inside in turmoil. I was going to have to handle this on my own. My breathing was all over the place – too loud, too fast. My hands slipped on the bannister as I raced up the stairs again.

'Where's Stuart?' I said.

Karen came out onto the landing with the boy and walked past me into her bedroom. 'Your guess is as good as mine,' she replied.

Chapter 43

A week earlier

I can't believe it. I thought I'd made it clear. I'm desperate to blurt it all out, but I've got to keep my cool. Been a bit lax and had a few more spliffs than I intended. Mustn't lose it. But how else am I meant to deal with what has happened?! I'm completely on my own with this total cock-up.

Charlie showed me a photo before he took the child; the infant was certainly a dead-ringer apart from the blonde hair – similar size, remarkable likeness in features and face shape – and I remember double-checking with him that the child was a GIRL. At that age it's not always easy to see the difference.

Charlie kept hold of the new baby in the caravan until after the police had done their house-to-house interviews. The police came to check out 'my baby', of course – and found she was a girl, so there was no issue from that point of view. I knew they'd be checking out my history, but I was ready for that.

When I collected my new child – I knew it was all over. As soon as I got him back to the cottage and changed him – total disaster! My new baby HAD to be a girl – everyone already knew about her.

Charlie must have been a total pillock. He'd got the most basic, most crucial part wrong! The stupid prat wasn't bloody well getting the rest of his money after that. That's why he turned up during the night, no doubt – to get his hands on that final payment. I didn't have it by then, anyway; with the police sniffing

330

around, I'd already passed it on to Pam for safe-keeping.
Obviously it didn't end well for him.

Chapter 44

I picked up the phone downstairs, heard the dial tone and put it down. I didn't want to do this to her. I wanted her to do the right thing and hand herself in.

I tapped on her door.

'Karen, you have to give him back,' I called out simply. 'His parents must be going crazy.'

'You're wrong, Alice, you're mistaken. You haven't been well.'

As she spoke, the pain beside my eye ignited again, as if she'd lashed out at me. I tried to blink it away.

'The child is a *boy*,' I protested, 'the one who was abducted. I can see that. Anyone can see that! You can't *keep* him.'

I tried the door handle, but Karen had locked herself in.

'I'm calling the police, Karen – I have to.'

'No – wait,' she called out. 'Don't call them yet. You're right – it's all over, but I need to tell you something first. I need to explain. Let me get him dressed.'

I could hear her fussing over him and went downstairs to try Stuart once more. His mobile connected again, but he didn't answer. This time I thought I heard a ringtone faintly in the background somewhere. I must have been mistaken.

Chapter 45

Two days before

Everything has gone so badly wrong, I just want to blot it out.

Of course, I recognised Charlie straight away. I hid the stool in my room, knowing I'd have to burn it. It was covered in his blood. Alice didn't see me take the mobile phone from his jacket, either, to dispose of later.

No one was going to miss Charlie so getting rid of him wasn't an issue. He deserved everything he got. Alice has turned into a liability, however – going flaky on me and I can't be sure she won't buckle under pressure if the police start asking more questions.

Couldn't relax once Charlie had handed over a boy. I did my best – I cut Brody's curly hair and dyed it much darker – I dressed him in pink and prayed that no one saw him naked. I did feel sorry for Brody's mum for a while – but she has another kid. I have no one.

I fell into a real depression as a result of Charlie's unforgiveable mistake. I've been using dope and drinking too much – probably giving the child too many sedatives, but I wanted to keep Brody out of the way as much as I could. Not been the world's best mum, to be honest. It's not his fault – but I'm stuck with the wrong child.

Chapter 46

I went into the hall, about to call up to say she was running out of time, when Karen appeared on the landing. For a second, she reminded me of my mother. She had the same expression on her face: pity, mixed with disdain and a dash of impatience for good measure.

It reminded me of a long-forgotten memory. I'd been helping my father in the garden one afternoon, holding the ladders and handing him tools as he fixed the guttering. Dad hadn't realised I'd followed him into the house and was standing right behind him. I overheard him say it was a shame I wasn't a boy. Mum hadn't spotted me either and replied without disguising the disappointment in her voice that it was also a pity I wasn't gifted, intelligent or pretty. 'She'll never find a husband,' she'd said.

I was about eleven at the time. Those words had stuck like thorns in my skin that day and had never fallen away.

I realised, as Karen stood still waiting for me to say something, that I'd spent my entire life trying to be small; trying to keep out of everyone's way, so I'd be no bother. My sole aim in life, it now occurred to me, was to be useful. Like holding the ladders and passing the tools to my dad; like stealing the exam paper and spying for Jodie. I thought that at least would give me a reason for people to like me, because there was so little else going for me. But all that was in the past. I'd had enough of feeling diminished a long time ago. And I wasn't going back.

I wasn't going to wait.

I was about to turn away and finally make the call, when something struck me. I had to stay near the phone, but as long as Karen was out of my sight I didn't know what she was up to. And Brody – I needed him right by me to make sure he was safe.

'Get Brody and come right down.' I told her. 'I'm waiting here right by the phone until you do.'

Chapter 47

Present Day

Big problem. Should have locked the bathroom door! So close to getting away with it – damn it. Alice has found out and my cover is blown. I need to stop and think this through.

Will have to lay things on a bit heavier now – she's no longer the pushover she was at Leeds. At least I don't need to pretend we're friends anymore. Nevertheless, got to think quickly to minimise the damage.

How can she possibly understand? How can anyone? She doesn't know what happened to me and how much I lost. Being a mother is a primitive drive for me – as basic as breathing and I can't fight it.

She's waiting – the time has come. I need to face her. She's about to call the police. I've got to stop her. It's as simple as that.

I'm ready.

Chapter 48

I had the receiver in my hand when Karen reached the bottom of the stairs holding Brody.

'After everything I've done for you – you'd turn me in?' she said. She lifted Brody into the playhouse and approached me, looking broken.

'Am I supposed to be indebted to you for ever?' I said.

'I thought we were better than this, Alice.' Her words were soft, enticing, but a voice inside me said, *Enough*. I wasn't going to get pulled into this again; get tricked into believing she thought our relationship was worth something.

Only as this fiasco unfolded had I realised how one-sided our relationship had always been. I'd confided everything to Karen at Uni and she'd listened, cajoled, given advice – whatever I'd needed, but it had never worked the other way around. I hadn't noticed it at the time, but she'd never told me anything deeply personal or shared her worries, her doubts, her failings. It was never equal. We weren't best friends; she was *my* best friend – there was a difference.

I was always so grateful to have someone in my corner that it hadn't been an issue, but now I saw it was all false. When we were at Uni, I thought I had to 'earn' my right to be her friend, but real friends don't operate like that. They support each other, share and stand up for each other – they don't set tasks and offer token friendship as the reward.

It was time for some straight talking, some home truths. 'Karen, be honest. You've never really liked me, have you?'

Her face dropped.

'You've only ever *used* me. All that chumminess at Leeds was about getting me to do your little jobs for you and Jodie. I'm deeply ashamed of that now – sneaking around for you, lying, stealing, spying for you. I did it so you'd like me. I admired you, you know. I thought you were terrific – so courageous and inspiring. I wanted to be like you. Now, I'd much rather be *me*; plain and unsophisticated. At least I've never been to prison!'

'I told you I didn't kill my baby,' she said.

I only had her word for it and that didn't mean much anymore.

'I kept trying to work out why you'd invited me here, but I get it now. This whole escapade was a charade to cover up the abduction of a child. Unbelievable!'

I wanted her to deny it. To insist that it hadn't only been about that. To claim that she'd missed me and wanted to renew our friendship, but, of course, she didn't.

'You knew I'd come, because I owed you for the way you helped me – and you banked on me doing as I was told.' My voice was cracking with anger and loss, but I kept going. 'You also needed me to keep quiet. You could be sure I wouldn't tell anyone you killed Charlie –

but I've worked it all out, Karen. You were in on the abduction with him and something went wrong. *You* hit Charlie over the head…'

She glanced at the phone; it was still purring in my hand. 'Don't forget – you covered up Charlie's death and that carries a prison sentence,' she sneered. 'If you say anything, you're going to be in very deep shit yourself, Honey.'

'Well – you should know. Being jailed for killing your baby! Making out you were in Hollywood, when all the time you were locked up in Holloway! It's gone too far, Karen. I'm sick of playing the doormat – feeble little Alice who always goes along with everything. I don't care what happens to me – I've had enough of owing you. I've had enough of leverage and blackmail. I'm calling the police.'

'Wait, Alice.' She reached out, but I took a step away. 'Please hear my side of things. At least allow me that, will you?' Her voice was strained. 'I want you to know what it was like for me. Will you hear me out?'

I put the receiver down, but warily kept my hand on it. Throughout my misty adoration of her I'd never considered what she might truly be capable of until now.

I glanced over at Brody to check he was okay. He was playing with the little piano Mark had brought and chuckling away to himself.

She leant wearily against the doorframe.

'I didn't know enough about shaken baby syndrome at the time and there was no one to help me. I was left completely on my own with a useless lawyer who had it in for me. No one likes a woman who attacks a kid.'

She picked at stray paint on the door frame without looking at me. 'I was already two months pregnant when we finished at Leeds.'

I gasped. Of course. If she'd had a baby in early 2008 that would be right. She hadn't said a word at the time.

'I met a guy called Travis one night at the local cinema and we hung out for a while, but he wasn't about to ditch his wife and family for me – I knew that.'

'But weren't you with Roland, then?'

'Only as a fall-back. He wasn't the father.'

She said it so casually. By now, I shouldn't have been surprised at the way Karen treated relationships with such indifference.

She carried on. 'Mel was always a sickly child and she seemed to cry non-stop. A number of people – I thought they were my friends – had seen me fly off the handle about it, but never at Mel herself. I never touched her. I punched cushions, I screamed, I threw chairs at the wall, but I never laid a finger on her.

'It tore the inside out of me, feeling her go limp in my arms, like that. I fought to get her to breathe, I tried everything…' I heard the bones crunch in her jaw. This wasn't an act.

'Can you imagine what that was like?' she said, desolation flooding her voice.

'Dreadful…awful…it must have been,' I said, meaning it.

'I didn't know then that it was going to get worse.'

She went over to Brody and picked him up. Straight away, he became agitated, flapping his arms against her chest and kicking out.

'Mammaa…' he cried, pulling away from her.

'I know, sweetheart…I'm sorry.'

She tenderly kissed his forehead and held him like he was the most precious thing in the world.

'The trial was torture – I was trying to grieve with everyone around me pointing the finger and hating me. Then getting put away like that nearly finished me off. I kept looking for her in prison, even though I knew she wasn't there. I ached with a pain I never knew was possible.'

I let out a whimper, like an injured cat.

Brody reached out for the playhouse, so she put him back and held up a mobile of feathers and sparkly butterflies for him. 'I made this,' she said. 'He seems to like it.'

She hooked it over the side of the box and returned to me as I stayed where I was, hovering by the phone. I was horrified to my core by what she was telling me.

She pressed her fingers into her forehead, fighting back tears. 'I don't know how I got through the rest of my sentence. I lived like a small shrew, going in and out of my cage to get fed and going back in again to sleep. The other inmates hated me being amongst them. I wasn't one of *them*, I was a monster in their eyes. They could only see me as a child hater, a baby-killer, and they made me pay for it.

I was beaten over and over. They knew where to cause the most damage. In the end I was rushed to intensive care and they all got what they wanted. I lost the chance to have another child ever again. I was pronounced infertile.'

She dropped her gaze to the carpet and I wanted nothing more than to scoop her into my arms and let her slump against me. But I stayed still. I knew if I moved I might lose my nerve and give in to her. I had to stand against her on this. I just had to.

'Weeks and months turned into years and then my release day finally came in May and I was out.' She took a step towards me. 'I'm not a bad person, Alice. I've just learnt new ways to defend myself. I've had to toughen up. Prison does that to you.'

'I can't imagine how you coped,' I said with conviction. I held out my arm towards the boy. 'But you've taken someone else's child – he doesn't belong to you. Remember how *you* felt when your baby was gone? Well – his mother is in agony now.'

'Poetic justice,' she said wryly.

I tapped my lip. I was thinking back to our first few days here. 'When did you do the swap? You were at the cottage when the boy was seen being handed over.'

'The night Brody was taken, a witness flagged up a car, that's true – but it wasn't mine – it was Charlie handing the baby over to a go-between couple. I never met them and they didn't have the whole picture, but they looked after the child until the handover to me at the pick-up point, miles from here, the following night.

'Mark didn't take much persuading to head off to the pursuit centre with Jodie earlier that evening. I offered them a lift and took Mel, remember?'

I thought about it and nodded slowly.

'I did the swap after I'd dropped them at the pub. It was just you I had to worry about, but it turned out really easy. I got back here in time to give you a nightcap, with Brody already fast asleep after a sedative.'

'Why resort to this?' I glanced over at him. 'I know you couldn't have another baby of your own, but why didn't you adopt a child or set about fostering?'

She laughed. 'With *my* criminal record? Think about it. I tried – of course I did – but all my efforts were blocked, especially as my offence involved a child. But I made a friend in prison and she's been amazing.'

She snatched a breath.

'Pam got out before me, but we stayed in touch. She let me 'borrow' her daughter, Daisy. She was used to babysitters and she's about the same age as Mel when she died. Pam knew from our time together in Holloway how much losing Mel had destroyed me – and she named her own baby Daisy Melanie as a way of remembering her. I paid for Pam to stay in Fort William while I rented this place.'

She was tripping over her words, getting it all out.

'Daisy was just a stand-in until I picked up the baby I was going to keep. I needed witnesses to see her with me when the other child went missing.'

She slowed down, her eyes roaming around the room.

'There were times when I almost felt she was mine. Like going back in time with *my* Melanie. I couldn't wait to do it for real.'

I felt my head shake from side to side in disbelief as the pieces continued to slot into place.

'The day before my birthday you said you'd gone to the hospital…' I said.

'I took Daisy back to Pam for a while, just to keep

them both happy. I never set a foot inside the hospital.'

She was looking pleased with herself, even though her plan had gone completely off the rails.

'Didn't the police here want to see a birth certificate? Didn't they know you lost your own baby? Weren't they suspicious about the baby girl being yours?'

She smiled. 'That's where I need to give you the full picture.' She stroked a knot in the wood on the open door. 'As far as the police know, I've been looking after my friend's child. They knew my history and I told them I was babysitting for Pam to give her a break. They checked up with Pam, of course, and everything was above board.'

'So why the big pretence to all of us that the baby was *yours*?'

'Because I was going back to London a mother, bringing home the baby girl who's been ill for so long. That's the story everyone around me was meant to know. Pam and I set this up months ago.'

'But, the baby's a boy...'

She rested her head against the doorframe and sighed. 'Yeah – and I'm going to have to rethink everything. I might not go back. I might have to start again somewhere new.'

She stared over towards the window, no doubt dreaming up fresh schemes for her future.

I wanted to bring her back. 'So, Mark's not involved?'

'No – he just provided some of the money.'

'Won't the police back home ask questions? About this new baby you have, out of the blue?'

'Why? There's nothing to link me with Brody's

disappearance. The police are looking for Charlie – your new friend, Nina, put them on to him. Pam's child is back safe and sound. Why would anyone be snooping around after me?'

'But social services will, surely? They'll want to watch you like a hawk with your record.'

'I'm not worried about them. They're concerned about me *harming* a child and there's no way that's going to happen. Someone's preparing me a fake birth certificate and I can easily get fake hospital records if I need them – I've got friends underground now.'

I could see how this might – just – have worked, but not now she had a boy on her hands. There was so much to tell Stuart – it was mind-boggling.

'You have to give him back, Karen.'

'Don't you see that I can't face the horror of going back to square one after all the hope and anticipation, the longing, the waiting I've endured to finally get my baby back?'

'He's not yours, Karen. You'll get caught and it will all be terrible.'

She put her hands on her hips. 'I won't get caught,' she said, shooting me a fierce stare through narrowed eyes.

I picked up the receiver. 'I can't stand by – even after what you've told me. It's still wrong.'

'Don't do this, Alice. Don't make me hurt you.'

She lurched forward, but I was too quick for her. I let go of the phone and slammed the sitting room door in her face pushing her out into the hall, then shoved a wooden chair under the handle. She rattled it, then threw her weight against it, trying to get in.

'Alice – don't do this. It will end very badly.'

I picked up the antiquated handset again and dialled nine three times. I could hear it ringing at the other end. Any minute now and the police really would be on their way, this time.

Then I looked up. I realised too late. I'd forgotten about the door at the other end of the room that connected to the kitchen. The cord was only a metre long and I couldn't reach that far with the phone still in my hand.

Come on – pick up.

Chapter 49

Karen burst in through the far door before I could say a word to anyone in emergency services. She stormed past me and slammed her hand down on the cradle.

Snapping the wire out of the wall with one hand, she made a grab for me with the other. I winced as she got a tight grip on my hair and pulled me backwards so that my back arched too far. I fell to my knees. She caught the side of my bruised forehead with her elbow and I cried out as the pain multiplied.

'I'm sorry, Alice. But, I thought you were my loyal friend. The one who would stand by me, no matter what.'

She forced me onto my front, pulled my arms around my back and wrapped the wire from the phone around my wrists.

'I don't want to have to do this, Alice – but I'm not going to sit here and wait for you to tell the police where Brody is.' She dragged me to my feet, hauled me over to the cellar and thrust me down the steps.

At the bottom, she pushed me onto a broken wooden chair and tied my ankles together with a piece of old washing line. She rummaged in a couple of drawers in the bench against the wall and drew out a roll of tape. It was tacky, the sort used to patch up guttering, and smelt of tar. As she pressed it across my mouth, it made me gag. As an afterthought she brought down my anorak and a blanket, both of which she tucked around me.

'I don't want you to freeze down here,' she said. 'Someone will find you before long, I'm sure.'

I thought of Stuart. He would come back to the cottage any time now, surely, and wonder where I was. He'd come looking for me.

'I'm going to pack now.' She was leaning over me, her hands on her knees, articulating her words as if I was deaf. 'Then I'm leaving with the boy. I'm sorry this didn't turn out to be the happy holiday we planned.'

I didn't struggle or moan; there wasn't much point. I stared at her, hoping my eyes would convey sufficient distress to make her change her mind. But she clambered up the steps again and I heard the key snap shut in the lock. Then she flipped off the light-switch in the hallway and was gone.

As my eyes got used to the darkness there was just enough daylight from the small grubby window at ground level to turn the black mass into shapes with corners and shadows. There were boxes to my right and a large chest to my left with a bundle of clothes behind it on the floor.

After a few seconds, I realised that the bundle wasn't a pile of clothes. There was a leg sticking out, and another beside it. Someone else was down here with me.

I called out *Hello?*, but it came out as an indistinguishable muffle through the tape. I stared at the shape above the chest, trying to make out who it was.

Shuffling closer, I pressed my arm against a stockinged foot – a man's foot. It was cold. Not only that – it was stiff.

Oh, God – what has she done?

With tiny wriggles, I managed to kneel so my face was next to his. I knew then. From the smell of his skin. That distinctive peppery fragrance, starting to go stale.

Stuart? No! Stuart!

I pressed my face against his, but drew back. His cheek felt like a briefcase that had been left out all night. I wanted to shake him, wake him up, bring him back. I cried out, but the moan stayed solid in my mouth. I nuzzled into him and realised my nose and cheek were sticky. Blood. *What did she do to you?*

There was just enough light for me to see that half his head was glistening and torn. I fought for air as my tongue felt like it was clogging up my throat. I couldn't see properly after that; tears had claimed my eyes and I had no way of wiping them away.

Not my lovely Stuart. I sank beside him and wept; my body shaking in huge sobs as I thought of how wonderful he was. He seemed to appreciate me exactly as I was and I had such hopes that could have had some kind of future together. Now it was all over. Karen had killed him. She'd battered him to death. He must have confronted her about Charlie – or the boy. Why had he not waited until we were together? Why had he faced her on his own? After all, *he* had warned *me* about how dangerous she was.

I listened. I could hear Karen moving around upstairs. Then I heard her footsteps as she came down again, humping luggage with her. A terrifying thought occurred to me. Maybe she was coming back to finish me off.

I listened again, trying to work out where she was and what she was doing. Her footsteps receded and I decided she must be in the kitchen. There was the clunk of a cupboard closing, the whoosh of a tap running and then a sound I wasn't expecting. The front door knocker.

'Hello,' came a woman's voice. 'Ms Morley?'

'Yes.' I could hear every word.

'I'm DS McKenzie and this is Sergeant Harris, you'll remember from before. May we come in?'

'Yeah – no problem.'

My heart flung itself up to the base of my throat. *The police! They were here. Stuart must have managed to call them after all.*

'It's just a courtesy call,' said McKenzie. 'We're sending in a team shortly to look over the byre again.'

'Oh…' Karen sounded surprised. 'Is it the boy?'

'We're not in a position to release any details, I'm afraid,' said McKenzie. 'It's nothing to worry about. It's just to let you know we'll be here.'

'Yes – yes, of course.'

I could hear shuffling footsteps but they were all still in the hall; Karen hadn't invited them any further inside.

'Have you seen anyone hanging around in the area since we last spoke to you? Anything suspicious? Cars around at unusual hours?'

There was a stunted silence. 'Er, no – I don't think so.'

'We need to speak to the other holiday makers who're

350

staying with you. Are they here?'

Yes – I'm down here! I grabbed Stuart's arm instinctively. It felt brittle and stiff, but I didn't want to let go.

'No – I'm afraid not. I'm on my own with the baby. Jodie Farringday and Mark Leverton left in separate taxis this morning. They went to Fort William to catch trains south. I don't know where Alice is – her gear is still upstairs.' *No – don't listen to her. I'm in the cellar. I'm right under your feet!*

'Right, I see. Are you leaving yourself, today?' They must have seen her bags in the hall.

'Probably,' she said. I could hear the smile in her voice. 'It's a lot colder than I expected up here and I don't want the child I'm baby-sitting to catch a chill. I thought the cottage would have central heating, but it doesn't – and, you know, with a small infant – you can't afford to take risks. I need to get her back to her mother.'

'I understand,' said the female voice. 'We'll leave you to it, then. If Alice returns before you leave, can you give us a call?'

'Of course.'

'And the Land Rover that's out there? That belongs to Mr Wishart?'

'Yes – he and Alice seem to have teamed up. They're probably out walking somewhere.'

'Okay, then,' said the male officer. 'We'll be on our way. I'm afraid it's snowing again, so be careful in the car. Have a safe trip.'

No – don't go – help me! She's killed two people – she's stolen the boy. It's Brody – she's got him upstairs. Ask again to see the baby! Ask again!

The stomp of footsteps carried overhead towards the front door. I needed to make some noise. I should have done it sooner. *Stupid! Stupid!* I'd wasted precious time listening to what they were saying when I should have been getting them to hear me.

I thumped my feet against the side of the chest, banging and banging. The chest was solid and had no give in it, but it was the only thing near enough to lash out at. I was still wearing slippers and after about ten swings at it, I felt like my heels had cracked in half.

'That's the baby making a fuss,' she said. 'I'd better go to her.'

No – it's ME. I'm in the cellar. Listen to where the sound's coming from... I carried on through the pain barrier, making my feet numb.

'We'll just need your contact details before we go,' said the detective sergeant. 'Just in case we need to speak to you again.'

'Yes, of course. I'll write everything down.'

I heard the patter of feet, a silence and then the front door opening.

'Thanks again.'

I gave one final thrust at the chest, but all it did was set off renewed pain in the tender spot on my temple. Clunk – the front door closed. The footsteps disappeared and I was left with silence crushing down on me.

Chapter 50

I curled up into a tight ball. My feet were on fire now. If the pain was anything to go by, I'd beaten them to a pulp trying to get the police upstairs to hear me.

The officers had gone. I heard the engine rev up and then fade away, taking my chance of escape with them. Was I going to die down here? Was Karen just going to leave me with no food or water?

I kept thinking about Stuart; kept seeing him out of the corner of my eye. All I'd wanted was to be with him – and here he was right beside me – but of course he *wasn't* here at all. And never would be – ever again.

The finality of it hit me, grief clutching at my insides. His life was over. And my chance of happiness was gone. I could just sink down and give up. Wait for thirst, cold and starvation to claim me – so I'd be able to join him.

A yawning gap of time seemed to pass before a sound outside startled me. A car door, then another. I hitched over to the side wall and pressed my ear against it. I felt like a seal, lumbering around out of water. Voices. Muffled footsteps muted in the snow.

I sat back, lamenting the fact that the only window was on the other side, with bars on, facing the wrong way. The wall I was next to was brick and mostly underground, but there were places near the top where it had crumbled and a botch-job had been done with plaster and thin timbers to patch it up.

With my ankles tied, I managed to roll onto an upturned plastic box and hitch my way onto my knees. Searching the damaged brickwork, I found that at one point, there was a tiny hole. I lined my eye up to it and had to pull away as the blast of cold air stung me. I tried again, blinking to protect my iris.

Karen's 2CV had gone. She really had left me here to die. After everything we'd been through, this was how much she valued me. There was a police van parked on the track and several figures in white boiler suits were gravitating towards the byre.

Two figures disappeared inside and I pictured the interior. The snow we piled over Charlie would have melted, then maybe frozen again into a dome of ice.

What had we left behind? I didn't care anymore about any incriminating evidence – I just wanted them to find something. Anything to give them a reason to come back to the cottage. We weren't due to leave for three more days and Mrs Ellington might not bother to clean straight away, if she was planning renovations.

I thought about Charlie and the awful smell that had come from his corpse, then took a sideways glance at Stuart. My beautiful, kind Stuart. He, too, would start to decompose in the next day or so. How could I let that happen to him?

In that instant, I felt a surge of energy. I sent up desperate prayers to any god who might be listening to help me.

Stuart wouldn't want me to give up. He'd want me to fight. I was the only one who knew the truth; I had to see it through.

It must have been mid-afternoon and what little light there was, was receding like a fast tide. I needed to find something sharp I could rub against my ankles to snap the washing line. The wire around my wrists wasn't going to be easy to break, but the washing line was old.

When I'd been down here before looking for the phone, there had been tools hooked onto the wall. Somehow I managed to get to my feet. I hopped to the bench and felt around, my hands still firmly fastened together. I had to do everything backwards as my hands were tied behind me.

I felt the knobbly head of a hammer, a wrench – then a hacksaw. Luckily, it was small and I was able to hook it over my fingers. I squatted down and lined my heels up either side of the blade. It tore a hole in my socks and cut into the skin, but I kept going, up and down, knowing the alternatives were far worse. Before long, the outer plastic gave way, then the rope inside snapped.

I hurried back to the front wall and leapt on the box again. The police were congregating by the van. One of the officers nodded and looked at his watch. They started loading up their gear.

No – wait!

I was desperate. I hurried back to the bench with the hacksaw and sat on the handle, then worked the wire around my wrists up and down across the blade. Nothing seemed to be happening and I was about to give up when it broke in two. I peeled the gummy tape away from my mouth and spat to get rid of the industrial taste.

The police were leaving. I had to find some way to alert them. What could I do? I screamed at the top of my voice, but I knew it would never reach them. I needed something louder. What would they be able to hear way down the track?

I'd seen a bell from a bicycle earlier, but that was useless. Then I had an idea. I'd spotted them when I'd looked down here for the phone. I rummaged in the first box, doing everything by touch as there was so little light left. Wrong one. I nudged it aside and tried the next. I found them under what felt like a pair of curtains.

I picked one out and went back to the peephole in the wall. I took off the lid and prayed it wasn't empty. I stuck the nozzle against the tiny gap in the wall and pressed with all my might. There was a fizzle, then a splutter. I was firing it the wrong way. I tried again and this time there was a hearty hiss. I kept pressing until it choked to a halt. Then I grabbed the first thing I could find – a cricket bat – and began walloping it against the wall with both hands. It sounded deafening to me, but I knew that fifteen, twenty metres down the track, it was probably inaudible.

Look back at the cottage – please look back…

Sobbing in great surges, I reached up again to the peephole. Two officers were already in the van, another was talking to the woman with an apron under her coat.

Please look up.

The woman – presumably Mrs Ellington – shook the officer's hand and stood back. He got in the passenger side and shut the door.

No – you can't go. This is it. This is my last chance…

Mrs Ellington took one final look at the cottage.

She stopped and put her hand up to shield her eyes from the dying sun. The police van was reversing. She stepped forward and tapped on the bonnet. The vehicle stopped and the passenger window slipped down. Mrs Ellington leaned in and then pointed at the cottage – she was moving her arms from side to side looking straight at me.

Had they seen it?

Two officers got out of the van and the three of them, Mrs Ellington in the middle, tramped up the track towards the cottage.

I could hear their voices now. '…wasn't there earlier…'

'No – it's bright red – it looks like blood.'

'That's the cellar…' said Mrs Ellington, sounding baffled.

'Can we have your key, Mrs Ellington? I think we need to take a look.'

I had to move fast. I grabbed the cricket bat, got up the steps and walloped it as hard as I could against the door to the hall – slam, slam – over and over.

I don't remember a great deal after that. I rushed back to Stuart's body, but they dragged me away. It was a crime scene, so they had to leave him where he was and call out a pathologist. I recall only the words of one of the younger officers as the ambulance arrived: 'Just as well it had been snowing, Miss,' he said. 'That red spray paint would never have shown up like that on brown soil.'

Chapter 51

As soon as we reached the hospital, I was fast-tracked through A&E. I'm not sure why I got to see a doctor so quickly – I wasn't injured – just a bit cold and stiff from being stuck in the damp for a few hours. And devastated about what had happened to Stuart. He'd been innocently caught up in Karen's audacious plan and she was going to pay for it.

The doctor checked my pulse, my heart rate, looked in my ears, my eyes and held fingers up in front of me. He asked about the bruise on my forehead.

'That looks nasty,' he said, peering at it. 'How did you do it?'

'Oh – it's completely innocent. Just banged my head under the sink. I was checking a leak.'

'When was that?'

'The day I got here. November the thirtieth.' It felt like months ago.

'Did you get to see anyone about it?'

'No. We were a bit too far from anywhere…'

He gave me a look that suggested he wasn't happy with me.

'I think we might need to do more tests, but the police will need to speak to you first, okay?'

I let myself be led to the police car. I was feeling fairly

blasé about everything at that point. Perhaps it was relief at being rescued, but I was also elated to be away from Karen, to be finally going home.

Shortly after, a weird kind of lethargic stupor came over me. I kept thinking about Stuart and how I'd never see him again. All my hopes had been crushed. Of course, I told the police that Karen had killed him, but it was only once I'd said it out loud that I really started to cry.

They asked if they could go through my belongings and I agreed without hesitation. I knew there was nothing there, but I did warn them that Karen could have messed with my things and planted something to make me look guilty.

After the initial chat with the police, there was an odd hiatus and I was left in a room and told to wait. I told them I wanted to go home or failing that I was at least supposed to go back for more tests at the hospital, but they asked me to stay.

I was left for ages with only a lukewarm cup of tea for company. There was a lot of coming and going in the corridor and I gathered from snippets here and there that they must have been searching the cottage. I bit my nails. Would they find a link to Charlie? What if they found something belonging to Brody and realised what Karen had done? They'd think I was in on it.

Time passed and still they kept me there. I was starting to think they'd forgotten me. I tried to leave the room but as soon as I opened the door an officer came from nowhere, took my arm and led me back to the chair. There was a mirror on the wall and they must have had someone in there, watching me the whole time.

I heard shouting and then it went quiet. Where was Karen? Hadn't they arrested her by now? Had she put the blame on me?

Finally, another officer came back. They allowed me to make a call and not wishing to worry my parents, I rang Nina. I gave her a quick résumé to let her know where I was. She was appalled by what had happened. After batting questions and answers back and forth about my horrendous experience, she asked how I was coping.

'Not great, obviously…I'm heartbroken about Stuart. I know I barely knew him, but…'

She said all the right things in an attempt to comfort me.

'Why do you have to go back to the hospital?' she asked.

'I'm very headachy. The doctor thought the bump was quite bad,' I said. 'He told me off for not getting proper medical attention.'

'You've been through the most unimaginable horror. You need to be out of there. How long are they going to keep you?'

'I don't know. It's all a terrible mess.'

'Hang on in there, girl. Just tell them everything you know and it'll be alright.'

My eyes welled up and I couldn't answer her straight away. 'I'd love to see you again before you head back to London,' she added.

'Absolutely,' I croaked. 'As soon as I'm out, I'll ring you.'

'Take care.'

I never got the chance to call her again.

Chapter 52

Alice was found in the cellar before any more harm was done. I didn't want her to suffer down there – I just needed her out of the way.

On the way to offer my information at the police station, I stopped off at The Holland's farm and left Brody asleep inside the porch. I heard voices inside so, wearing gloves, I rang the doorbell and fled, knowing he'd be found quickly and his parents would be over the moon.

I'd rinsed the wash-in, wash-out dye from his hair and dressed him in the clothes Charlie took him in – so he barely looked any different from the day he disappeared. I knew by then that my scheme was untenable. I'd told too many people about my baby girl – a boy wouldn't work. The plan was doomed.

The police have been searching our cottage, of course, since they discovered Stuart's body in the cellar. I'd done a thorough job earlier of wiping away any possible prints left by Charlie in the kitchen, the bannister and Alice's room. Of course, there will be the odd stray hair and bits of skin with his DNA, but they will be mixed up with hundreds from other people who've stayed there over the years. I found out he doesn't have a police record, so his details won't be on file, anyway.

We've been lucky too. We'd kept Charlie's head well wrapped in the sheet when we dragged him down the stairs, and the rug where he fell was thick enough to soak up all his blood. Because I'd burnt everything, there were no incriminating traces inside the cottage.

I'll need to wait until they get all the test results back, but I'm banking on the police not knowing there was an earlier crime.

Chapter 53

They kept me waiting for hours before they took my fingerprints and a DNA swab. They asked if I wanted a lawyer. I didn't like the sound of that. Karen must have told them a pack of lies about me. She must have been prepared for this and set up a trail of false clues I knew nothing about.

The next day, the police took me back to the interview room and everything was more serious this time. It was no longer a friendly chat. I was very careful about what I said; I didn't want to fall into a readymade trap.

They asked me about Stuart. Of course my DNA was on his body – I'd found him down there in the cellar in the dark. I'd held him and cradled him, because we were in love and about to embark on a wonderful journey together. No, I didn't know he was there! No, I didn't know how he died – except there was blood on his face and his head was caved in. *Ask Karen*, I said.

They brought in Exhibit A inside a plastic bag and asked if I recognised it. Yes, it was my pyjama top, but no – I had *no idea* how it got covered in Stuart's blood. *Karen*, I said. *It has to be her doing.*

Then there was Exhibit B; did it belong to me. Yes, it was my camera; I'd taken shots of the mountains, the trees, the lake.

Later that day, I was taken back to the hospital and a different doctor came to see me, a police officer at her side. She asked about my headaches.

'Quite bad, actually,' I told her.

'And how many sleeping tablets did you take?'

'Just the odd one – and only since I'd been at the cottage, as a last resort. Nothing for anyone to worry about,' I insisted.

Her questions went on and on. Had I been feeling unwell at any time? Had I taken any other medication? Didn't I have some kind of seizure in the bathroom?

'Yes, I'd had a little episode, but it was just a panic attack.'

I knew it. Karen had told them all my private, personal things and was making out I was some kind of deranged nutcase. But I kept my cool. I knew that once they probed deeper, the truth would come out and I'd be going home.

'What about when you hit your head, did you black out?'

I remembered the clocks. Karen had told me it was only a second or two, I told her, when *I* thought it was more like twenty minutes. The doctor shared a knowing look with the police officer and I smiled, because I knew then that Karen was going to be in trouble for lying through her teeth.

Chapter 54

It was Alice's camera that sealed it.

The night Charlie broke in, there was a photo of the open kitchen window, with the time logged at 2.45am. The police never worked out what that picture signified and only Alice's fingerprints were on the camera, with a few partials from Nina, the woman she met by the loch. But I knew that it proved Alice was up and about that night.

She was the one who brought down the stool on the back of Charlie's head. It must have been the last thing he was expecting!

Why Alice would have taken a picture of the spot where he broke in, I have no idea. She had no recollection of any of it, but then people do strange things when they're sleepwalking.

I heard the noise of him falling in Alice's room during the night and rushed in to see what had happened. She was back in bed by then, curled up like a baby.

That's when I took the stool. I knew what I was doing. Alice would have freaked out if she'd known she'd killed him. She would have insisted on giving herself up and the police would have been crawling all over the place, getting in the way of my plan to steal the child. I couldn't afford to let her mess things up.

It was better for her to think it was a freak accident at first. Then the possibility it could have been me – or even her – kept her on her toes. By then it was too late to alert the police – we'd handled the body, messed with a crime scene.

The police asked me to stay in the area for questioning, so while Alice was being interviewed, I picked up a local paper to find the latest news on the loch.

Charlie hadn't been found and the police had called off the search. The first two dives brought up only a battered oil drum, a fishing seat and an old cast-iron meat mincer. As soon as Brody was discovered back at home, the police looked at other lines of enquiry – no one else had been reported missing so they didn't know there was still a body in the water. They were looking for Charlie, but they thought he was on the run, they didn't know he was dead.

None of the witnesses could be certain what had been dumped that night – there was evidence of a smashed-up boat, that's all – assumed to be the work of drunken tourists.

Charlie was hidden for good.

Chapter 55

My world collapsed after that. I didn't even get to see Stuart at the mortuary to say a proper goodbye. The police fired the same questions at me over and over: *When had I last seen Stuart? Did I remember taking photographs at the cottage?* They started talking again about my camera and fingerprints and sleepwalking and suddenly a psychiatrist was shining lights into my eyes.

Before I knew it, I was in a ward full of mad people; they must have run out of hospital beds or something. Lying there with no one sensible to talk to, I decided to go right back to the beginning in my mind and run through everything I could remember about the last two weeks. I wanted to secure it inside my head and remind myself about the parts I had to keep secret, before the sedatives they forced me to take turned the whole experience to fog.

I was right to do it; it wasn't long before everything was a blur – they must have put me on even stronger tablets. I think Karen came to see me at one point, but I had no idea what she said. I could just picture her walking away. Although, when I thought about it later, I couldn't even be sure it was her.

Chapter 56

Finding Stuart that final morning was a ghastly shock. He'd stayed over on the sofa in the sitting room and Alice must have taken another sleeping tablet.

At some stage during the early hours, she'd battered him with a rolling pin from the kitchen drawer. The evidence was on her camera, including a selfie she'd taken with the automatic timer. It showed her beaming face pressed next to Stuart's, with his head split open – timed at 3.05am. Once the police saw that one, there was no question that Alice was seriously unhinged.

They asked me about finding his body.

'Alice must have dragged him into the cellar after she'd killed him.' I said. 'I had no idea he was down there until I went to find the vacuum cleaner for a last-minute tidy up.'

'What made you think Alice had killed him, Ms Morley?'

'I didn't think it could have been anyone else. There was no sign of a break-in and there were no fresh footsteps or tyre-tracks outside in the snow.'

'Alice Flemming is your friend, isn't she? Did you think she was capable of that?'

'Well – I hadn't seen her in a while. She used to be very quiet, but she's come out of herself since then. She's certainly more assertive. I should tell you that Alice had been having panic attacks and periods of anxiety. I think, on reflection, she was probably quite unbalanced.'

I knew what was coming. 'This bang on the head – how long was she unconscious for?'

I pretended to think about it. 'It would have been around fifteen to twenty minutes. I was quite worried.'

'But you didn't suggest she went to hospital?'

'Oh, yes,' I corrected, without a beat. 'I insisted on taking her, but she categorically refused. She was adamant that she was fine. I kept an eye on her as far as I could. To be honest, I thought she was okay – until I found Stuart, obviously.'

'Why didn't you ring the police as soon as you found the body?' they asked.

'I panicked. I was terrified for myself and the little girl I was looking after.'

'Did you touch the body?'

'I think I might have touched him to check if he was still alive.'

I knew there was a chance they'd find my DNA on him when I'd hidden him in the cellar. In fact, I'd moved Stuart before Alice got up that morning, because I didn't want her dragging the police in again before I'd decided what to do about Brody. That was my only crime. Otherwise, my conscience was clear.

I hadn't killed anyone.

'What exactly was your reason for tying up your friend, Ms Morley, and leaving her there in the cold?'

'I was scared! – desperate to get out of the house and I knew if she was tied up, she couldn't hurt us. I rang the police as soon as I got a signal outside.'

The officers could see that I'd left water and food at the top of the steps in the cellar and I hadn't even locked her in. That stood in my favour. I didn't tell them I'd rattled the key in the lock to make it sound like I'd shut her in.

Apparently, forensics found her fingerprints – and hers alone –

on the rolling pin in the sitting room; it had rolled under the sofa out of sight. She had blood spattered on her night clothes too. Poor Alice. During the night, she turned into a different person.

Chapter 57

Psychiatrist Report - Patient Alice Flemming
Dr Henry Macleod – 23 December

Following a series of medical examinations, mental assessments and in-lab sleep tests, I conclude the following:

Head injury

During her recent holiday in Scotland, Alice suffered a trauma to the head, causing damage to the left frontal lobe. Alice claimed she lost consciousness for no more than a few seconds, but given the nature of the injury I believe this to be an underestimation. Alice made no attempt to seek professional advice in spite of subsequent headaches.

The trauma to Alice's left temporal lobe appears to have affected the amygdala. Head injuries of this sort are known to cause a number of psychological changes to the personality, often swift and dramatic, including loss of control over emotions such as anger, rage and risk-taking. If Alice had sought medical attention immediately after the injury, a full series of tests (including a PET scan) would have highlighted this.

It is common knowledge in the medical profession that a disturbingly high proportion of serial killers have sustained head injuries at some stage in their lives.

The head injury alone, however, does not fully explain the dramatic shift in Alice's behaviour.

Aggression during sleep

Alice was prescribed sleeping tablets (Zoltratin) in September this year and took the recommended dose (10g) on several occasions during the holiday.

A series of EEG-monitored nocturnal tests were undertaken over seven nights in the London Sleep Clinic as part of my assessment. The results confirmed that following the administration of sleeping tablets, Alice experienced four episodes of sleepwalking during this period.

During one of these episodes, Alice forcibly removed the monitoring electrodes and attempted to smash the bed into the door of the sealed chamber. When restrained by the technician, she acquiesced immediately and climbed back into bed. When shown a CCTV replay of the activity the following morning, Alice responded with shock and disbelief. The analysis of nocturnal rapid eye movement and slow-wave sleep confirms my assessment that she had no knowledge of her actions.

Conclusions

I conclude that this unique combination of factors led to uncharacteristic aggressive and violent behaviour in this patient. I believe Alice was not aware of her actions and requires treatment in a secure psychiatric facility until the prognosis regarding her condition is fully established.

Chapter 58

Two weeks later

I heard on the news that Alice had been arrested and charged with Stuart's murder. She went straight to a secure psychiatric hospital. She hadn't confessed; she had no recollection of doing anything wrong. It's not every day an old friend turns out to be a serial killer! I'm so relieved it's over.

So – what happened to me?

I didn't get off scot-free. I was back where I started – a mother without a child. And my lawyer reckons I'll get a nine-month suspended sentence for detaining Alice against her will. I hadn't harmed her, and as Alice was proven to be a danger to others, I had mitigating circumstances. My lawyer fell back on a statement that went something like this:

'Any person detaining another person must have an honest belief that detention is necessary and reasonable grounds for that belief.'

Until Alice burst in and saw Brody in the bathroom, I'd fooled everyone with the switch. Done such a good job of making sure no one saw the baby's face properly. Alice tried to tell the police I'd taken the boy, but by then no one was paying much attention to her. During her first night in hospital, before they started all the tests, Alice had to be restrained for attacking a nurse with a bed pan. She was a completely unreliable witness by then.

Apart from the obvious glitches, I chose my alibis well. Alice was going to be a teacher, but when I first planned the reunion, I did a bit of background research on her. I knew she was single, without children, and at Leeds, she'd never been the least bit interested in babies.

Jodie and Mark were the same. Mark had a child, but he was nothing more than a fly-by-night parent. Infants of a young age can look similar and their gender isn't always obvious. I read up about it when I first started hatching my plan in Holloway, with Pam. My house guests didn't pay much attention and that was exactly what I wanted. The police contacted Mark and Jodie, of course, but they both said Alice's accusations were rubbish.

Charlie's whereabouts is still a mystery and I pray it stays that way. Thank goodness Alice didn't take any photos when she killed him, or I really would have been in trouble.

I had to intervene, otherwise my own scheme would have been in jeopardy. We had to get rid of him and there was no way she could have got him to the lake on her own. In any case, the whole business about Charlie has gone quiet.

Right until the end, Alice kept her word and didn't mention him. I'm not sure if that was because, by then, her mind was broken into pieces or whether she still had an ounce of loyalty left towards me. I think, to be honest, it was probably because she was never quite sure about her own part in his death.

Alice turned out to be the most shocking and unpredictable of us all. Who would have thought it? I started locking my bedroom door after we found Charlie, because I knew how dangerous she could be.

I sent Stuart after her when she tried to take off that morning, because we HAD to have one last conversation. I needed to make sure our stories were solid and an assurance that she'd keep her mouth shut about Charlie. One little chat to get everything straight was all I needed. Just like the old days.

How mistaken I was in choosing her.
Alice – the one I thought I could trust.
Alice – the solid, law-abiding, dependable one.

~

Coming soon from AJ Waines:

Inside the Whispers

(Samantha Willerby Series Book 1)

The first in a series of three haunting Psychological
Thrillers that will keep you awake at night

Clinical psychologist, Samantha Willerby, is mystified
when three patients with Post Traumatic Stress Disorder
recount scenes from the same Tube disaster – an
incident, she discovers, that they were never involved in.
She is horrified when, one by one, instead of recovering,
they start committing suicide.

When her partner, Conrad, begins to suffer the same
terrifying flashbacks, Sam is desperate to find out who
or what is behind them and a mysterious and chilling
crime begins to unravel.

Then the flashbacks begin for Sam…